# OFFSIDES

# OFFSIDES

*A Novel*

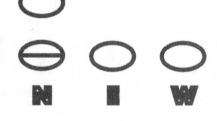

**Kerry Madden-Lunsford**

William Morrow and Company, Inc.  New York

It is the policy of William Morrow and Company, Inc., and its imprints and affiliates, recognizing the importance of preserving what has been written, to print the books we publish on acid-free paper, and we exert our best efforts to that end.

Library of Congress Cataloging-in-Publication Data

Madden-Lunsford, Kerry.
    Offsides : a novel / Kerry Madden-Lunsford.— 1st ed.
      p.   cm.
    ISBN 0-688-14935-9
    I. Title.
PS3563.A33934038   1996
813'.54—dc20                                                          96-17164
                                                                     CIP

Printed in the United States of America

First Edition

1 2 3 4 5 6 7 8 9 10

BOOK DESIGN BY LEAH CARLSON

*In Memory of Jeanne Baker Luecke and Michael Madden*

*For my mother, Janis, and her love of art and music and life. For my father, Joe, and his great dedication to a career he loved and his gift of teaching me never to quit.*

*And most of all for Lucy, Flannery, and Kiffen*

# CONTENTS

*1.* The Fake Out    1

*2.* The Hurricane Inn    9

*3.* Aunt Betty Arrives    16

*4.* A Strange Fever    26

*5.* The End of the World    35

*6.* The Five Cents    43

*7.* The Cardinal and Gold Pantsuit    52

*8.* The Hunchback of Orphanage Hell    60

*9.* The Siesta Bowl    70

*10.* The Ugly Little House on the Prairie    77

*11.* Track Camp Bitches    90

*12.* Leaving Bobcat Country    100

*13.* Jag-offs    110

*14.* The Joy of Sex    122

*15.* C'est la Vie by the Sea    134

*16.* A Tempest of Relatives    148

*17.* Girls Rule the School    162

*18.* National Champions    171

*19.* Hello, Stinking Creek Road    178

*20.* Tennessee Catholic    188

*21.* If You Want to Be a Christian—You Can!
(And the Folks Are Friendly!)    201

*22.* Getting into the Tennessee Spirit    213

*23.* "Danny Boy"    223

*24.* Beam and Stream    236

*25.* Big Fight and a Frozen Dog Funeral    244

*26.* Praise the Lord    257

*27.* True Catholic Love Under the Magnolias    269

*28.* Vocations    283

*29.* Kudzu    295

*30.* Leavenworth    307

Look at the sky and don't blink and you will see angels.

*Anton Chekhov, "Peasants," 1899*

# OFFSIDES

# THE FAKE OUT

*"I Left Opposite Toss 38 Straight X*
*Reverse Left"*

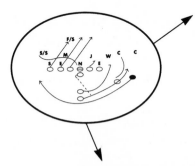

**A REVERSE** presents the illusion that the offensive intent
is to attack the defensive front in the direction of the initial flow
of the play, concealing the actual point of attack, which is opposite
the play's origin. This is an excellent strategy in slowing down a
quick pursuing defensive unit. The **QUARTERBACK** reverse-
pivots, and tosses the ball to the **RUNNING BACK;** he in
turn hands off to the "X" **WIDE RECEIVER** on the reverse.

"Don't give me that face." Mama popped her gum by the country
club pool in Leavenworth, her eyes glued to her book, *Daily Recipes for
Smiles,* the pages sticky with coconut Coppertone.

"What face is that?" I gazed toward the heavens, wondering if it was
my destiny to spend every summer of my life in penitentiary towns. Besides Leavenworth, where my grandparents lived, Daddy always insisted
we stop in Marion, Illinois, to visit a coaching buddy and his six children,
who loathed each other with such passion that it made us look like the
von Trapp family.

"You know what face . . . that long-suffering, how-could-you-do-it one," Mama sniffed.

"Well, how could you?" I slid my sunglasses over my prescription glasses, as she shut her book in annoyance, scintillas of oil splattering the air.

"Liz, honey"—Mama began cleaning her nails, her fingers arched—"you ought to fall down on your knees and be grateful that your daddy is ambitious."

"Maybe some other time."

"Fine, joke. *Joke.*" Mama gripped the arms of her chaise longue as if it were a mechanical bull. "But remember this, Lady Jane, football is our bread and butter."

The sun oozed, and the Leavenworth wind buffeted our faces, blowing Mama's latest permanent from Connie's Curl to smithereens.

"Y'all, this is our vacation," urged my ten-year-old sister, Peaches, from her Marilyn Monroe towel. "I think you should just quit and be nice."

Mama fixed an eye on Peaches. "If your big sister would simply try to have a good attitude, she might see that moving to Cincinnati is not the end of the world."

"It would be the end of the world for me. I've lived in eight states in seventeen years. I'm going to be a senior. I told you I wasn't moving again."

"Peaches," Mama cut in, "you tell your sister that I know she can do it. She can handle any difficult situation. All of you can. You're the children of a football coach . . ."

"Mother, spare me. I can see right through that cheerleader mentality," I replied, keeping my eyes fixed on *Anna Karenina.*

"When am I going to be old enough to be a cheerleader?" asked Peaches.

"We'll look into cheerleading squads when we move to Cincinnati, sugar." Mama smiled at Peaches. "At least you're trying to be positive." She glared at me. "If there's one thing I won't tolerate, it's a bad mood."

That wasn't news to me. My mother didn't believe in moodiness and insisted upon the same lack of it from her four children. "Life's too short. Here's fifty cents. Now cheer up." As the wife of a coach, Mama was expected to maintain an upbeat demeanor, no matter what the circumstances. One football season, after she had a bad miscarriage, the head coach, Donny Mac, caught up with her outside the locker room, jawing, "Hell, Sally, heard you lost that baby. I know what loss is like, honey. Game today was so important, and we had it and blew the sumbitch. Fumbled on the one-yard line. Talk about grief. Whooo-doggie. But you gotta look ahead now, sugarpie. Get a new game plan. Hell, you can be pregnant by the time we play 'Bama if you get to work, little gal."

After Mother told me the story when I was old enough to understand, I could never look Coach Donny Mac in the eye again. When I tried to explain why, she said, "Liz, he meant well. Now I didn't care for his comparison either, but sweetie, most men are under way too much pressure to be sensitive. They got ball games to win."

*Marco? Polo. Marco? POLO.* Kids in the water were shrieking, chasing each other. Peaches scooted down beside me. "You want me to paint your toenails, Liz?"

"No, thanks." I jammed my sun hat over my eyes.

Mama picked up a poncho and began sewing fringe to the bottom. She made ponchos for every football team, claiming it not only relieved the outrageous stress of being a coach's wife, it gave us all some "team spirit" to wear. Whenever she was measuring out loops of gold, purple, or tangerine fringe, she offered the same advice, "Remember, y'all will never have to make a hem in your life as long as you sew fringe on the bottom. Fringe covers up everything perfectly."

"Anyone want something from the snack bar?" Peaches offered.

"Get me a suicide. An icy cold one," I ordered.

Peaches draped the Marilyn Monroe towel over her shoulders like a stole, sauntering toward the snack counter, while Mama sipped diet tea from her Tennessee Fighting Game Cocks thermos.

I began doing sit-ups, and stated my position once again. "Don't take this personally, Mother, but I'm not like you. I can't follow him around anymore, and I will never understand how you gave up your music for football."

"Don't take it personally? How exactly should I take it, missy? And I did not give up my music. I sing in college choirs. I teach."

I could hear her snapping the justifications for a life of yard lines and state lines, but I turned on her other voice in my head. The dazzling one that made you hold still to listen as it soared right up to the living-room ceiling. She also played a whiz-bang version of Mozart and Joplin, and when she hit the final notes with a look of rapture on her face, she patted our upright Yamaha, boasting, "This piano was our first piece of furniture besides a rattan couch." I learned to read only the treble clef myself, but listening to her sing when she wasn't praying for Daddy's team to perform miracles sure beat freezing in the bleachers, watching guys named "Heavy" or "Suppa" knock the crap out of each other.

"Liz, didn't you ever want to be a cheerleader?" Peaches appeared with the drinks and a plate of salty fries bathed in ketchup.

"No, I didn't," I said, smearing sunscreen on my face. "In order to be a cheerleader, Peach Pie, you have to have a sizzling pair of legs, plus masses of long hair, preferably platinum."

"Lord have mercy on us," Mama heaved, digging around in her purse. "Did I bring my aspirin, girls?"

"In fact, if you're even going to belong to the hallowed inner sanctum of football, you have three choices. You can be a bubbly coach's wife, a cheerleader, or grow a penis. Otherwise, there's no place for you."

"I will not listen to this vulgar nonsense," Mama ordered, swallowing two aspirin.

"Peaches, maybe you'll be a cheerleader, but maybe not, which means you could end up like me . . . Lurking around the edges of locker rooms, trying to figure out your place, until it dawns on you, you have no role . . . even if you are related by blood."

"I pick cheerleader." Peaches didn't worry about lurking around the edges.

4

# The Fake Out

"Liz, you get the Oscar." Mama picked up her book again. "Satisfied? I swear, you and your high drama. It's like that time we moved out of Winston-Salem . . ."

I had heard this story about a million times. *I am six years old, wearing a long blue dress, clicking my high heels together in a pair of Mama's red shoes (ruby slippers), clutching our dachshund, Knute Rockne—Toto—in a basket, howling from the blackberry bushes, "There's no place like home."*

*"Liz, there you are." Mama, very pregnant, begging me to come out. "Sweetie, come on. You'll love Iowa. You'll forget all about North Carolina in a few months."*

*"I'm not going."*

*The wicked wizard bellows, "GET YOUR ASS IN THE CAR." He appears in his cardinal and gold coaching clothes, hauls me out of the bushes, throws me into the backseat of the car, tossing Knute Rockne in after me. My ruby slippers are left behind in the scramble. He hits the gas, peeling out of town, as I try to memorize each tree and landmark of North Carolina, my nose and fingers pressed to the back window. There's no place like home, there's no place like home.*

"So, Mama, why did you marry Daddy?" I turned off the transistor radio, which was blasting static and Steely Dan. I couldn't see her eyes under her sunglasses, but I knew she'd probably just rolled them around, royally irked at being asked once again to justify her life.

"What was Daddy like then?" I prodded.

"Oh—fun. Ambitious. Handsome. He liked steak and gin, and he wasn't cheap. Whatever you do, Liz, don't marry somebody cheap. You'll regret it all your days. Look at Betty and Leroy."

Aunt Betty and her ex-husband had run a hotel in Tallahassee called C'est la Vie by the Sea. They never had much business, because Betty preferred to sit in a tub drinking sloe gin and reading mysteries, while Leroy watched TV at top volume. After Leroy split, Aunt Betty continued the business for a while. Her lifestyle scared the daylights out of Mama, so she made sure when she started dating Daddy that he wasn't some stingy SOB who wouldn't take her out for dinner and treat her right.

5

"What was your first date like?"

"I can't remember yesterday; don't ask me to go back twenty years. I know I made him stop and buy pajamas on our wedding night, since I didn't want some naked man in my bed."

"That's kind of the point, isn't it?"

"I am not going to dignify that coarse remark."

"All right . . . give me one word that describes your first year of marriage."

"Starkville."

"Was that where the lady peeked in my stroller and said . . . ?"

" 'My, my . . . she looks as happy as a dead pig in the sunshine.' The same. I typed sixty letters to every college team Daddy could think of . . . and Starkville hired him. That's where he first met Coach Donny Mac. Only thing good about Starkville was Mary Martha Mac. She knew how to make the best gin and tonics and Chattanooga cheese grits. I hated everything else, all the grandiose brass cuspidors in every coach's office and the flea epidemic. I made a tuna noodle casserole every Friday and watched *The Fugitive*. Daddy was on the road constantly, wooing Alligator prospects, since the NCAA had no recruiting rules back then. Anyway, I learned one thing there."

"What?"

"I learned that women could be serious about football, because they didn't chitchat during the games." Mama rolled over on her stomach. Visions of Starkville rose like helium in my brain as I watched Peaches glide through the blue water doing the butterfly stroke, then glisten as she climbed out of the pool. Flopping down on Marilyn, she announced, "Okay, my turn, Lizzie. Scoot."

I walked over to the edge of the pool and hung my legs in the water. I watched Peaches lie down next to Mama. The two of them were close. It had something to do with not being afraid of being a girl, the way I was. Peaches never thought her head would blow off if she put on panty hose, and she never wanted a hysterectomy the way I did after my first period dragged on for sixteen days.

Peaches asked, "Mama, did Daddy really have his football season schedule printed on your wedding napkins?"

"What's wrong with that? He needed to build support for his team."

"Lizzie says she's not about to follow some guy around after marriage or marry one who prints his—"

"I didn't say exactly that," I yelled from the shallow end, the water lapping at my legs as Peaches sang back, "You did say it, Liz. And I agreed. Hey, Mama, who was that mean old coach who used to say he was going to cut off my ears? He even showed me the blade of the big silver knife he was going to do it with! I thought I was a goner."

"Peaches, darlin', he was just pulling your leg."

"Some sense of humor. Terrorize the crap out of a three-year-old," I snorted. "Anyway, I did say, there is no way I'm going to follow some guy around from football team to football team. I also want a husband who will help with dishes and the kids and give me some freedom to take off and have my own adventures."

"Well, girls," Mama bristled. "I guess I just wasn't as smart as y'all, but did you ever think about where you'd be right now if I hadn't followed that 'guy' around? However, I'm sure when you get married, you'll have all the answers. Now, two minutes of peace is all I ask."

"Peace" was not a high priority in a football family. During one of our many moves, Daddy roared as he was packing the Rambler, "Hell, Aunt Gertrude, you'll make new friends. I love you, sweetheart, but world you rather I was a goddamn insurance salesman, clocking in at five, doing your homework with you and all that crap? What kind of asshole life is that?"

I heard a snatch of big-band music from a transistor, which made me think about Mama's own father, a serene man who played the Wurlitzer for the silent movies in Kansas City and later was an organist for roller rinks, funerals, and Sunday services at the penitentiary in Leavenworth. Poppy never attended a football game in his life, and his wife, Catherine, said the rosary three times a day, smoking Lucky Strikes.

With that sort of upbringing, Mama simply wasn't born knowing about blitzes and long bombs, but Daddy was thrilled to coach her on the football facts of life. "Don't be a quitter." "Don't show your ass in public." "Action dispels fear." I often thought of my father, Coach Jack Donegal, as a sort of "football Polonius," except he was infinitely more surly, especially after a loss.

★   ★   ★

From the shallow end through the trees, I saw Daddy and the boys arguing on the ninth hole of the golf course. I couldn't hear them, but I saw my eleven-year-old brother, Leo, hurl the flag down on the green, Daddy's arms flailing after him in rage. Joe-Sam, who was just a year younger than me, leaned tranquilly on his putter, watching.

Mama sighed, "Put some oil on my back, Peach Pie, but don't get it in my hair."

Peaches reached for the oil, and I dove toward the deep end. The water suddenly felt familiar, like the pool at the Ames Golf & Country Club. Ames, Iowa, the first place I was old enough to realize my station in the world. On summer days, the smells of cornfields and manure came roiling up through the midwestern air. In the winter, I helped Daddy shovel snow out of the driveway to prove to him I could take it as good as any boy, but to him, I was only "Aunt Gertrude," the one who didn't get jokes or speak the right football rhetoric; the one who moped and walked like a hunchback. He'd yell, "STAND UP STRAIGHT. YOU'RE ATTRACTIVE AS HELL, NOW STRAIGHTEN THAT SPINE." *I promise to be better, Daddy.* "ONLY A LOSER MAKES PROMISES; A WINNER MAKES COMMITMENTS. YOU'RE TOUGH, NOW GET IN THERE AND FIGHT FOR WHAT YOU WANT." *Yes, sir, I swear I won't stand screaming in the dust at our Sisters of Mercy. I'll even stop being a girl for you. Watch.* But he didn't. "YOU'RE THE OLDEST, GODDAMMIT. NOW GET THE JOB DONE." *But watch me throw the football like you taught me.* "YOUR BROTHERS ARE USELESS IN THE KITCHEN. THAT'S YOUR AREA OF EXPERTISE." *Who cares about dirty dishes? I'm becoming a boy for you. It's a miracle.*

In Ames, a war heated up between me and Daddy, a war whose beginning went back so far, we couldn't say when it began.

# THE HURRICANE INN

*"I Right P12 Trap"*

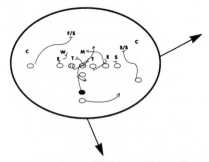

**The OFFSIDE GUARD pulls and executes a trap block on the first color (defender) to show past the CENTER. The QUARTERBACK opens away from the point of attack, and hands off to the FULLBACK. This play is utilized to take advantage of a hard-charging DEFENSIVE LINEMAN. Also an effective method in slowing down the pass rush.**

When we first moved to Ames, Iowa, we lived at the Hurricane Inn, a dinky motel stuck way out by some farms, where Mama got us kids out of her hair by ordering us outside to the cornfields to play.

"Okay, Leo buddy, crawl deep for a pass," Joe-Sam hollered one morning, setting our baby brother's snowsuited body on the icy ground, aiming the football at his head. "Come on. A long bomb, ya big baby. Go long."

"He's too little," I snarled, pushing Joe-Sam into a snowbank.

"OWWWW." The football rolled away. At the age of six, I dominated his world. "Daddy says you're never too young to play football. Now get off, I can't breathe."

"Make me, sowsucker." I dribbled milk from Leo's bottle onto Joe-Sam's face, which Knute Rockne slurped off joyfully.

"Wiener dog kisses! Gross!" Joe-Sam yelled.

"Want more, my pretty?" I cackled a wicked witch laugh, but I allowed the toad to wriggle free. He sprinted toward the motel, bleating, "Wait till Daddy gets home."

"Daddy's never getting home, Joe-Sam," I tortured him, hauling Leo out of the snow, hefting him onto my hip. "He can't 'cause he lives in the stadium now."

"He does not! Does he? You . . . you . . . girl!" He hopped up and down, aghast.

"Face it, bud. He's turned into a real Hurricane, but I bet we'll be able to wave to him during halftime. He might even remember your name, but don't count on it," I laughed, as Leo gurgled his first words, "Hut, hut, hike!"

I never minded Daddy being gone so much, since we royally got on his nerves when he was around. One winter morning, he walloped us after he discovered we had unhitched his U-Haul trailer, filled with football films, from the back of his Rambler. As he accelerated out of the parking lot, snow chains clanked behind him. He glanced in the rearview mirror to see the trailer sitting by the dog kennels. He flew out of the car, bellowing, "Liz, Joe-Sam, y'all sumbitches perambulate your skinny ass over here, pronto." He scooped us up one under each arm, marched inside, threw us facedown on the bed, and whomped us before dashing out to practice, proclaiming, "My ass is late."

After the trailer incident, Mama took the matter of discipline into her own hands. Eight months pregnant and sick to death of living with three kids in a motel, she purchased three items: a flyswatter to smack on the dashboard when we got too restless on outings; a book titled *Dare to Discipline;* and a toy called The Bolo, which was really a Ping-Pong paddle with a rubber ball attached by an elastic string. She ripped off the rubber ball right in front of our eyes, warning us, "This is not a toy. Y'all don't make me have to use this."

# The Hurricane Inn

★　★　★

Our room at the Hurricane Inn seemed to shrink by the second. Late one night, a fight that had been brewing between Mama and Daddy finally erupted. Daddy had just stomped in after another late-night defensive meeting, and Mama challenged him, "Did you ever try to scrub a greasy electric skillet in a motel sink?" The wind was howling outside, and she was down on her knees scraping SpaghettiOs out of the carpet while Johnny Carson cracked jokes on TV.

"Hell, Sally," muttered Daddy hoarsely, yanking off his cardinal and gold muffler, "If my defense goes to shit, what am I but a big limp dick?"

"I'll give you 'limp,' " her green eyes fiery. " 'Limp' is eating pancakes and beanie-wienies in this freaking motel. We need to find a house."

"What the hell do you want from me? You've got Liz. You can get out."

"She's six. Good God, I can't leave her alone with a five-year-old and a baby."

"All right, all right . . . I'll check with one of the players . . . see if they have any girlfriends who are masochists."

"Very funny."

"A little levity, Sally, a little goddamn levity." Daddy tried out one of his new dictionary words, mixing himself a bourbon and soda. He spent thirty minutes a night reading the dictionary to find words to use in his Booster Club speeches while raising money for the Hurricanes. "Prevail," "conquer," and "fortissimo" were his favorites.

"I also want to go out to dinner, Jack," Mama whispered, setting a clean stack of Leo's diapers on top of the TV. "I want a thick juicy steak and a twice-baked potato with sour cream, chives, and cheese. And I want to dance. I used to be a fun person . . . I used to *be* a person." She rubbed her gigantic belly underneath her Hurricane jersey.

"Sweetie," Daddy answered, mirroring Johnny Carson's golf swing, "I've had so much goddamn steak at the training table lately . . . what about—"

Mama's voice got stuck way back in her throat, "You've had too much steak?"

"But, hey," Daddy dived in trying to save himself, "steak sounds great, darling."

"I want steak too." Joe-Sam popped up, boxing the air. *Jab, jab, right cross.*

"Me too!" I smothered him with the pillow as he howled his protests.

"What the hell is all this goddamned assiduity?" Daddy snapped.

"I'm a man," Joe-Sam yelped. "A man needs steak." He kicked me in the stomach. I pinched him hard. Leo whimpered from his crib. Chaos.

"Son, apologize like a man to your sister. And Liz, you can apologize too! You're the oldest. Act like it."

Joe-Sam and I squared off. *Apologize?* Never. *Let the cross-eyed rodent contract leprosy and fester away to hell for all I cared.*

"Now y'all cut that crap out," Daddy demanded. "The person you're mad at could die in the night, and then where would you be? Answer me that one."

"Sorry, Lizzie," Joe-Sam finally squeaked.

"I hate your leper guts," I raised my fists again.

"You'd better get with the goddamned program, Aunt Gertrude, and apologize!" Daddy pounded on the wall.

"No," I fumed, but I was beginning to crack. I could no longer stomach the venom dilating inside. Awash in weakness, I jumped out of bed and fell into Daddy's arms, sobbing, "Forgive me, Daddy. I beg your forgiveness."

"Jesus Christ." Daddy peeled me off. "Forget about it. It's in the past now. What are you? A goddamn actress? Now get to sleep. No more bullshit."

As we settled back down, Mama strained to wedge herself into a vinyl chair of cardinal and gold. Daddy sat on the edge of the bed and picked up one of her feet, rubbing her swollen ankle. At least they weren't mad at each other anymore. I breathed a sigh of relief; the divorce wasn't going to happen, which meant Mama's new baby, when it arrived, would have married parents.

★ ★ ★

# The Hurricane Inn

The next morning, while Mama sliced open packages of pick-a-pack for breakfast, pouring milk from the ice chest right into the cardboard cereal "bowls," a knock came on the door. Mama's friend Mary Martha Mac swirled inside wearing an angora cape of cardinal and gold, a fleecy fedora perched on her curls. Her voice sang out, "Sally Donegal, would you just look at all these children?"

Mama hadn't seen Mary Martha since her Starkville days and grabbed her, hugging her as if she were her own personal savior from motel hell. The two of them hooted about how great it was that Coach Mac was now the Hurricanes' head coach with Daddy as his defensive coordinator. When Joe-Sam body-slammed her son, Buster, to the floor, the boys became instant best friends and galloped off into the bathroom to play Tarzan. Mary Martha slipped her own baby, Beth, into the crib with Leo, and the two of them started patting each other's rosy faces.

Mary Martha assured Mama, "You go on now. Take just as long as you need to find yourself a pretty house. We're gonna do fine here."

As soon as Mama ducked gratefully out of the motel, Mary Martha flipped on *As the World Turns*. Sitting next to her, I reached out to caress her fedora, drinking in her heady fragrance of spearmint, orchids, and snow. Smiling, Mary Martha drawled, "Elizabeth, you look just like your Uncle Whitey."

*Uncle Whitey? The guy with sweaty hair, a bumpy nose, and seven kids?*

"Mama says I look like Julie Andrews."

"Sure you do with that pixie, but your Uncle Whitey could have spit you right out of his mouth, sugar-pig."

I pretended to concentrate on the spinning globe of *As the World Turns,* even though Uncle Whitey kept looming up like a hot whistle in my ears. We had gone with him to the beach once, where he stood on shore with a real whistle, his glasses sliding down his nose, screaming as we waded into the ocean, "Jesus, Mary, and Joseph. You'll drown. Watch it. Holy Mary Mother of God. I can't stand it. Get out of that water now." It gave me a sinking feeling in the pit of my stomach to realize I was a female version of Uncle Whitey. I avoided mirrors for a long time afterward so that I didn't have to face the truth.

Mama found a house on Clark Street, and we all were about to take in a deep breath and let it out, when Joe-Sam decided to play one last game of Tarzan. He took one of Daddy's belts, lobbed it over the bar separating the bathroom from the bedroom, got out only half a Tarzan yell, "Auh-a-uh," before he crashed, the bar piercing his head. I thought he was dead, except he was screaming, and Mama, mopping up the blood, yelled that was a good sign.

Daddy blasted in the door several hours later, after Mama and Joe-Sam got back from the hospital. "Hey, hey? How's Tarzan?"

"Shhh. Sleeping. Ten stitches. There's a Hurricane Slammer for you."

"Thanks, sweetie, but I ate at the office. They brought up a mess of barbecued spareribs."

"How nice for you, Jack. How—very—nice—for—you." She went into the bathroom, turned on the water, and shut the door. I watched the steam ebb out.

Daddy knew better than to follow her. He leaned over the bed to inspect Joe-Sam's injury. I heard him mutter, "Crap. How ya doing, buddy?"

"Can we go chase rabbits, Daddy, like we did?" Joe-Sam's eyes fluttered as he half-smiled at Daddy. "I think I'm almost as fast as a jackrabbit now," he slurred.

"We'll do it soon, son." Daddy patted Joe-Sam's shoulder.

"Hi, Daddy," I grinned.

"Are you still awake? How you doing? Helping your mama?"

"Course I am."

"Good." Daddy kissed me good night, settling himself into the vinyl chair. He shook driblets of milk off the sports page and started to read. A few minutes later, Mama appeared with a wide-awake look on her face.

"Jack? We have to go to the hospital."

"Jesus Christ. Do I have time to take a shower first?"

"Hell, no, you don't have time to—*ow*." A barbed wound seemed to jab her belly.

"Our ass is gone. We will prevail."

"What about a sitter?"

I sat up in bed. "I can do it. I know how to feed Leo, and Joe-Sam can eat cereal. I'll call you if there's an emergency."

She looked at Daddy. "I don't know."

Daddy snapped, "Well, I do. Liz, stay away from matches, don't let anyone leave or come in the room. That's a good girl."

Mama clung to Daddy as they stepped out into the night, locking the motel door behind them. I climbed out of bed and started cleaning up everything—old cereal boxes, plastic cups, hamburger trash. I wanted the room to be fresh. I peeked outside to find flowers, but there were just a few snowy bushes. I slipped on the icy sidewalk coming back into the room, skinning my knees raw, but I ignored the pain. I cut out flowery shapes from yellow construction paper, and pasting them to the mirror, I sprayed them with Mama's springtime bottle of Jean Naté perfume. Finishing up the final touches, I opened a drawer only to find The Bolo, which I picked up and threw in the trash. I knew Mama hated it too, since she hadn't used it once. It also seemed like bad luck to have it around a new baby.

I knelt down in the clean motel room to pray, grinding my sore knees into the scratchy Hurricane carpet, grateful to suffer like a real saint. I had studied Saint Lucy in kindergarten, when Sister Mary de Porres showed us a painting of her holding her eyes in a bowl. She was the patron saint of eyesight, and she loved everybody. If I worked hard at it, I could be the next Saint Lucy, and my family would grow to love me and admire me for all my good deeds. I made a vow to be more like the saints. What did it matter if I looked like Uncle Whitey, moved all the time, and spent my life in stadiums? God knew I was strong enough to handle it. I had the potential to be all-powerful. Hadn't he made me the oldest child, the leader of men? My knees on fire, I prayed passionately for grace and redemption, while my sister was making her entrance into the world.

# AUNT BETTY ARRIVES

*"60–70 Outside Ghost"*

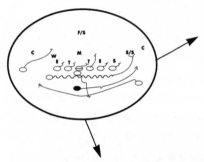

**A "Change-up" off the REVERSE, utilized when the DEFENSIVE
SECONDARY pursues quickly to defend the REVERSE.**

Mama stayed in the hospital for ten days after having my sister, Mary
Clancy Donegal (aka Peaches), not for medical reasons but because she
needed a break from life. Her doctor assured her during labor, "You'll
get a vacation after this is over." No visitors were allowed except Daddy,
which suited her just fine.

Later, Mama told me about the first night Peaches was born. When
the nurses brought her in for a two A.M. feeding, Mama said, "I'm not a
breast-feeder. Y'all can have her tonight, and I'll start the whole formula
business tomorrow." The next afternoon, when a new mother murmured
to her, "Did you hear about that mother who didn't want her baby?,"
Mama pretended to be shocked. "My goodness, you don't say? That poor

little baby." When I asked her why she never breast-fed, she declared, "In my day it was considered common, just the same as natural childbirth. Before they knocked me out during one labor, your Aunt Betty braided plastic flowers in my hair so I'd look pretty afterward for Daddy. I looked like hell, and those flowers got stuck, but I had drugs for all my births. I had gas with you, a saddle block with Joe-Sam, and Demerol for the others, and Lord knows what else. I'm no martyr, and y'all turned out fine. I'm sure your generation will be full of wonderful earth mothers, but it just wasn't my style. Now, have you seen my tweezers? I need to pluck my neck. I feel a hair."

With Mama in the hospital, Daddy continued his own brand of discipline, speaking to us as if we had one collective family ass. "Get your ass in the car now!" he'd say, or, "Get your ass moving; let's go, let's go, let's go!"

"Why do you have to say 'ass' all the time?" I asked him one morning in the car, weary of his blustering control. *The saints never had to put up with the word "ass."*

"If you don't like it, Liz, don't let the doorknob hit you on the ass," he thundered, balancing scalding coffee, turning on the ignition, lighting up a cigar, and scanning the sports page.

Whenever we went anywhere, it felt like our car was just one big ass. The first two days of Mama's recovery we prowled around the football office, and I noticed that all Daddy's football players wore Hurricane sweatshirts with huge letters G.A.T.A. on the back. When I asked Daddy what they meant, he growled, "It's an acronym for Get After Their Ass. And come football season, baby, that's just what's gonna happen. Balls to the walls and dicks in the dirt."

How we missed Mama! So did Daddy, who by the second night had convinced Mama's sister, my aunt Betty Thomas (who didn't have any children of her own), to close up the C'est la Vie by the Sea in Florida so she could move us into our new house on Clark Street. The snow melted,

Daddy left on a recruiting trip, and April dawned sunny, as Aunt Betty directed all the unpacking and arranging of furniture. She even brought books with her about Clara Barton, Florence Nightingale, and fairy tales. Every night, after she put the boys to sleep, she would read to me, and like her mother, light up Lucky Strikes and sip a bourbon highball. As I curled up in her arms, her voice flowed out of her mouth like nectar. It sounded that way even when she described how Uncle Leroy had just filed for divorce, since he wanted to marry a woman with whom he'd found the Baptist religion.

"Aunt Betty, do you still love him?" I traced the tropical patterns in her jungle dress, the tigers, jaguars, and leopards leaping out of lush rain forests.

She laughed easily. "Shoot, Liz, maybe I did. Once. Until the two of them came to visit me after their swanky Gatlinburg church convention."

"What's he like?" I held her hand.

"Let's see. He's real good at squashing palmetto bugs, and when you live in Florida, that's a nice talent to have."

"You going to get married again?" I sniffed her glass, the waves of Old Crow bourbon making my eyes water.

"Lord, I hope not."

"Aunt Betty, if I tried to be a saint, would I have to get stabbed in the throat first?"

"I don't believe so. They don't do that so much anymore. Now let's read about this old village of Pompeii."

"I bet I don't get married."

"If you do, make sure he likes books more than TV. You'll have better conversations." She took a drag on her cigarette, staring off into our shadowy portrait of the North Sea that Mama had bought on her honeymoon at Myrtle Beach.

The golden chain of days with Aunt Betty was deliciously uncomplicated. In the mornings, we made French toast with lots of syrup and butter, and ice-cold orange juice. She insisted we eat breakfast outside under the apple tree, even hauling out Leo's high chair, so we could all breathe in the first air of the day. She read to us constantly, and once she recited a poem called "I Heard a Fly Buzz When I Died" and told us all about this poet named Emily, who hung out in her own garden in white dresses, thinking about birds, and how Emily wasn't famous until after she died, when her sister discovered thousands of her poems in a secret box.

After pancakes and poetry, Aunt Betty drove us to the florist, where we'd buy roses for Mama, since Aunt Betty claimed roses meant a celebration of life. She loved to bury her face in the petals, and each time she bought a different color: yellow, red, pink, lavender. Aunt Betty always bought a half dozen, and we'd drive over to the hospital with the scent of roses filling the Rambler. Another of the most remarkable things about my aunt was her perfect aim, and as we stood under Mama's window holding our breath, she'd wing the bunch of roses up to Mama, who'd catch them from her third-floor perch every time. I loved to watch those roses sailing right up toward Mama, landing in her arms.

After the rose toss, Aunt Betty would lean on the hood with Leo in her arms, wearing sunglasses and a royal-blue scarf, resembling a stouter version of Greta Garbo. Mama smiled down from her Rapunzel perch, her black hair glossy in the sun.

One morning, Joe-Sam squealed up to her, "Hey, Mama, you want to see me do the squeak?" Before she could answer, he licked his hand, placed it under his arm, and flapped it up and down to make a fart noise.

"That's real good, honey," Mama cheered down from the hospital window. "Are y'all behaving yourselves for Aunt Betty?"

"They're loves, Sally," Aunt Betty waved. "How you feeling, sug?"

"I'm in postpartum heaven. Private room, three good meals a day, heat treatments. Lord, just call me Queen of Sheba. I can't thank you enough for helping out and for my roses. I believe Peaches is the prettiest baby girl I've ever seen."

*What about meeeeeee, Mama?* I wanted to bay like an old hound dog as her words zinged down, but I bit them back because I knew I'd sound like a spoilsport. I grinned into the flinty sunlight, pretending not to give two hoots that the pretty one was up there with Mama. Joe-Sam quit doing the squeak long enough to look at me and ask, "What's wrong with your face?"

"Nothing."

"Looks like you stuck it in the freezer for a few years."

"Shut up, pissant!" I tackled him, going for his jugular, forgetting all my vows as the future Saint Lucy of Ames, Iowa.

Mama cried from the window, "Liz, for shame. That boy wasn't hurting you."

Aunt Betty opened the car door, calling, "All right, children, I believe the Dairy Queen is going to close if we don't get on over there. Hop in."

I let him up and edged sullenly into the front seat, sitting as far away from the vermin as possible. As we sped off down 13th Street, Mama's voice reverberated in my ears: *prettiest baby girl I've ever seen . . . prettiest . . .* Then Aunt Betty patted the place next to her, indicating for me to move closer. She whispered, "You know, Liz, I was seven when my sister was born too, and my mother said the exact same thing."

"Really?"

"You betcha, and oh, how I wanted to claw my face, but I wasn't ugly, and you aren't either. You're beautiful. Okay? Now I've got a big surprise for you coming up."

The surprise was the musical *Oliver!,* which turned out to be one of the most influential nights of my life. I longed to fly down from the balcony and join the troupe of orphans, singing for gruel, while the wicked schoolmasters hoarded their "Food, Glorious Food."

After the show was over, Aunt Betty bought the record album in the lobby, which we played the minute we got home. We started performing our favorite songs in character, and I was relieved Daddy was still recruiting with National Signing Day approaching, the date players had to sign with colleges. He never would have stood for an impromptu musical at midnight.

The next morning, I got down wooden salad bowls and large soup spoons from the cupboard, mixing flour and water in them. I made an orphanage in the front yard with sheets, while Joe-Sam sampled the gruel. We wrapped up Leo in orphan blankets, placing him in a wicker laundry basket to be the orphan Oliver. When he started squalling, a lady with blue hair came out of her house, snipping, "Where's that baby's mama?"

"His name's Oliver. His mama's away having another baby named Mary Clancy, only we're calling her Peaches."

"Mama's the Queen of Sheba," Joe-Sam hollered.

"Well, where's the daddy?"

"At a stadium," said Joe-Sam. "He's a coach who's going to whip ass so the Hurricanes can win the Big Eight title. And that baby's name is not really Oliver."

"Shut up, Joe-Sam." I elbowed him in the gut.

"My, my, a coach and the Queen of Sheba?" the woman stuck her hands in the pockets of her apron just as Aunt Betty pushed open the screen door, carrying a clean diaper, a novel, and a cup of coffee, calling, "Y'all all right, out here?" She waved at the blue-haired lady, "Yoo-hoo, I hope these children are not annoying you."

"Well . . ." she began.

"Because frankly, I think there's nothing finer than children using their imaginations. Don't you agree?" Aunt Betty beamed at the woman.

"I'm sure I do" was all the lady said, before ducking back inside.

Aunt Betty knelt down to change Leo's diaper in the grass.

"Hey, Aunt Betty, you want to try some gruel?" Joe-Sam asked.

"Not at the moment, sugar. I prefer my coffee."

"What's that book, Aunt Betty?" I asked.

"It's called *The Heart Is a Lonely Hunter*. I like the title, don't you?"

"It's okay. When are you going to watch our play?"

"Soon, my love. Now let your old aunt have her coffee." She handed Leo to me.

As she glided to the front steps, sipping her coffee and reading her book, I began playing all the other characters of Mr. Bumble, Fagin, The Artful Dodger, Nancy, and Bill Sikes, with Joe-Sam yelping the only line he could remember, "Please, sir, I want some more." Leo crawled back into the basket and fell asleep.

Aunt Betty stretched out in the chaise longue under our apple tree, never once taking her eyes off the pages of her book. We included her in the play by pretending she was the ghost of Oliver's mother: a silvery, coffee-drinking angel, who liked watching over her boy, while sighing into the pages of satisfying stories. We even let Knute Rockne play one of the orphans, since he lapped up the gruel with gusto.

Four days later, my grandmother Catherine (who insisted we call her by her name, not a tacky derivative like Granny) arrived on Clark Street to give Aunt Betty some help. One evening, as we were gobbling up her peppery supper of pork chops and potatoes boiled in milk, Mama walked in the front door, wearing a clingy yellow dress, holding Peaches in her arms. It seemed like a dream, seeing Mama and Peaches standing there in a splash of sunlight. Nobody spoke or moved to greet them; Joe-Sam took another slow bite of pork chops, Leo drooled, his eyes glazed. I felt ladled with warm sorghum. My brain kept trying to tell me that Mama was home with my new sister, but all I wanted to do was to bury my head in Aunt Betty's neck and beg her not to leave.

Catherine, in her cat-eye glasses, salmon-pink rosary beads dripping out of her housedress, harped at us, "Are you just going to sit there like bumps. Say hello to Mary Clancy! Move it." That snapped us to attention. We flung our forks down and clustered around Mama and baby, touching her soft petal fingers. Mama sighed. "She's a peach. My Peaches." Our grandfather Poppy sat down at the piano to play "My Blue Heaven," and Mama handed me Peaches, whom I rocked gently to the music. Joe-Sam walked on his hands around the living room, while Mama gathered Leo in her arms, smothering him with kisses.

That night, when Aunt Betty finished reading me "Snow White," I swore to her that if she ever died, I would not let her get buried in the cold ground; instead, I planned to keep her in my closet, upright in her jungle dress, in a glass coffin, just like Snow White's. Then I whispered one last time, "Please don't leave."

"You'd better visit me, Lizzie. I'll fix up a room all special for you. I promise, honey," she said, crooking her little finger around mine. The smiles we shared switched fragments of our souls, linking us together for all time.

# Aunt Betty Arrives

*   *   *

After Aunt Betty left, we weren't allowed to play *Oliver!* except very softly when the baby was awake, since loud music gave Mama migraines. Joe-Sam stopped eating gruel, wanting only to play Speedy Gonzales, and then, worst of all, football season began, which meant at least eight hours in a stadium every Saturday. Daddy still wasn't home much either, but when he was, our bickering began. One evening while Joe-Sam and I were rolling Leo back and forth across the rug like a beach ball, Daddy, tripping over toys, yelled, "Sally, this house still has no goddamn order and discipline."

"I couldn't agree more, Jack," Mama said, rocking Peaches. "Have at it."

"Liz," he howled. "Big girl like you, I expect you to take more responsibility."

"Yes, sir."

"Thatta girl. I like your attitude. You can begin by putting your brothers to bed."

"Yes, sir. Let's go, men."

"We don't gotta listen to that oaf." Joe-Sam stood his ground.

"The hell you don't," Daddy roared. "She's in charge."

"Move it," I snarled, snapping my fingers. After I chased them into their bunks, I slipped into my room and concentrated on the album cover of Herb Alpert and the Tijuana Brass's *A Taste of Honey,* trying to feel delicate, instead of like Godzilla. I loved that music with its cool beat and flashy rhythms, but I also liked gazing at the dark-haired lady sitting beneath a mountain of whipped cream, sucking on her finger. I wanted to bury my face in all that white sweetness, lapping up the cream that would fill my soul with goodness like the saints, the heroes, and the whipped-cream lady.

"Daddy, were you born knowing you wanted to be a coach?" I asked, dusting the furniture energetically, so he couldn't say I wasn't helping enough.

23

"Hell, no, I was all over the place as a kid, but I decided in college, and when Joe-Sam grows up, he'll play football too. He has God-given talent."

"What's my God-given talent? In your opinion?"

"You can accomplish anything as long as you put your mind to it."

"Really? But what's my talent?"

"Just don't be a quitter, and don't make excuses."

"Yes, sir." Then I tried to steer the conversation to things he was interested in. "Daddy, why are we the Hurricanes when our mascot isn't really a Hurricane? And why is Alabama called the Crimson Tide, but their mascot is an elephant?"

"Goddammit, Liz, honey, it makes perfect sense if you just think about it. When the boys from Alabama run down the field, they look like a goddamn red ocean wave."

"Okay . . . but what about the elephant? And what about our rooster?"

"Because the University of Iowa has a hawk for a mascot, and the Iowa Hurricanes wanted to have a bird too. He's Harry the Hurricane, don't complicate it."

I couldn't stop. "Can girls be mascots? And why can't girls play football?"

"American tradition."

"Well, why are the ugly girls in the band and the pretty ones are all cheerleaders?"

"Jesus Christ, honey, I'm going out for cigars."

"Wait, Daddy." My brain scrambled, trying to find a way to talk to him like I could Aunt Betty. "Have you ever read the book *The Heart Is a Lonely Hunter*?"

"I don't know what the hell you're talking about. Now scrub those chili bowls."

Later, as I scraped shellacked chili off the Frosty the Snowman bowls Mama had finished in her ceramics class, I knew I never was going to figure out how to talk to him. Why was it so easy to talk to my aunt, but so impossible to talk to my own father? He liked everybody else: Joe-Sam made him proud with his inbred talent; Leo was learning to throw a football at the age of two, and already Peaches had her first baby cheer-leader outfit. He called me Aunt Gertrude, since I reminded him of his Irish aunts who forced him to eat soda bread and drink tea, while he itched to get outside to play ball. The name Aunt Gertrude made me feel stern, too, and humorless. Late at night, I tried to remember Aunt Betty calling me beautiful, the flying roses, and Emily, the poet in white dresses. *I'm nobody who are you are you nobody too?* I'd already written my aunt three letters, but so far, no answers.

# A STRANGE FEVER

*"Illegal Procedure"*

**An OFFENSIVE BACK, WIDE RECEIVER, or TIGHT END aligned
in the Backfield moves toward the line of scrimmage from a stationary
position or while in motion before the ball is snapped.**

It was a sizzling Sunday when we piled into St. Cecilia's Church, along with Daddy. We were late as usual but, according to Mama, God forgave us because Daddy was a coach. Daddy rarely attended church during football season, but he attempted to fulfill his Sunday obligation by inviting a priest out to the stadium to offer a team blessing before games. By the time we streamed out of St. Cecilia's after noon mass, the skies had flushed a sour yellow, like something out of *Dark Shadows*.

Daddy sized things up, trumpeting, "Damn, looks like a tornado, ya turkeys."

I began leaping in the air, the phantom of Barnabas Collins nipping at my heels. "Not a tornado. We'll die. We'll get sucked up and die."

# A Strange Fever

"It's probably just a little funnel something," Mama yelled. "Get in the car."

My stomach knotted, I couldn't swallow. I tried warbling "Over the Rainbow," remembering the days when I insisted everyone call me Dorothy. As we pulled into the driveway, earsplitting tornado sirens began to shrill. *Danger. Danger. Danger.*

Daddy hallooed, "We'd better get our ass in the basement."

I yowled all the way, thinking the siren itself was the tornado.

"You'd better get tough, Gertrude. Show some prowess. The rest of you, too, suck it up. Nobody needs a pansy-ass in a time of crisis!" Daddy ordered.

"Is the tornado going to tear up our house?" Joe-Sam asked.

I couldn't help it: "Death is near!" I shrieked. As Daddy moved to comfort me, I vomited all over him. "Daddy, don't die! Mama, don't die! Nobody die!"

"Jesus Christ," he decreed, "nobody's gonna die. Where's a sum-bitching towel?"

We stayed down in the basement for maybe an hour, until the radio said it was safe to go upstairs. Leo toddled around the floor, playing with his blocks, and Peaches snoozed as if everything were normal, unfazed by my sobs.

"Poor fools," I shuddered, my face cupped in my knees, despite the fact I never saw or even heard the tornado myself. Later, we learned it had touched down in Boone, a town thirty or so miles away, with no injuries reported.

The day after the tornado scare, my teacher, Sister Mary Analise, her mouth coiled, introduced us to Helen Keller in between the scorching death of Saint Eulalia, Saint Agatha's breasts being sliced off, and Saint Cecilia's execution by three decapitating sword whacks. The saints captured my attention, but Helen Keller seemed much more tantalizing than all the martyrs. The thought of going blind and deaf sent chills up my spine, puncturing my eardrums and severing my optic nerve.

While I was engrossed in Helen Keller, Daddy remained consumed with winning football prospects. "Folks, I'm gone," he snorted one morning, hightailing it out of the house to pick up a superstar recruit at the airport. I had just climbed up into our tree to read more about Helen when I saw him glance at his front tire, bellowing, "Goddammit, I got a sumbitching flat. Crap." Helen, already at the water pump with Annie Sullivan, was about to utter her first word, so I concentrated on the story.

"I can't wait, folks. My ass is behind schedule." His new coaching car was blocking Mama's Rambler in the driveway. I figured he'd change the tire, but instead, he hopped into her Rambler, ground it up the side of the house, floored it past the swing set in the back, and finally plowed it back down through the front yard over the curb into the street, leaving ruts in the seeded grass. I peeked through the branches where Mama stood with Leo and Peaches, one on each hip, her face purple.

When I wasn't reading about Helen Keller, I was sharing my knowledge of her with my family. One night at the dinner table, as Mama slipped into the kitchen to get more milk, I challenged Joe-Sam, "Who am I? See if you can guess, quick?"

"Okay," he answered, swallowing his peas one at a time as if they were pills.

I fell on my knees, clawing around the tablecloth, sniffing the dinner plates. Sensing I had their attention, I bawled out, "Wa-wa," cramming a dinner roll into my mouth. Peaches whimpered, Leo slurped his juice, and just as Joe-Sam hooted, "A freak," I felt Mama's fingers pinch the back of my neck. Breathing into my ear, she warned, "I am not raising pigs. Is that clear? Sit down now."

"I am teaching this family about Helen Keller," I retorted, my eyes still clamped shut as I fumbled back to my chair. "I think we should learn about other things besides Joe Namath or Vince Lombardi or Johnny Who-Cares Unitas."

"Hey! Those guys are great," Joe-Sam argued as Leo belched, grinning.

"But they're not the only people in the world. Helen Keller once said, 'Life is either a daring adventure, or nothing.' How can we have daring adventures if all we ever talk about are guys who play football? The world is a big place, you know."

"I don't have time for this mess, do y'all hear?" Mama downed two aspirin.

"Who's Helen Keller?" Joe-Sam wanted to know.

"Nobody," heaved Mama. "Now could we just finish our dinner in peace?"

"Nobody?" I scowled, stabbing my fish sticks. "Helen Keller is not nobody."

I persisted in making sense of Helen's fate. "Mama?" I asked the day Daddy made our yard look like a racetrack. "If you had no choice, would you want to be blind or deaf?"

"Shhh." She was winding up Peaches's port-a-swing.

"If Jesus came down from heaven right now and said to you, 'Sally, bad news. You can have your ears or your eyes, but you can't have both,' what would you do?"

"For God's sakes. I guess blindness, because then I could still listen to music."

She wasn't convincing. I was about to question her further when Daddy breezed in, swinging keys. Mama lashed out, "Jack, I planted that grass seed myself."

"I had to get my ass to the airport," Daddy snorted, as I yanked my black turtleneck sweater over my eyes and ears, pawing my way along the walls.

Mama didn't back down. "All I need now are a few black checkered flags, and we'll have our own Indy 500."

I sidled toward the upstairs. *Helen, Helen, Helen.*

Daddy crabbed, "Jesus, Mary, and Joseph, we can plant more grass seed."

"You've never planted anything in your life. Your idea of a yard is AstroTurf with woodchips."

I made it to the archway separating the kitchen and upstairs. *Utter darkness.*

29

"I'll tell you one goddamn thing, Sally, it's a lot less of a pain in the ass."

I found the shag carpeting on the steps. I used its loops as a guide. As I bumped blindly up the stairs, Daddy snarled, "How long is this Helen Keller crap supposed to go on? It can't be customary."

*Customary? Don't insult me, Coach Donegal.* I reached the top, pulled the sweater from my face, breathing in other worlds, stars, and breezes from the cracked window. Downstairs, their words volleyed and fell, no longer bayonets but tennis balls; lime-green, rolling away. The Liz part of me decided to listen carefully.

"I hope you at least signed that player," the woman downstairs finally said.

"Hell, no," the man answered. "He flew here to tell me he was signing with the Huskers, but the sorry SOB waits until after steak at the Ramada to parlay it to me." He banged the ice trays on the counter to loosen the ice for his Scotch.

With the approach of football season, my eyes began noticing colors, every hue, tone, and shade of them. I wanted to make up for all Helen missed in her life. I could be her eyes and ears even though she was dead, because I was alive. I fell especially in love with the color blue, drinking in all its incarnations for Helen: sky, sapphire, indigo, royal, ocean, Della Robbia, and midnight.

"You're wearing the colors of the other team!" Joe-Sam accused me on the way to a home game one Saturday.

"Shut up. I've got red on."

"They're still going to think you're a Jayhawk with that blue shirt!" he lamented. "You look like a traitor."

"So what?"

"You're such a girl," he scoffed.

The coaches themselves didn't have to worry about colors, since they received a new set of outfits for every team they coached; but in Ames, the wives started a fashion show where they all modeled cardinal and gold outfits at the country club to jack up team spirit. Plus, according to Mama and Mary Martha Mac, regular women needed to be educated on how they could be involved in football. In Mama's phone conversations to plan the fashion show, and other events that cropped up over the years, the phrase *coacheswives* came up so regularly that Peaches grew up thinking of *coacheswives* as one word.

Sometimes, during the tailgate parties before home games in the stadium parking lot, I studied the *coacheswives* from the bumper of our Rambler, knowing I would never look like them with my boy genes multiplying by the second. They were chatty women who stirred their Bloody Marys with Hurricane swizzle sticks, making an autumn sports bouquet in their cardinal and gold miniskirts, vests, frilly blouses, with chain belts looped around their waists, hair poofed high, and white go-go boots.

At the first country club fashion show, Mama and Mary Martha swept on stage, tap-dancing to the Iowa fight song in their ponchos that dripped cardinal birds of fringe. Mama made me model sweatshirts with Joe-Sam and Buster Mac, and I also had to wheel out Peaches, Leo, and Beth Mac in a triple stroller, so they could show off their Hurricane baby jumpsuits. Knute Rockne even wore a Hurricane dog sweater, designed for a dachshund body. He was a hit.

Daddy also went to that first luncheon because Donny Mac asked him to give a speech. To get prepared, he highlighted a book with a chapter in it called "How to Teach Ladies About Football," which advised he bring along a real football player to demonstrate. A running back came in only his cleats, sanitaries (tight white football underwear), and jock strap. The player stood in front of the ladies, his face lobster-red, while Daddy had him dress in shoulder pads, pants, jersey, and helmet, explaining the purpose of each item to the ladies.

The luncheon was a big success, and a few women even came up to Daddy afterward to tell him they had a much clearer understanding of the game. One of them smiled, nodding toward me, "Your oldest boy sure is a good baby sitter, isn't he? Your little ones are just darling. Especially that baby girl."

All Daddy did was smile and mutter, "Yep, yep, yep. Sure was veracious of y'all ladies to make it out here today."

I bit my lip, tasted blood, letting the words wash over me, "Your oldest boy . . ." I was a boy in their eyes, make no mistake, and my own father didn't correct them. Blindness. I closed my ears to the conversation. Deafness.

*Epiphany.* With Daddy's, "Yep, yep," I hunkered my shoulders, *yep,* slapped my thighs, and downed a glass of milk like it was white lightning. *Yep.* Before departing the banquet room, I tipped my imaginary hat to a few of the ladies, swaggered out of the club to the putting green to practice putts like a man. Honor, pride, respect. *Yep.* With each putt, I began to plot my escape from my destiny as a girl. I would become Helen Keller to all things feminine, girlish, and weak. It would be my key to survival in a world of football. Fearless. *Yep, yep.*

For the first eight years of my life, my vision had been fine, but the afternoon the ophthalmologist announced I needed glasses, I knew my own blindness was coming true. Not only was I evolving into a boy in the eyes of the world, I would soon need a Seeing Eye dog and a white cane. A few days later, I picked up my pair of thick-lensed octagon-shaped glasses, I looked in the mirror, and sure enough, Uncle Whitey was blinking right back at me.

That night, sitting around the table, we were all playing Daddy's favorite dice game, 21. Daddy was blowing on the dice, shaking them in the cup, yelling, "Hey, I feel lucky! Hot!" While the dice rattled, I tried to memorize the faces of my family. The thought of never being able to look at them again was unbearable. As the dice rolled, I saw Helen Keller's face float over the tablecloth along with Uncle Whitey's, wearing dark octagon glasses for the blind, and I rushed into the bathroom to throw up.

Daddy followed, booming, "Goddammit. Nobody's going blind in this house!"

"The eye doctor said I was legally blind . . . I would be blind without glasses."

"You're not blind, goddammit, you're myopic. You got that, slick?"

"I'm scared. Plus I'm getting uglier. I look just like Uncle Whitey."

"Now Liz, your Uncle Whitey isn't a bad-looking guy."

"Daddy!"

"It's a joke. Jesus Christ, where's your sense of humor?" he yelled as I bent over the toilet to vomit some more.

Daddy came into my room later that night. "Liz, honey, are you awake?" He bumped his head on my canopy as he sat down on the edge of my bed. Rubbing his head, he mumbled, "I did some checking for you, and the reason we're called the Hurricanes is because a sportswriter in the 1930s described Iowa as a hurricane when they whipped Northwestern's ass on the football field."

"Oh."

"Iowa liked the name, and so they became the Hurricanes."

"I guess it makes sense."

"You bet your ass it does. . . . Now goddammit, be proud of yourself. I'm proud of you. You're strong as an ox, and you're not going blind. So get some sleep." He kissed me on the forehead and slipped out of my room, shutting the door. I pulled my Raggedy Ann doll close to me, sniffing her curls of yarn. *Strong as an ox.* Out of the blue, my baby sister, Peaches, popped into my head. Peaches: dimpled and fragrant. Peaches: golden hair, the same color as Helen's when the scarlet fever got her. At that moment, I knew I was saved.

The next day, I dragged a blindfolded Peaches into the attic. "God, don't let my baby go blind. Please save my Helen." I was her mother, father, and Annie Sullivan.

"Me not Hewen!" Peaches bawled, terrified of the hot blackness enveloping us.

I shoved off the blindfold, shining the light at her, but she blinked. "No do dat."

I pretended it was a miracle, shouting, "My baby can see. . . . Helen, you're cured."

*Life is either a daring adventure, or nothing.* Despite what Helen Keller said, I didn't want her adventure; instead, I longed for one of my own. I began scaling trees to the very highest branches. I swung from tire swings and river vines, letting go at the peak, falling. When cretinous boys performed Helen Keller tricks to torment me, I karate-flipped them, stomping on their entrails. I practiced lining up my fingers with the neat threads of the football, throwing the ball with a spiraled arc, not a wobbly girl throw. When I grew bored proving my strength, I climbed up to the attic crawl space off Peaches's room, reading for hours: fairy tales, *Children's Digest, Sports Illustrated,* biographies like the one of Louisa May Alcott, who I realized was a girl very much like me. She didn't have time to waste being a priss-pot either.

One evening, as Daddy was starting on a recruiting trip, he left his suitcases in the living room to kiss the kids good-bye. I picked up his bags effortlessly, swinging them from my arms like feathers, and tossed them into the trunk. When Daddy came outside, I was just closing the hood.

"Where the hell are my grips?" he demanded.

"In the trunk, sir. You're all packed. Have a great trip. Best of luck signing some decent talent. I'll take care of things while you're gone." I walked up to where he was standing, stuck out my hand, and gripped his in a firm handshake, just like any other superstar recruit with one ounce of respect, pride, and honor would do.

# CHAPTER 5

# THE END OF THE WORLD

*"Eagle Nasty Lightning Y 1 Combo"*

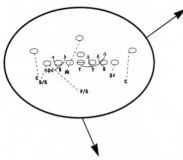

**Pass rush games are typically executed by
the DOWN LINEMAN and are effective in disrupting pass protection
blocking schemes. The intent is to free one or more PASS RUSHERS,
resulting in a hurried pass, an interception, or a sack.**

"Here's your present, honey." Mama handed me the biggest box of all from under the Christmas tree, and I just knew Thumbelina was inside waiting. I had told her and Daddy exactly what I wanted, so I knew they had to get it right.

"Hurry!" Mama was excited. I picked at the wrapping, savoring the moment.

"I am," I said, imagining Thumbelina's flaxen hair, rosy cheeks, dancing toes. I knew she was definitely a doll for a girl, but I didn't care. I wanted her. Some secret part of me longed to be Thumbelina, but as I tore off the last sheet, Mrs. Beasley fell into my arms. I grinned into the movie camera's blinding light that Daddy was aiming at my face. I knew how to appear appreciative, but *Mrs. Beasley?*

"Thanks . . ." I stared at the spongy feet, the hideous polka-dot body, crushed.

The boys, ages three and eight, received Hot Wheels sets, in addition to football junk: pennants, shoulder pads, posters, rawhide leather footballs, chin guards, mouth guards, electronic football fields with magnetic cleated players. Peaches, age two, got Barbies, dresses, frilly socks, high heels, and a pink feather boa.

I gathered my gifts: Mrs. Beasley, dog candle, nightgown, and game, Sorry. *Old lady, old dog, old lady. Sorry. Sorry.*

The one bright spot of the holiday was Uncle Peter, Daddy's youngest brother, who was visiting us from Nashville. Peter was born when Daddy was twenty-two, which made him only five years older than me, more of a brother than an uncle. He was also the opposite of Daddy, and he knew what I liked because he paid attention. For Christmas, he gave me the books *Amelia Earhart* and *The Diary of Anne Frank.* Another book, *Charlotte's Web,* was under the tree from Aunt Betty. It amazed me how Mama's sister and Daddy's brother knew by instinct what to get me. Peter was also an artist, always drawing cartoons and sketches of us. Daddy was proud of Peter's drawings, which he hung in his football office. Peter idolized his big brother, even though Daddy was always signing him up for boys' football camps, despite the fact that Peter confided to me he didn't like playing football very much.

At the age of nine, when I stopped believing in my girlhood, I quit believing in Santa Claus, too, after Mama announced on Christmas Eve that Peter and I could be Santa Claus, since she and Daddy had to go to a party for the coaching staff. All the kids were in bed, so Peter and I worked late together getting the packages stacked under the tree. Then I crumbled up cookies and left out half a glass of milk to make it look like Santa's snack. Peter put on *Bing Crosby's Christmas Album,* tapped my shoulder, and solemnly asked, "Liz, do you want to movie kiss?"

"Movie kiss?" I looked at him, wondering how old he was. Fourteen?

Movie kissing was certainly an unexpected turn in our relationship. "But I wear glasses."

"Who cares? Take 'em off, and come here and lie down." He patted the rug.

I thought about it. He was my uncle, I loved him even when he irritated me, and it wouldn't at all be like kissing Uncle Whitey (yikes). As I lay down next to him, he kissed me on the mouth. "Isn't that nice?" he drawled.

"Not so wet." I wiped off his slobber.

"Sorry, darlin'," he answered, swabbing his mouth with his sleeve. He bent over and kissed me again. It was drier the second time, better. Without my glasses, the Christmas lights foamed into one blinking orangy starburst. "I'm dreaming of a white Christmas," crooned Bing. Breath on my face, on my neck. My stomach dipped a few times, my brain layered into hard right angles. What if Mama or Daddy walked in? But I knew that was impossible; coaching parties always lasted a long time. More kissing. *Oh, was this why it was called movie kissing? We're in the movies, me and Peter are the stars. People are watching. Sister Mary Analise is frowning.* I felt his braces brush against my lips, back and forth, back and forth. Uncle Peter. He smelled like cookies, acne cream, and pine needles.

The next morning, after we finished opening the presents, Peter took Joe-Sam and Leo out sledding. He seemed embarrassed to be around me, but I said nothing. Daddy didn't feel like playing Sorry, but I didn't mind because he was so grouchy. I kept a watchful eye on him as he lit one cigar after another, drinking cans of Coors, watching bowl games, which I knew could make any person edgy, especially a coach who'd just finished a 3–8 season. I decided to cure his foul mood and save his life—kind of a quarterback fake—hiking his cigars out the window.

"Which one of you sumbitches touched my cigars?" he demanded, turning to see a third-quarter kickoff but finding no smokes.

"Couldn't tell you," I sighed, lying on the floor playing Sorry by myself.

When he finally found them by the end of the fourth quarter of game three, frozen like twigs in the snow on the window ledge, he kicked the Sorry game, scattering pieces everywhere.

"Liz, you mind your own goddamned business!" he raged, trying to blow each cigar dry, one by one, with the hair dryer from the fireplace, his "electric billows."

"You are my business, Daddy." I blinked back tears as I gathered up cards. "I don't think you should smoke. You might die. Sister Mary Analise says—"

"I don't give a good goddamn what Sister Mary Whoever says."

"But she's a *nun,* Daddy."

"I know what the hell she is. . . . Look, I know you mean well, honey, but Jesus Christ, I say you can both mind your own business," he said, tramping out the door.

I wasn't about to let him get away with that, so I chased him out to the Rambler through the snow, screaming, "Daddy . . . I was only trying to save your life."

As he peeled off without looking back, I tried to swallow the gourd in my throat, gazing up at gray clouds hanging in the sky. Not so different, I realized, from Sister Mary Analise's drawings of tobacco-infested lungs.

Daddy's mood didn't improve between Christmas and New Year's. He had never spent so much time locked inside a house with four kids. He announced daily, as he monitored Peaches's eating or tied Leo's shoes, "I gotta get on the road and recruit. Enough of these goddamn holidays." But he had nowhere to go, since all the players were on vacation too. By New Year's Eve, he began ripping ornaments off the tree, decreeing that Christmas was over. To drown him out, Joe-Sam cranked up the TV.

"Turn off that idiot box, ya sorry sumbitches. No more TV unless it's a bowl game. New law!" Daddy blasted, trying to wrench the tree out of the stand.

"Wrap it up in plastic, and you won't shed so many pine needles," Mama said.

"Goddammit, it's easier to do it my way." He lugged the tree up the steps, needles shedding everywhere, hooking themselves to the pea-green carpeting.

Mama tried vacuuming, but the shards of pine were stuck tight. "See, Jack"—she spoke through clenched teeth, flipping off the vacuum—"if just for once you'd listen—"

"All right, I want every one of you kids picking up pine needles. Nobody's leaving this basement until every swinging one is picked up . . . and you, Aunt Gertrude . . . untangle these Christmas lights while you're at it. Didn't you have a nice Christmas? Didn't you get a Mrs. Baizley?"

"Mrs. Beasley, Daddy, and I'm sorry to tell you, but I didn't want her. I wanted Thumbelina. I told you. Remember? Thumbelina is a beautiful doll who dances."

"You don't want Mrs. Beasley? Fine." He picked up Mrs. Beasley and flung her against the mantel, toppling Mama's antique clock onto the hearth with a crash.

"Look what you've done, Jack. I loved that clock!" Mama wailed.

"I'll fix it, Sally! I'll fix the SOB."

"You've never fixed anything in your life."

Without looking at Daddy, I gingerly inched across the room to pick up Mrs. Beasley, while he gazed at the bits of broken clock. I propped her up where she would be staring at him, in her grinning silence, while he watched bowl games. I stuck a pack of cigars on her lap.

Later, after Daddy superglued the clock back together (it never actually kept time again), he perked up enough to take Mama to a New Year's Eve party at Coach Mac's house, armed with Doritos and a case of cold duck. They sprang out of the house, calling, "See you next year, y'all. Clean that kitchen too. It's a wreck." The heaviness of the day rose like a hawk when the door clicked behind them. I knew I felt the way grown-ups did when their children finally went outside to play.

Peter drank half a bottle of Rebel Yell and went to sleep on the sofa. While he dozed, I went into the kitchen, got out raisins, unwrapped Kraft American cheese singles, and spread them on paper towels across the dining-room table. I made smiling faces with the raisins on each square of cheese. At about 11:30 P.M., I dialed Aunt Betty's number. She answered after ten rings. Her voice seemed wrong, slower.

"Aunt Betty, it's Liz. Happy New Year. Thanks for the book."

"You're welcome . . . sugar. Is your mama there?"

"No, they're at a party. I already read my book. Charlotte's great."

She didn't seem to hear me. "Well, you give them my love, okay?"

"I will. Hey, what did you think about the part where—"

"Liz, I'm real tired tonight. I'll call you when we can talk longer."

"Wait. Aunt Betty?"

But she hung up. I stared at the phone a minute, hating it. *Stupid phone. I'm no good. Letters or face-to-face. She didn't want to talk to you anyway, loser.*

Determined to have a happy New Year's, I got Joe-Sam to stop playing with his Hot Wheels, woke up Leo, and pulled Peaches out of her crib. We sat them down at the table, and I pronounced, "It's midnight. New Year's. Happy 1971, everybody. CHEERS." Banging our juice cups together, we ate the happy faces fast and stepped out onto the porch, banging on pots and pans with spatulas.

"HAPPY NEW YEAR!" our voices twisted in the December winds. We retreated into the warmth of the living room to play *A Taste of Honey* at explosive decibels on the Philco. I held Peaches close, dancing her around the floor to the music. My little girl. I sniffed her head, which smelled like fresh bread, and a giddiness flooded over me. The boys were comets, leaping over couches with candlesticks as microphones, inventing words to the Tijuana Brass. When Peter woke up, groggy, I cried, "Come on, Uncle Peter, dance!" He jumped up and put on Loretta Lynn and Ernest Tubb singing cheating songs. He taught us the two-step, with a beer bottle in his back pocket, the way real folks dance down in Nashville.

When January gave birth to a series of savage Iowa thunderstorms and blizzards, Sister Mary Analise didn't have to convince me the end of the world was coming any day. We learned how Jesus would be returning to earth when least anticipated; therefore, it was vital to keep a pure soul washed clean with Christ's blood.

# The End of the World

As I walked home from school one freezing afternoon, I noticed flashes of lightning in the sky, followed by claps of thunder. I skidded down the sidewalks in my boots, the wind cutting my legs. I reached Clark Street, breathless, to find Mama in the kitchen making manicotti. I hung up my coat on a hook, trying to think of an easy way to inform her about the end of the world. The words were on the tip of my tongue as Daddy banged through the door earlier than usual, announcing, "Practice was short today. Froze my ass off on the field. What's to eat?" He grabbed the sports page.

"Did you by chance notice how it's thundering and lightning outside?" I began, determined to be strong, unlike my weaker days of tornadoes and Helen Keller.

"Goodness . . . Is it still snowing too?" Mama asked. "Lord, these Iowa winters. You need to get a coaching job in Arizona or California."

"Yeah, yeah. Holy shit, they traded him to the 49ers. Can you believe it?"

"It's thundering and lightning in January." I realized they didn't want to face the truth, for neither seemed to be listening.

"So? Put a beer in the freezer for Daddy, Aunt Gertrude."

"No, Jack," Mama argued. "You always forget and then they explode."

"The hell I do!"

"Thunder, lightning, and snow are not supposed to happen at the same time."

"Imbecilic weather." Daddy didn't look up.

"Not just imbecilic weather. It means . . . the end of the world."

My parents stared at me in silence.

"There will be fire," I warned, "and more lightning, thunder, snow, tornadoes, floods, hurricanes, and Jesus Christ himself will fly down on fiery angel wings!"

From the looks on their faces, they still weren't getting it, so I rushed to the living-room window, flinging open the curtains for effect. "Then the whole earth will burn to a crisp, and the next thing you know, we'll all be in heaven for eternity singing Alleluia on our knees with the saints. The end of the world is coming. Maybe tonight!" I was gasping hard, pointing to the sky, which was sure to burst into searing, pink flames at any second.

"Well, goddamn," I heard Daddy chuckle. "How would you like to have her ass around in a time of crisis?"

I questioned Sister Mary Analise in class the next day. "Is heaven like church? Are we really going to kneel there forever singing Alleluia? What if we get bored?"

She glared, enunciating each syllable, "You will never grow bored with praising Jesus Christ, when your soul has been bathed by the blood of Christ in heaven."

"But how long does eternity last? Suppose I want to read books in heaven?"

She fixed an eye on me. "Today is the day we are going to learn about the Stations of the Cross. Lent is next month. Who knows why we celebrate Lent?"

"My mother hates lint, Sister." Michael Bolling raised his hand. "It gets in her dryer and on our clothes."

Sister Mary Analise seemed to be sniffing rotten eggs as she smacked her lips together, drawing her yardstick from the lectern to begin indicating each wound of Jesus Christ. In agony on his cross, between a wall clock and a poster with rainbow lettering that read, IT'S NOT WHO YOU ARE THAT MATTERS, BUT WHOSE YOU ARE, I felt sympathy for him strung up there like that, for I perceived my own world narrowing too.

Anchored at my desk, in a sea of antsy third graders, I wondered if there was a third something available that a person could be, other than "boy" or "girl." A kind of third sex, where it didn't matter what you were. You just were, and nobody thought a thing about it and liked you anyway. I looked at Jesus nailed to his lonesome perch, wondering what answers he might have. He looked way too miserable to carry on a conversation. I suddenly wished that Jesus had had a sister. Surely she would've had some great advice for me.

# THE FIVE CENTS

*"Playbook General Information"*

**Playbook: We expect you to keep your playbook neat
and orderly. Keep a record of everything that is discussed.
Become an expert. Take notes. No one is smart enough
to remember everything the first time.**

"You want to hear about sex?" hummed Sarah Camp, my friend who lived across the street, as we rested against the wall inside the snow tunnel we'd sculpted.

"I already know," I assured her. "It's when a woman and man love each other so much that a miracle occurs by their love getting mixed up, and a baby is born."

"Nice try, Saint Joan"—her breath came out in blue circles—"but you're missing the part of how a man's thingy gets real stiff and goes inside a woman's thingy."

"That's a hot damn lie."

"Swear to God. That's how babies are made. You ever seen one?"

"My brothers' but they're nothing . . . a couple of acorns with a thingy."

"It won't look like that when they're big."

"I don't want to talk about it, Sarah."

"Okay, but I just thought you should know. You hungry?"

"Not anymore."

"Come on. My mom made cookies." She crawled toward the opening of the tunnel.

I tried not to look too jarred as I crept out after her, despite the fact my stomach was churning. Peter flashed through my mind. Had his thingy been stiff during our kissing? Mama had never made it too clear how the seed traveled, so I suspected Sarah was right. The mechanics of it sickened me. If I became a boy, was I supposed to do it with girls? Or if I stayed a girl, did I want some guy doing that to me? *Hell no.*

Sarah Camp was one of the girls on Clark Street who taught me the latest chants, plus dirty Tarzan and Jane jokes like, "Jane, Jane, turn on your headlights; Tarzan's snake is caught in your grass." After Sarah's revelations in the snow tunnel, Tarzan and Jane took on a whole new meaning. We also spent the night at each other's houses, standing on guard at the window for the Hook Man, a sinister man with a steel-hook hand, said to be on the loose from the mental home, who preyed on couples in cars. I mimicked my friends' faces, matched their tones, and never tattled on them, and so I was accepted. I loved them dearly.

Sarah Camp knew the most because her Dad was a Presbyterian minister and her mom took night classes in psychology. They had real conversations in that house, where everyone was expected to participate, no matter what your age. I loved it. Everyone's opinion mattered to Mrs. Camp, who used to instigate "Edith and Archie" discussions on feminism whenever we were in Sarah's basement pounding away on her piano, playing "Those Were the Days."

I also loved the way Mrs. Camp looked at her daughter, as if Sarah were the most engaging person she'd ever met in her life. Sarah was the younger sister of two high school brothers, so maybe that's why her mother looked at her that way, since there were no little kids around anymore to wear a person flat-out in that house.

After a visit to the Camps, I slid on my own Sarah mask at home by initiating stimulating conversation. One night, while Mama was bathing Peaches and Leo, the bathroom pungent with steam and soap, I pulled Knute Rockne on my lap and announced, "Edith and Archie are the generation's Alpha and Omega."

"Oh, really?" Mama answered, lathering up Leo.

"Mrs. Camp takes psychology classes," I continued.

"My, my. She must enjoy that."

"You could too. Wouldn't you like to take a class so we could have good talks?"

"We have good talks."

"I mean about interesting things, like—"

"I sing in the Hurricane chorus, and I bowl with the *coacheswives* on Fridays, and I take ceramics. You want to talk ceramics? I just made a basset-hound nose for my mother to rest her reading glasses on. Hand me a towel." She lifted Leo out of the tub.

"That's not what I meant. Mrs. Camp—" I began again, handing her a towel.

"Is not married to a football coach. Now, get some fresh pajamas for the kids." She dried off Leo, who squealed with giggles as she tickled him.


I sometimes tagged along with Sarah to the Presbyterian church on Sundays to listen to her father preach, but it was bewildering not to be worshiping in a Catholic church. Nobody ever knelt, genuflected, or crossed themselves, plus they had no saints or even statues of Mary around, just Jesus and the apostles on stained-glass windows near an empty cross. Communion consisted of banana bread and grape juice, which Sarah said they had only once a month. To top it off, even when I went to Sarah's church, Mama still made me attend early mass first so that I wouldn't commit a mortal sin by breaking the third commandment of missing a holy day of obligation.

So far, I had met only "Christians" in my life, and I now longed to make some Jewish friends. I sometimes wished Sarah were Jewish, because I had just finished reading Peter's gift of *Anne Frank*, and I wanted to race back through time to rescue her from the concentration camp. I pretended that Sarah was really Anne, and I thought of ways of saving her from danger, but she never seemed to require any rescuing. I also needed details about Judaism, but Mama and Daddy weren't much help.

"I wish I could help Anne Frank." I cornered Mama one afternoon while she was ironing: a chore she despised more than anything.

"Liz, turn up the Mozart. It make this job less tedious." Mama looked harried.

"I'd have helped her if I'd known. Wouldn't you have? You were nine when she died in 1945. Didn't Catherine and Poppy want to try to stop the war? Did you ever try to learn about concentration camps and gas chambers?"

"Good God, Liz, I was a kid in Leavenworth, Kansas. I didn't know."

"But if you'd known, would you have done something? Did you read her book when it was published? It must have been a huge thing."

"I suppose I read it. I can't remember."

"You can't *remember*? How can you not *remember* something so important? Did Daddy read it? Did he *care* about all those people who died?"

"Of course he cares, Liz."

"Could it happen again today?"

"Lord, no."

"Are there any Jewish football coaches with kids my age or Jewish players?"

"I don't think so. . . . Most Jewish people are too intelligent to play football."

"Really? Why? I want to know more. How can I do it?"

"Fine, but let's not make this into another Helen Keller thing, all right? It was a tragedy, yes, but we have her diary, okay? That's something. Now please, let me finish these shirts before I scream. Take Peaches outside for a walk." Peaches sprang up, ready to go anywhere. I grabbed her by the hand and we went outside, but my mind was far away, listening to the words of Anne Frank, kissing her boyfriend named Peter, hidden away in that warehouse, waiting to get free. We were kindred spirits. Didn't I have a Peter too? Wasn't I longing to break free? But she was way smarter and braver, and—I glanced down at Peaches, who tugged at my hand.

"What are we going to play today?" she asked.

I thought for a minute, then I smiled. "All right. Your name is Anne Frank, and I'm your big sister, Margo, and we have to go hide in the attic when the German lady who is ironing isn't looking. Okay? I'll even protect you from the air raids and bombs."

"I don't like that attic," Peaches balked.

"Do you want to get sent to the gas chamber instead?" My eyes bored into her.

"No." She popped her knuckles one at a time.

"Then don't ask questions. I'm trying to save your life."

"Okay." She nodded her head, clutching my hand.

"Now I'll gather bread and cheese for our rationed supplies."

"Great." Peaches excitedly followed me as we sneaked through the breezeway. The German lady was still ironing to Mozart in the living room. She never saw a thing.


A few days after our Anne Frank game in the attic, I dragged Peaches into our neighbor's garden and whispered in her ear, "I have bad news, but I know you're going to be brave." I held her hand as we sat among the rhubarb, lettuce, and juicy tomatoes. Peaches had proven to be a wonderful Anne Frank, ducking bombs, hiding from soldiers, eating rations, so I was ready to prime her for our next game, Orphan Child.

"Bad news about what?" Her lower lip stuck out.

"Mama and Daddy can't afford to keep you anymore. They felt too sad to tell you themselves. They wanted me to do it. They can only afford three kids, not four."

"Why?" She looked at me, fat tears welling up in her eyes.

"Look, don't feel bad. You can live here in the garden and eat the vegetables that grow all summer, and in the winter you can build a snow fort to keep warm. Okay?"

Peaches glowered, pulling up a stalk of rhubarb to suck on. "That's a yucky idea," she finally spoke up.

"Please try to understand. Anyway, I have to go now, but I swear I'll visit you and leave you notes. You'll always be my sister. I love you." I hugged her tightly, on the verge of tears myself, the story was working so well. As I waved good-bye and tiptoed out of the garden to the sidewalk, I heard this bloodcurdling scream, and I glanced behind me to discover her ripping around the side of the garage after me. I knew I would be in huge trouble if caught telling so evil a lie, so I rushed back toward her, grabbing her up in my arms, swinging her around, crying, "It's okay, Peaches, they'll take you back. They're so sorry. I talked them into it. You can come home forever."

"Thank you, Lizzie, thank you!" Peaches wept on my shoulder. It was an incredible reunion. Maybe I was her tormentor, but I was also her savior. I'd finally found someone to rescue.

"One thing, honey," I warned her.

"What?"

"Don't ever mention it. Ever. They feel too bad about it already. Just say nothing about it, and everything will be okay. Promise?" I whispered into her ear, carrying her down the sidewalk piggyback.

"I promise, Liz." She wrapped her arms around my neck, relieved.


The next day when I came home from school, I discovered a new brown diary on my pillow with a tiny gold key, plus a library card with my name and address on it. I walked out of my room to find Mama where she was playing Joplin. When she looked up to see me standing there, she said, "Yes, it's for you . . . for your own private stories."

"Thank you, and for the library card too." I wrapped my arms around her neck.

"I'm not a big reader, Liz. Betty always read way more than me."

"I want to write Aunt Betty and tell her about my diary. I owe her a letter. She finally wrote me after about a million years."

"Listen, you write her. She'd love it. She really needs letters now."

"Mama, what did you like to read when you were my age?"

# The Five Cents

"*Lassie Come Home* was one of my favorites, anything with a dog in it . . . but the way you eat up books, I thought you might also like to write things, just like your Anne Frank friend." Her fingers danced on the keys. I leaned against her, watching her work the notes. I wondered why Aunt Betty needed letters now, but I didn't want to interrupt Mama's playing to ask. She had to grab her moments of freedom before someone else did.

Sex came up again the spring after Sarah and I built the snow tunnel. May Day was a big deal in Ames, Iowa. At St. Cecilia's we sang "Mary, We Crown Thee with Blossoms in May," and we placed May baskets around the dilapidated statue, which had suffered from too many Iowa winters. We also made secular baskets crammed with suckers, and trekked around with them, dropping them on people's doorsteps, ringing the doorbells, and running like hellfire so we didn't get caught being sweet.

On May Day, after I placed my very last basket on a door handle, I jumped the fence, snagging my Brownie dress, when an old lady sang out, "Are you the big girl who left me a May basket?"

"It wasn't me, lady," I hollered, bolting off to find Sarah and the Banger girls, three sisters who also lived on the block.

They were in Sarah's backyard, next to her raspberry bushes, lounging on a simple set of monkey bars with their skinny legs wrapped tightly around the poles. Sarah and Barby kept hanging there, smiling as if they had some great secret between them. I backed off, knowing it had something to do with things I wanted no part of. As I tried to sneak away, Sarah spotted me, "It feels good, Liz, especially when you move up and down." To demonstrate, she and Barby began sliding up and down the poles. I made no reply, but then Terri appeared and said, "Let me have a turn."

"Yeah, let me," echoed Mony, following behind her.

Mony was so little that Barby had to boost her up to grab the top bar. Terri just jumped up and hung on. "Now wrap your legs tight around the poles."

Mony whimpered, "I don't feel nothing. My arms hurt."

49

"Just move a little. You'll feel something good." Barby smiled.

Terri and Mony scooted up and down.

"I still don't feel nothing," whined Mony, "plus, I'm tired. Help me down."

Terri didn't say anything, but she was smiling. Mony nudged down, but Terri hung on rubbing quietly. Nobody breathed as she moved a little faster. Finally, she slunk down, and we watched her in petrified awe. I checked for stray lightning bolts.

"Not bad," Terri acknowledged, as she glided away from us. When she disappeared around the side of the house, Sarah asked, "Do you want a turn, Liz?"

"No. Thanks anyway." I flashed a busy grin their way, but I felt every inch of my face burst with shame. I was physically self-conscious for a damn good reason. I saw what other girls looked like naked, and they didn't look like me. I hadn't become all-boy yet, but like Jane in the Tarzan jokes, I got "grass" down there at the age of six, which made me akin to a woolly mammoth freak. I glinted severely at Sarah, wondering if she'd revealed my secret. Recently we went swimming, and by accident, my towel slipped, and in the middle of the girls' locker room, she hissed, "You got hair?"

Humiliated, I scoped out the room, which thankfully was empty. I grabbed her shoulders, calming her, "It's okay, it's okay."

"You got hair. You got hair." She was getting hysterical.

"Sarah, some girls just mature faster. Everybody catches up, sooner or later," I stammered, impersonating my mother's voice.

"But you got—"

"Would you shut up? We can still be friends. Right? Who cares?" Though of course, I cared desperately, for I'd never met anyone who'd "matured" as fast as me.

As my friends stared at me, I swallowed. "I promised I'd do my homework. I have to write a paragraph about the five cents."

"What five cents?" Sarah wanted to know.

"You know, the five cents . . . hearing, tasting, smelling, touching, and seeing. Helen Keller only had three of them," I added.

# The Five Cents

"Five cents is a nickel, brain. You mean 'senses.' " Sarah rolled her eyes.

I knew she was right, because she was never wrong, but I started walking, fast, without retorting, cursing whatever force had turned me into a hairy monstrosity.

When I got home Mama was squashing eggs into raw hamburger for meat loaf, and I asked her, "Don't you think it's strange I *matured* so early? I was six. It didn't happen to Anne Frank or to Helen Keller or to Louisa May Alcott or to Saint Lucy for that matter. Why didn't you do something? I'm a freak."

"I'm telling you, every one of those girls is going to catch up sooner or later."

"What's a freak?" Peaches cooed from the kitchen table, chewing a banana.

"When will they catch up? I can't even spend the night at anyone's house in case their moms make us take a shower together. That would be disastrous."

"I got my period when I was ten. It's in your genes. You can't change nature."

"I hate nature," I shrieked, running out of the kitchen, adding, "Dammit." I just wanted to be normal. I detested wearing thick underwear beneath my girl bathing suits, so people couldn't see anything. Even though I adored my friends, I hated their normal little-girl bodies, loathing my own most of all. I picked up my new diary and wrote: *You want to hear about sex? I'm not a girl, and I haven't been able to become a boy. Warning, evil freak alert. Don't look at me. How could I become a saint with all these disgusting things happening to my body . . . and why weren't there any Jewish saints? What made Saint Lucy a better person than Anne Frank? I didn't buy it for an instant.*

# THE CARDINAL AND GOLD PANTSUIT

*"Split Rip"*

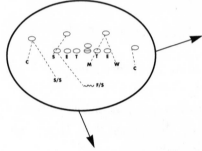

**Man-to-man coverage in the
SECONDARY with the STRONG SIDE CORNER
and STRONG SAFETY in double coverage
(in & out) on the WIDE RECEIVER.**

"I'm sorry, but I am not going to be able to go to Daddy's football game today," I declared to Mama. Her mouth was crammed with bobby pins as she tried to attach a French twist to her head, so she couldn't answer back. I played with the iron crucifix, swinging it like a pendulum above the pompoms lobbed over the headboard. I unscrewed her tub of Vicks, breathing in the eucalyptus. Three Styrofoam heads for her wigs sat on her dressing table: afro, bouffant, and French twist. I carved faces in the heads with my fingernails, filling the Styrofoam eyes with blood-red nail polish.

"I have other plans," I explained, as she anchored the French twist to her skull. I loved hearing my mouth form those words. It made me feel in sync with the universe. I continued, "We're going to the nursing home to play checkers with the old folks."

"God, don't start in today . . . we're in a hurry, Liz."

"Hey!" Joe-Sam hollered from the other room. "I can't find my Hurricane socks."

"Me either, Mama. Joe-Sam stole my good ones," echoed Leo.

"Did not, you punk." There was a sound of tackling, grunting. Knute Rockne began barking, running from room to room in a panic. He hated wrestling.

"Don't you care about old people?" I asked with dignity.

"Of course I care, but your place is with your family when your Daddy has a game. Go visit the old folks tomorrow. I'll drop you off after mass. Now help your brothers find their socks, and check to see if Peaches is dressed."

"Ouch," yelped Peaches from her bedroom. "The brush is stuck."

"None of my friends are going tomorrow," I hissed.

"You're going to your father's football game, and that is that. Did you make the peanut butter and apple jelly sandwiches like I told you?" She stretched her poncho over her head, so she wouldn't muss the spectacular weight of hair on her head.

"Mama, who would miss me if I didn't go to the game?"

"Liz, why do you push and push?" She was on the floor zipping up her red boots. She shoved her calf muscles inside so they wouldn't get pinched by the zipper.

"Yes, but I think I'm sick. I feel hot, feverish . . . I may have . . . consumption." I had no idea what that was, but a girl died of it in the movie *Jane Eyre*.

"You march in and get dressed now and put on some cardinal and gold." She began dabbing blush to her cheeks. She certainly didn't need it.


During the off-season, I had gone to the Ames Golden Age Nursing Home with my friends. We loved going together, where the rich odors of age, cleansers, and institutional food mingled together, filling our nostrils as we squeezed into the lobby. We felt like powerful do-gooders on the sure-fire track to heaven, skidding in and out of patients' rooms, listening to them jibber-jabber about the good old days.

Once, Sarah and I tried to fix up Blind Barney with chatty Agnes. I wheeled Agnes to Barney's door, announcing, "Hey, Barney, this is Agnes."

Agnes pushed me away, wheeling herself straight into Barney's room. "Well, howdy do, Barney? They say a big tornader may touch down come Thursday."

"Get out!" screeched Barney.

"Don't fight, you guys!" Sarah ordered. "Have you ever heard this song?" She began to sing, "Barges," while Agnes and I clapped in time. Barney began to bawl.

"Put that book down and watch the game," Mama yelled from where she was sitting with the *coacheswives* the Saturday my friends went to the nursing home without me.

"His games make me nervous. What if he loses?" I kept my eyes on my book, breathing in the smell of hot dogs, Cracker Jack, and burning autumn leaves.

"His players have made seven interceptions. If you're going to be a writer, you ought to pay attention to what's going on around you." People were starting to look.

"I don't plan on writing for *Sports Illustrated*," I yelled up to the *coacheswives* section, chewing on a Hydrox cookie, but my words got sucked into the roar of the crowd. At every game, while the Hurricanes were either smearing or getting smeared, I was deep into stories like *Amy and Laura* (about two opposite sisters like me and Peaches) or *Queenie* (a tomboy like me who catches squirrels) or *Follow My Leader* (a boy who gets blinded by firecrackers and has to get a Seeing Eye dog—didn't that bring back memories). These characters fired hot coals of hope in me as I identified with the adventures of their worlds, far more palpable than my own.

★   ★   ★

54

# The Cardinal and Gold Pantsuit

During that same football season, I woke up in the middle of one night to the clicking of the Lady Singer machine. I peeked out of my bedroom, and there was Mama at the dining-room table, bent over, lining up fabric, ripping out seams, and stitching them up again. The material had tiny red and gold squares that zigzagged up and down the arms and legs, plus a zipper that stretched from crotch to neck with a rooster button to pull it up and down. She finally modeled it for us one night, her face red.

"Looks like you're caught in a trap," Joe-Sam quipped.

"It's a little snug, that's all. I'm sure it will give a little." Mama stepped around the room like Frankenstein's monster. "It's not like I'm pregnant. I'm wearing this to the Nebraska game."

I picked up the pattern package, and I noticed the warning, "Recommended for Stretch Material Only."

"What kind of material is that, Mama?" I asked.

Her face was getting red. "Bonded wool, I think. Why?"

"This package says something about 'Stretch Material Only.' "

"Give me that," she yanked the package out of my hand and studied it for a minute before tossing it onto a pile of sheet music.

"This will just have to do." She tried working the zipper down. "I worked too hard on it not to wear it."


On the day of the Nebraska game, Daddy arranged for me to go down on the sidelines, a genuine press pass hooked to my belt. I pretended to be a journalist capturing the aura of the October afternoon by breathing in the acrid sweat, Gatorade, and mud chunks stuck in cleats. *They do their long stretches and high kicks, grunting out "Hut one, hut two, hut three, hike." What animals.*

The Hurricanes didn't perform well against Nebraska, and I spent most of the game near the thirty-yard line, watching Coach Mac pace, barking out plays in his checkered pants, blazer, and derby hat. During tense moments, he grabbed chunks of ice, chomping on them, swallowing with no hint of a brain-freeze headache.

Looking into the stands, I could see Mama decked out in her bonded-wool pantsuit, sitting with the *coacheswives* as usual, but she was studying the scoreboard clock. I noticed this only because I was a scoreboard watcher myself. The clicking down of numbers, 14:59, 14:58, 14:57, was the only way I knew for sure we weren't suspended in a football time warp; real seconds were passing; we would eventually go home.

Iowa got creamed 37–10. At the final whistle, Mama appeared on the sidelines with Peaches and Leo in her arms and hustled me and Joe-Sam out of the stadium. Waiting by our car, we found "Cussin' Tom," a rabid but somewhat tongue-tied football fan (aside from his bursts of profanity) who usually took us kids home after the games in exchange for free football tickets. The arrangement freed up Mama and Daddy to hit the Sheldon Mudd Bar on Main Street with the coaching staff for either a celebration or commiseration gathering.

"I'm taking the kids home myself today, Tom," Mama informed him, pushing us into the car.

Cussin' Tom's eyes looked left, right, left-right, before he finally replied, "Shit, shit, shit. Okay by me."

"But Daddy will think we don't love him if we don't wait for him at the locker room. The Hurricanes lost today!" Joe-Sam kicked the seat, then turned his wrath on me. "It's your fault. You shouldn't have been on the sidelines. You lost the game."

"I didn't lose any game for anybody." I vowed to get even with the midget who resented me just because I outweighed him by at least thirty pounds.

"Stop the car, Mama. I want to see Daddy." Joe-Sam tried opening the door of the moving car. "We always go to the locker room."

"Joe-Sam, you want to get killed?!! No *Speed Racer* show for a week, damn you!" Mama hit the brakes to unzip her pantsuit, but the zipper wouldn't budge.

"What's the matter?" I asked, staring at her face, which seemed to be puffing up.

"This pantsuit is a little constricting, that's all. Hold Peaches and give her some juice while we're driving. Joe-Sam, shut the damn door this instant."

# The Cardinal and Gold Pantsuit

"Mama, can we get doughnuts on the way home?" Leo asked.

"Yummy. With pink sprinkles," Peaches echoed.

"No. Now y'all just sit still back there. Don't make me have to use this flyswatter!" She picked it up off the dash, waving it around. All the way home, she whispered, "Son of a bitch, son of a bitch, son of a bitch."


My tenth birthday fell on the Hurricanes vs. Tigers game; we had to have a quick family party before we left for the stadium. I opened my presents with Mama hurrying me along, finally handing me the last gift. As I ripped the wrapping, the bonded-wool pantsuit fell out.

"I know what you're thinking," she jumped on defense. "But honestly, I couldn't even release the emergency brake in this thing, and you're such a skinny-minny, it will look really cute on you. Just give it a chance."

I prayed she'd yell, "Surprise. It's a joke. Here's your real present, sweetie." But "Oh, Happy Birthday, honey," was all that came.

"Run, try it on," Mama insisted, walking me to the bedroom, singing, "Now you'll have even more cardinal and gold to wear to your father's football games."

While I was yanking up the zipper, trying not to cry, an inspiration hit me. I did wild jumping jacks until the middle seam split up the butt. I slipped it off, dressed again in my jeans and sweatshirt, and walked out of my room to show the split seam.

"It didn't fit" was all I said.

"Not at all?"

"Nope."

"Oh, what a shame . . . I worked so hard," she sighed, grieving her loss, not mine.


After football season, we celebrated my birthday with Daddy at the country club, where we went once a month to "Eat Up Our Minimum." All the Hurricane families were charged fifteen dollars a month for food at the country club whether they ate there or not, and Mama was not about to let any cash go to waste. When we arrived that evening, Joe-Sam and I began with our usual: pink fizzy Shirley Temples; Mama and Daddy drank bourbon and sodas with a twist; Peaches and Leo had milk.

I kept an eye on Joe-Sam, who stole maraschino cherries from my drink whenever he could. He gobbled his cherry, while I licked mine, savoring the sweetness.

On my birthday night he grabbed it again, but this time I lunged across the table, zipping past my father drawing his inky football plays on a white napkin, whooshing by Mama sipping her whiskey sour. I punched the thief as hard as I could in his Adam's apple; he gagged up my maraschino cherry onto his plate.

Daddy hauled me up by the back of the neck. "What the hell? Haven't I edified it clearly enough that you don't show your ass in public?"

Peaches started crying, while Mama hissed, "For God's sakes, Liz, if you think you're getting another maraschino cherry after that display—"

"Did Joe-Sam just throw up his tongue?" Leo wanted to know.

The pig himself was sobbing, gasping for air. I knew I looked big, mean, and ugly to everyone at the country club that night, but I didn't care. Revenge was mine.

I ordered, "Tell the truth, Joe-Sam. Was it my fault we lost to Nebraska? Was it?"

Joe-Sam's eyes revealed nothing. Mama and Daddy exchanged glances.

"Did I make us lose by being on the sidelines?" I persisted.

His mouth finally started working, and he whispered, "Nope."

Vindication. He had stolen his last maraschino cherry, plus he'd admitted that I had no control over Daddy's wins and losses.


My triumph was short-lived. When we pulled into the driveway, we saw something sticking out of the bushes. Daddy got out to examine it. Coming back to the car, he announced, "Folks, get tough. Looks like Knute Rockne has gone to dog heaven."

"No, no," I sobbed. "I'm sorry I socked Joe-Sam."

"Come on, sugar-pigs, let's go inside." Mama was crying too.

# The Cardinal and Gold Pantsuit

Joe-Sam flew out of the car, grasping Knute Rockne's frozen hot-dog body, trying to yank him out of the bushes, while Daddy got the little ones inside.

As we sat by the bushes, Mama aimed for the bright side. "You know what makes me feel better? I know when I die, all the dogs I had in this life will be waiting for me in heaven."

"Knute Rockne too?" Joe-Sam asked, his lips blue from the cold.

"Of course Knute Rockne. They'll all be waiting there to greet me . . . to greet all of us. We'll get another dog soon. Dogs and kids belong together."

After somebody in a dogcatcher truck came to get Knute Rockne, Daddy took me and Joe-Sam into the living room to say our prayers. Mama preferred the rosaries, but Daddy liked freestyle prayer. "All right, children, on your knees for Knute . . . Let us pray. Dear Lord, I love you very much."

"Dear Lord, I love you very much."

"Please help the poor folks."

"Please help the poor folks."

"Please let it be a safe world for a boy and girl to grow up."

"Please let it be a safe world for a boy and girl to grow up."

"Please help Daddy get a good head job."

"Please help Daddy get a good head job." Joe-Sam tried not to cry.

"Please help all the poor souls in purgatory."

"Please help all the poor souls in purgatory." I licked a tear.

"Take Knute Rockne to dog heaven."

"Take Knute Rockne to dog heaven." We both burst out blubbering.

"And, God, please help us whip Nebraska next season and kick ass against LSU in the Siesta Bowl." Reality dried our tears.

"All right, end of prayers. Thank you, God. Give me and your Mama a kiss good night and y'all get your little ass in bed. And brush those teeth."

"Yes, sir. Thank you, God. Good night, Daddy. Good night, Mama."

Later, Joe-Sam sneaked in and slept at the foot of my bed, but I didn't say a word. I was glad for the company.

# CHAPTER 8

# THE HUNCHBACK OF ORPHANAGE HELL

*"Double Single"*

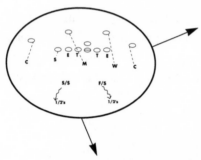

**A two-deep coverage in the SECONDARY.**
**The CORNERS lock on the WIDE OUTS in man-to-man coverage**
**and the SAFETIES play a zone coverage in their**
**respective halves of the field.**

Whenever I got a letter from Aunt Betty, I ripped it open, praying to find out when she was coming again, but she never mentioned it. Her letters were few, and when she called, Mama mostly did the talking, but then I finally got a letter and a gift.

> *Dear Liz,*
>
> *I've been thinking about you. You're already ten. I can't believe it. You must be so tall. I thought my jungle dress might fit you by now. I hope you like it. If it's too much of a dress for a lady, don't wear it until you're ready, but I remember how you liked it. Not much is going on. I closed up the C'est la Vie*

# The Hunchback of Orphanage Hell

*by the Sea. Business wasn't so good. Kiss your Mama. Keep writing in your diary.*

   *I love you, sweetie. Aunt Betty*


I had the jungle dress on as I reread the letter. It was the first dress I'd worn in three years, and it fit me perfectly. The leopards, tigers, and jaguars had faded a little, but it looked great on me. I was about to describe the dress to my diary when Daddy's voice sliced through my thoughts, as he flipped burgers on the grill. "Ladies and gentlemen, this is as close to camping as I ever want to get."

I sighed, writing down the date. "November 1, 1972." We were on our usual Sunday picnic with the Macs. *Dear Diary. It's November and guess where we are?*

"That's right, that's right," echoed Coach Mac, who always spoke so fast he said the same thing twice. *The boys are killing each other somewhere. Peaches and Beth get to be princesses.*

"Y'all are no fun," Mary Martha chided, mixing marshmallows into the salad.

"Hey, Sally"—Daddy poured barbecue sauce on the grill—"I always said, 'Don't ever ask me to shave out of a coffee can.'" *Big HAHAHA from all the adults.*

"I used to go on camping trips all the time with my boarding school when I was a girl," Mary Martha remarked.

"Boarding school?" I perked up, closing the diary. "Like in *Jane Eyre?*"

"Be warned, Mary Martha"—Mama stirred the grits—"Liz has this very romantic idea of boarding school. She thinks it's castles and bells out of the nineteenth century."

"Well, it wasn't as dramatic as all that, Liz." Mary Martha patted my hand. "But we did camp up in the Smoky Mountains of East Tennessee once in a while."

"And you won't catch me hiking either," Daddy continued on his roll. "If you're going to go to the trouble of surmounting a hill, at least have a damn golf club in your hand, right, Donny?"

Coach Mac nodded, slurping his Coors as he and Daddy hovered over the barbecue flames, ladling the steaks with piquant sauce.

"Golf. What a game. Everyone should learn to play." Daddy swung his spatula like a seven iron.

"I'm the queen of worm-burners," Mama admitted. "Jack's idea of a date when we first got together was going to the driving range. He'd say, 'Sally, swing at the tee to practice, and then I'll give you a ball.' He'd hit bucket after bucket. I was such a fool."

"How come I never learned?" I watched Mama shred cheese on the grits.

"Hell, I don't know, Gertrude. You never showed any interest. I think these are almost done." Daddy stabbed the burgers to check for raw meat.

"Did Joe-Sam and Leo show interest?" I challenged.

"Sweetie, boys should learn to play. It's good for them. Go watch the kids. Let the adults have a little time? I'll teach you golf soon if you really want to learn."

I knew a dismissal when I heard one, so I wandered just far enough away to spy from a tree. I stuck my diary in the pocket of my jungle dress, climbing up to a secluded branch above the action, where I could see the kids, all five of them, Peaches, Leo, Beth, Joe-Sam, and Buster, playing freeze tag in the field nearby, but I was more interested in the grown-ups. Lately, I was beginning to notice that the *coacheswives*, regardless of their costume, hair, and tailgate fun, swayed easily with the ups and downs of football, maintaining equilibrium for the family.

I watched the adults sipping their gin and tonics and Coors, their easy mirth cutting into the November air. We considered ourselves full-fledged Iowans after three years of Iowa winters, especially me. I now belonged to this place just as much as anybody, because I had friends who liked me, who called me on the phone just to hear my voice, who invited me to their houses. I planned on being a teenager in Ames, who tasseled corn in cornfields for a summer job.

As the voices grew noticeably quiet down below, I strained to hear what was being said. The words "An interview with the Kansas Bobcats?" wafted up through the leaves, carrying Mary Martha's shocked voice.

"Shhh." Mama clutched her arm. "I wasn't supposed to tell."

*Kansas Bobcats?* That couldn't mean us. My lungs bucked against my ribs.

"On Tuesday. They're flying Jack into Manhattan, Kansas, to discuss the defensive coordinator position."

*Defensive coordinator? Manhattan, Kansas?* I slipped off the branch, then landed on the one below. I tried not to breathe as I clung to the trunk, struggling not to plummet to the ground. *Coaches don't leave when they win. They stay and keep on winning. We were finally winning; it was our job to stay.*

"It makes me sick to think of moving." Mama leaned into Mary Martha. "I love Ames, but Jack's very ambitious."

I inched back up on the branch for now I knew a secret, and I was not about to give it up. Coach Mac's voice cut through the trees as the two men squared off around the barbecue. "What? What?" he roared, hearing the news for the first time too.

"Goddammit. It's an opportunity, Donny. Advantageous, goddam-mit."

*We have opportunities here*, I wanted to scream.

"Opportunity bullshit, opportunity bullshit." Coach Mac flailed the spatula around, flecks of sauce spraying the air. "Riddled with recruiting violations. Riddled."

*Oh, so they were cheaters too. Great. Just great.*

"Shit, they'll be off probation in two years," Daddy said, forever op-timistic.

"Can't win down there. Can't win down there."

*If we can't win, let's not go. We'll lose and have to move again. And again.*

"If he doesn't take a chance, Donny, he'll never know," Mama spoke up.

*She was on his side? We had no chance if she wanted to go.*

"Kids, get your ass to the table. Time to eat." Daddy whistled like a hunter.

Leo, Peaches, and Beth Mac came zipping through the trees like bird dogs, while Buster and Joe-Sam tackled each other on the way to the table.

"Liz!" Mama called. "Where is she?"

"Aunt Gertrude. Your burger is getting cold!" Daddy hollered.

"I'm coming," I yelled, muffling my voice to sound far away. I slid down the tree, edging up to the kids' table, trying to plaster a normal "kid" expression on my face.

The grown-ups were very quiet at their own table. Mary Martha shivered in her cardinal and gold motif, but then, to brighten up the strained picnic, she announced, "Hey, did I tell y'all I'm going on an archaeological dig?"

They kept right on eating. Mama said, "That's nice."

"I'm thinking of getting a degree in it," Mary Martha continued.

All I could hear was food chewing and wind blowing. God, it was freezing.

Daddy suddenly snapped out, "Did y'all hear about Jackal? New offensive line coach? Wants to have a bull brought into the stadium to have it castrated in front of the players to get them geared up for the Siesta Bowl."

"That's right, that's right." Coach Mac finally laughed.

"Crazy SOB," Daddy laughed, a little too heartily.

Mama and Mary Martha began to laugh, too loudly, as if that was just what they'd been dying to do.

"What's castration mean?" Peaches asked.

Before they could answer, Joe-Sam squealed. "It's when they cut your willy off."

"Aw, honey. It ain't gonna happen," Daddy cried, wiping the tears from his eyes.

"Crazy SOB! Crazy SOB!" was all Coach Mac could get out.

The four adults struck a careful truce. After all, they'd been friends a long time. While they finished their supper of thick steaks, green salad, and grits, it grew darker, until it seemed the November night had swallowed us up. When I woke up hours later in my own bed, I felt like I was at the bottom of a murky dream, but I was really peering at the light of the streetlamp coming through my window, trying to figure out if its pale glow was the dying barbecue, wondering where the voices had gone.

# The Hunchback of Orphanage Hell

★   ★   ★

A few weeks after the picnic, we spent Thanksgiving with the Macs. Daddy and Coach Mac sat around watching football games nonstop. Daddy even helped Coach Mac drag up his other TV from the basement, so there were two televisions, sitting side by side with different games on, the sound muted on the less important one.

While Mama and Mary Martha were creating Thanksgiving in the kitchen, I slunk past the football room with a stack of *Ladies' Home Journals* and *Redbooks* tucked in a brown bag. I intended to circle the telephone numbers of boarding schools advertised on the back pages, including one from England. Daddy still hadn't officially told us he had accepted the job with the Kansas Bobcats, but I was preparing for my future. I climbed up into the Macs' attic, the only room in the house where you couldn't hear football, to peruse potential boarding schools. Within minutes, Beth Mac barged into the attic, demanding, "Play with us." She was a chubby little girl with brown eyes and golden hair, a kind of triplet to Leo and Peaches.

"Yeah, please." Peaches skipped in right behind Beth.

"Come on!" Leo stomped through the attic door.

Their determined faces gave me an idea. If I couldn't have the privacy to look at boarding schools, then I sure as hell could create one, and torment my intruders at the same time. "Okay, but you have to do what I say. It's a tragedy with a happy ending."

"What's tragedy?" asked Peaches.

"Something terrible, but your soul gets cleaned out in the process."

They followed me through the coils of the attic as I dug through Mary Martha's wardrobe, where I found the garments I needed. I began adorning all three in old-fashioned clothes, combining the stories of Oliver Twist, David Copperfield, Sarah Crewe, and *Little House on the Prairie* into a brand-new game called Boarding School. First came three dresses apiece, followed by petticoats, scarves wrapped around the heads, and sensible brown shoes. On Leo, I placed kneesocks, short boots, blazer, bow tie, and a boy's black derby hat. An old record player sat in the attic so I put on a beat-up Brahms album, a melodious overture to foreshadow the disaster.

"What are we playing again?" Beth asked.

"Boarding school," I spat. "Now, silence, while I get you ready for your journey."

They stood quietly as I braided the girls' hair in tight ropes and slicked back Leo's with gel.

"This gunk better come out," Leo sulked.

"Quiet, whippersnapper." I felt this odd voice coming out of me, giving me the power to dominate. "This is my attic. Stand up straight." I poked his spine. "Now," I commanded them, "I'm the mother, and you're on the brink of becoming tragic triplet orphans, since cancer is eating away at my innards and entrails."

"What are entrails?" asked Leo.

"Guts." I staggered to my deathbed. "Mama's guts are turning black, rotted with disease. Therefore, y'all must go to boarding school. I adore you. You're my angels."

"No, Mama," cried Peaches and Beth, immediately getting into it. "Don't die."

"This is a stupid story," Leo accused, picking at his kneesocks.

"Play the game or you're dead," I ordered from the bed.

He rolled his eyes, folding his stubborn arms across his chest.

"I mean it." I reached up, pinching his ear like Mr. Bumble in *Oliver!*

"Ow! Don't die, Mother," he uttered flatly, without a shred of enthusiasm.

"Say it right," I hissed. "Like you care that I'm dying."

"Like this." Beth cried, "Oh, mother, mother, mother! Don't die!"

"I'll sound so stupid." He looked miserable.

"God, can't you just act, Leo?"

"Don't die, Mama," Peaches wailed again in an effort to keep up the momentum.

"Exactly. Oh, my girls"—I held them close—"how I want to be with you forever. Be brave in boarding school, no matter what happens."

"Oh, brother." Leo rolled his eyes.

After I kissed each of them good-bye, I sent them to the train station for their long journey. Then I switched into an evil train conductor, followed by a drunken passenger who harassed the young triplets. I set up chairs in the hallway to indicate the train, but the poor things kept getting knocked off their seats because of random earthquakes.

"When does the game end?" Beth wanted to know.

"Is it almost Thanksgiving?" Peaches inquired.

"Do not speak until you are spoken to. I am Miss Minchin." I launched into my hunchbacked matron character, watching them shrink. I heard Mary Martha call to Mama, "Lord, would you look at that? She's got them all dressed up. It's great how she plays with them. She'll make such a good mother."

At last, by a miracle of God, just as things were getting too awful for the poor triplet orphans, I sprang back into the gentle Mother, who'd made a miraculous recovery. I came to their rescue to bring them home from Boarding School.

"Finally," muttered Leo.

"Oh mother, mother, mother," squalled Peaches and Beth, now crying real tears, trying to yank off their sweaty orphan layers.

"I'm going to find Joe-Sam and Buster to make them play with me." Leo wrenched off his bow tie and derby hat and scooted out of the room.

Amid the wreck of orphan props and costumes, we heard Daddy yell up the stairs, "Y'all come on now, it's time for Thanksgiving. I set up a kids' table. Liz, make sure you put all that crap away."

After my invention of Boarding School, I fell even more deeply in love with the idea of attending one myself. I could handle the pain and terror of becoming an orphan heroine like Jane Eyre much more easily than hunkering down in a new football town with a pack of loser Bobcats. Having plotted my scheme, I began to enact it one morning at the crack of dawn, sneaking downstairs with a list of very important phone numbers in my hand. I picked up the phone and dialed the first of ten numbers. I heard the line crackle with static, then start ringing in sharp double rings. After six rings, a British accent announced, "Treeves Boarding School for Girls."

"Is this England?" I asked.

"Yes, quite right."

"Yes, um, my parents want to send to me . . . I mean . . . to send . . . me, their daughter, to a good boarding school and they said to call a few and check out the . . . uh?"

"Certainly, we would like to help, but may I speak to your mother first or perhaps she would like to contact me herself?"

"She's out at the moment. She and my father, that is. Aside from her cancer, they're very busy in the world of football."

"Did you say cancer?"

I was beginning to sweat. This phone call was taking forever. "It has nothing to do with me, and since *they* move around so much, *they* decided that a boarding school would be best for my education."

"Have you been to boarding school before?"

"Well, no, but I've read up on it. I'm sure I could get the swing of it." I wondered if it cost more to call England, since I knew there was six hours' difference in time. "Um, my address is 1411 Clark Street. Ames, Iowa 50010. USA. Send it to Liz Donegal."

"We'll put a brochure in the post straightaway."

"Thank you." I hung up, thrilled at my bravery. Yes. Yes. I had called England. I was in charge of my life. Let my family join the Bobcats; I was off to England. I would write them loving letters and visit on holidays *after* football season.

To prepare my parents for the future, I began leaving notes by their bed that said only, "Boarding school," a sort of subliminal message, so they wouldn't be shocked when my England application arrived. To play it safe, I called up a few in Florida and New York to ask them to send information in case England didn't pan out.

One Saturday morning in December, as we were packing for the Siesta Bowl, Mama burst into my room, waving the phone bill and brochure from Treeves School. Fuming, unable to utter a sound, she whacked me over the head alternately with the bill and packet. Finally, when she could speak, her words poured out, "Liz, I swear to God, if I hear one more word about boarding school, I'm going to scream."

"I just—" I ducked the blows.

"You actually want us to give up our country club membership to send your royal fanny to boarding school in England? Is that what you want?"

"Yes, ma'am, that's exactly what I want."

Her eyes flamed scarlet. "You're going to the Siesta Bowl tomorrow. How many kids in your class are going to the Siesta Bowl? What do you want from me?"

"I want adventure the way Jane Eyre had adventure. I want to see where Cathy and Heathcliff played in *Wuthering Heights*. Smell the heather."

"Of all the selfish . . . Boarding school tuition would mean no more swimming for your brothers or sister or me or golf for your daddy. And you're paying for this phone bill. Dishes for a month plus baby-sitting."

"I do that anyway."

"Boarding school! No kid in their right mind wants that. They want Disneyland or a trip to the circus, but God in heaven, boarding school? You've a got a screw loose somewhere, and you'd better tighten it up, pronto!" She slammed out of the room.

I picked up the foreign envelope smothered with Queen Elizabeth stamps and slid out the brochure for a peek. The pictures of the boarding school looked just like I imagined: mysterious castles where bells gonged and girls in plaited brown braids and clean white socks and saddle shoes walked arm in arm under sheltering trees, sharing secrets. My hair grew barely an inch from my head because Mama refused to deal with tangles, but I could let it grow, couldn't I? Within the walls of privilege, I envisioned clusters of my dearest friends gathered by fireplaces, discussing life's meaning, until the headmistress came around to do bed check. Even the word "headmistress" sounded regal and profound. I belonged with them.

Oh, for that world instead of my own. Tomorrow I was to board a plane for the Siesta Bowl. In one or two months, I would be expected to change from the responsible daughter of a Hurricane coach to that of a Bobcat coach. If my parents refused to stay in Ames, and I couldn't go to boarding school, then what? Trapped. What would Jane Eyre have done? No clue. Maybe she would have moved in with the Camps. After all, Sarah needed a sister, didn't she?

C H A P T E R

*9*

# THE SIESTA BOWL

*"I Right, Toss 37, Turn"*

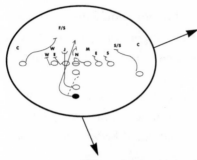

**This action presents the illusion of a toss sweep,
but in actuality, it is a cut back toss with the RUNNING
BACK keying the block on the NOSEMAN.**

We flew out of Ames in a snowstorm but arrived in a sun-drenched paradise at our Siesta Bowl hotel. Mama, close to tears of joy, sighed, "This must be what heaven's like, minus all my dogs." I tried to be loyal to Ames and not enjoy this new place, but I was excited to be surrounded by orange trees, bougainvillea vines cascading over walls, and birds of paradise pluming near juicy jade plants. The only thing that worried me was that our home in Ames might sell while we were gone.

When Daddy's new job became official the week before, I had taken a stand, asking, "Why are we moving?" The secret burst out of me and hung in the air before Daddy lassoed it in a fury.

# The Siesta Bowl

"Who the hell said we were moving?" He mashed his lips together.

"I know what Realtors do; I also know Bobcat Country isn't in Iowa, and I can read the sports pages."

"Goddammit to hell!" Daddy looked volcanic. "A man's gotta do what a man's gotta do, and his kids need to learn to be supportive."

"But what if those Realtors sell our house before we get back?"

"I'll tell you one thing right now. Nobody needs a pain-in-the-ass. We're a football family, and you'd better adapt and get with the program."

My voice stuck in my throat. Our home would be gone. No good-byes, even. I wanted to be there to protect it from strangers. How could I two thousand miles away?

At the Siesta Bowl, Mama and the *coacheswives* fell immediately into the routine of sunning themselves on the adult side of the pineapple-shaped pool, sipping zombies with dinky parasols and cherry chunks floating in them, while the coaches and players geared up to win a game in a stadium surrounded by palm trees.

Everything about California was in direct contrast to the life we'd flown away from in Iowa. Even Christmas seemed out of whack when Mama explained that our Christmas tree was to be the gigantic one in the hotel lobby, since we didn't have time to put one up before we left Ames. *Dear Diary . . . Smelling the scent of pine and ocean roiling in through the hotel windows doesn't really convince me of Christmas. I wonder what Aunt Betty has planned for Christmas. She hasn't answered any of my letters in a long time. Maybe she's got new friends now.*

*The Siesta Bowl, The Siesta Bowl, The Siesta Bowl . . .* it was written in cheerful letters on everything, plus tiny Siesta Bowl stickers stuck to all the fruit. One night, the coaches decided to take their wives into Tijuana to dance with mariachis, and the hosts of the Siesta Bowl arranged a baby-sitter for all the coaches' kids, since there were too many boys for me to watch by myself. Her name was Hortensia, and she taught me bits of

71

Spanish, letting the boys run wild. Six sons of coaches were busted by the management for dropping water balloons off the balcony. Hortensia got fired for teaching me Spanish instead of being a responsible baby-sitter.

The next day, the Siesta Bowl people took us all into T. J. for a kind of family field trip. On the way down, Mama kept a washcloth on her head.

"*Qué pasa*, Mama?" I asked, since she looked quite sick.

"Please, don't talk," she whispered.

"Leave your mama alone, Liz. She kicked it up with one too many mariachis last night." Daddy was reading the San Diego sports page.

"What are mariachis?" I asked.

"Short Mexican men who play music." Daddy didn't look up from the paper.

"Please, don't talk," Mama whispered.

I was quiet the rest of the way into Tijuana, where we were dropped off at the markets around Revolución Boulevard.

"Barter with those Mexicans now," Daddy coaxed me and Joe-Sam. "Barter 'em down. They're just selling junk, and you gotta get 'em to bring the price down."

I really didn't know how to make anyone bring the price down, but I had twenty dollars of baby-sitting money in my pocket, and I wanted to spend it. After a few minutes of browsing, I spied a golden glass swan. I had never seen anything so beautiful, roosting there in the sunshine of the bustling market.

"How much?" I asked the man with a droopy mustache.

"Fifteen dollars."

"Okay," I squeaked, buying it. "*Buenos días.*"

"*Buenos días,*" he said without smiling, handing me the hefty swan by its neck.

When I found Mama, she was carrying a globular swag lamp on a chain. Daddy was behind her with straw wine holders, wearing a sombrero. "What did you buy?" Mama exclaimed, staring at my swan, which was about the size of a two-year-old.

"A swan. It's kind of cardinal and gold. See? For the Hurricanes."

"How much that sumbitch weigh?" Daddy eyed it critically.

"How are we supposed to get it back home?" Mama wanted to know.

I didn't answer them as they crabbed at me all the way back to the Siesta Bowl bus, where I heard Daddy whisper to Mama, "We could offer to hold it for her and then drop it." She laughed, feeling better after a lunch of enchiladas.

Me and my swan boarded the coach in silence. It was big enough to sit next to me in its own seat. I stroked its cold glassy feathers as the two of us stared straight ahead, waiting to be driven back to San Diego. I didn't care what Mama and Daddy thought. Everyone knew swans were beautiful. Even me.

On the afternoon before the bowl game, Daddy burst into our rooms, shouting, "Guess what! We're going to the San Diego Golf and Country Club golf to see Lee Trevino play golf, so get the hell ready to go, ya big turkeys." I knew this was supposed to be great news, so I got ready fast. I brought my swan along with me.

Upon our arrival at the country club, the Siesta Bowl people guided us over to the first tee to watch. Lee Trevino smiled, taking his club, thwacking his ball into the air. Everyone clapped with respect. I couldn't clap, because I was holding my swan. The two head coaches hit their balls. Coach Mac hit a pitiful worm-burner, but nobody dared laugh. He whispered, "Goddamn you, goddamn you."

Lee Trevino smiled again, waving to his fans. We waved back, but then his caddy grabbed his club and golf bag, and Lee and the two coaches jumped into their golf carts, speeding off to find their balls. I thought we were finished with them then, but soon discovered we were just beginning. We had to follow Lee and the coaches on foot. I couldn't believe this was the actual plan. This was Daddy's "great news"? I looked at him to make sure I had it right. He caught me looking and carped, "What'd you bring that goddamn swan for? Sumbitch don't belong on a golf course."

I didn't answer him. Whenever anyone looked at me, I grinned until my teeth throbbed, so they wouldn't suspect what I was thinking. I swung my swan by her neck. She was dead bored too. By the fifth hole, I couldn't

73

take it anymore. It wasn't just the golf game. It was my whole life. I let the crowd get ahead, before allowing my knees to crumple under me, giving way so I slid to the ground, lying flat on my back in the middle of the crisp green fairway thinking, *I'll find a phone, call Sarah, ask if I can be her sister, if my swan and I could move in.* I began making grass angels, leisurely moving my arms up and down, the way I made snow angels.

I gazed at the cobalt sky, the sun gushing through waltzing clouds. I turned my head to watch Lee Trevino and his disciples get farther away, until the very last head dipped down over the hill. I was alone, completely free. Oh, peace. My swan sat reverently beside me, a serene guardian angel on the fairway. After a while, my legs stopped tingling and felt stronger too, so I got up to go order a Coke at the clubhouse. It looked similar to the one at the Ames Golf & Country Club, only much fancier, with live pink flamingos standing on one leg hoofing it around the fountains of shooting water. I was still at the clubhouse sipping my Coke when Lee Trevino and his entourage, including Daddy, came back. His snappy blue eyes were on fire as he yanked me by the arm toward the bus.

"Well, goddamn!" he heaved. "Why didn't you just try to mortify me a little? I told your mama to leave you there . . . 'Just pretend you don't know the sumbitch.' "

"I'm sorry." I tried to squirm away from him, but Mama swooped from around the side of the bus, squawking, "Are you nuts?"

"Sorry, sorry, sorry."

"Damn right you're sorry. You lay your ass down in the middle of the fairway with a freaking Mexican swan. I just hope to God nobody noticed."

"They noticed," Mama sneered.

His head looked ready to blow off his neck. "Aw bullshit. Give me that swan."

"No, don't," I yelled as he raised my golden swan high above his head, ready to smash it into a trillion sharp crystals. I screamed, feeling like I'd be smashed right along with her. Just then, Mary Martha appeared, "There y'all are. About time to go now."

Daddy let the swan down, since he couldn't very well crash it at the feet of the head coach's wife. As he turned away, I picked up the swan, crying, "Daddy? What about me? What about Ames? Are you even sad about leaving Ames?"

"Get on the bus. Get on the bus." Daddy spoke like it was his mantra.

I stood in the gravel, looking up at Daddy's face. There were tears biting his eyes. There was nothing else for me to do. I got on the bus.

On the last day in San Diego, LSU kicked our cardinal and gold ass at the Siesta Bowl, so the Hurricanes finished the football season 8–4 instead of 9–3. Nobody really cared. We all felt too bad because of the Montezuma's revenge that hit. During the game, a few coaches, players, and families were either sneaking out of the stands or off the football field to find toilets. I think the kids got it because we ate way too many suppers at McDonald's, and the grown-ups succumbed to the spicy chile rellenos, enchiladas, and salty margaritas in T. J. It didn't affect Daddy, who had decided early on that the best way to eat Mexican food was to chase each bite with swigs of Kaopectate right out of the bottle at the table, which is what he did for most of the bowl trip.

At the beginning of the third quarter, a potbellied drunk fell on me in the stadium stands. He smashed me between the bleachers when his body just fell over on mine. It felt like slow-motion crushing. Fortunately, Uncle Whitey and Uncle Peter, who'd flown in for the game, dragged him off me, ordering him to go home.

During the fourth quarter, Peter said, "I heard about your swan."

"Everybody hates it."

"I'd like to see it."

"Don't lie."

"I'm not. I would," he smiled at me.

I picked up the swan from under the bleachers and handed her to him.

He studied her for a minute, letting the sun glint off her proud gold back. "She's lovely," he said. "Just like you."

I studied the moons on my fingernails, ready to burst with affection for him.

"You know, you're lucky, Liz."

"Lucky? How?"

"You're moving. Do you know I've been in the same house my whole life? Sixteen years. At least you get to have adventures. See new places and people."

I didn't answer him. He placed the swan in my arms, and we watched the rest of the game together in silence, holding hands.

Afterward, I went around the Siesta Bowl hospitality room, asking all the *coacheswives* if any of their husbands were accepting new coaching jobs at other universities, recording the answers in my diary. After about the fifth wife, Mama pulled me aside. "Stop asking everyone such personal questions."

"I'm not trying to be personal. I'm trying to find out the truth."

"The truth is your daddy is a great coach, and the Bobcats want him."

Finally, after all the coaches and players had cleared out, Daddy appeared, always the last one out of the showers. Mama hugged him since he looked so sad at not winning his last game as a Hurricane coach. Then, as he reached down to pick up his duffel bag, I asked, "Daddy, could you just tell me why we are the only ones moving, and I won't say anything else."

His shoulders sank. "Goddammit, darling. This is my dream. I want to be a head coach. If I don't take risks, I'll never get that opportunity."

"What about my dreams?"

"Sweetheart, you can follow your dreams when you get grown up, but for right now, it's my show. My shot. And you need to get your skinny ass on the team. Got it?"

"Yes, sir," I said quietly.

Outside the stadium, we said a brief good-bye to Peter and Uncle Whitey. Peter whispered, "Liz, you write me if you ever need anything. Okay? I can drive now." I was impressed as I hugged my uncle, my friend. At least I had him. We boarded the airport bus with the other coaches and families, because our flight back to Ames left in an hour. Daddy didn't come. He took a taxi to catch a plane to Bobcat Country to follow his own dream.

# THE UGLY LITTLE HOUSE ON THE PRAIRIE

*"Bobcat Policies"*

**It is each player's responsibility to be on time.
Women are not permitted in a player's dorm at any time.
Unauthorized use of drugs is prohibited. Use of marijuana is also
definitely prohibited. Players are not permitted to associate with gamblers
or frequent places where gambling occurs.**

"Look closely, folks," Daddy commanded from the driver's seat as we careened along the Kansas highway the following February. "Watch the horizon, and you can almost imagine Indians riding over the plains." I looked but saw no Kansas Indians, no wild horses piercing the horizon. I was smashed into the backseat, crammed against our new black Lab puppy, Bear Bryant, who was drooling his brains out. He was supposed to be kind of a consolation prize for leaving Ames, but I knew the score. I propped my feet up on the ice chest, ignoring the boys' wrestling match, Peaches's chattering, Daddy's blasting sports-talk station, Mama reciting the joyful and sorrowful mysteries.

It all became too much. I began yodeling, "Iowa, Iowa, that's where the tall corn grows," with enthusiasm. Joe-Sam joined me.

"That's enough, you two!" Daddy yelled after the third rendition.

"Iowa, Iowa, that's where the TALL CORN GROWS." Joe-Sam and I were hot.

The coach swerved over to the shoulder of the freeway, gravel spitting from his tires as the ground the Buick to a halt. Silence swallowed the car, as we kids scrunched down in our seats to dodge his gold-ringed knuckles, chopping the air, determined to snuff out acts of insubordination.

"IOWA-IOWA-IOWA," we piped out in a final rush.

Just inches out of his range, I could feel jet streams of air as his hand slapped at the emptiness surrounding me.

"Ow, Daddy," Leo protested as Daddy's Siesta Bowl ring impacted his skull. "I didn't do nothing. I'm just eating Little Debbies."

"It's for all the stuff you're gonna do, Big Time."

"Come on," Mama sighed. "Here, Liz, why don't you eat an apple and think of this move as one big adventure."

"I don't want another big adventure."

Daddy arched his body from the driver's seat over into the backseat, reached for my door, flinging it open. Wind rocked the car, semi trucks yowled past, as I squinted at the road stretching on the other side of the windshield.

"Don't let the doorknob hit you on the ass on the way out, Aunt Gertrude."

"Can we just have pleasantness, please?" Mama sang, her lap spread with bologna and sandwich spread. "Who wants a sandwich? Yummy bologna, kids."

A brick farmhouse with a windmill and tractor in front stood about a hundred yards away. A woman in a bulky sweater standing on the porch seemed to be staring, asking, "Do I know you? Are you in trouble?" I considered jogging over to introduce myself just as Bear Bryant leaped out my door, but Daddy grabbed him by the tail. "Get your ass in here, Bear Bryant."

Bear Bryant reluctantly crept backward, panting sorrowfully at all of us with his limpid brown eyes, his toenails digging into the Styrofoam lid of the ice chest.

"Are you a part of this family or not, Liz?"

Peaches began to cry. "Don't make her get out, Daddy. She's sorry. Right, Liz?" She draped her hand over mine, her little fingers sweaty with concern. I closed the door, curled up on the seat under a beach towel to stifle my sobs, self-loathing pouring into my soul like gasoline. Daddy revved the engine. My ears closed, I willed reality to be absorbed into the fabric of the Hurricane team towel as I drifted back to the last week in Ames. I resolved to chisel the details into memory forever.


Mary Martha threw an afternoon surprise party for Mama the week before we left. Everything and everyone at the party was decked out in purple to prepare Mama for the Kansas move; the violet water in the fishbowl, going-away presents, a sequined bra and panties, grape-juice daiquiris, candies, cookies, Jell-O mold, streamers, and sweet breads. I watched from the basement where I was baby-sitting.

That same night, Sarah Camp threw me the first surprise/slumber party of my life, inviting lots of St. Cecilia's girls. When I walked into her basement to find my friends waiting for me, Mrs. Camp playing "Those Were the Days" on the piano, I grew dizzy with love for all of them. I wanted the night to go on forever and ever. I kept having perfect moments with my friends, one right after the other.

"Liz, I'm really going to miss you. Thanks for never telling on me at school."

"Liz, I always liked your glasses. They make you look smart."

"I wish I were tall like you. I'm so short, everyone makes fun of me."

We kept hugging each other. The girls with long hair let me brush and braid it. We played the radio for hours. A song we all adored, "Killing Me Softly," suffused the midnight air. Everyone fell asleep, but Sarah and I stayed awake, swearing to stay friends, no matter how the domination of grown-ups orchestrated our lives.

"Are you sure I can't live with you?" I asked her for the millionth time.

"Lizzie, I want you to, and even my mom said she'd think about it. It's your parents who refused. They called up my mom and told her just to humor you, that there was no way they were leaving you behind, especially in the fourth grade. . . ."

"I hate that."

"I know. Liz?" Sarah looked very serious. "When you grow up, be a Democrat."

"Why?"

"Because John F. Kennedy was one."

"Okay," I answered, wondering how she could already know about such things as politics. All I knew was Nixon and the Vietnam War. Some girls in my class wore a silver chain bracelet with P.O.W. and the missing man's name etched on it. The war was not discussed in our home. Daddy's only connections with wars were opposing teams.

The day we left for Kansas, Sarah and the Banger girls came to say good-bye. We sat on the curb, doomed. As the yellow moving truck backed out of the driveway, I gave those moving guys the finger, and so did all my friends. The men just drove off laughing, as Daddy banged out of the house, ordering, "All right now, girls, say your *arrivedercis* and get it over with."

We hugged, cried, swearing to write forever, and by three P.M. that afternoon, the Iowa sun slated against the marble sky, Ames became a memory as we took the highways toward Des Moines, Kansas City, and ultimately, Manhattan.

"Iowa, Iowa, that's where the tall corn grows." I vowed never to forget my home.

When we first arrived, we lived in the football dorm, because Mama and Daddy couldn't decide which ugly little house on the prairie to buy, plus it had to be a brand-new house, since Daddy couldn't fix anything. When one Realtor attempted to take us all on a tour of one of the older neighborhoods in town, Daddy balked, saying, "Nope, sorry, folks, this won't do. We need a new house on a new lot in a new subdivision. My ass isn't the least mechanically inclined, if I may speak frankly."

"You always do," sighed Mama.

"Well goddamn, all I'm saying is we need a house with no problems. Best to buy one that's never been lived in. No leaky sumbitching faucets and all that other crap. No surprises, just a house that works."

Mama was in complete agreement, because she knew she'd be the one making small talk with any plumbers or repairmen, so after that, the Realtor always drove us down streets with lots of construction and the skeletons of new houses being formed. There was always at least one completed home sitting up on a large hill of black dirt or red clay (depending on the state), which was typically Daddy's choice. He'd also tell the construction guys to convert the garage into a rec room big enough to hold a pool table and a wet bar. As far as he was concerned, a garage was a big damn waste of living space.

Until they found it in Kansas, we remained in the football dorm. Peaches and I slept in dorm beds, while the boys crashed on the floor in sleeping bags. One night, when Mama was kissing us good night before returning to her own dorm room, Daddy barged in, "Coach Eliot's invited us for a cookout Friday night."

The ugly face of Coach Eliot loomed before my eyes in the darkness. He was the fast-talker who had lured Daddy away from Ames in the first place.

"His wife is the alcoholic?" Mama zipped up Leo's sleeping bag.

"What the hell's that got to do with anything, Sally?"

"What's an alcoholic?" I asked. As far as I knew, I'd never met one before.

"Jesus, Sally," Daddy fumed. "Now what'll she do with that?"

"What, Jack? I just thought you said not to expect much partying in Bobcat Country. You said that we should watch—"

"What's an alcoholic?" I asked again.

"Shhh," Mama whispered. "I thought you were asleep, Liz. An alcoholic is a person who drinks liquor and can't stop."

"You guys drink."

"Yes, we do, socially, but we know our limits. That's the key. Knowing your limits. Now go to sleep and don't mention a word of this on Friday night. Do you understand? I'm sure Mrs. Eliot is a very sweet lady with a lot of pressures."

"Do you know any other alcoholics?"

She stopped, then sat down on the bed. "Your Aunt Betty is an alcoholic."

"That is a bold-faced lie." I was outraged.

"Why would I make that up?" Mama's eyes widened.

"I don't believe you. Maybe it's because she never comes to visit us anymore. She's lonely. If you'd just invite her, maybe she'd get better."

"Betty would like to live with us, but I told her no. I can't look after her and four children. Football is very demanding. I don't have a lot of support at home with Daddy gone all the time, and the last thing I need is for Betty to bring all her problems here. I love her, but—"

"She looked after us when Peaches was a baby. She was a great story-teller. She loves me very much. I have her jungle dress. I would look after her."

"I bet you would. Now I'm only telling you all this because you're mature and can handle it. I don't want you discussing it with any-one."

"I miss her . . . I haven't seen her since I was a kid."

"Get to sleep now . . . okay?"

"I'm not tired."

"Say the rosary. It helps."

"No, thanks. I just want to think awhile."

"I love you, Liz." Mama put her hand on my head.

"Yes, ma'am." I closed my eyes, seeing *Oliver!* with Aunt Betty and Joe-Sam. It seemed like another life, but every so often, I could hear her velvety voice speaking to me in my dreams.

On Friday night, when we went to the Eliots', Mrs. Eliot opened the door and, speaking in the raspiest twang I'd ever heard, drawled, "Hey y'all, welcome to Bobcat Country." Her voice died away, like she was too whipped to say another word.

"Thank you," Mama spoke up. "I'm Sally, Jack's wife, and these are our children . . . Liz, Leo, Joe-Sam, and Peaches. Say hello, children."

"Hi, hello, hey, howdy," we muttered.

Mrs. Eliot smiled at our foreheads; her arms dangled like limp celery.

Mama pressed her palm against my spine, which was the signal for me to stand up straight, but I slunk off to the side of the porch to get out of her range.

"Woo-hoo! Is that Sally Donegal?" boomed a hearty voice. "Lord, gal, get in here. Jack's told me so much about you." Coach Eliot appeared in the doorway with Daddy following. He was a burly man with a silly grin; strands of frizz matted across his shiny head. Both men wore purple and held cans of beer.

"There she is now! Miss America!" Coach Eliot grabbed Mama and goosed her.

"Oh my." Mama tried to jump away.

"Lord God, gal, you gotta passel of 'em." Coach Eliot winked at her. "Just like us. Come on in, y'all. Let me git a look at you."

"Yes," echoed Mrs. Eliot. "Bless your heart, come on in."

Mama wrenched free of Coach Eliot's grasp, giving Daddy a warning look that he ignored, as we all trooped into the foyer. Then she grabbed me by the arm. "Liz honey, get Peaches and Leo dressed, and y'all can go for a swim. Joe-Sam, you help too." We ducked down the basement steps, which led to a rec room, where the walls, rugs, pool table, pompoms, pennants, and furniture were all various shades of purple.

"I like purple, but pink with purple dots is my favorite," Peaches announced, pulling her swimsuit over her chubby hips.

Later, by the pool, I studied Mrs. Eliot, trying to figure out what made her an alcoholic; I noticed she downed glass after glass of purple Kool-Aid in a Bobcat glass.

"You have children?" Mama took a crack at conversation.

"Four boys," Mrs. Eliot sighed.

"Four linebackers," corrected Mr. Eliot, chugging the last of his beer.

I wondered where those linebackers were, but then I figured they'd ditched the party because they knew the new kids were coming. I spoke, up, "No girls?"

"No, biscuit." Her voice was barely audible, as she stared into a bowl of Cheez Whiz as though she were looking for answers.

"How are you, big gal?" Coach Eliot directed this at me, as he trotted off the deck over to the diving board.

"Fine."

"Good for you. You going into high school?"

"Liz'll be in fifth grade," Daddy piped up.

"Well, they sure grow 'em big in Iowa, don't they?" Coach Eliot honked.

"Liz can eat, that's for sure. I tell her she'd better marry a farmer when she grows up so she'll have plenty of food. Voracious appetite."

I tried to scrinch my bones into a delicate position. *Impossible.*

As the boys bobbed up for air in the water, Coach Eliot yelled at them, "You're gonna love Bobcat Country, young men. Noooow leess-sen heeeerre, y'all. We gonna win. Isn't that right, Mrs. Eliot? We gonna knock some balls to the walls."

"That's right, Coach Eliot," she sighed, drinking more Kool-Aid without looking at anyone.

"Y'all be sure to watch my highlight show too," Coach Eliot contin-ued. "On after every game. I sell stuff that the fans send in. Purple baby blankets, sweaters, socks, caps. You can buy it right off the TV. A little lady from Atchison sent in the prettiest purple pig last year. Crocheted it herself."

"How about that now, folks?" Daddy's tone sounded forced.

"Purple is pretty," Peaches laughed.

"My, my," Mama hummed, dipping a chip into the Cheez Whiz.

Mrs. Eliot smiled toward the stars winking over the prairie.

The purple pool was warm, shaped like a bobcat, but much smaller than the pineapple pool at the Siesta Bowl. A snarling bobcat, in a football jersey, was painted in the bottom. The lights under the water gave off a violet glow. I let Peaches ride on my back in the water, Joe-Sam let Leo ride on his, and we had chicken fights. Naturally, we smeared them. I was the queen of chicken fights.

★   ★   ★

# The Ugly Little House on the Prairie

When Mama wasn't watching *The Guiding Light* in the football dorm lobby, she was out with Manhattan Realtors discussing new split-levels, foyers, and the Catholic school in town. Whenever she was gone, I baby-sat the kids, and college girls would come up to me, inquiring if I would go upstairs to retrieve their boyfriends. I always obliged, climbing the stairs where I would see hallways of guys, some naked, some not. One morning, I knocked on a door. An impatient voice droned, "Yeah?"

"Um . . . Your girlfriend . . . she . . ."

"I don't have a damn girlfriend," whipped the voice. He opened the door to look at me, wearing only a grimy jockstrap. I forced myself not to notice.

"Your girlfriend, I mean, Mary . . . she's downstairs."

"Thanks, kid. Now tell her to get lost. Can you do that?

"Uh . . ."

"You play football, kid?"

"Uh . . . uh . . . yeah . . . Sure." I dug my hands into my letter jacket, one of Daddy's.

"Cool. Stick with football, stay away from women. They'll ruin you. Got it?"

I got it.

"Now go tell that whiny bitch to beat it. See ya."

I lurched past three naked guys who swaggered down the hall.

Downstairs, I ran smack into Mama in the lobby chatting with a Realtor.

"Excuse me a minute." She flashed her teeth at the Realtor, before taking me outside. "Liz, you've been up in the men's dormitory again, haven't you?"

I stared past her shoulder, trying to see a future.

"Listen, those college girls may think you're a boy, and maybe their boyfriends do too, but you're a girl, and I don't want you going up there anymore."

"You don't understand." I jerked away, walking to where Mary was waiting.

I broke the news gently to Mary. "He's a creep. You should know that."

"Yeah, I guess I do. Thanks anyway." She jumped on her bike and pedaled off.

Another college girl approached me, but before she could speak, I said, "I'm sorry. I'm not going up there anymore."

"Why not?"

"Because I'm a girl." I didn't look at her. "I really am. Ask my mother."

"I'm so sorry," the college girl stammered, leaving fast.

I turned to look at Mama, her pretty animated face in conversation with the Realtor on the dorm steps. *Miss America.*

> *Dear Diary,*
>
> *Miss America hates Bobcat Country, and it's not just because the Bobcats are losers, although that doesn't help matters. She hates it because the people aren't fun like the Ames folks were. Miss America is a party girl, and the Ames folks were party people. Everybody was always getting together, going trick or treating or snowmobiling, but nobody does anything like that in Manhattan, plus there is no Mary Martha to laugh at the soaps with, so she fills her days decorating our new house, which smells so awfully brand-new. Fresh-cut wood, thick shag carpets, and lots of perfect paneling and Formica. Even the faucets look like the display models. I'm afraid to touch anything. I don't want to leave fingerprints. No proof that this is my house. My house is in Ames, Iowa. It's five hours by car, eight by bus. I already checked.*

"How does this look?" Mama asked one afternoon as I watched her hang straw wine-bottle holders and ponchos on every wall. "And what about this?" She pointed to the ceramic bulls on the shelves and three fringed leather vests draped over hooks. "And last of all . . . ta-da." She waved her hand at a series of sombreros swinging from the bar light, and the globular swag lamp shining on the furrowed statue of the Virgin of Guadalupe, next to three iron balls with spikes adorning the wet bar.

"Where's my swan?" I asked, realizing something was missing.

"Swan?" Mama pretended not to know what I was talking about. "Oh, that swan. It's in the garage. Did you really want it in your room?"

"Yes, I want T. J. in my room. That's her name, by the way," I snapped, barreling into the garage. I found her sitting in a cold corner behind some flat tires. I picked her up, dusted her off, and brought her into the warm house, where I fixed her a comfortable nest. As I placed the swan in her own bed, Mama walked into my room with a mug of hot cocoa. She stared at the swan. "Here, drink this while it's hot. I must say, Liz, old T. J. isn't half bad." Mama gave her a pat on the head as she walked out.

After Mama finished decorating, Daddy decided to have his players over for dinner, so they could all bond. I was reading *Little Women* when the entire defense pounded in the front door. Peaches heard them and cartwheeled into the living room, wearing a purple cheerleader outfit, shouting:

*Firecracker, firecracker, boom, boom, boom.*
*The boys got the muscles,*
*The coaches got the brains,*
*The girls got the sexy legs,*
*So we win the game.*

She jumped into the air, squealing, "Rah rah. Go, team," as she'd seen the real cheerleaders do. Everyone applauded, except me. I was going to have to teach that brazen prima donna a thing or two about the dangers of parading around like a four-year-old hussy.

After a few months on Wind Chime Drive, the Rolands moved in down the street, a family with fourteen adopted kids, including three sets of twins, their names all beginning with "R." An added bonus was that a few had missing fingers or hands.

"Don't you think it's neat that fourteen orphans moved in down the street?" I asked Mama one day while she was sewing more purple curtains.

Mama gave me a look. "No people in their right minds adopt fourteen children."

"Can we at least invite the Rolands over sometime?"

"Fine, as long as they don't all come at once. Okay? I couldn't take it." Mama snipped off yards of purple fringe to sew to the hems.

Before I even had the chance to invite Mr. and Mrs. Roland and their kids over to our house, they began dropping by anyway, unannounced, for a cup of coffee or a chat. I liked their noisy social calls, but I could tell they set Mama on edge. To thwart these visits, Mama began making us switch off all the lights in the house, so the Rolands would think we weren't home.

"Get quiet," she hissed the evenings we were out late, turning off the headlights as we drove into the driveway, trying to sneak into the house without getting caught.

"Just tell them to go away," Daddy said one night when he came home to find us sitting in the dark.

"I can't tell them to go away," Mama snapped. "You tell them to go away."

"Look, Sally, if you don't want the sumbitches around, be forthright with them."

"You be forthright with them!" Her voice scaled up several octaves. "Oh, but you can't. You're not here, are you?"

Joe-Sam turned up the sound on *Creature Feature* to drown out the argument, but Mama dove for the television. "Y'all kids keep the sound down, or they'll know we're here. I mean it."

None of Mama's precautions worked. The Rolands kept coming in droves. In desperation, she roped me into her plot to rid herself of them. "Liz, you go down right now and tell those people your mother has *nerve* problems," she said one afternoon when I got home from school. A few minutes later, I found myself standing in Mrs. Roland's crowded kitchen, explaining it to her. Mrs. Roland nodded her head sympathetically, and the next day, the twins Rosy and Rex appeared with two apple pies to speed along Mama's "nerve problem" recovery, and left without coming in. Mama considered this a real victory.

"This is delicious. Thank you, honey," Mama smiled, relief washing her eyes. "Do you realize that Mr. and Mrs. Roland haven't visited in twenty-four hours. . . . Those twins didn't stay . . . it's a good sign. You must have been very convincing."

"I tried." I swallowed a sweet apple morsel.

"How's your nerves, Mama?" Peaches' eyebrows arched.

"They're fine, sugar, much better," Mama laughed, scooping up another bite.

Joe-Sam and Leo burst into the room, grimy from a game of kick the can. They stared at us devouring one of the pies out of the pan.

"That's sick," Joe-Sam accused. "Why don't you get a knife and cut a piece."

"I want some too," ordered Leo, grabbing a fork, unfazed by germs.

Peaches and Mama and I looked at each other and started laughing. Finally Mama said, "Joe-Sam, you can have a piece of the other pie. It hasn't been touched by human mouths yet. We're doing just fine here, aren't we, children?"

Mama fed me another big bite of pie. As I swallowed, I felt so close to her, so glad that she had nerve problems too. It made me realize we had something in common.

# T R A C K   C A M P   B I T C H E S

*"Dogging System"*

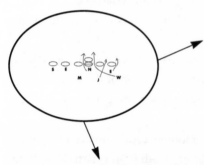

**Penetration of the line of scrimmage by a
LINEBACKER or consortium of LINEBACKERS on the
snap of the football, e.g.: "Nose Strong, Will/Jack Invert."
The Purpose of a "Dogging Defense"
To create a big play on defense
—a turnover or tackle for a loss.
To pressure or sack the quarterback.
To cause confusion in the opponent's pass protection
assignments. To confound or destroy blocking
coordination on running plays.**

"By the way, you, whatever your name is, I get dibs on this bed."
Sandy's voice swirled around my head on our first day of track camp.

"Yeah, you," began Lacy, the other one. "The bed on that side is
mine. Sorry, I guess you don't get one." She bared her braces at me in a
smirk.

She reminded me of a lizard, unblinking, ready to strike, as I shrank
by the cold radiator, feeling like Frankenstein meets the Lolita twins.

"We heard your dad is a Bobcat coach. So do you think you're great because of it?" Sandy oozed onto the floor in a split.

"Great?" I ventured.

"You know. Stuck-up?" Sandy's belly was flat on the floor, her chin pressing into her palms.

"Hot shit?" Lacy slid to the floor to join her: their small bodies, agile, arched, flawless. The whispering began, followed by peals of laughter, bodies still molded into perfect splits. I could tell they hoped I would cry, but I was not about to satisfy them. I opted for a lame smile, but my facial muscles froze. As their stares baited me, a fury settled behind my eyes: the kind where you have visions of twisting a telephone cord around your enemy's scrawny neck or mowing her down with one of the tractors that sits on the lonesome prairie, watching her limbs gush up in a fountain of blood.

"Ew." Lacy got up to inspect my mouth. "What's wrong with your teeth? One's kinda black and the other's chipped. Gross."

"Yick," Sandy echoed, jumping back as if it were contagious.

"It was an accident." I choked out the words, my hand clamping over my mouth. I ran my tongue across the jagged grooves of my front teeth, cursing Daddy, cursing the fake cap that had begun to darken, loathing my life.

Right before track camp, he and I were bolting through the house playing a game of chase with Mama warning us to settle down. We wouldn't. At one point, he shoved me into my room, laughing, pulling the door shut tight. I tried to twist it open with all my might, just as he let go from his side. The oak door hit me full in the face, knocking out most of my two front teeth. It hurt so much . . . like someone spearing a sword into your gums. I saw his face looking down at me, ashen.

"Are they loose?" I screamed. My fingers fumbled to touch the pain.

As Daddy bent down, I saw him scoop up bits of broken teeth. He and Mama packed me into the car to go to the team dentist, who put temporary caps on my teeth that same night, but they still looked fake.

He informed me I could get real porcelain caps when I was sixteen, but for now, these would have to do.

Mama tried to make me buck up about the situation a few days later. I was sucking bites of cereal with my side teeth, because of the throbbing ache in my front teeth, when she crowed, "Liz, this may be a good thing. I always thought your permanent teeth were too long anyway. They'll look better shorter."

"The capth look fake."

"They do not!" She swabbed the harvest-gold counters with a sponge.

"They do too," Joe-Sam assured us, drinking milk straight from the bottle, wiping his chin. "Rex and Rupert Roland asked why you got some dentures."

"Would you get out of this house, boy!" Mama snapped a dish towel at his head.


"Do you want to be a football player?" Sandy's ice-pick voice jerked me back to the room, which now felt like a violent kaleidoscope . . . *jazzy with heat, tangled with crayon colors.* "Is that why you dress like one and wear that stupid letter jacket even in July?"

Lacy exchanged looks with Sandy. "You want to come swimming with us?"

"I don't know." I moved blindly toward the door, fingering the knob, my escape.

Lacy upped the challenge. "Why don't you put on your bathing suit?"

"I'm putting mine on . . . I'm not shy. See?" Sandy strolled about naked, her body hairless, fatless, unblemished. She was both elf and eel; the bile rose in my throat.

"Where's the bathroom?" I turned the knob on the door, eyes set on the floor.

"Just do it here . . . we're all girls. Aren't we?" Lacy pulled off her top.

Their naked bodies were identical; I hated them. "I'll meet you at the pool."

"Chicken."

"Fuck you." The words plunged like icicles melting free. "Fuck you maggots in the head until you're dead." I shocked myself, I was so calm.

"We're telling that you said the 'F' word," they chanted in unison.

"I don't care. Tell. You, you . . . flat-chested rodents. I bet your mom still shops for you in the baby girls' section."

They were both taken aback, but it took only a few seconds for Sandy's eyes to slit. "Well, did anyone ever tell you you need a bra? It really shows when you run."

"Yeah, and you should shave your hairy legs, too," sneered Lacy.

Suddenly a smile spread across Sandy's face, her eyes dancing. "Hey, Lacy," she cried, "she's hairy, but she jiggles. Maybe she's a boy-girl. Are you a he-she? That's what my papaw calls 'em."

As I galloped down the corridor toward the exit doors, I heard their giggles scorching the air and imagined their heads chasing after me, disconnected from their bodies, bobbling behind me like swollen balloons. I didn't know what they wanted from me, nor why they so instantly despised me, but I knew they spoke the truth. I was hairy, I did jiggle, and I deserved death. I dashed through the campus, ran across prairies and over a highway, where I made it back to Wind Chime Drive by sundown.

"How did you get home?" Mama found me panting in the driveway.

"I'm not going back. Not ever . . . You don't know what those girls said. I didn't do anything to them," I yelled, my eyes stinging from prairie dirt.

"Why don't you take a shower, honey? You'll feel better after all that running. I'd like to call up those girls now. Talk to their parents. What did they say?"

"Oh, God. Don't. Don't ever."

"Honey, sometimes girls are just plain meaner than boys. I mean with boys it's sheer physical combat, but with girls, it's this kind of mental torture."

"I hate their guts."

"Fine, now come inside and eat. I'll make your favorite. Pork chop and potato casserole. Okay?" Mama draped her arm around me as we went into the house.

★　★　★

Daddy was home when I got out of the shower. He came into my room while I was looking up the word *hate* in his thesaurus, because *hate* was not strong enough for what I felt toward those track camp bitches. I wanted real words I could store as ammunition, and I found them: *abhor, loathe, abominate, detest.*

"I'm quitting track camp," I told him as I copied down my list of hate words.

"You're not a goddamned quitter."

"Oh, yes, I am."

"Aw bullshit, you tell those snotty tramp-tails to go defecate in their headgear. You're not going to let a couple of morons ruin a decent opportunity for you to develop some skills as an athlete."

"I don't give a crap about skills as an athlete. I'll run across the prairie every day for a month, ten times, a hundred times if it'll make you happy; just don't make me go back." I grabbed him around the waist for emphasis. "I implore you, Papa."

"You're going," he ordered, unpeeling me from his body. "If you quit, you'll be doing exactly what they expect you to do, goddammit. You're gonna show those no-good turds a thing or two."

The next day, I hung out at the track and hid under the stadium during breaks. Both Sandy and Lacy were sprinters, so I asked to be a long-distance runner. I also requested a room change, but the counselor said room assignments were permanent. When we gathered for lunch, I steeled myself not to look at their faces as I stabbed at the glossy yellow gravy with turkey floating in it.

In the afternoon as I dove into the pool, "Hey, He-She!" sailed through the air, just before my head cut through the water. I stayed under until I thought my lungs would explode, then burst to the surface, sucking in air, lunging to the depths again.

That night, I cornered Joe-Sam, pulling down a sweat sock. "Does this look like a girl's leg to you?" I asked.

"No way, man," he said respectfully, dribbling his basketball.

" 'Cause it's not and don't you ever forget it," I warned him.

"I won't, man, I swear," he nodded.

But it was a girl's leg . . . I knew it, and I hated it. I went into my parents' bathroom and picked up Daddy's razor, contemplating the double-edged sharpness. Then I reached for the shaving cream, squirting the cool lather from thigh to toe, from fingers to elbow and I began the business of shaving. It took forever. I changed blades three times and used ten Band-Aids for all the raw nicks, but by the time I was finished, no one could call me a he-she anymore. Mama peeked into the bathroom at one point and yelled, "My God. What are you doing in there?"

"Nothing." I shoved her out, bolting the door.

Jiggling the handle, she cried, "Oh, Lord, Liz. What did you do?"

"Don't worry, Miss America," I spoke calmly . . . scrape . . . strip . . . peel . . . scour.

"If you call me that again, I'll smack your smart-alec mouth."

"It's a compliment."

"The hell it is."

"What would you know about being a low-down hairy dog?"

"What? You're not!" She waited. Silence. "Oh, fine, Liz. Have it your way. Shave your head if it will make you happy," she railed through the keyhole. "But you'd better clean out that sink, 'cause I don't want to see one stray hair. You got that?"

"Yes, ma'am."

"And Liz? For God's sakes, be careful with that razor. You're not even eleven."

"That's true, Mama, but remember . . . I'm very M-A-T-U-R-E."


Daily, the Nazi track coach insisted on everyone doing sprints together. "Hey, He-She, don't trip over your huge boat feet," snickered Sandy as we lined up to race.

"I shaved my legs," I snarled in a whisper, adding, "You stinkbug from hell." I resisted the urge to rake her face with my fingernails, drawing blood.

As the gun popped, so did something inside my chest. I was faster than Sandy, and as I hit the finish line ahead of her, I sideswiped into her body, sending her sprawling toward the long jump, but I just kept running. I flew past the stadium, the dormitories, the cafeterias. I was soaring. I actually felt my feet leaving the ground as if I were about to cruise into the air, high above Bobcat Country, far from the slinging insults. My plan was to jog to Ames. I could actually see the cornfields beckoning me, when a counselor, Jo, grabbed me by the collar.

Jo was everyone's favorite counselor, but I was shy of her. I didn't want to be deemed camp loser. She guided me over to the campus library steps and handed me a grape soda, which I chugalugged. Then I studied the tiny print on the soda can.

"I grew up on a farm . . . summers were the best time," she remarked after a while.

I read the ingredients: fructose, sucrose, benzoate . . .

She tried again. "So what's your favorite season?"

Fall was my favorite season, but I was goddamned if I was going to tell her that. I crunched the can in my hand, bending it into two halves.

"How'd you get all those cuts on your legs?" She studied my wounds.

I didn't reply, pulling my T-shirt over my arms, stretching it down over my legs, hiding my body dotted with nicks and Band-Aids. *None of your business, babe.*

"I heard you just moved here."

"Yes, but it's very temporary."

"Very temporary, as in you're going to run away?"

I burst into tears. Humiliated to be crying where everyone could see me, I slunk behind some tall bushes. The salt from my sweat and tears stung my cuts.

Jo reached behind the bushes, patting me on the back, as I wept for the loss of my home, my teeth, and most of all because of those poisonous girls.

When I'd cried the last of my tears, we took a walk across campus, breathing in the scent of honeysuckle, and then Jo offered a magic antidote. "How would you like to change rooms?"

My heart danced with possibility, hope.

"I don't have a roommate," she continued, "and since you're a day-camper, it's not like you're going to be in my way. Of course, I'm on another floor."

"Another floor?" It was beyond a miracle. Jo smiled at me, and for the first time, I felt like I had a big sister, and I felt thrilled to be strolling next to such a divine angel.

By that afternoon, I was moved in. All I had was one grocery sack with a change of clothes, soap, and toothbrush. Jo taught me to play gin rummy during breaks, how to shave my legs without slicing myself to ribbons, plus she never said a word about my dressing in the closet.

> *Dear Diary,*
>
> *The cretinous, disgusting, psycho track camp bitches from the underworld still follow me around, but Jo is great protection. They hate me more than ever for living with the best counselor at track camp, but I don't care. As I learn to walk past those two lowlifes with my head held high, I get stronger. I am not their roommate, and I will never ever be their friend. Even though it's not saintly, I pray they burn in hell. I belong with Jo, who is smart and kind. It feels great being a girl around her, because I look at her as my own future model. If I have to stay a girl, I accept my fate if I can be one like Jo. She even looks like Laurie Partridge.*

After track camp, just when I was ready to celebrate being home free, I got my first period, which lasted for a marathon of sixteen days. Mama, thinking it was the greatest thing, pulled out her econo-size box of sanitary pads from under the sink, plus some belts to demonstrate their workings. Mortified, I watched her hike the belt and pad up over her brush velour purple pants to demonstrate.

"Women have been doing this since the beginning of time," Mama beamed.

"How can this be happening? I've been a boy for so long." I tried to make sense of my body's betrayal.

"You were never a boy," Mama said. "You just got that into your head is all. But if it will make you feel any better, it won't last forever. I can promise you that."

By day ten in the cycle, I knew she was lying like a dog. She kept buying more Stay-Free at the store, tossing the boxes into the shopping cart at Bobcat Grocery like they were bags of apples. I despised the girl on the box running across a beach like a free-floating fairy. I was terrified Daddy would find out. I knew I had his respect as a powerful girl, but if he were to find out the truth, I was sure he'd be disappointed in me that I wasn't tough enough to stop it. I made Mama promise not to tell.

One night he came home after practice, muttering, "Jesus Christ. Worst team I ever saw. Bunch of crap." Then he called over the banister, "Hey Liz, your feminine supplies are on the top of the refrigerator." My face burned. Watching *Brian's Song* on the TV, I concentrated on Brian Piccolo dying of lung cancer. Daddy had coached Brian in North Carolina, but I didn't remember him. Gale Sayers was holding Brian's hand in the hospital room when Daddy called again, "Hey, Liz."

"I heard you!" My lip trembled; Brian was barely breathing.

Leo glanced up. "What's female supplies?"

"You promised!" I hissed at Mama, who was matching socks.

"Oh, honey, it's just Daddy. His mama and his grandmother and his great-grandmother all had periods. It's no big deal. He's proud of you."

"AAAGGGGG. I can't believe you!"

"You're on the rag?" Joe-Sam laughed.

"What rag?" Leo looked confused.

"Shut up, you pricks!" I lunged at them, but Mama body-blocked me, railing, "Don't you ever use that word again."

"Why? They are pricks. *Relax.* It just means they're like the prick of a pin."

"That's not the definition. You are not to use that word. Ever. Got it?"

"Fine."

"No, not fine."

"Yes, ma'am! Fine! Fine!"

Then Brian Piccolo died. We missed it screaming about pricks.

# Track Camp Bitches

★    ★    ★

My next move was to plan a hysterectomy. Mama had been talking about Mrs. Coach Eliot having had one, and it seemed like just the ticket. I called Jo to get the lowdown. "What exactly is a hysterectomy?" I asked her.

"It's just an operation that means you won't get your period anymore. They kind of gut out your insides."

"Gut?"

"Pretty much."

"Oh."

"It'll get more regular, you know. Your period."

I didn't know what to say to that, so I just said, "When? I feel like Moses in the Red Sea," and hung up. Mama passed by with a sack of groceries. "Boys don't have to go through this." I followed her. "And from the way the girls in fifth grade look at me, I'm the only one. And don't say they'll catch up. I've heard that lie since I was five."

"It is not a lie."

"And I'll never forgive you for telling *him*!" I went into the bathroom and soaked my hands under scalding water to rid myself of this rush of womanhood.

"I'm very sorry," she called from the keyhole. "Now, be grateful you're becoming a woman. You'll be glad for it if you ever want to have children."

"I'll adopt, thank you."

I waited for her response, but there was none coming. I heard her footsteps as she walked down the hall. A few minutes later, she was singing softly, crooning, "Someone's in the kitchen with Dinah, someone's in the kitchen I know oh-oh-oh." I knew she was rocking Peaches on her lap.

I got on the scale: 133 pounds. Mama weighed 110. "Someone's in the kitchen with Dinah, strummin' on the old banjo." I longed to be five years old again and have my mother sing to me. If I sat on her lap now, I'd crush her petite bones.

99

# LEAVING BOBCAT COUNTRY

*"40–50 Wham"*

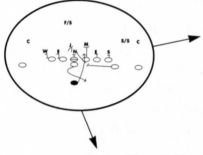

**Featured in a ONE BACK style offense. A most
effective method in separating the defense and creating blocking
angles for the OFFENSIVE LINEMAN. The "H" BACK utilizes "bang"
motion and "wham blocks" the first down lineman from
the center box to the backside.**

The Bobcat football team finished the season 0–11. The final indignity occurred when Coach Donny Mac's Hurricanes came down from Ames to womp us on our own turf. It was strange to be cheering for the loser Bobcats after rooting for the Hurricanes for so long. It was like changing religions from Catholic to Baptist. We had worshiped Harry the Rooster, who symbolized a sort of "Hurricane Jesus," but suddenly, there we were in our purple vestments, praying for the Bobcats. Nobody on our side of the stadium was even cheering. The closest thing we had to a mascot was a caged baby bobcat brought in for every game from the Kansas City Zoo. You couldn't even see it unless you knew where to look and had a pair of binoculars.

# Leaving Bobcat Country

As hulking flashes of cardinal, gold, and purple flailed across the field, I sat in the stands, reading *A Tree Grows in Brooklyn*, about an eleven-year-old girl named Francie Nolan, who would have been my best friend if I could have reached back to 1911 to grab her by the hand. I also wanted Daddy to become Johnny Nolan, Francie's father, without the drinking. He was gone so much, I was beginning to fantasize about him quitting coaching to become a singing waiter, dreaming of spending more time with me.

> *Dear Diary,*
>
> *I've been dressing up Bear Bryant like a ballerina for shows with Peaches. My brothers get even by dressing him up in football pads. He doesn't seem to mind either way. I wish I could see my father more. He works so hard for our family because he couldn't live without us, but I miss him so much. He's like the "Phantom of the Opera"—or I guess I should say "stadium." I hear him late at night and early in the morning. I smell his cigars and Scotch and soap, but when I look, he's not there. Where are you, Daddy? I can see you in the press box of the stadium if I squint hard enough or on the sidelines on TV during the away games. Daddy? Daddy? Hello. Hello. Let's you and me take a trip down south where the cotton blossoms grow, just like Johnny wants to take Francie. You take Joe-Sam recruiting. Why not me?*

By the third game of the season, Coach Eliot had stopped hollering, "We gonna win," and took to silently dipping Skoal from a tin he kept in his coaching pants. I managed to get a sidelines pass once, where I watched him spit stream after stream of tobacco juice during every fumble. Mrs. Eliot didn't go to the games at all, but Mama took her place among the other purple wives, where she sat in her poncho, sharing a thermos of Irish coffee to keep warm during the games. The Bobcat wives were a solemn group of women, each realizing her husband was on the verge of being fired.

After the final massacre by Coach Mac's Hurricanes, Daddy emerged from the steaming locker room, grinning, "Alleluia, folks. The sumbitch is over."

Mama clung to his arm as the boys and Peaches scampered after them.

I followed, wondering if he was going to get fired, as was the rumor. What would happen to us then? Maybe we could move back to Ames? Maybe Coach Mac would give him his old job. After all, they were our friends, right? I decided the only thing to do was ask Coach Mac myself, since they were coming over for dinner that night.

Daddy pretended to be jovial for Coach Mac and Mary Martha, cooking ribs on his new Mr. Smoker out on the deck. I greeted the Macs at the door, as if I'd been starved for their company all these months.

"How are you, Mrs. Mac? Coach Mac?" I smiled my best Francie Nolan smile, shy but intelligent, making my eyes brim with understanding. "I need to talk to you about something, but come in out of the cold. Please." I hauled them both inside.

Mary Martha hugged me, saying, "How are you, sugar? Where's your mama?" and then swept past me before I could stop her.

"Coach Mac," I grabbed him. "Would you like coffee? You know, I could stick a lump of chicory in it . . . My friend from Brooklyn, New York, makes it that way. It tastes strong, but I put milk in too." I could feel Francie Nolan coursing through my veins, but Coach Mac only stared at me strangely while stomping the snow off his shoes.

"Hey, Donny! You down there?" Daddy hollered.

"Coach Mac"—I blocked him in the foyer—"I'm a proud person, but I have a favor to ask before you go upstairs." I tried to be gentle like Francie, but I was desperate.

"What is it, darlin'? What is it?" he edged away a little, concerned.

"My-Daddy-wants-his-old-job-back-in-the-worst-way-so-could-you-give-it-to-him-and-don't-say-I-told-or-he'll-kill-me-please."

Coach Mac, the king of fast talk, smiled. He gripped my shoulder, nodded his head, and then went upstairs, yelling, "Got any Jack Daniel's up there? Any J. D.?"

*Deliverance*. All I had to do was ask. The head coach had agreed. He even liked me as Francie Nolan; he had comprehended the gravity of the situation, and now we were going home. To Ames. Sarah Camp. The Bangers. Clark Street.

A few minutes later, as they all raised their glasses for a toast, Coach Mac announced, "I've accepted the Pittsburgh Sharks job, Pittsburgh Sharks job."

My heart stopped.

"Pittsburgh. Whooo-doggie. Hell, Donny, that's great," Daddy congratulated him, shaking his hand. His voice oozed enthusiasm, but his eyes glowed regret.

*Pittsburgh?* Why had Coach Mac betrayed me?

"That's wonderful, Donny." Mama's voice sounded hollow. I knew she was worried about Daddy, plus heartsick at facing the long winter ahead on the prairie.

"Want you to come with me, Jack," Coach Mac commanded. "As my assistant head coach! Assistant head coach!" He looked at me and winked.

I was sick. I realized I should have been more specific, but before I could think how Francie would react, Daddy wiggled his hips, juggled some ribs, and did the goosestep, rejoicing, "Goddamn, Donny, my ass is there."

"Hell," Coach Donny Mac grinned, "let's win the damn National Championship, the National Championship."

"You bet your ass, buddy." Daddy's gloom over the Bobcat football season evaporated, and he was back in business, the coach who knew how to win.

"What about Ames? Coach Mac? Sir?" I spoke up, trying to appear calm.

"Hell, sugar, done all I could in Ames, all I could. Took 'em to two bowl games. Rebuilt the program. Now's a chance to move on, move on to new opportunities."

"Well, I've never been so relieved to see a football season end," Mama sighed, putting her head on Mary Martha's shoulder.

"Honey, you're going to love Pittsburgh. They even fly the *coaches-wives* to the away games on a special charter jet, so you'll never have to miss any."

I was the wart in the room, loathing my life being turned upside down. Again. "I'm not moving," I said. "Unless it's back to Ames."

"The hell you're not. Now eat a rib, you'll feel better!" Daddy ordered.

"What are the colors of the Pittsburgh team?" Peaches asked.

"Blue and gold, little gal, blue and gold," cheered Coach Mac.

"Then I need blue and gold pompoms," Peaches announced.

"Great. Now I can give all this purple crap to Goodwill," Mama cried, dancing and dipping Mary Martha around the living room to the stereo's "Knock Three Times."

"Things are looking up. Lordy, we're gonna be Pittsburghers. Haw. Who needs another beer?" Daddy cracked them open with jubilation.

When I told my Kansas schoolmates that I was moving, they looked at me in confusion, "You just got here, didn't you?"

"That's what happens in the crazy world of football."

"When are you leaving?"

"My daddy's already gone. I guess as soon as my mother sells the house. She hammered a For Sale sign in the snow yesterday."

"Your mother is going to sell it herself?"

"She's going to try, so they won't have to deal with Realtors and lose money."

They looked at me as if I were from some foreign planet. They'd all been together since birth, and nobody had ever moved away.

"You ever coming back to visit?" one asked.

"Sure," I said, secretly vowing to revisit all the places I'd been wrenched from when I was finally old enough to do so.

"Boy, I wish I could move. I've lived in the same house my whole life," one girl sighed. "How many states you lived in?"

"Florida, I was born there, but then we moved to Mississippi, Kentucky, North Carolina, Iowa, Kansas, and now Pennsylvania."

"How can you remember them all?"

"I can only remember bits of North Carolina, but all of Iowa. It's one of the best states in the whole country, but I may go for a visit to Florida to visit my aunt who used to have a very upscale resort by the sea and plans on reopening it any day now."*Liar, liar, liar,* the saints sang in my head.

Before the conversation could continue, the bell rang, and as I followed my class inside, I wondered if I should try to look more like Francie Nolan by the time we moved to Pittsburgh. I touched my hair, which was hacked in a short shag. At this rate, I didn't even look related to Francie. If only we could wait until I had long braids.

With Daddy gone to Pittsburgh, our days fell into a routine of schooldays, and a treat after Saturday night mass of going to Mr. Steak. I figured the waitresses thought we were a divorced family, since we were in there every weekend without a father.

"Remember Papa? Coach Jack Donegal?" I began one evening after we were halfway through our steak dinners. "Francie Nolan's papa died when she was fourteen, but mine is very alive. Right?"

"He'd better be. Could we have extra ketchup?" Mama smiled at the waitress.

"Papa says ketchup ruins a perfectly good steak; he says you should only use it on eggs," I warned her.

"Well, good"—Mama cut up steak for Peaches—"you don't have to have any."

"Why are you calling him 'Papa' now?" Leo looked suspicious.

"He personally asked me to," I smiled. "Hey, Joe-Sam, you think the Pittsburgh Sharks are going to win any games?"

"Sure they are with Daddy coaching." Joe-Sam blew milk bubbles until Mama slapped at him under the table to quit.

As Leo chomped on his steak, spitting out the meat when he grew bored with chewing, Mama spoke in a low voice. "Swallow your meat, sir, this minute, or you'll stand in the corner when we get home."

"I'm too tired." Leo flicked at the pile of jawed-up beef on his plate. "Can I get some coconut cream pie now?"

"You're such a Pillsbury Dough Boy," laughed Joe-Sam.

"I bet Papa's heart is *rupturing* with loneliness for us," I burst out to get Mama's mind off Leo's jawed-up steak carcass. "Does anybody remember what color his eyes are? I've been trying to remember, but for the life of me, I can't."

"I miss my papa." Peaches's lower lip trembled dangerously.

"Peaches, sweetie," Mama sighed, "Daddy misses y'all kids very much; now hurry and eat up. Coconut cream pie is coming."

"Why don't he call us ever?" Peaches looked worried.

"Peaches," I rushed to assure her, "I talk to Papa every night. He simply can't wait for us to join him in Pittsburgh so we can be a true family once again."

"May I ask what book you're reading now, Liz?" Mama set down her fork.

"*A Tree Grows in Brooklyn,* and Francie's papa calls her 'Prima Donna,' and he sings her Irish songs like '*In Dublin's fair city where the girls are so pretty, it was there I met sweet Molly Malone.*' Why can't Papa call me Prima Donna?"

"Papa's been gone forever," Peaches whispered, hot tears spilling.

"Wine refill?" asked the waitress to Mama.

"Please." Mama shoved her glass toward the waitress.

"Next time he calls, Peaches, I promise, I'll put him on." I squeezed her hand as sympathetically as Francie would.

"You lie like a dog," remarked Joe-Sam.

I kicked him hard under the table, all the while smiling at my baby sister who needed my comfort and love.

"Children," Mama's voice arched through the air, giving the other Mr. Steak patrons pause to glance at our table. She lowered her voice. "Next person who says anything unpleasant is finishing their Mr. Steak in the Rambler!"

Sometime in February, Mama left to go house-hunting in Pittsburgh, but instead of a new puppy to atone for the disruption of our lives, she hired Jo as our baby-sitter, which made us roommates again. I was her shadow as she taught me how to play the guitar and drive a pickup truck. Mama was gone for only two weeks, but I spent some time in her closet, smelling her clothes and perfume. I loved having Jo, but I also needed to know Mama and Daddy weren't dead like Johnny Nolan; I made vows to be a better daughter to both of them. The days I was extra lonesome for Mama, I listened to Jo from Mama's closet, playing John Denver melodies to the kids or some of her own homemade songs on the guitar with lyrics like

*Nettie, Nettie lying on the bed . . . one boob out and one boob in . . .*
*Nettie, Nettie led a life of sin . . . one boob out and one boob in . . .*

One day, Jo took us on an adventure in her pickup across the prairie to spin 360s, but after one swivel, her truck got stuck in the mud.

"Hell's bells." She kicked the wheel as she got out.

We all climbed down to look.

"Maybe we could get a board," I offered.

"What for?" she asked.

"I'll tell you if you do something for me."

"What?"

"Buy me a bra, so I don't jiggle anymore," I whispered in her ear.

"Get us out of here, and I'll get you one. No big deal."

"All right, stick the board at the back of the truck under the wheel. For traction."

After we speared the wood under the tire, she said, "You drive, I'll push."

"Okay." I turned the key, gave it some gas, and floored it out of the mud.

"Well, aren't you something?" Jo said, climbing into the pickup. "Move over."

As we drove off the prairie, she took the road out to Sears to buy me my first bra. It was lacy with a rose stitched between the cups. It was a little snug, but I was willing to suffer. The kids got A & W chili dogs.

On the morning Mama was due back, Peaches and I played orphanage in the driveway. Jo was inside cleaning the house, and the boys were playing kick-the-can down the street. Peaches wore my old Brownie uniform, and I tied a thick scarf on her head, commanding her, "Sweep, orphan child . . . ungrateful little beast. Sweep for your supper." The broom was a foot taller than she was.

"I'm sweeping," she cried, "see?," just as Mama drove up in the taxi.

"How are my girls?" She grabbed us up with big kisses. "Listen, y'all, I've found a pretty new house in Pittsburgh in a cul-de-sac, and every room has shag carpeting. How do you like them apples?"

"When's Papa coming home?"

"As soon as this bastard of a house sells. You know, I'm tempted to leave it with a Realtor after all. Did anyone come look at it while I was gone?"

"No."

"By the way, all the Iowa coaches are now Pittsburgh coaches, so we'll get to be with all our old friends again. Isn't that great? It won't be so much like starting over. Now I've got to pay Jo." She started to walk inside.

"Hey, Mama, wait." I smiled. "Look what Jo bought me." I stretched my T-shirt flat to reveal what was underneath.

"What is that, honey?" Mama stared.

"Look. It's real." I snapped the bra strap for effect.

She got a funny look on her face. "I could have gotten you one."

"I didn't want one before."

"Peaches"—Mama turned on her suddenly—"when you're ready for a bra, you let me know. That's what mothers do. Understand, missy?"

"Yes, ma'am," said Peaches, wide-eyed.

"And Liz," Mama sniffed, "congratulations."

"Thanks," I said, tracing the rose between the cups, knowing it was beautiful.

"Am I still gonna be an orphan?" Peaches asked.

"No," I said. "Now you're Francie, and I'm your aunt Sissy, and we live in Brooklyn, but you still have to do what I say, only I'm nice, and my bra's a corset."

"Okay." Peaches took my hand. "What do I do?"

# Leaving Bobcat Country

★　　★　　★

One year after leaving Ames, Daddy returned to Manhattan, Kansas, to move us to Pittsburgh. At the baggage claim, I carried his suitcases for him, the way I always did. He slapped me on the back, looking so handsome. I walked close to him to make sure every single person at the airport knew this man was my father.

"Daddy, let's sing the way Francie and Johnny sing to each other," I pleaded.

"Who the hell are they?" He carried Peaches in his arms; the boys had their fingers looped on his belt.

"A father and daughter who are crazy for each other. They know Irish songs. 'When Irish eyes are smiling,' " I sang.

"Sweetheart, I can't sing a lick. Besides, I never heard of 'em."

"But, Daddy. . . ."

"Sally"—Daddy kissed Mama—"you're gonna love Pittsburgh. It's got nightlife and action. I even checked into the Pittsburgh Symphony Chorus for you."

Mama smiled, her arm linked around Daddy's. I kept up a steady pace with the suitcase, concentrating on getting to the car with them without breaking stride. Maybe I would read him *A Tree Grows in Brooklyn* aloud on the trip to Pittsburgh, so he could learn about other kinds of fathers and daughters. I took a deep breath and beamed a gentle Francie Nolan smile with my mouth closed. (Francie had lovely white teeth.) Why, even if Daddy couldn't be Johnny I could be Francie Nolan on my own without any help from him, thank you very much. If I could just remember to be like her at all times, then the ugly, boring parts of myself would disintegrate, and I would be loved by one and all upon my arrival in Pittsburgh. Some new friend, a friend like Jo, might even say to me, "Hey, Francie, baby, where've you been all my life?"

# JAG-OFFS

*"Butt 'em in the Mouth, Knock 'em in the Dirt"*
*—Larry Beightol*
*Offensive Line Coach*
*and Assistant Head Coach*
*Miami Dolphins*

**The heart and soul of any good offensive football team
is its offensive line. There is no position that requires more discipline
or technique. Our success as an offensive football team hinges
on our ability to control the line of scrimmage. Our battle cry:
"Butt 'em in the mouth and knock 'em in the dirt."**

As Francie Nolan, I was certainly not loved by one and all at my new school, St. Sebastian's, in the north hills of Pittsburgh. I wore a wig of brown braids bobby-pinned to my skull and a heavy muslin dress with a petticoat. Jo had encouraged me to be more like Francie Nolan, but I doubt heavy muslin was what she had in mind. I purchased the clothes at a Cincinnati thrift shop on the trip out from the ten dollars Grandmother Catherine had given me to "cheer up and pray to Saint Jude once in a while for guidance." I couldn't find any lace-up boots from around 1910, so I wore hightops and a black stretch bodysuit of Mama's underneath the entire ensemble. I stuck my octagon glasses in my pocket (Francie had strong, clear eyes) and fumbled out of our brand new house through a dirt yard to the new Buick in a blur. I could only hear Mama gasp, "You can't go to school like that, especially your first day. You look like Lorna Doone."

The boys didn't say anything. They were laughing too hard.

"I like the way I look," I declared. "You want me to be a girl; finally, I'm a girl, plus, Francie's a writer, and I'm a writer." I tossed my braids around, then added, "A woman's hair is her crowning glory."

"Her what? Oh, never mind. I've got the movers coming to the house today. Be the Girl of the Limberlost if it makes you happy." Mama gunned the engine.

As we drove to the new school, my thoughts drifted to *A Girl of the Limberlost,* an old-timey novel given to me by Meemaw, Daddy's mother. The heroine was Elnora Comstock, "a girl who collects moths to pay for her education, and lives by the Golden Rule." Each chapter began with a *Wherein.* . . . "Chapter One: Wherein Elnora Goes to High School and Learns Many Lessons Not Found in Her Books. Chapter Two: Wherein Wesley and Margaret Go Shopping, and Elnora's Wardrobe Is Replenished." I began making up my own: *Chapter One: Wherein Liz decides to kill herself by leaping off the church steeple in the parking lot of St. Sebastian's School. Chapter Two: Wherein Liz refuses to baby-sit and her parents disown her but not before torturing her by making her watch football nonstop. Chapter Three: Wherein football—*

"Liz! Liz, wake up, we're here!" Mama shouted, pulling up in front of a marble statue of Saint Sebastian. I snapped out of my Elnora Comstock dream, Mama hooting, "Children, one word of advice. Don't talk about where you've moved from. Nobody here is interested. If you rattle on about where you're from, they'll just say, 'Why don't you go back there if you like it so much!' So y'all just focus on the here and now, and if you've got any gumption, and I know you do, you'll march right up to somebody and say, 'How do you do? I'm new in town, and I would like to be your friend.' "

"There is no way in hell I am about to make a fool of myself like that!" I said.

"Fine, it's just a suggestion," she replied, shoving brown sacks into our hands, adding, "Look alive. There's Velveeta for lunch," as she prodded us across the parking into the principal's office.

Anchored behind her desk was the principal, Sister Marcia, under a three-foot crucifix. Dried palm fronds were stuck in Jesus' toes. Peaches stared. Leo fidgeted. Joe-Sam combed his hair over and over, until it looked skewered to his head.

"Sister Marcia," Mama addressed her. "I'm Mrs. Jack Donegal. We spoke several weeks ago about my children. Here they are. Speak up, y'all." Mama prodded, but Sister Marcia's leaky eyes cast a foreboding spell.

"My oldest daughter," Mama plunged on doggedly, "is in sixth grade, and Lord, is she a reader." I prayed to blend into the scenery, transforming into a filing cabinet.

Sister Marcia studied my braids for a minute. "Maybe she has a vocation? Good readers often have a calling to the religious life?" She raised her voice at the end, like she was asking a question.

"Wouldn't that be something," Mama agreed before pointing to Joe-Sam. "My son Joe-Sam here is in the fifth grade . . . he's a real athlete, but he also knows if he complains, he vacuums the whole house, so be on guard for griping."

Sister Marcia didn't say a word.

"And the little ones, Leo and Peaches," Mama continued, "are in first grade and kindergarten. Here are birth certificates, shot records, and report cards." Mama gave Sister Marcia a coach's wife's victory smile.

Sister Marcia reflected for a minute, then asked, "Where are yoonz guys from?"

*Yoonz?*

"We're from Manhattan, Kansas; actually we're from Ames, Iowa, too. We move a lot because of football. My husband is with the Pitt Sharks now."

"I'm a hockey fan myself?" smacked Sister Marcia; her inflection was jarring. Were we supposed to tell her she was a hockey fan? Mama didn't seem fazed.

"Well, Sister Marcia, when the season begins, perhaps you can spare a few Hail Marys for the Sharks. We could sure use them." Mama laughed, her gales walloping the walls of the muted office. A secretary in the next room stopped typing.

"I'll see what I can do?" said Sister Marcia when Mama finished. "Now, when would yoonz like your children to start school?"

"Uh, this minute . . . if that's possible. I got a moving van coming, a Labrador in the car outside, plus my husband is heavy into spring practice. I just need a few hours to unpack before these wild ones hit the house."

"I—could—help—you," I mouthed, but Mama refused to catch my eye. I was growing dizzy, my braids felt like weights, and sweat pinched my neck.

"Let's get yoonz guys to class then?" Sister Marcia stood up.

"Sister Marcia"—Mama gathered Leo and Peaches to her—"I'll walk the little ones to their rooms. Would you be able to tell the kids which bus to catch home? I just think it's great that y'all bus 'em here. I never lived where they bused the Catholic kids."

I couldn't believe she was making us take the bus on our first day. But before I could grumble, Sister Marcia had summoned the vice principal, Sister Karen, to take Mama to the kindergarten and first-grade classrooms, while Joe-Sam and I followed Sister Marcia down a long corridor. I longed to grasp Joe-Sam's hand, a thought that hadn't occurred to me in years. I did, and he didn't yank it away. In that instant, he became Neeley Nolan, Francie's little brother. Our sweaty palms clasped together until we came to a stop in front of a door that said, "Sister Celine, Fifth Grade," and underneath, "He Who Hath a Sharp Tongue Slices His Own Throat."

Joe-Sam nudged me. "What's 'hath'?" Before I could answer, Sister Marcia pushed him through the door with her. After she emerged, beckoning me with an arched finger, we stopped at a door with another sign, "Sister Matilda, Sixth Grade," and underneath, "Seven Days Without Prayer Makes One Weak." I felt knots harden in my stomach as Sister Marcia propelled me inside, droning, "Yoonz listen up? This is a Shark's coach's daughter from Nebraska someplace? Welcome her, class?"

There were a few "heys," but mostly smeary leers. I hunched my shoulders in Francie's muslin dress, feeling the underarm seams straining.

I scanned the room for an empty seat. Sister Matilda, a jowly nun who came up to my shoulder, stepped forward, decreeing, "You're big. You must be an alto. Sit back there or the littler ones won't be able to see over your head. And no jagging around."

*Jagging?* My Francie Nolan persona was not working. At lunchtime, I took out my diary.

> *Dear Diary,*
>
> *The Pittsburgh kids behave the way I'd always been warned about public school kids. I'm on a typical Catholic school playground now (a blacktop parking lot), but kids in tight jeans are climbing up over the cinder piles to smoke cigarettes. One girl just slipped on the sooty hills, causing a Rolling Rock beer to splatter down the black coals. She crawled back up, laughing, "Goddamn, did yoonz see me fall on my ass?" I wish I could go home, but I forget where home is. Is it Ames? Is it Manhattan? Why am I so ugly?*

Nobody spoke to me at recess or at any other time that day, except for a ringleader, Scott Fishley, who baptized me "Moose" and "Skyscraper," both of which caught on. Several smart-ass jerks joined in. "Hey, Moose?" "How's the weather up there, Skyscraper?" I found a place to hide behind a janitor's shed, where I could see Joe-Sam across the playground, playing quarterback for his class, already the star.

After school, Scott Fishley ripped off my Francie braids while we were waiting for the bus, tearing several strands of my hair with them. I felt naked, my short hair matted, and I thought of Jo, five states away, unable to rescue me from evil this time. He swung the braids in a lasso, daring me to catch them. "Come on, Moose." I inhaled a sharp whiff of steel mills, before walking over to punch him in the stomach with all my might. He flung them back at me, vomiting and wheezing. A chorus of "Ews" rose from the other kids. I hoisted Peaches and Leo up onto the bus, but Joe-Sam leaped over the rank puddle, grinning back at the crowd, "That's my sister." When I studied Fishley's face as he crept onto the bus, I knew he wouldn't snitch because it would mean admitting that a lowly girl could knock the crap out of him.

# Jag-offs

★   ★   ★

I was with Sister Matilda for homeroom, plus three subjects: math, religion, and music. I never took my eyes off her, because I'd seen what she'd done to kids who flaked during class, bringing a pointer down hard, *thwack,* on their desks. She kept a used hankie stuffed in the sleeve of her habit, which she was always hauling out, scouring the insides of her nostrils. When singing class started, we stood on rickety risers, practicing hymns and singing a song in the round called "Coffee" with the lyrics, "C-O-F-F-E-E, coffee is not for me."

Since Fishley was only an inch shorter than me, Sister Matilda made me stand next to him, but he couldn't sing, and I edged as far away from him as possible. I learned he hated me not only because of my pummeling ability but because he used to be the tallest person in the class before I hit town.

"Why do you wear those dresses?" Fishley asked me one day after he challenged me to an arm-wrestling competition on the bus to prove who was tougher.

"Because I'm a girl," I said, keeping my arm steady, but it was tricky with the bus jolting us in and out of the Pittsburgh potholes.

He considered this, then bragged, "Well, I'm a man. When I went to kiss my dad on my eight-year-old birthday, he slapped me real hard. On the face."

"What'd you do to get hit?" I thrust his arm back, lower.

"Nothing!" he pushed my arm upright. "He was just mad 'cause I kissed him. He yelled, 'Hey, boy, you don't kiss me no more. You're a man now.' "

I watched Fishley's face as he told this story; he glowed at his father shoving manhood into him. He wrenched my arm down, claiming victory, "I did it. I beat your girl's ass. Who's tough now? Huh?"

I stared out the bus window at the dense foliage roaring by. I didn't care that he won. In fact, I was glad. I was glad, too, that my own daddy, who was tough, never slapped any of us in the face, and when we kissed him, he kissed us back, boy or girl.

# Kerry Madden-Lunsford

$\star$   $\star$   $\star$

As the Pittsburgh days trundled by, belching forth the stench of steel mangled with the smells of bread-baking factories, and every sentence sounding like a question, I learned about funerals. Pittsburgh sixth graders of St. Sebastian's had to sing at funeral masses on Wednesdays. Sister Matilda marched us up the hill to the church, where we sang hymns for the deceased, trying not to stare too much at the sealed coffin. For openers, we belted out "The Old Rugged Cross"; at the offertory, "Make Me a Channel of Your Peace"; for communion, "Let There Be Peace on Earth"; and for the recessional hymn, we blasted, "Go Forth Among the People."

Some Wednesdays, it was a colossal funeral with the church packed; but most often, there was just a casket covered with a holy sheet and crucifix, plus a couple of droopy family members reaching for us as we hurried by to receive the Eucharist first, so we could hoof it back up to the choir loft for the communion hymn. Sister Matilda insisted on high vocal standards, and after one mass, when we didn't sing well, she gave us the evil eye. She leaned over the balcony to see if the priest was gone and the casket wheeled out. When the coast was clear, she whipped back round, jowls quivering, whooping, "YOU WERE ALL FLAT. YA BUNCH OF JAGGING-AROUND JAG-OFFS." Then, as if to enlarge my guilt, she arched her arm through the air, decreeing, "Donegal? You were the flattest. And you were running your mouth at consecration."

"I'm sorry, Sister," I whispered, even though I hadn't been, but one did not contradict Sister Matilda and expect to live.

"You got detention for diarrhea of the mouth. Next time, you stand in the trash can in the classroom if you don't shape up."

"Yes, Sister," I whispered as the class snickered.

Once her rage was spent, we trekked back down the hill for religion class, to take a multiple-choice test on saints, apostles, and miracles.

After the tongue-lashing Sister Matilda visited upon me, and what with me being a far better domestic servant than any baby-sitter Mama could hope to hire, the rough climate of Pittsburgh gave me the perfect opportunity to parcel out my humiliation and grief. The words "yoonz," "jag-off," and "jagging" became part of my own vocabulary. "Cut it out, you little jag-offs!" I hissed at Joe-Sam and Leo, who were wrestling under my feet while I was fixing hamburger patties and a can of green beans. The outsides of the burgers were burning, but the meat was a solid brick red inside.

"I heard what you said," Mama appeared, thrusting a finger in my face.

"Sister Matilda says it all the time. Jag-off, jagging around, so what?"

"She can say whatever the hell she likes, but in this house, we are not common people, and we don't use those words." With that, Mama chased the boys downstairs with a spatula, before ducking back to the living room to finish her piano lesson.

I learned to say jag-off only when Mama and Daddy were out of the house, which was a lot, because the Pittsburghers knew how to party.


Everyone in the family soon acclimated to Pittsburgh like they were natives—everyone except me. I was the holdout as far as Mama was concerned. It also became evident that she didn't know what to do with me, but that didn't mean she stopped trying. The new neighborhoods of the Pittsburgh suburbs were called *plans;* and Mama's own plan hatched in ours, Brookseed. While Mama had no interest in associating with the ladies of Brookseed, with their frosted hair and squishy bosoms pushing out of their tube tops, she looked on their offspring as a treasure trove of potential friends for me. She knocked on my bedroom door at regular intervals, trying to entice me into a social life. "You can't sit here listening to sad music and writing letters the rest of your life. That Beryl Merzlak seems like a nice girl."

"Why don't you make friends with Beryl Merzlak if you like her so much."

"Fine, be a mole. Be a pitiful little mole listening to your depressing music."

"Paul Simon is not depressing!" I yelled.

"Watch your tone with me, lady!" she snapped.

"I am watching it. And by the way, did you ever give Aunt Betty our new address? How is she supposed to know where to send letters?"

"I wrote Aunt Betty everything."

"Then, why haven't we heard from her?"

"I don't know. Don't ask me things I don't know. Now what about Beryl?"

Beryl Merzlak never stopped trying, and neither did Mama. The two of them seemed to be in cahoots. One night when Mama invited Beryl inside without even asking my permission, I heard them talking downstairs. Mama was saying, "It's so sweet of you to come by to see Liz, honey."

"You think she wants to go for a walk around the plan this time?" Beryl asked.

"No can do," I yelled from the top of the stairs.

"Okay, see yoonz guys later . . ." Beryl said cheerfully, walking out the door.

"That poor girl isn't going to keep trying forever," Mama warned.

"Oh, darn," I whispered, strolling downstairs once the coast was clear to turn on *Love Story,* ready to weep with Oliver over Jenny's cancer. I'd already read the book, so I was prepared. Then the phone rang. I answered it, and a nasal voice said, "Are yoonz guys ever gonna do jackshit about your goddamn dog?"

Bear Bryant was loose again, and it was one of the Brookseed women on the phone. They called at least three times a week.

"It's for you, Mama." I handed her the phone.

"Hello?" Mama tried to be nice.

I could hear the shrill tone on the other end. "Are yoonz ever gonna tie him up? That black dog is a menace to the plan, and we're gonna report yoonz to *The Babbling Brook.*" That was the plan's monthly newspaper.

"I am so sorry," Mama breathed. "I'll get him in right away. And would anyone in y'all's family be interested in free tickets to a Sharks game?"

The voice on the other end softened until she and Mama were laughing about how dogs will be dogs and kids will be kids. Mama always pulled that free football tickets–southern lady stuff whenever she wanted to make peace with the neighbors.


The men of Brookseed mowed their lawns on Saturdays, after which they met in the circle to drink Rolling Rock in the late afternoon. As usual, Daddy bought wood chips and added railroad ties to avoid the hassle of grass, but once in a while in the off-season, he joined the Brookseed men for a beer, sports talk, or to shoot hoops in the circle. Sometimes the men let me shoot baskets with them because I was so tall. I was still struggling to stay Francie Nolan, but as I kept ripping the hems and petticoats playing basketball, my latest personality began to unravel.

Then I figured that if I lost weight it would help, and I wouldn't be such a moose.

"What do you mean, you're not hungry again?" Mama said one morning after she fixed a big breakfast of blueberry pancakes.

"I'm sorry, I can't eat it." I nibbled a bite.

"Well, I'm not going to bother cooking all this garbage if you won't eat it."

"We're eating it." Leo indicated Joe-Sam and Peaches, who were blissfully inhaling their pancakes without a care in the world. Simpletons.

"That's because you have no sensitivity, and you don't care if you're despised by everyone at school." I gathered my things and walked out the door to the bus stop, wondering why I had no friends. The only girls who ever spoke to me wanted information about my cute younger brother. *Does he have a girlfriend? Is he smart?*

I tried to be really nice back to them, so they'd like me too. *Yes, he does have a girlfriend at the moment, but he has a new one every month, so get in line, and he's pretty smart at football; however, I'm available for friendship. Any takers?* There never were, except for girls like Winifred Stack and Velvet

Sneller, whom nobody wanted to be friends with because of their crooked teeth, no brains, and greasy hair. I, too, kept a wide berth, refusing to be lumped in with the outcasts of the class.

One night after supper as Joe-Sam and I were playing crazy eights, he whispered, "You know what I heard about you from Scott Fishley?" Before I could answer, he caught himself, "Aw, never mind. Too mean." He shuffled the cards, slap, slap, slap.

"Just say it. Nothing that lowlife says affects me in any way."

"Well? He wanted to know where I got a sister with such an ugly dog-face."

Something snapped inside my lungs, like brass knuckles whacking my chest cavity: no air, no breath. "Is that it? You were afraid to tell me that?"

"You're not mad?"

"Mad? Come on, I thought it was really something. That's nothing. That's zero." I slipped upstairs, ears roaring. *Breathe. Breathe. Breathe.* As soon as I shut the door to my plum-colored bedroom, I choked into the privacy of my pillow, ugliness seeping in and out of my skin. I smothered the sobs, but they kept creeping back up in defiance. A few seconds later, Mama pushed open my door, hauling Joe-Sam inside by the hair, "See! You big mean dummy."

"Ouch. My hair. Yes. Yes, ma'am, I'm sorry. Sorry, Liz."

"Now you will vacuum the whole house for a month, boy." She pushed him out the door and slammed it in his protesting face. She came over and sat on the bed.

"I hate this stinking place," I wailed from under the blankets. "I've tried everything. Nothing works."

"Look, I know you miss Jo. When we go to Leavenworth this summer, how about I get you a bus ticket to Manhattan? Then you can visit her. On your own."

"All right. What about Aunt Betty? I'd really like to see her too."

"I'll think about it. And how about we plan a date for Sunday afternoon? Just you and me. Let's go see *The Way We Were.*"

"With Robert Redford?"

# Jag-offs

"That man could cheer up any woman," Mama teased, smiling down at me. I put my head in her lap, gazing at the pink-checkered spread.

Later that night, Joe-Sam tapped at the door. His raspy voice said, "I'm sorry, Liz, but you told me to tell you."

"I know," I whispered back. "But you don't have to do everything I tell you to do. I'm not your mother, you know?"

I could tell he was thinking hard. "I know that, Liz, but listen to me. Everybody knows Fishley is the biggest jag-off in the whole school."

# 14

# THE JOY OF SEX

*"Peter, Peter, Don't Play with It"*

**On punt returns, never be indecisive. Either handle the kick or get away from it. If there is a sliced or short punt situation, and you can't handle it, make the "Peter" call.**

"Way to knock the hell out of the ball tonight." Daddy slapped me on the back as we drove home from my softball game on a spring evening a year after we moved to Pittsburgh. I was playing catcher for the Space Cadettes, a name our coach coined, which we all considered extraordinarily witty.

"Thanks." I smiled, thrilled Daddy had come to see me in action. I wasn't a horrible catcher, but I struck out most times at bat. The most I ever hit was a double, but still it was exciting to watch the ball arc over center field. I also worked consistently at pleasing my teammates by listening to them, admiring their athletic prowess, and laughing at all the jokes, whether I got them or not.

"So how's seventh grade?" Daddy stopped at a red light.

"It's okay," I said. "I hate math."

"Math's a royal vexation, but I'm proud of you for doing your best."

"And for extra credit in religion class," I continued, "Sister Matilda told us to keep a sharp eye on the communion host when the priest lifts it into the air, and if it's round and white, everything's normal, but if we see the face of Christ crying on it, then we might be witnessing a miracle."

"I thought you had Sister Matilda last year."

"She got moved up to seventh grade."

"Jesus H. Christ. So how's Joe-Sam doing?"

"Not so hot in school, but he's the star quarterback."

"Good for him. What about Leo?"

"He'd like to be the star quarterback, but he gets a lot of As."

"I bet that's right. And Peaches? What do you think of your little sister?"

"She's fine. Loves pink things . . . and feather boas . . . girl stuff. It's kind of sad."

"Why is that sad? She's all girl," Daddy smiled in the growing darkness.

He loved hearing about the boys, and when he asked about Peaches, his voice beamed with a father's pride. That confused me. I'd always figured he'd wanted a daughter who could take it like a man, not some girly-girl, but I was beginning to sense I was wrong. He loved her how she was.

We drove past a couple kissing, silhouetted in the glow of a streetlamp. The girl's back was to us, but she looked luminous in her jeans, hair hanging to her waist, arms linked around her lover's neck. Daddy noticed them too.

"Attractive, wasn't she?" he said. "She takes care of her figure."

I could see where this was going, so I didn't answer. My green polyester stretch shorts were incandescent in the dark car, straining at the seams.

"You might want to take it easy on the starch and sugar is all I'm saying," Daddy advised. "Look at it this way, sweetheart—no boy is ever going to want to kiss you if you don't lose a little weight."

*Screw you, screw you, screw you.*
"Understand what I'm saying to you?" he asked finally.
"Yes, sir," I sighed, wishing we were home already.


I decided to prove the coach absolutely wrong about the kissing, so I threw myself a belated thirteenth birthday party, inviting the most popular boys and girls from my class over on a Friday night. I even wrote the same poem on all the invitations:

*It's not Christmas, it's not New Year's, it's not Halloween . . .*
*It's my birthday, it's a great day, 'cause I'll be thirteen.*

Surprisingly, everyone came, and after I opened my presents, I whispered to Mama, "Can you make Joe-Sam, Leo, and Peaches go upstairs now? Please?"

Mama understood. "All right kids, let's go, bedtime," she insisted.

"No, we want to stay!" shrieked Peaches, but Mama dragged them upstairs, yelling behind her, "Y'all have fun now."

We warmed up with spin the bottle, where I got tongued once, but then Norbie Klank turned off the lights to signal a more daring game called switch. Each couple was allowed five minutes to do whatever they liked, until somebody yelled, *"Switch!"* and the girls rotated to the next guy. During the game, the boys sprawled all over the basement, by the pool table, under the bar, waiting for each new chick to emerge from the darkness. After a few rounds, most people stopped switching and got with the one they really wanted to be with for the night.

I didn't know how to join in, so I smiled like a good hostess, studying my new Beach Boy albums, offering Cokes to those who came up for air. I tried to be admitted at one point, but I chose a boy who turned out to be more petrified than I was, and so we sat next to one another, rigidly discussing football strategies, until everyone had had enough of switch, and started slow-dancing to "Jackie-Blue," "Angie Baby," and "Seasons in the Sun."

As I played the records for my guests, I tripped over the last switch couple, who turned out to be Joe-Sam and Beryl Merzlak, whom Mama had forced me to invite. I couldn't believe she'd lowered herself to be with my brother. He scrambled upstairs, while trashy Beryl slunk off into the arms of somebody else.

Peaches was also growing prettier by the second, and I loathed feeling like an old hag at thirteen with a darling princess nipping at my heels. When I studied her, slipping on Mama's pantyhose like a second skin, playing in her makeup, strutting downstairs in stiletto heels, I caught a glimpse of the future. She would be the star, and I would be forgotten. Just like Aunt Betty, I would disappear from life, possibly to live someplace like the C'est la Vie by the Sea in Tallahassee—cut off from civilization and family: the weird one nobody discussed.

I swallowed my jealousy, knowing that Peaches was too young to understand. I loved her, but I had to be in control of her, lording our seven years' difference over her. I created a new fantasy universe for the two of us as sisters, where I ditched all pretense of the good and kind Francie Nolan and emerged into a character named Angela, who was beyond horrific. Poor Peaches hated Angela's guts even more than she despised playing Helen Keller and Anne Frank, for Angela made her entrance through my body, chanting in a booming baritone, "I AM ANN-GELL-AA. . . ." Peaches always screamed, attempting to dash off, but Angela grabbed her, warning, "Say a word, and your sickening sister, Liz, is dead. Gone. Forever. If you dare try to scream for help." Ripples of guilt swept through my soul as I watched Peaches in her petrified anguish, but her belief in my transformation made it all so irresistible that I couldn't stop Angela from entering me to spark up a dull Sunday.

One rainy afternoon, as Angela put Mozart's *Requiem* on the Philco, she whirled around when the strains of music began, bellowing at Peaches, "Liz is drowning in a pit of alligators. See that speck?" Angela held up a clear vase of crusty rose soaps. "There she is. At the very cataclysmic edge of death. Look closely."

Peaches thought she saw something Lilliputian move amid the salmon soaps and began wailing, "Bring her back, bring my sister back."

Angela held the soap vase high above her head, shouting, "Never. I'm your new sister now. Atrocious Beast. And you will suffer."

"No, I love her! Please, please bring her back!" Peaches wept, an Academy Award performance.

"Never. You are mine." I picked her up, squirming, spinning her round and round in a terrifying dance, the music enveloping us in wind, glass, and dead leaves. When we finally fell on the shag rug, gasping, Peaches looked deeply into Angela's eyes, pleading, "Liz, are you in there?" which caused Angela to writhe on the floor. "Wait, I'm dying," Angela rasped. "I can't breathe, but I'll be back, I'll be back. Just when you least suspect, you prissy Shirley Temple. I'll be waiting. You little golden-haired princess. Thinking your looks will carry you forever in this life. HAHAHA."

Then, staggering awake, I returned as Liz, feigning absolute bewilderment. "Peaches, what happened? My head. Where am I?"

"Please don't let Angela come back. Please!" She began hiccuping with wrenching sobs, patting my shoulder.

"Oh, sweetheart, I love you. I love you so much. I'll never go away. I won't let Angela take over. I'll fight her off. Oh, my poor angel." I stroked her teary face and, beginning to feel remorseful, I carried her downstairs to fix her a bowl of chocolate-chip ice milk. As we ate our snack, we curled up close together in the rocking chair to watch an old Debbie Reynolds movie. We each drew a deep breath, feeling purged and at peace, far from the lurking Angela. At least for the moment.

Inspired by my tremendously successful transformation into Angela, I attempted to become Alexander for Leo, but he took one look and muttered "Yeah, right. Psycho."

"You have no imagination!" I screamed, hating him for not kowtowing to my iron will.

"Fine with me. You're not gonna do me the way you do her. She goes nuts, and it'll be your fault if she grows up to be a lune." Leo stalked off.

"You, boy, have no understanding of theater. That's your problem."

"Yeah, and your problem is you're jealous." He flew out the door before I could grab him, take him into the bathroom, and wet his hair into a slicked-back version of Oliver Twist and whack him with a yard-stick like he deserved.


The first thing I usually did after the kids were asleep on Saturday nights, when my parents were out celebrating another Shark win, was to make sure the kitchen passed inspection, by slinging Comet around. To "not clean" was a direct affront to my mother, who *slaved* during the week, and who didn't want to wake up on Sunday morning to a sink full of filthy dishes.

Once everything was more or less grittily presentable, I stole into the living room to begin my solo concert; a repertoire of Helen Reddy, Lou Reed, and Karen Carpenter. I brushed out the braids of my old Francie wig, fashioning it into a Karen Carpenter coiffure. I wore bell-bottoms, beads, and Mama's silk blouse. Sometimes I screwed a black lightbulb into one of the lamps before I made my entrance, singing to the expectant living room. On other Saturdays, I sang along with Helen Reddy, feeling very much like "Angie Baby," with the whole house eerily quiet, the walls an inky resplendence of shadows. Or I took off my shirt and shoes to swagger about as Lou Reed, taking "A Walk on the Wild Side." I crooned, swayed, and reeled to lyrics that touched me in ways the funeral hymns never could.


After one of my more exhilarating Saturday night concerts, I was packed with energy, so I decided to prowl around upstairs in Mama and Daddy's room for an inspection of any questionable materials. I soon dis-covered a tantalizing stack of sex books and a bundle of private letters, which I spread across the king-size bed for further elucidation. The sex books were Daddy's, but I knew the letters belonged to Mama, because I recognized Aunt Betty's hurried scrawl, which was very similar to my own. I also knew that only a true low-down sneak would snoop into those letters, but I couldn't help myself. I thought she'd quit writing to everyone, but here was a stack of recent letters to Mama. The return address was fairly illegible, but I could make out the words "Saint Bridget's" on most of them. Saint Bridget's? What happened to the C'est la Vie she was going to reopen?

> *Dear Sally,*
>
> *I miss you. How are the children? Please forgive my shaking fingers. They have me on Thorazine, and it's supposed to help my nerves. Lord, I never thought I'd be on it myself. When I was working as a nurse, I used to give it to patients, and the ones who got it in big doses, we called them the "Thorazine Shufflers," because of how they walked. I sure didn't plan to land back in here. I had every intention of working as a home nurse after I got let go at the hospital. I prefer home nursing anyway. I still hope to someday. I did well while it lasted. The nuns at this place aren't the happiest women in the world, but I suppose it will help with my drinking in the end . . . but after two years on and off, I really want to leave. I would love to see y'all again. We have prayer meetings to discuss things, but I'd rather be reading. How is Liz? She's my special one. What about the baby? The boys? If I came to visit, I swear I wouldn't drink.*
>
> *I love you—don't worry. Betty*

I was still her special one? Don't worry? Oh, Aunt Betty. I reached for the next letter, hands shaking. I was itching to call the bus station, so I could get the schedule to Tallahassee, where I could hail a taxi to this Catholic drunk tank or whatever it was.

> *Dear Sally,*
>
> *Remember Leroy, my ex-husband, from a million years ago? He still comes to see me every so often with his wife, Rhonda. She looks like her name. They've given me more Bibles and prayer books, which I just give away as soon as they're gone. He and his wife never had any children either. I wish I'd had children. Why don't you send Liz down to visit? I'm sure I'll be leaving this place any day. I'm feeling so much stronger since they cut back on my Thorazine. It was making me stupid. I'll take Liz to the movies. Hope you can read this?*
>
> *I love you—don't worry. Betty*

# The Joy of Sex

I was furious. My loving aunt had been inviting me all along, but I was a prisoner in my own house. How dare Mama not tell me. It was a big fat conspiracy to keep me captive and Aunt Betty lonesome.

> *Dear Sally,*
>
> *My roommate slapped me hard. She's not right in the head, but look who's talking. I've got to get out of here. I hate this place. I'm thinking of reopening the C'est la Vie by the Sea, if the home-nursing thing takes a while for me to get it started again. Best thing about this place is "Mash." I watch it faithfully. The nuns would prefer I went to mass, instead of "Mash." Ha, ha. I pray. I do pray. I think I need glasses. Or maybe you'll need glasses to read this letter. I was a good nurse before all of this too. I don't know why I stopped. Do you? I write Mama and Daddy once a week. I'm thinking of visiting them . . . maybe I could visit you on the way back.*
>
> *I love you—don't worry. Betty*

Fearful, I unfolded another one.

> *Dear Sally,*
>
> *Remember when we were girls and Mama and Daddy would go to church (we'd have gone already), and Mama expected the roast to be on by the time they got back? I was always reading, and then ten minutes before they were expected home, I'd have us chopping vegetables, trying to get dinner on, so she wouldn't go crazy. Remember that awful hand-crank laundry machine? Remember when I told you after I got my first nursing job that I was going to buy you a present every week. I never did, did I? I still love big band and swing music. I listen to it as I do my housework in this room. Of course, I don't play it when my roommate is around. I'm doing much better. I pray all the time. God's grace will see me through this.*
>
> *I love you—don't worry. Betty.*

I knew that feeling. Kitchen cleaned *before* they got home so they wouldn't get *mad*. Or dinner ready or laundry folded. Betty, we're the same person—in some ways. And I play loud music all the time, not big band but maybe I'll try it sometime. Wait for me, Aunt Betty.

*Dear Sally,*

*You know I've put on 100 pounds. I look awful. I don't know how I did it. I didn't use to look this way. You always were so pretty. Remember when I used to sneak Cokes into my bed? Mama always caught me. "Enjoying your Coke?" she'd say when she'd hear me open it. What razor hearing. I'm back on Thorazine. I'm sure it won't be for too long. I'm going to lose the weight. I don't know when, but I sure don't want visitors looking like Moby Dick. How's your weight? Mama called the other day right after they'd given me another dose of electric-shock therapy, and first thing she said to me was "Betty, how's your stomach?"*

*I love you—don't worry. Betty*

One hundred pounds? How could this be? My beautiful aunt.

*Dear Sally,*

*I have to remember to wrap my womanly pride around me to get out of bed these days. God has held me together so far, and the last few months, believe me, I've actually been praying in tongues. I bought my first Charismatic book. Can't remember the title. Will write soon. I have made friends who speak in tongues and have seen the face of Jesus. It's a comfort. They're giving me more shock.*

*I love you—don't worry. Betty*

By the time I'd finished reading all the letters, I was sobbing. What did it all mean? I found Mama's directory and dialed Aunt Betty's number in Florida, but a voice said, "Good evening. Saint Bridget's Asylum."

"I would like to speak to Betty Thomas, please."

"I'm sorry. All the patients are sleeping now."

I hung up the phone quietly, wondering what Mama had replied in her letters. I thought of Aunt Betty, a lonely figure walking along the Florida beach, watching *M\*A\*S\*H,* thinking deep thoughts, longing for adventure, but not welcome anywhere. If it was true, if she was an alcoholic, why couldn't she just stop drinking? The woman I remembered certainly could. Maybe she was just different, and people were too busy to fool with her, including her own sister. I hated thinking about Mama this way, judging her, but I couldn't stop myself, plus the whole speaking in tongues and shock therapy news made me nervous. I felt I ought to get down there quick to check things out.

I found the phone book and looked up "Greyhound." I dialed the number, and a voice said, "Greyhound bus, downtown Pittsburgh."

"I need your bus schedule and price from Pittsburgh to Tallahassee."

"Just a minute, please," answered a very Pittsburgh voice. "The fare is fifty-eight dollars, and we have buses leaving at twelve noon and midnight."

After I hung up from Greyhound, I lay on the stack of her letters spread across the bed, mixing them up with the sex books, feeling her words soak into my skin. *Betty, of the jungle dress.* I closed my eyes, trying to picture her, send her a message telepathically.

When I opened my eyes, a picture from Daddy's book *The Joy of Sex* caught my eye—called "Oral Sex." As I realized where the man's mouth was, my brain zapped, and I shivered at the thought of mouths "down there." I slapped the book shut, opened it again, slapped it shut, slowly opening it again. I began perusing all the books, garnering information about orgies, sexual ceremonies, orgasms, blue balls, cheap johns, flagpole erections, and something called "a zipless fuck," which seemed very mysterious. I pored over the stash like a scientist until two in the morning, before putting everything back in perfect order: letters in one pile, sex books in the other. Good Catholic gumshoe.

As I crawled into bed, listening for Mama and Daddy's car to crunch into the gravel driveway, I wondered what kind of sin I'd committed by nosing around. Was it "mortal" or "venial"? And who would I confess to? I had been avoiding the Sacrament of Penance lately because of the chic concept of face-to-face confessions. Gone were the days of confidentiality; now we were supposed to be hip, revealing to the priest our low-down dirty sins in the sacristy. I did it once and found the experience so mortifying, I vowed to keep my wicked ways, which were multiplying by leaps and bounds, to myself, and to God.

★   ★   ★

One night I was still up when Mama and Daddy got home. I had finished with the letters and sex books early and was watching an old Sally Fields movie, *Maybe I'll Come Home in the Spring,* about a family torn apart by drugs. As Mama and Daddy ushered in the fragrances of icicles, bourbon, and perfume, I turned to look at them. Daddy had his arms around Mama, and suddenly, there in the middle of the night, my parents appeared dazzling. They carried with them a spirit of nightlife and action. For a split second, I almost forgot who they were. They were just two radiant strangers stopping by to ask directions, and I was the cronelike spinster of the house, watching late night TV. My parents were winners.

"Turn that crap off," Daddy ordered, hating to watch anybody who had problems.

"You're up too late." Mama shrugged off her coat.

"I couldn't sleep . . . this is almost over," I hinted, moving closer to the TV.

"The kitchen is just sparkling," Mama called from the kitchen. "Oh, good. You used Comet in the sink. That's terrific. See, I told you it really makes a difference."

"How were the kids tonight?" Daddy looked at me.

"Fine. They went to bed around eleven. After Carol Burnett."

"Christ Almighty, I don't see how you can watch such bullshit." The parents were now tearing apart their daughter's room, searching for drugs.

"It's fascinating," I huffed, refusing to feel guilty.

"We danced for hours." Mama twirled into the den. "Did the kids eat the Tuna Helper? You know you should be in bed. Were there any calls for us?"

"You're too intelligent for this." Daddy walked over to the TV and turned it off.

I seethed, but it was also almost three o'clock in the morning, and I didn't have the energy to fight his fascism. I committed the movie's title to memory, so I could watch it in the future when I had my own television and my own life. *Maybe I'll Come Home in the Spring. Maybe I'll Come Home in the Spring.*

"You need to get to bed, sugar, church tomorrow," Mama said.

"Mama?"

"Yes?"

I knew I was taking a chance, but I had to do it. "Mama, why don't we invite Aunt Betty to visit us sometime? I bet she's never even seen Pittsburgh. I haven't seen her in almost five years. Or maybe I could go visit her? A Greyhound bus ticket from Pittsburgh to Tallahassee isn't that expensive."

"Don't get any ideas."

"I have some baby-sitting money saved, and I think it would do Aunt Betty good."

Silence. I backed out of the kitchen and was halfway up the stairs when I heard Mama call, "Why do you ask that now?" Her voice sounded suspicious.

"No reason, but is she okay?" I said quickly.

"I hope you haven't been reading anything addressed to me, Lady Jane."

"I don't know what you're talking about," I replied, as innocently as possible. "I just want to see my *favorite* aunt. Gosh, I'm tired. Good night, yoonz guys." And I dashed off to bed.

# C'EST LA VIE BY THE SEA

*"Monster Left"*

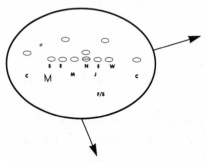

**A term that was employed in college football to
identify the STRONG SAFETY. The SAFETY aligned to the strength
of the formation. The MONSTER would declare his alignment by calling
"Monster Right" or "Monster Left." The next call would relate to who
would provide the primary run support; either the MONSTER, or the
STRONG SIDE LINEBACKER, or the STRONG SIDE CORNERBACK.**

Another Saturday night. I was grounded for having tried to catch the bus to Tallahassee. The day it happened, Daddy had to leave football practice (unheard of) to find me in the bus station. I almost made it onto the bus, looking forward to lively conversations with new folks on my adventure south. I'd already met an old blind lady who knew how to play "Amazing Grace" on the harmonica, but as I was boarding, I heard his voice boom, "Get your ass over here now."

"I'm going to Florida." I kept moving. "Call you when I get there."

"NOW!" his face was on fire, his cleats stomping across the asphalt.

"I'm going to see my aunt, Coach Donegal."

He pushed through the line, grabbing me hard by the arm. The Greyhound passengers gazed at him in his Shark coaching gear, as he yanked me toward the car. He didn't speak to me the whole way home, except to say I was grounded for three months, which included baby-sitting on Saturday nights. I continued to write and call my aunt, but never got a response. I felt like a dead person. *I must be dead, which is why she doesn't write.* All I wanted was one letter, one line. Anything but the silence. The everlasting, sickening silence.

One night after I put the kids to bed, I began my performance of Karen Carpenter, Lou Reed, and Paul Simon songs, but the music made me so lonesome that I bowed out of the rest of the show to research more of the sex literature and to reread Aunt Betty's letters, saving them for last. I studied a sketch of a man sucking a woman's bosom. I noticed the same woman gripping the guy's penis, with the recommendation: "Notice how she gently cups the testicles," and "A wife's breasts can become a man's playground."

From the looks on their faces, it suddenly made sense to "gently cup the testicles," because Joe-Sam always fell on the floor writhing in agony whenever Leo "racked" him in one of their wrestling matches.

I tried to imagine some man sucking on my breast while I fondled his balls. I grew dizzy. I couldn't begin to picture it. The phone jangled shrilly, knifing me back to the present. I dived for it, trying to speak in my "mature daughter" voice, so whoever was calling wouldn't suspect that I was drifting in a sea of sex. "Hello?"

"Liz, this is your grandfather. From Leavenworth."

"Hi, Poppy, how are you?"

"I'm all right. Is your Mama home?"

"No, she and Daddy are out celebrating. They're at the Huki Orchid. Pitt smeared the Bulldogs by two points." I realized how shallow my words rang, as I tried to ignore a diagram of the woman on her knees with the man directly behind her. "Are you okay? Is Catherine okay, Poppy?"

"We're fine, honey." He sounded so far away. "You just ask your mother to call me immediately. It's an emergency."

"Okay." I hung up and dialed the Huki Orchid. I could hear a loud fight song in the background. "Cheers to Pitt, cheers to Pitt . . . Every loyal fan . . ."

Mama came to the phone after a few minutes, tense. "What's the matter?"

"Poppy called and wants you to call him at home tonight."

"Dear God. Is Catherine all right?"

"He said she was, but it's an emergency."

"Okay, thank you. How are the kids? Asleep?"

"Fine. Yes."

"Okay, don't stay up reading forever, I don't care how good it is."

"No, ma'am. I won't. Bye."

Fifteen minutes later, I heard a car grinding in the driveway. I jammed *The Joy of Sex, Playboy, The Happy Hooker, Fear of Flying* on Daddy's shelf, and Aunt Betty's letters into Mama's drawer, before rushing downstairs.

"Hey," I squeaked, trying my hardest to be normal.

Daddy's arms were around Mama, who looked dazed. "Why are you still up?"

"Me? Well, it's only eleven-thirty. Yoonz are never back this soon."

"You should be asleep, goddammit."

"What do you expect? I have to keep a watch on things. Why is Mama crying?"

Easing Mama out of her coat, he sighed, "Honey, your mama has to go to Florida. Aunt Betty's not doing real well."

"What?"

"I need to go see my sister." Mama spoke to the banister.

"When?"

"Tomorrow. I'm getting a plane tomorrow."

"Let me go too!" I begged.

"Sweetheart"—he tried to phrase his words—"Betty had a reaction to some shock-therapy treatments she was getting."

"What kind of reaction?"

"Hell, I have no idea. She's been having treatments to . . . to . . . to get her thinking straight again and to cheer her up. She's had a little problem with depression."

136

"Lord have mercy." Mama gripped the banister.

"I'm going with you, Mama."

She looked at me. "No. No, you're not. Betty wouldn't want you to see this."

"I don't care." I grabbed her hands.

"I do, Liz. She would absolutely hate you seeing her like this. I need you to stay home with the children. I'm going to ask Peter and Meemaw to come help out too."

"I don't care what she looks like. I'm not the maid around here. I'm going to Florida. I'll clean up the C'est la Vie by the Sea for her. You can't stop me."

"Bullshit," Daddy fumed. "Your mama needs to get on down there and assess the goddamn situation, and your ass needs to do what we expect you to do. You're not in charge yet, slick."

I despised them both at that moment—him, forbidding me to see my sick aunt—her, refusing to understand. As we stood there, each cloaked in separate loss, Mama gradually picked her words, "We'll talk about it in the morning when we can all think more clearly. No one ever solved anything at midnight."

"Go to sleep, Liz!" Daddy ordered, then a softer, "Honey, please."

"I'm so sorry, I'm so sorry" came Mama's voice, flat, unnatural.

My parents looked like strangers; they weren't dashing anymore. All I could see was crooked spines propping one another up, wrapped in smells of snow, tears, and Kentucky bourbon. Daddy kept holding on to Mama, who was sobbing silently.

I backed out of the room, feeling their grief follow me. I didn't know what to do. I crawled inside my closet, where I curled up the whole night through. I struggled to recall my aunt's face. I could only recollect a black-and-white photograph of Mama and Betty as girls. Betty stood solemnly with her socks rolled down like chocolate doughnuts around her ankles, while Mama looked dimply, hanging off her daddy's neck. I tried to re-member every detail, but snapshots of Mama kept crowding into my brain as she grinned from baby pictures, school pictures with pretty teeth, piano recitals, beauty contests. The more I tried to see Aunt Betty, the more I saw my mother smiling at me. I held my diary, but I could only write a bit, recalling the Limberlost girl. *Wherein Aunt Betty's shock treatments don't work, and her niece doesn't know what that means. Wherein . . .*

Mama worked fast, and by the next afternoon, Meemaw and Uncle Peter arrived to stay with us. Since it was football season, Daddy couldn't very well take off time to accompany Mama, much less be around to watch us. When Peaches and I opened the door, Meemaw was already gabbing, "Hello, girls. We took the cab, and what service, I tell y'all, he took us right to the front door, didn't he, Peter? And such reasonable rates for a big city. I'm worried about leaving Papa Sweetheart home alone, but he should be all right with the colored girl checking in on him, and I left him a freezer full of meat, he shot pheasants out near Shelbyville, but oh my it's all such a tragedy. Did I tell you he retired from podiatry? Course, he'll still do my feet, but—"

When Peter stepped away from the curb after paying the taxi, I saw he was no longer a boy. He stood more than six feet tall with big shoulders, a mustache, and lustrous brown hair, which fell into his eyes. He smiled at me as he strolled toward the house, pulling me into a big hug. The boy in braces who'd drooled on me under the Christmas tree to the music of Bing Crosby was gone. He carried a portfolio with him, which I would later learn held his paintings and photographs.

Meemaw kept talking. "Well, thank the saints that Peter had a short break from Notre Dame, he's on scholarship there. The priests just love him. Don't know what I would have done, but I do know—" and then Mama banged downstairs with her suitcase, hugging Peter and Meemaw, explaining, "My sister Betty's been asking me to visit for years. It's about time I did."

"Well, isn't it a little late for that?" I spoke up, not caring how it sounded. "I mean, considering her brain's been electrocuted? Isn't that what shock treatments are? Little jolts of electricity?" I'd spent the morning reading up on them.

"Electrocuted?" Peaches squeaked, popping her knuckles one at a time, as the boys muttered, "Huh?" in unison, gawking at Mama.

"Liz, may I see you in the kitchen?" Mama asked pointedly.

I followed her, waiting.

"I know you blame me," she began in a low voice. "Fine, go right ahead. But until you're a mother, don't judge me too harshly."

"We could have gone together last summer, not during football season. I should be going with you now."

"I've got three other little children. They need you here. I'm doing the best I can." She was almost crying, thrusting her fingers into her gloves. "I don't even know what to expect." She walked stiffly to the front door. "Kids, your grandmother, uncle, and big sister are in charge." Mary Martha's car horn tooted outside. Mama didn't even glance back as she walked out the door to catch a plane to visit her sister. I dove into the hall closet, where I was hiding six roses I'd bought after church. I ran outside after Mama, but she was already in the car. As I banged on the window, she looked up. I thrust the roses inside, begging her, "Take them."

"I can't carry roses all the way to Florida."

"Please? Aunt Betty always said a person could never have too many."

Mama hesitated and then reached for them, squeezing my hand, as Mary Martha pulled out of the cul-de-sac with my mother, who was off—*to catch—a plane—to visit—her sister. Simple. Simple Simon. Simple Simon met a pie-man. Going to the fair. No fairs, not today, just a sister whose mind probably wasn't working right anymore. I knew Aunt Betty; she knew me. They'd kept us apart for so long—they shouldn't keep on doing it now. To—catch—a plane—to visit—her sister . . . her sister living with the nuns of Saint Bridget who were feeding too much electricity into her brain. Shame on them. Shame on all of us.*

We stood on the street in silence, before Meemaw began chewing the fat again, "Well, I'm sure you kids must be hungry. How's the price of meat these days? It's a sin where I'm from, but when I was a girl, Mama used to saw the heads off chickens, while Daddy'd come home from work to play the violin. Come on inside now."

Peaches and I followed, trying to figure out where her story was going, but the boys vanished by the second sentence, dragging Peter with them to escape into the backyard. From the kitchen window, I could see

139

them lobbing the football back and forth, tackling each other up and down the hill. Freedom. Footloose and fancy-free. Unleashed from a hot house of endless women words. How I longed for wings.

Meemaw chattered nonstop the entire week. When she got up in the morning, she started in. When she went to bed at night, she was still buzzing. Her tone never rose in anger or dropped in sorrow. Over meals, on the way to church, from behind the bathroom door, she rambled on about details and people we'd never heard of. She had a habit of drawling on about every situation and applying it to her own life with strands of fact and monologue that twisted, dissected, and meandered until the listener saw spots. One day I escaped into the forest, leaving Peaches to fend for herself against the gush of words. Peter, Leo, and Joe-Sam found me. I could hear them coming a mile off, since Peter was teaching them the words to Creedence Clearwater Revival's "Proud Mary."

When they spotted me, I muttered, "Hey," wishing I had Peter to myself for a few minutes, as Leo and Joe-Sam collapsed on him. But I knew that was impossible. The boys adored him too much to let him out of their grasp.

"Why are you sad, Lizzie?" asked Leo. "We don't even know her."

"I know her. I know her very, very well."

"She likes me," Joe-Sam whispered. "A lot."

"How d'you guys know her so good?" Leo demanded, hating to be left out.

"She took care of you when you were a baby, Leo, you just can't remember."

"How come they put her in the electric chair?" he asked.

"Not the electric chair, idiot," I said. "Electric-shock therapy. They stick wires on your temples and hit a button that zaps you."

"No way?" Joe-Sam looked at Peter to see if it was true.

"Like Frankenstein." Leo got excited. "I definitely want to see her sometime."

"Shut up." My head throbbed the way it did after reading for hours on end.

"I remember her," Peter broke in, and we all turned to him. "She was fun," he continued. "I met her when I was four. She took me out for ice cream. Your mama and daddy were about to get married. We got our picture taken as a present for them."

"I miss her so badly." I dug my nails in the moist earth as we listened to woodpeckers tapping against the trees, their steady echoes saturating the forest. Peter glanced down at me, and whispered, "I know how you feel, Liz. I really do. But remember, your Aunt Betty might get better, and no matter what happens, the best part of her—it's still here . . . in you."

I glanced up. Before I could catch the moment, he whirled around, arms outstretched: "All right. Who wants ice cream? How about we practice a fine Aunt Betty tradition and go to Farrell's to get the Zoo."

"She preferred the Dairy Queen," I replied sadly.

"Duh, they don't have Dairy Queens in Pittsburgh, Liz," Joe-Sam said.

"I love Farrell's. I want the biggest scoop of vanilla." Leo danced around.

"You would, doughnut-boy," laughed Joe-Sam.

We were all on our feet in seconds, tromping through the woods to retrieve Peaches and Meemaw. Suddenly, the thought of a Farrell's Zoo, a whopping extravaganza of fifteen scoops of ice cream piled high in a huge tin bowl, covered with Cool Whip, syrups, sauces, nuts, sprinkles, and cherries, seemed like a slice of sweet heaven. Maybe we could even fib and say it was one of our birthdays, so the waiters in their bow ties would ring the cowbells and blow sirens to deliver the Zoo on the trough, a sort of ice-cream stretcher, and the waitresses in their miniskirts and garters would gather to sing "Happy Birthday." I grabbed Peter's hand as we followed the boys up out of the gully, delivered from the weight of electric shocks for a while.


When Mama came back from Florida, I waited until everyone was asleep to approach her. She sat at the table, exhausted. I began rubbing her neck, which she craved. "How was it?" I asked softly.

"Let's not do this now, love."

"Please, if we don't talk now, when will we? It'll just get farther and farther away, and then it'll be a memory, and you'll say, 'Why bring it up now? It was years ago.' "

"All right, all right. I get the point. She's doing all right. She's comfortable. She recognized me," she sighed. "Lord, that feels so good, honey."

"Why wouldn't she have recognized you?"

"She had a mild heart attack, Liz, during the shock therapy, and her brain lost a little oxygen. But she's getting stronger. The nuns adore her. They call her an angel."

"Can she visit us again?" I massaged gently, trying to picture Betty, the angel.

"Oh, maybe someday, but not right now."

"Why?"

"I loved Betty dearly, but my children have, and will always, come first. It wouldn't be fair to y'all. She may never be herself again."

"Why not?"

"I don't know why not. Don't ask me questions I can't possibly have answers to."

"Why didn't you let her visit us? Just one time?"

"The AA people told me not to have her come. . . . I asked their advice. She wanted to live here. . . . She had problems you don't know about . . . pills . . . alcohol. Now, the nuns know how to take care of her best. She doesn't belong here."

"How does she look?"

"She looks all right. . . . It was a terrible thing to have to go through, but now we've got things to look forward to. Pitt's bound to be going to a bowl game in a month. That's exciting. I know your Aunt Betty will be rooting for us from Florida. She has a television set, and we even watched some ball games together."

I know Mama meant well, but at the mention of football, like life just goes back to normal, a mercurial wrath welled up inside of me. "I don't think I would ever abandon Peaches that way." I watched the words march out of my mouth. "I couldn't do what you did. What if I become like Betty? Will you forget me too? Will I be the crazy one down at the C'est la Vie? Or with the nuns? She's my sweet friend, my aunt, she loved me. She's like a great sad queen living in an asylum near the water."

Mama scraped her chair across the linoleum, sucking in her breath before she clawed out, "You have all the answers, don't you?"

"No, I don't."

"Fourteen, and you think you know exactly what you will do at every stage in your life, and you're just so certain it will be the right thing."

"No, I never—"

"Maybe I was an awful sister, but until someone you love with all your heart changes so radically into a terrifying stranger, who can't even get on a plane because she's too drunk, and they have to remove her, don't you dare stand there, criticizing—"

"I'm sorry."

"And tell me what you would do, because *you don't know what you would do.*"

"But—"

"You *can't* know, because you haven't been there. Yes, maybe I was wrong. Maybe I could have done something to avoid this whole mess, but that's something that I will have to live with for the rest of my life. Not you, Lady Jane."

"I want to see her."

"Liz"—Mama looked me straight in the eye—"listen to me. She doesn't want to see you. She doesn't want to see anybody until she decides she's ready. The nuns feel this is the best thing too."

She walked over to the sink, uncapping an aspirin bottle, removing three white tablets. She swallowed them at once, then speaking in a whisper, "I have a box to give you. It has your name on it. She must have gathered the things over the years. Mostly books she wanted you to have. But as for everything else you feel for her, you're simply going to have to write about it, because I can't talk about it anymore. It breaks my heart, and I miss the sister I knew too much."

The box was heavy. I waited until she walked out of the room to open it. Inside were Louisa May Alcott books, the Betty Smith books, *Oliver Twist,* a Helen Keller biography, tons of *Reader's Digest* condensed books, a set of children's encyclopedias, a Bible, and Carson McCullers's *The Heart Is a Lonely Hunter*. I did as my mother wished; I read all the books to find the answers. The next day in school, Sister Matilda asked us to write a paragraph about a saint, so I wrote:

### AUNT BETTY AND THE NIECE

*Aunt Betty is a goddess with a voice like rippling silk who makes people feel beautiful, even her rather unattractive niece. Nobody, however, really makes Aunt Betty feel needed, which can get very lonely after a while. In her younger days, Betty drove her mother crazy, because she preferred reading to cleaning, and it took her all day to scrub clothes on the hand machine. Read, crank, read, crank. Mondays were wash days, and when her mother wasn't looking, Betty lounged in the Kansas sun with a book, her feet propped up on the wash bucket, her fingers trailing the cool suds as she turned the pages. One time, Aunt Betty dressed up her niece in a pink robe, fluffed her pillow, and brought her breakfast in bed. . . . Aunt Betty was the only person in her niece's life to bring her breakfast in bed. Aunt Betty used to be a nurse, tending to the sick in their homes.*

*Aunt Betty had a sense of humor too. Once she and her best friend, Bernadette, caught a bunch of lightning bugs in a jar. They took the jar into religion class, and when the Mother Superior sat down to doze as she always did, Betty and Bernadette released the lightning bugs under the Mother Superior's long black veil. You could see hundreds of flashing lights beneath her habit. Betty said she and Bernadette didn't stop laughing for a week.*

*Aunt Betty loves books about people. She gobbles up mysteries, biographies, and stories, soaking in the tub until her fingers and toes prune and the water turns cold. She also keeps a black cigarette case with silver trim, which holds her "Philip Morris Special Blend" smokes. Aunt Betty is fun and warm, large and generous. She is a lake on an August day in the early evening when everything burns golden. She smells sweet and musky, and a person could lie in her arms for days. She lets her niece lie in her arms, even though her niece is really too big to be held. Aunt Betty makes her niece feel wise. She isn't a real saint, but to her niece she always will be.*

THE END

"I told yoonz to write about saints." Sister Matilda's oily eyes zeroed in on me. "Yoonz think you can write about whatever you please? Do it over, Donegal, or you flunk."

"Yes, Sister."

Her tone softened a little as she continued, "Now, yoonz may think that because I'm a Sister of Mercy, I'm perfect?" She rapped the ruler on the lectern. "Well, I did bad things, too. When I was little . . . I stole an orange once?" She let her words linger in the air; nobody moved. "Yes, I stole it from my mother's fruit bowl. Yoonz may not believe it, but I did. And I flushed the peels down the commode, thinking I wouldn't get caught, but guess what got stopped up?"

*Who cares, you mean old jowly bat!*

She paused before exhaling, "The commode! My father, God rest his soul, and the priest had to plunge it, and what do you think came up?"

"Orange peels?" whispered a boy in awe.

"That's right, and I didn't eat supper for a week. But I learned to follow directions. Yoonz have to learn to follow directions." She gaped at me before erupting a great honk into her hankie, then stuffed it back in her habit sleeve as usual.


As the days went by, I tried to write to Aunt Betty but the words wouldn't come. Peter and I sat at the kitchen table the night before he left for Notre Dame. I was delicately sewing up a trembling baby rabbit that was barely alive after Joe-Sam nicked it with the lawn mower. Peter swallowed as I threaded the needle into its skin, using sterile gauze to wipe hydrogen peroxide into the wound. "Liz, you're not a vet," he winced.

"I am for now. There's no car here. No way to get to the doctor's, and I have to save this rabbit. If we don't attach this flap of skin, it will die, and it needs to go back to its mother. I'm going to save something for once in my life."

"Jesus, I feel sick watching this."

"Then don't," I replied, taking a few more careful stitches in silence.

"Are you going to write to your aunt Betty anymore?" Peter asked after a minute.

145

"I'll try . . . but . . ."

"But what?"

"I love her, but I'm not going to be like her, Peter. I can't. . . . Even though we liked some of the same things. Nobody's going to stick electricity in my brain. For any reason. And I don't plan on speaking in tongues. I just miss her so much."

"Of course you do. And Liz, trust me, you're your own person. You always have been, and God help the person who doesn't realize that and tries to push you around." He sipped a beer.

"That's right." I rubbed the baby rabbit's ears as it eyed me, quivering.

Peter sighed, "I just wish I could be mine."

"You are. You're an artist. You're a painter. A real painter. The best!"

"I put on a good show . . . artist, honor student, southern boy, Notre Dame, the priests, the Saint Mary's girls, but it's just an act."

"I don't see how you can say that. What's wrong?"

Suddenly Peter's eyes filled with tears. I didn't know where to look, so I just focused on saving the rabbit, connecting the skin again, suture by suture. Finally, he said, "Listen, you think and talk about Betty and anything else that's bothering you whenever you like. Fuck what anybody else says. It's the only way you'll ever begin to understand."


After he was gone, back to Notre Dame, I tried not to think too much about his brief rush of tears. Instead, I followed his advice, reeling in the memory of Aunt Betty. In my story, she was a young woman full of hope who had just opened the C'est la Vie by herself . . . before Leroy was in the picture. She was going to run the motel and practice home nursing. It was her first night to ever see the ocean after moving from Leavenworth, and she decided to take a walk along the beach. The October moon sparkled, the sand shone like diamonds as she dove into the waves. She swam strong strokes, watching the glow of the lights winking at her from the moonlit shore. Then she swam back to land ready to begin her new life.

In the months that followed, I decided if I ever had a daughter, I would tell her that she was beautiful and smart every day of her life, and

I'd tell my son the same thing. I wouldn't make my daughter clean the kitchen day after day or baby-sit a bunch of kids just because she was "the girl." I wouldn't give my son assorted sizes of footballs for his birthday just because he was "the boy." More than anything, I wouldn't tell them, "Things just happen"; I would try to explain "why" the best I could.

I yearned for a bigger kind of life; the kind Aunt Betty didn't have; the kind Meemaw didn't have; the kind my mother didn't have. I was not going to be the outcast: the lost aunt living with the nuns of Saint Bridget, or the sweet grandmother who didn't know how to quit jabbering, or the coach's wife with a keen eye toward a rosy future of bowl games and opportunities. I just had to figure how to get it.

# A TEMPEST OF RELATIVES

*"The Blitz System"*

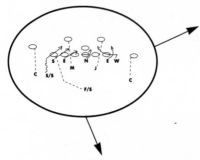

**The Blitz involves a DEFENSIVE BACK, THE DEFENSIVE LINE,
and possibly a LINEBACKER. The intent is to penetrate the line of
scrimmage with a defender that is not accounted for in the OFFENSIVE BLOCKING
SCHEME. We anticipate tackling the BALL CARRIER for a loss, possibly forcing
a turnover, or sacking the QUARTERBACK. This strategy is to disrupt the
OFFENSIVE SEQUENCE and place the OFFENSE "A Play Behind" in their
down and distance strategy. The Blitz may also force the
QUARTERBACK into an audible situation.**

**Base Crash Y Rifle Cover Zone**

The following summer we rented a cottage at a beach near Ocean
City, Maryland, for Daddy's three weeks of vacation from football. A
hurricane was ripping up and down the east coast, but Daddy claimed it'd
be over by the time we arrived. When it wasn't, he took the bad weather
personally, cursing the violet skies, bitter at not being able to get on the
golf course immediately.

I liked the beach, rain or shine, because it was about the only place in the world where football could not follow, except in the sports pages, and I never read them. Though nobody ever mentioned Aunt Betty, I still thought of her at night, and in my dreams, I told her about my days, of going into the eighth grade, the escape from Sister Matilda. I also wrote in my diary when I could, often writing down my memories of Aunt Betty, so she wouldn't slip into complete oblivion down in Florida.

Because our beach cottage wasn't ready the first night, we stayed at a motel called the Silver Spur. It had a blinking neon boot, proclaiming COLOR TV/TUB/WEEKLY RATES. Mama turned up her nose at the boot, while Daddy growled, "Hell, I know it's a fleabag, but we'll be in the beach cottage by nine A.M., so let's get a goddamn positive attitude going here, folks."

"Just make sure you get a good deal." Mama rolled down her window.

"Yeah, yeah." He stomped across the parking lot, trying to get the feeling back in his legs from hours of driving.

"And say we've got just two kids. The boys have their sleeping bags."

"No fair, the danged girls always get the bed," Joe-Sam yelled.

"Offer it up to the poor souls in purgatory," she hissed out the window, "Jack—!"

"Christ Almighty, Sally!" Daddy walked faster to dodge further instruction.

"Don't mention Bear Bryant either."

"Any other observations?" He kicked the gravel as an affable voice called out, "Can I be of service to you good folks?"

"Yes, sir, how do you do?" Daddy voice's drizzled professionalism.

"How do you do, too?" The grinning manager ambled across the parking lot.

"My name is Jack Donegal, and I'm a football coach with the Pittsburgh Sharks." He reeled off the speech he always gave whenever he hoped to earn a discount.

"A coach. How about that now," said the manager, wearing cowboy boots. "I see you got four kids. Isn't that wonderful. Five dollars extra for the dawg. Say you're from Pittsburgh? I'm a Long Horn man myself."

A few minutes after we checked in, Daddy went out for food, bringing back bulging sacks of french fries, hamburgers, and milk shakes, banging on the door. "Supper time." As he looked around the squalid room with all the flung-open suitcases, towels, and blankets strewn about, he thundered, "You sumbitches can tear up a room in flat-ass no time."

Ignoring him, we groped for our burgers, devouring them. While we were eating, Joe-Sam asked, "How come we only go two places on vacation: the beach or Leavenworth?"

"Right," I added. "Some of my friends have rustic cabins by lakes in Minnesota, and some of them go to New York City to climb the Empire State Building."

The last part was a lie. I didn't have any friends who'd ever gone to New York or even acted like they wanted to. But I wanted to visit Williamsburg in Brooklyn, New York, so I could walk down Francie Nolan's old street. Then I planned to tootle on over to Louisa May Alcott's home in Concord, Massachusetts.

"Yeah, how come we only ever go two places?" Peaches joined in. "That's two more than I ever went," Mama languished, sipping her gin and tonic. "I never went anywhere except for long Sunday drives on dusty Kansas roads."

"Why?"

"My father wasn't a football coach, that's why. Plus, we didn't have air-conditioning in those days. . . . Lord, Betty and I'd get thirsty, and Mama, carsick, belching over bridges, and Daddy'd keep right on driving."

"Wouldn't you get a drink?"

"Oh, sometimes, but mostly Mama said, 'If you're so thirsty, swallow your spit.' "

"Grrr-oss," Leo finger-punted a french fry through Joe-Sam's fingers, which were arched like a goal post.

"That's just the way it was. So y'all be grateful for what you got. Some kids never go anywhere or do anything." Mama swallowed two aspirin.

As Peaches and I snuggled into our bed, the boys in their sleeping bags, I watched Daddy staring at a lightbulb that hung on a string from the ceiling. He sighed, "Goddamn, look at this shithole. . . . I feel like I been fired. . . . But hell, it's only fourteen-fifty a night, including the price for the dog."

"Can't beat it with a stick," Mama smiled.

"That's for goddamn sure." Daddy reached over to hold her hand.

Our cottage near Ocean City had four large airy bedrooms with an odd assortment of beds in each one: twins, bunks, trundles, queen-size, king-size, plus a waterbed to boot. My grandfather, who had laid down the law long ago that no person was to ever call him "Grandpa" or "Gramps" and expect to live, had coined his own name choice of "Papa Sweetheart." Papa Sweetheart was the one treating everybody to this vacation, including our cousins who were due to arrive at any moment. We were all going to have to quadruple up, but that was fine by Mama and Daddy. Ever since the trauma of Aunt Betty's failed electric-shock therapy and shaky mental state in general, they spoke often of the importance of family—except we were visiting strictly Daddy's side, since there were lots more of them and not a single one had ever had therapy—a real plus in Daddy's book.

In the mornings, Daddy rose first to brave the hurricane rains to buy doughnuts and newspapers. He brought back at least three or four papers, plus custard long johns, cinnamon swirls, and apple fritters. After waking to the fragrance of black coffee, cigar smoke, and wet sand, I found him reading all the sports sections: his lifelines to the world. He was quiet those stormy mornings, as if he were conserving his energy. When he saw me, he murmured, "Doughnuts on the table. Don't eat 'em all."

I grabbed my doughnut and juice, sitting near him to read *Joy in the Morning, Tomorrow Will Be Better,* or *The Heart Is a Lonely Hunter* and *The Member of the Wedding.* As Daddy and I sank our teeth into printed words in the morning tranquility, I liked pretending we were close friends who didn't need conversation, since our silence together was understood.

Everything changed when the hurricane rains left, and the relatives blew into town from Nashville. First, Meemaw and Papa Sweetheart ar-

151

rived. Then Aunt Little and Uncle Whitey, plus their seven kids, and finally Peter and his new white-trash girlfriend, Cynthia Elspecker. Since every inch of bed space was taken, Peter slept in a sleeping bag in the bathtub, while Cynthia shared a room with me, Peaches, and our three little girl cousins, Mary, Molly, and Maggie. Although Miss Elspecker was nineteen, Peter's age, she needed a disgusting amount of coddling from Peter. She also wore a ton of makeup to the beach (on the days she agreed to go), warning every kid to steer clear of her towel, umbrella, and diet sodas. It didn't take long for me to dislike her, and I couldn't believe Peter was enslaved to such a southern-fried priss-pot.

"Do you go to Notre Dame, too?" I asked her one morning over a bowl of Cap'n Crunch with Crunchberries, after the men had departed for their daily thirty-six holes of golf.

"No," said Cynthia Elspecker, sipping her coffee, one pinkie finger sticking up. "I study dental hygiene in Goodlettsville outside Nashville. I met Peter at a Little Flower dance. We only get to see each other on vacations, so our time's very precious."

I nodded my head, feigning sympathy but feeling nauseated, as Peaches marched straight up to Cynthia Elspecker, giggling, "I like your hair and your pink eye shadow and eyeliner. Can I see your bra strap? Pretty please?"

I wanted to sink into the Crunchberries, but Cynthia patted Peaches's curls, cooing, "We girls will have to have us a makeover one night."

I ground my teeth, eyes slewed, watching the two of them immersed in girl talk. I considered sneaking into Cynthia's bed one night to slip a mess of live sand crabs into her goddamn frilly nightgown.


Each night, all the adults, including Cynthia Elspecker and Peter, bolted from the cottage to revive their spirits in Irish bars. As the oldest child of all the cousins, I was again the designated baby-sitter, a role I'd come to see as my destiny on earth; but I rebelled by refusing to clean. I figured I'd keep all ten kids alive in the evenings but, by God, I would scour counters for no man. Joe-Sam and Leo were tight with the boy cousins, while Peaches played with the girls, all close in age. The very youngest was a tolerant baby named Al. I carried him everywhere, because he hated being stuck in an infant seat. As long as he was being held, he observed the chaos with grins and gurgles.

Papa Sweetheart could have been a twin of Jackie Gleason's Ralph Kramden, and he loved practical jokes, like slipping plastic insects into a person's towel or electric buzzers in the couch. After each joke, he grabbed the victim in a bear hug, roaring, "God love you and I do too. . . ." I learned to laugh at the jokes played on me to prove I was a good sport, but I didn't trust him an inch, nor did he think much of me.

One morning, keeping quiet since Papa Sweetheart despised a racket, I put on my headphones to play *Jesus Christ Superstar.* Right away, Daddy reared up, flinging sports pages, screaming, "Goddammit to hell." Papa Sweetheart staggered out of his room, cursing, "Jesus, Mary, and Joseph." And I knew, for whatever reason, I was in for it.

"Way to go, way to go." Daddy ripped off my headphones, diving for the stereo to turn it off. "So circumspect of everyone else's sleep in the morning."

"I have on the headphones!" I cried.

"Well, the sumbitches aren't working, are they?"

"*JESUS CHRIST, SUPERSTAR*" sailed through the room.

"Hail Mary, full of grace." Papa Sweetheart was making the sign of the cross.

"It'll be a miracle if you didn't wake every poor bastard in the neighborhood." Daddy pulled out the plug, which caused the singing to grind to a stop.

"You're already doing that for me, aren't you?" I was shaking, but he wasn't listening. He had his arm around his trembling father, ordering, "Daddy, go on back to bed. I'll keep things quiet." He patted Papa Sweetheart on the back.

Meemaw appeared in the doorway, "It's all right, Liz darling, the music is so lovely. Though certain people in Nashville don't have a nice thing to say about us Catholics, *Jesus Christ Superstar* was a hit. I saw the show—"

"Not now, for the love of Christ in heaven," Papa Sweetheart begged her.

153

As her voice died away, Daddy and I locked stares, me brimming with rage, he ready to return to the sports pages now that the drama was over.

"Oh, so now you've got the red ass. That's great, Aunt Gertrude."

"You don't have to yell in front of my own grandparents."

"Oh, goddamn." He snapped back open a sports page. "Forget about it!"

"I don't forget." I struggled to stay unflappable.

"By God, you ought to learn. You're too goddamned sensitive, that's your problem, slick," he roared.

"No, that is not my problem, Coach Donegal," I spoke evenly. "You are." I slammed out of the cottage, leaving him sitting there with his cold coffee and half-smoked cigar. I needed to get some air.


Later that day, Daddy took my social life into his own hands by inviting Mary-Louise, a second cousin close to my age, to the beach. She had to take the Greyhound all the way from Nashville, so I tried to stay out of trouble until she arrived, but it was growing more lonesome in spite of all the relatives, none of whom fit me.

Once in a while I thought of Jo back in Kansas, who had stopped writing, the same way Sarah Camp had. I was beginning to get used to people dropping out of my life and new ones entering. It seemed to be part of the mathematical football formula. You can be friends for one or two years, but after four, forget about it.

On the evening before Mary-Louise came, the grown-ups stayed home to fix everyone a seafood feast, with crabs and shrimp; the beer was already flowing at sundown. Daddy, Papa Sweetheart, and Uncle Whitey poured bushel after bushel of steamy red crabs across a table covered with newspaper. With each bite or swill of beer, Papa Sweetheart wailed, "Aw, son, I'm so proud of you!" to his boys, while Daddy or Whitey or Peter sighed right back, "I love you, too." Why didn't they toast the women, too, I wondered, or why didn't the women toast each other? The little kids pressed in, squeezing between the browned elbows and legs of the laughing adults.

I sneaked sips of Peter's beers as Daddy bellowed, "Now, boys, you gotta use a wooden mallet to tap open the claws and dig out the soft white meat. Like this, son.''

The boys watched, but Peaches, Mary, Maggie, and Molly didn't; they were too busy cavorting with Barbie's Dream House in the corner.

The men and boys were gathered together at one end of the table in a kind of huddle. Uncle Whitey showed them how to chew on the claws, sucking the pinchers. The more beer I sipped, the more I stared at the blank eyes of the crab watching me eat him (or her).

"I don't like crabs," sniffed Cynthia Elspecker. "They smell something awful."

"I'll get you a Big Mac later, Cyn? Okay?" Peter squeezed her arm.

"Big Mac. Haw." Aunt Little, a woman who sized people up by their eyes, gave Cynthia Elspecker a look.

Cynthia Elspecker's lip twisted.

While I tapped on the spicy crab claws, Mama and Aunt Little talked about what an idiot Nixon was to leave those bugs all over that hotel, while Meemaw sighed, "Aw, the poor man . . . Now FDR . . . he was one gentleman to be reckoned with."

Papa Sweetheart snorted, "Yes, but what about horse-faced Eleanor."

"Sure, but there's been no one like her since," Meemaw defended.

"Women should stay out of politics. They—"

"Even though she did bring all the coloreds into the neighborhoods, I can appreciate her now. But she never did forgive FDR for his affair. . . ."

"Ah, Jesus, don't start—"

"It's no wonder he died in that secretary's arms. Eleanor kept the poor man at arm's length all those years and years, after she found out."

Papa Sweetheart grunted as Peaches wandered over to watch him dissect a crab. He got a gleam in his eye; he hammered his crab with a knife, and a single pale finger sailed through the air, landing splat on a beer can.

Peaches screamed bloody murder, diving into my lap. It was a fake, of course, but it looked real enough. Papa Sweetheart, roaring with laughter, wiped his tears, sighing, "Aw . . . Peaches, God love you and I do too."

Neither Aunt Little nor Mama even cracked a grin, but nobody dared cross the patriarch of the family, so we just sat there. Peaches buried her face in my neck, stiffening as Papa Sweetheart tried to give her a bear hug.

As I rocked her, I dug patterns into the molting newspaper, grubby beneath our fingers. Aunt Little told the little kids to brush their teeth and get ready for bed. Peaches stumbled off my lap to follow her cousins, since they'd set up a tent for a slumber party. The colors of the beach house grew blurry. Voices pierced the air. I realized I was a little drunk, just like "Sarah T" in *Portrait of a Teenage Alcoholic*.

"Tell us, Miss Elspecker," I whispered, pretending to be a sex psychologist. "What do you know about love? How do you love your man?"

She drew away from me, tensed. I gave her a wink as Uncle Whitey shouted, "All right, did you hear about the priest from Ireland?"

Daddy interrupted, "How about the Pitt player using the john the same time as the Notre Dame player? You'll love this, Peter, you sorry-ass Notre Damer, you."

Peter laughed, unabashed by his school loyalties.

Mama said, "Don't tell that joke in front of Liz."

"Oh, God, just tell it." My tongue was thickening.

"Okay, folks, I have permission from Aunt Gertrude. . . . So there's these two players, standing there, side by side, at these urinals." Daddy's eyes were twinkling. "The Pitt player finishes first, but doesn't wash his hands, and the Notre Dame player says, 'You know, at Notre Dame, we're taught to wash our hands after using the john,' and the Pitt player says, 'Well, at Pitt, we're taught not to piss on our hands.' "

The laughter at the table crescendoed, while Mama and Aunt Little expelled tiny identical sighs. More cans of Coors were snapped open. Cynthia Elspecker flounced off to the bedroom with a bodice-ripper romance. I began making a sculpture of crab carcasses in the middle of the table. Peter, his face immediately years younger upon his girlfriend's exit, helped me until the sculpture swelled higher and higher. The night of spices and ocean mingled over mountains of rosy shells, the jokes, conversations, and smoky air looming above us like a prayer.

★   ★   ★

"Okay, what's the most delicious thing to eat?" Mary-Louise asked me a few days after her arrival. We were stretched out together in the hammock at about one-thirty in the morning. I turned to look at her lovely face, her six-foot frame, her retainer shining on her teeth like a tiara. I steeled myself to utter the right answer, for I was beginning to sense that my second cousin always needed to be right, and she held no patience for people with wrong answers. I worshiped her, and she knew it.

"Uh. Cherry pie?" I was hopeful.

"God, you have no imagination at all," she twanged. "*Think, fool.*"

What could it be? I had no idea. What a lump. I stammered, "I don't know, Mary-Louise, what is the most delicious thing in the world to eat?"

"Hot bread pudding with chunks of almonds and pecans, topped with a scoop of gourmet vanilla ice cream, swimming in a sweet liqueur."

What was there to say to that? She was eloquent, descriptive, rich not only with beauty but with language.

I sighed, "Well, I lust for fresh mountain blueberries. Big juicy ones."

"Honey, you can't lust for blueberries." She sat up straight in the hammock.

"I can if I want. You lust for hot bread pudding."

"I do not lust for anything." She was outraged. "I never ever said that. Lust is a sexual thing, you idiot. You can't lust after food."

"I do."

"You don't either. Just look up the word in the dictionary, and you'll see it doesn't apply to food. . . . Lust is . . . only sexual."

"I read books too, Mary-Louise, for your high-and-mighty information. And from my own experience, lust is when you want something bad. And there is never a time when I don't want blueberries. Juice dribbling down the blueberry, with each tender . . ."

"I think you've had way too much sun or else you've been reading stuff you shouldn't. I'm going to bed."

"Fine." I swallowed, wondering how in the world she could have guessed.

She stopped in the doorway, looking very severe, "I'm going to say a prayer for you, because in my opinion, you are deeply disturbed." With that, she was gone. I grabbed my diary.

# Kerry Madden-Lunsford

*Dear Diary,*

*I rock the hammock back and forth. Alone. Missing her. I loathe her and love her. I can still smell her, the scent of her aloe vera lotion, Bonne Bell skin freshener, and grape lip gloss. She's like a teenage Mary Poppins of the south. I pick up a peach from the crate near the hammock and bite into it. I wish she'd love me back the way I adore her. I'd do anything for my cousin, the queen.*

Mary-Louise's being six feet tall didn't bother her one iota. Fifteen years old, and she carried her height like a Greek goddess, even wearing heels. She weighed a sophisticated 115 pounds, and I clocked in at 139. Someone was always snapping pictures of us at the beach, so I kept my thighs concealed under a towel, knowing what I looked liked next to the empress. For all her savoir-faire, she was even more modest than I. We never even saw each other naked, which was pretty astonishing, considering we shared a room with all the little girls and spent so much time together; bras and panties, yes, but naked around Mary-Louise? No way.

At the beach, Mary-Louise tanned a rich copper her first hour in the sun. Her goal was to get as brown as the tiny birthmark on her thigh. I couldn't stay in the sun too long because I got sickening sun sties, blisters, and bubbly cold sores that blossomed on my lips. I was forced to use sunscreen, and wear a hat with a brim and sunglasses. I looked more like Meemaw's sister than Mary-Louise's cousin.

I loved the hours with Mary-Louise, despite the pain I sometimes felt just being in her presence. Aside from her abhorrence of lust, things were great between us, especially the first few days. We baby-sat, walked, swam, rose for sunrises, feasted, and talked together. We slept back to back. I needed nothing else, for I had a living treasure: a girl near my own age. I couldn't get enough of her; she wrote poetry, she exuded beauty. I could only hang back in respect, admiring. Maybe I was a little in love? I didn't want to kiss her, I just wanted to become her. The day we realized we had the exact same great-grandmother was a gift. Her name was Bridy McLaughlin, an Irishwoman with her hair piled high into a bun. We could see us both in her.

Unfortunately, a dark cloud surfaced, and it became all too apparent that my goddesslike cousin enjoyed being with Joe-Sam as much as or more than she did being with me. Whenever we had the chance to be by ourselves, she deliberately invited him to tag along. At first I blamed it on the generosity of her heart, but when I realized they actually liked each other, I was appalled. For one thing, they looked ridiculous together. Mary-Louise had to bend down to talk to him, since he was a foot shorter. When I protested that we couldn't talk with Joe-Sam around, she laughed. "Of course we can. You've got the greatest brother in the world. Do you know how lucky you are?"

*But I want you all to myself.*

Things went from bad to worse. Joe-Sam and Mary-Louise acted like they were in love, never quite touching but never far apart either. *Don't you know you could have retarded babies?*

On our last night of vacation, the grown-ups dropped all of us off at Play-Land. They gave us money, ordering me to keep an eye on the little kids with the help of Mary-Louise. The second Daddy drove off, Mary-Louise and Joe-Sam cut loose, leaving me with nine children, including baby Al. I took them on the baby merry-go-round rides and bought them cotton candy, all the time looking for Mary-Louise and Joe-Sam. Onto the Ferris wheel, and there below were the viperous traitors, walking together, holding hands. I buried my face in baby Al's neck.

We met at the Roto, where they took the boys so they could all stick to the wall while it spun. I didn't go on, but I could feel them—Mary-Louise and Joe-Sam spinning together, exchanging dizzy glances, fingers entwined. I jerked my attention back to the girls. "Who wants to go in the haunted house with me?"

"No, we don't want to." They licked their red apples.

Before I could insist further, Mary-Louise stalked down the ramp, trumpeting, "That boy Leo threw up on the Roto—how revolting." I rushed to find Leo, Al clinging to my neck. Joe-Sam was patting his back, and a man was helping him down off the Roto, which they had to shut down to clean.

"I think I ate too many hot dogs." Leo collapsed on Joe-Sam's lap. The cousins gathered around to make sure he was going to live, but within minutes, he recovered, demanding to go in the haunted house.

"Come on," I wheedled the girls. "I'll be right there. Let's go in the haunted house too. You'll be glad you did it."

"Why?" asked Peaches, skeptically.

"Because you just will." I was dying to show them the woman's hands reaching out of a flushing toilet. Peaches, sensing Angela's threatening presence, started squalling, "No! NO!"

Mary, Molly, and Maggie took the cue. "Help us. Help us!"

Mary-Louise glanced at me accusingly, and hissed, "I just can't believe how mean you are, trying to scare these poor little girls." She turned to them, sweetly cooing, "Let's go on the Donald Duck ride." They buzzed at her like honeybees.

I blared, "You weren't exactly Clara Barton with Leo on the Roto, now were you? And where have you been for the last two hours while I was watching all nine of them?" It felt great to let it all out. But Mary-Louise just tossed her hair and replied, "Don't be such a boring martyr. If it was too much for you, you should have just asked for help." Then she walked off.

A miracle happened the morning after Play-Land. Joe-Sam farted in front of Mary-Louise. Now, if he had shown a smidgen of remorse, she might have forgiven him; but he and the other boys fell to the floor, congratulating each other with glee.

"Way to cut the cheese, man."

Mary-Louise practically dove back into my company. I longed to say, I told you so but instead forgave her, since it was our last day, and Mary-Louise was catching a ride back to Nashville with Peter and Cynthia Elspecker, which Cynthia looked none too pleased about. Mary-Louise turned to give me a hug good-bye.

"I'll write, okay?"

"I'm a terrible letter writer," she avoided.

"I'm not. We have to stay in touch. It's our destiny."

"Lord, you're such an actress, Liz," she smiled. My heart slipped down into my gut.

I watched my queenlike cousin step very ladylike into the backseat of

Peter's Gold Duster to speed off with him and Cynthia Elspecker, who flashed us a toothy smile. It took Mary-Louise only a few moments to forget all about me.

It was the six of us again. With everyone gone, the beach house felt soggy, silent, and used up. I could smell all the crab shells rotting in bags at the side of the house. When Daddy whistled for us to get in the car, Mama refused. She stood outside the Buick, staring at the ocean. "I'm not ready to go back." I looked at her face to see if she meant it. I suddenly imagined Mama, Peaches, and me staying on at the beach house for the whole entire year, while Daddy and the boys went back for football season. The thought gleamed like a radiant promise.

"Sally, let's traverse our ass down the road."

"I told you, I need more time to smell the sea air."

"Sweetheart, I love you. Now get in the car so I can get ready to whip 'Bama's ass. We'll stop for some softshell crabs on our way out of town." He turned and saw us watching the action. "What the hell are you two staring at?"

"Nothing," I said.

"Nothing," echoed Peaches.

Mama looked at my face. She seemed to read my thoughts, yearning for the same year at the beach that I was. Maybe she didn't feel like facing her life either for a little while; the roller-coaster of football. "I sure would like that softshell crab sandwich." Her eyes were like warm green oceans. "How about y'all?" She got in the front seat, found her rosary, and put on her sunglasses.

When we got back to Pittsburgh, Daddy went straight to the football office and Mama hung up paintings of the sea at sunset, adding shells with netting and a mounted shark to the Tijuana and football motifs. She stuck red plastic crabs on the coffee table and mantel. She promised me she would make softshell crabs, but somehow she never got around to it.

# GIRLS RULE THE SCHOOL

*"Trips Right P 10—An Attitude Play"*

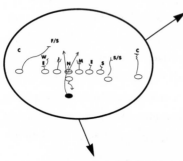

**A quick-hitting play designed to attack the
DEFENSIVE FRONT before they are set, or in a short yardage
situation with the BALL CARRIER going over the top. The BALL CARRIER
leaps over the DEFENSIVE LINE to avoid penetration.**

The day Mama finished redecorating the house, we learned that Papa
Sweetheart had died of a massive coronary while he was in a courtroom
giving evidence in a podiatry insurance-fraud case. He was going strong
on the witness stand when suddenly he collapsed, announcing that an
elephant was sitting on his chest. When they first told me, I wondered for
a second if he'd been pulling one of his practical jokes, but that wasn't the
case at all. In just one minute, he was dead. According to Uncle Whitey,
he was already up in heaven sharing a Guinness with Jesus Christ Himself,
but Daddy had very little to say about his father's death. He kept quiet
the whole funeral week, studying the pictures of his boyhood home on
the walls, sitting in corners by himself. Mama warned us to leave him

alone until he worked through losing his daddy, so we were all extra gentle with him, bringing him chilled beer or black coffee, depending on the time of day. Peaches was the most comforting. She stood right next to him, her little arm crooked around his neck, not saying a word.

I stayed for a month after the funeral, with Meemaw, who soon felt strong enough to go to a wedding in Bon Aqua, Tennessee, two weeks after Papa Sweetheart's death, insisting I come along too. In her attic, she found a floor-length pink bridesmaid's dress, which made swishing noises. The material was covered with soft pink roses, and the dress zipped up the back. Peter called it a Renoir dress, but I didn't know what he meant at the time. I didn't bother to shave my legs the day of the wedding because I knew no one was going to see anything with me in a Renoir maxidress.

On the way to the church, the strap of my wedgie sandal snapped, so I pinned it with a large safety pin. At the reception, I knew no one, so I hunkered down close to Meemaw. But when the bride went to throw the bouquet, Meemaw pushed me toward the group of ladies, urging, "Go on, see if you can catch that ole bouquet. Goodness knows you've caught enough footballs in your life, gal."

As I stood with the other ladies, tense, wondering if any of them were going into the ninth grade, too, the bouquet hit me smack in the face before it dropped to the floor. I didn't even have time to try to catch it, but because it touched me first, I was considered the one who caught it. I had to get in a picture with the man who had caught the garter. He had a big furry mustache, and he smiled at me as he lifted up my pink dress, revealing to all my prickly leg sticking out of the broken wedgie sandal. I clenched my teeth, gripping the bouquet, sweat pouring in hot rivers through my Renoir dress, while he slipped the garter up my leg to just above my hairy knee.

Peter roared with laughter as I told him the story on our three-mile night jog through the neighborhoods of Nashville. Then he took me and Mary-Louise for a ride in his new Gold Duster to Dipper Dan's for ice cream, but during those weeks after the funeral, he also grew increasingly testy.

★　　★　　★

"Liz, I told you not to wear my cut-off shorts," he snapped, watching me pull down the attic ladder on my way to seek out old photographs.

"Okay, okay." I scaled the ladder quickly, but his voice followed me.

"Don't wear them again, goddammit."

"I can't hear you," I sang, high above him in the rafters of the sizzling summer attic. I couldn't believe he was that uptight over a pair of shorts. I loved those shorts. They were the only article of clothing that was baggy on me.

Late one afternoon while I was preparing a pie, he nagged accusingly, "You're leaving the peels on the apples?"

"I like apple peel."

"But not for apple pie. It doesn't taste right."

"Then don't eat it." I thrust my hand into the Mixmaster to scrape the dough from the sides. Blindly, I got my fingers too close to the beaters, which chewed them inside.

Peter gently pried them loose from the steel blades, pleading, "Hold still, Liz."

"I'm sorry, Peter," I wept.

"No, it's my fault. I'm not myself these days. I can't believe Daddy's gone."

He gave me ice to put on my hand and finished making the apple pie himself. It was delicious, and he was right; it did taste better without the peels.

"I miss him very much," he admitted one night, before he left for Notre Dame.

"I know," I replied, lying. I hadn't realized Peter missed his daddy at all, because I certainly didn't. I found the house liberated from Papa Sweetheart's dominating Irish will, his *"Meg. Get me a beer!"* and the TV blaring from his bedroom at all hours, while he sat propped up like the sultan of the south.

"I would never do anything to hurt him." Peter spoke more to himself than to me.

"Of course you wouldn't, silly." I punched him lightly in the arm, but he didn't even notice. He was drawing a series of sketches of Papa Sweetheart, Daddy, and Uncle Whitey. The men in the family. The hunter, the coach, and the lawyer. He brought their faces to life in smooth black strokes.

"Who's your favorite artist, Peter?"

"Edward Hopper. He painted the way I feel."

In the late midnight hour, the sound of his pencil scratching the pad was underscored only by the recital of a single mockingbird, warbling and chirping at us from the rosebushes through the porch window. I leaned against the screen, breathing in the smell of roses, recalling Aunt Betty's flying bouquets of Ames, Iowa, when Peaches was born. If I were an artist like Peter, that's what I would have drawn.

After Peter left for Notre Dame, it dawned on Meemaw that she was cut loose from husband and son. With her new freedom, she began planning trips with Catholic Church tours to places all over the world. She made reservations to go to Hawaii, Jerusalem, Ireland, Las Vegas, France, Scotland, and New York—just for starters.

When I couldn't listen to her prattle about Europe or the Middle East, I'd go down into the cool of the basement. In the freezer was a frozen pheasant with stiffened emerald-green and black feathers. I'd lift the bird out of the freezer and cradle it in my arms. I named it after Saint Hubert, the patron saint of hunters and trappers. Nobody had the heart to eat the bird, since he was Papa Sweetheart's last shot.

At the end of August, when Meemaw left for Rome, I returned to Pittsburgh and my quest to love it as my real home.

Right before high school started, I begged Mama and Daddy to get me gold-wired glasses and pierced ears, but they took it one step further, insisting upon contact lenses. At first, the hard contacts felt like wet dimes on my corneas, but pitching out my octagon frames was so emancipating that I was willing to endure all optical agony.

To celebrate the beginning of high school, Mary Martha Mac also gave me a three-tiered tray of fifty eye shadows, ranging from indigo blue to canary yellow to aquamarine, and I began experimenting by dabbing

Mama's lipstick on my cheeks and lips. With my contact lenses, pierced ears, and splashes of makeup, I no longer resembled a defective John-John Kennedy, and nobody ever uttered the word "Moose."

My St. Joan's uniform consisted of a pleated skirt, white blouse with Peter Pan collar, and sweater, which I bellyached about with all my freshman friends, but secretly loved. We were a team, a troupe, a chorus, and for the first time, I belonged. I didn't have a best friend, but I had good friends because we were all new together. It was idyllic to start off fresh with everyone instead of alone, the way I always had.

The turning point came when I found a sport in which I excelled, and I made the St. Joan of Arc's field hockey team, elevating me far beyond the level of softball Space Cadette. The coach, Big Phyll, wore a windbreaker, a whistle, and a scowl, as she commanded that we run nonstop for ten minutes. She was smart enough to start me at halfback. We wore blue and yellow rugby shirts, rugby socks, white shorts, and cleats. During one of our first games, I made an assist to a forward who scored the winning goal, thrilling my teammates. I felt honored to belong to a group of girls who admired me as an athlete and friend and, by a miracle, were as tall as I was, or even taller. I was no longer the freak, towering over the masses.

The autumn afternoons blazed with gold-dusted leaves and azure skies. I knew I would burst with joy, sprout wings, and soar over the hockey field, kissing all the invisible angels who had bestowed upon me such tremendous fortune. I adored darting across the field with my stick, kneepads, and shin guards, whacking the ball, at last respected for my relentless aggression. We were girls of height and strength, free from smarmy boys with cracked voices and zitted faces.

*Dear Diary,*

*Few people ever actually attend our field hockey games, which is irritating since Joe-Sam's and Leo's J.V. and Peewee football games are always packed, but the people who do come know we're hot. Daddy's never seen one of my games either, because we play during football season, but he taught me how to ease the ache of my charley horses by pointing my toes toward the ceiling with*

*each stabbing cramp. I'm too tired to write anymore. I have a very busy life now.*
*I can't remember when I've ever been so happy. Is it normal to love a school so*
*much?*

As a freshman I registered for biology, English, French, music, religion, world history, physical education, and algebra I. Home ec, my avocation for all the years prior to high school, was the only elective offered. I was bad news at algebra, which was taught by a man named Mr. Swallow, who wore his pants hiked up to his ribs. In biology, I discovered I had O positive blood, very handy in case of catastrophe. I loved my English class, where I wrote a saga called "Meghan: The Migrant Worker Girl." (I had a crush on a senior named Meghan, who played hockey, smoked cigarettes, and was my "big sister" at school.) During French, I discovered the Eiffel Tower, masculine and feminine nouns, and a desire to travel overseas to lap it all up for myself. I felt my mind popping open in religion, where I learned that polytheism meant many gods. I was intrigued by polytheism—Zeus, Hippolyta, Aphrodite striding about the earth—but Sister Rose breezed through that section, so we could get to Exodus. As for world history, I probed into the tragedies and comedies of the Greek theaters, where thousands gathered in gigantic arenas to experience raging purgation and catharsis. I attempted to sew a wraparound skirt in home economics. I sang with the sopranos for all the concerts, conducted by a teacher who adored music and never forced us to attend funerals. I longed to beam Sister Matilda in for just one concert, to watch me perform in all my glory, but the latest word was she'd recently retired to the Sisters of Mercy Motherhouse to polish silverware for the rest of her days.

"Hey listen, yoonz guys. Buffy from *Family Affair* is dead. I just heard."

"No way. You're lying," I challenged.

"Buffy?" cried Anne Adams, one of the other field hockey halfbacks.

"Swear to God!" yelled Laurie, the goalie. "The radio said she OD'd."

My heart thudded. "But she was way young."

"I know. Seventeen. They said it was heroin."

"That's terrible."

Big Phyll stepped up. "All right, yoonz quit the jabbering and start the running."

"But Buffy—"

"Yeah, I know, I heard. A real tragedy. Now yoonz do your laps."

We started running without speaking, Big Phyll barking orders: "Take the corner, around the field, pace yourself, move it, move it, move it. Get those knees up. You're awful. Pitiful. Donegal, you run like my grandmother for Christ's sake." She blew her piercing whistle, checked her stopwatch, occasionally chasing us as we hustled around the track. I launched her a winning smile when I ran past for a third time, longing to win her over. She spat out, "Who are you supposed to be, Donegal? The smiling opponent? Get going."

I kept moving, sucking in any hint of Buffy, dead somewhere in Hollywood. It seemed absolutely impossible. She was only seventeen, three years older than me. It made me feel almost guilty. Buffy's face, her short pigtails, and Mrs. Beasley swarmed over me the rest of practice. I thought back to that Ames Christmas of digging pine needles out of the carpet, Mrs. Beasley, and kissing Peter. Why did Buffy take heroin anyway? When I got home, I retrieved Mrs. Beasley from Peaches's closet and stuck her on my dresser. I wanted to pull the string in her stomach, so she could give me an explanation for Buffy's untimely death, but she'd stopped talking a long time ago. Peaches walked in. "I thought you gave her to me."

"Well, I need her back for a minute," I explained.

"I don't have anybody to play with."

"You're too young for me."

"You used to play with me lots. I'll be an orphan! You can even be Angela if you want." She squeezed her eyes shut.

"I can't. I'm in mourning."

"It's not morning."

"You don't understand anything, do you? It's because you're so young."

"I hate when people say that."

"Peaches, I'll play with you later if you'll just scat."

She paused at the door, giving me the once-over. "I think you should know you've got stubby legs, and they need shaving."

She gave me no choice. I whipped around, eyes bulging, fingers curling toward her pink throat, booming, "I AM AN–GE–LA."

She was off like a shot, bounding downstairs to safety. I turned back to Mrs. Beasley, who hadn't moved her thin lips an inch.


In December of my freshman year, Daddy's big dream came true. He and Coach Donny Mac had an undefeated season, and the Pitt Sharks were invited to play the Georgia Hound Dogs in the Sugar Bowl for the National Championship. Mama was giddy with excitement, preparing for the most prestigious bowl game of our lives.

Before we left for the Sugar Bowl, to create the idea of Christmas she looped strings of lights and tinsel around a jade plant. Leo got mad because we didn't set up the artificial one. Mama had bought one the year before, since she'd grown sick of begging the neighbors of Brookseed to help her drag real ones into the house with Daddy gone recruiting all the time.

When Leo laid eyes on the puny decorated jade, he pitched a fit, yelling, "That's not a Christmas tree."

"Leo's right, Mama." I patted him on the back.

"It's better than a real Christmas tree," Mama warned.

"But I like sticking branches in the 'ortificial' one and spraying it to smell like Christmas. It was my job to do that." He was really upset.

Peaches piped up. "Go get the can of pine scent. You can spray the jade."

"It's not the same," Leo glowered.

"Leo, we have to catch a plane in three days, and then we'll be gone for weeks. Nobody's going to be here to enjoy a big Christmas tree."

"We could just set it up for one night," I suggested.

"Yeah!" yelled Leo. "Just one night."

Mama gave me a see-what-you've-started look.

"It's tradition," Leo mumbled.

"Well, dammit"—Mama arched her back—"I've started a new tradition. Now quit the crabbing, and let's have Christmas. We're going to the Sugar Bowl, by God."

"Hey, Leo," said Joe-Sam, flexing his muscles.

"What?" he sulked.

"Be cool."

"Shut up, fag."

"You're the fag, fag."

"Mama?" I tried to drown them out. "Do you ever wonder what it would be like if you and Mary Martha were the coaches? What if you two flew ahead to get the team ready for a win, while Daddy and Coach Mac brought the kids on the plane later?"

"What are you talking about?"

"Role reversal. What if you weren't stuck with us all the time? What if you and Daddy switched? Do you ever think about that?"

"No, I don't."

"Wouldn't it be nice if the women were the ones who did the taking off for once?"

"Yes, I suppose it would, but it won't happen in my lifetime."

"What a joke." Joe-Sam shook his head.

"Hey"—I grabbed his biceps, giving it a good pinch—"that's how my life is going to be, punk. I'm not going to be left behind."

"Me either!" Peaches jumped up, excited. "My husband can bring the babies to meet me. We'll have things to do, won't we, Liz?"

"Could we just have Christmas?" Mama replied, pouring eggnog into glasses, moving to the piano to play carols. "And settle the problem of women's liberation some other time? Now, has anyone seen my aspirin? I feel a headache coming on."

# NATIONAL CHAMPIONS

*"Vince Lombardi Philosophy"*

**Winning isn't everything. It's the only thing.**

To go to the Sugar Bowl, I had to leave St. Joan's a week before school was dismissed for Christmas vacation, but my field hockey friends made a cake for me and wished me luck—as if I had anything to do with the outcome of the National Championship. I really didn't want to leave them to face three weeks of football, because ugly rumors were circulating about this being Coach Mac's final year at Pitt, rumors I chose to ignore. I threw up repeatedly the night before we had to board the Sugar Bowl plane, something I had done during other bowl trips, too. I never knew what caused this sudden sickness to hit, but when Mama pushed me into the backseat of the Buick at about five A.M. that icy morning, she declared, "Well, it wouldn't be a bowl trip without you vomiting."

By the time we landed in Biloxi, Mississippi, for a week of pre–bowl game training, I was feeling much better. I sent postcards back to all my friends at St. Joan's to describe the Sugar Bowl follies, which began with a kiss in the Pitt Hospitality Room of the hotel. I was standing with Daddy drinking a Shirley Temple when, out of the blue, he nudged me toward a famous TV star who had entered the room, announcing, "Liz, honey. Meet The Six Million Dollar Man. In the flesh."

"Hey," I mumbled, as I reached out to shake his hand. He flicked his bionic eyes off the football game above the bar, leaning over to kiss me on the cheek, whispering, "Merry Christmas, darling."

"Amen," I breathed, flustered. *I wasn't in church. God, what a fool.*

As Daddy and I walked back to meet Mama at the hotel restaurant, he squeezed the back of my neck. "Hell, partner, what do you think? You just been kissed by The Six Million Dollar Man. Goddamn, isn't that something?"

"Daddy." I blushed.

"Aunt Gertrude, you need to loosen up."

"I am. I will," I informed him severely, but already I felt loose, for I loved the fact that I would be able to gloss up this Six Million Dollar Kiss in worldly postcards to Pittsburgh, impressing my friends. They didn't need to know *all* the details. I would simply rewrite the scene the way it should have happened.

Whether it was the air or the water off the Gulf of Mexico, the boys of the coaches went absolutely hog-wild at the hotel, wrestling near the fountain, ordering room service at midnight, tackling each other in the flower beds of the hotel gardens. You could hear them coming, like a pack of wild dogs. One afternoon, I was reading *Lisa, Bright and Dark,* about a girl who goes crazy, when I noticed them throwing rocks. I went back to my book, thinking, "Idiots," when one of their stones grazed an empty golf cart parked next to the hotel office. Joe-Sam sprang behind the steering wheel, with all the other boys leaping on behind him like flying caterpillars.

"Give it some gas," Buster ordered.

"You can't drive," laughed Leo.

"Come on, just do it," yelled another coach's son.

Joe-Sam floored it across the parking lot like a bumper car, attempting to do wheelies and 360s, squealing, rocking it violently with each slam of the brakes. Within a minute, he smashed into a Cadillac just as a lady walked out of the hotel office. Unable to figure out reverse, he began grinding the cart even more deeply into the car, gripping the steering wheel, sobbing. Hotel security nabbed him and hauled him inside the office, while I ran to get Mama, who was furious. When Mama shoved Joe-Sam back into the hotel room, the phone was ringing. As I answered it, Leo's voice ordered, "Put Mama on right now."

"You're in for it, punk," I whispered, handing over the phone.

Her face turned violet, and within seconds she hissed into it, "You creep. Your brother is in trouble, y'all were involved, and all you can do is cover your own ass?"

When she banged down the phone, I asked, "What did the scum-wad say?"

She answered with a mimic of Leo: "Mother, I want you to know one thing. Joe-Sam is guilty, and me and Buster and everybody else are all innocent."

That night, Coach Mac held a disciplinary meeting for all the coaches' sons. His eyes blistered into every boy, "I'm telling you this, men. . . . You better watch your little ass. Watch your little ass." What he really meant was "Liz, you'll be watching their little asses, watching their little asses," because for the remainder of the week in Biloxi, I was the "designated adult" when the "real" ones were out. In an attempt to make me feel better, Mary Martha crowned me "Mother of the Year," a role I politely declined. I had other things on my mind.

*Dear Diary,*

*In these days of breathing bowl fever, I have finally discovered one handsome player on the Pitt team named Sal. He is one of the best-looking men I've ever seen in my life, with his thick black hair, wide shoulders, and smile. I like to watch him, all clean-smelling with damp hair in the hotel lobby. Once he actually looked at me, and said, "Hey, how's it going?" I choked out a "Hi." How original. I'm glad none of my hockey friends are around to see me act so shivery. When I see him, I try to concentrate on* Lisa, Bright and Dark, *but it's difficult with him in the vicinity. He's graceful for a football player. My knees itch whenever I catch him wrapping his arms around various waifs with caked-on makeup. Then I remind myself that he is old, at least twenty-two, and I am fifteen, but he is one well-formed man. Mama likes him too, but in the same way she admires Robert Redford. She happened to meet Sal's father in the lobby the other day, and gushed, "Oh, Mr. Bondano, how do you do? I'm Jack Donegal's wife, and I have to tell you, you have such a handsome son."*

*Mr. Bondano took her hand, and smiled. "My dear lady, when you plant tomatoes, you get tomatoes." His son is one tomato, that's for sure.*

Being on a bowl trip, I always felt like something big was about to happen, and for some people, I suppose it was. I liked the feeling of anticipation, of losing myself in a new city, since at age fifteen I was deemed old enough to be on my own. In Biloxi, whenever I ran into one of the *coacheswives* on the elevator, she'd sigh, "Oh, honey, aren't we all just lucky to be here?" I'd reply, "Oh, yes, ma'am," and be on my merry way, exploring shops, wondering if Biloxi was actually supposed to feel like heaven on earth. In some ways it was, but every event was geared toward football: trophy banquets, stadium visits, the drone of speeches about athletes, winning, and champions. *A winner says, Let's find out. A loser says, Nobody knows. A winning team goes through a problem. A losing team goes around it and never gets past it.* Blah, blah, blah. I began to feel very removed from the testosterone storm of festivities, except in being happy for my father, who'd been working all his life for this opportunity.

Once we were out of the sleepiness of Biloxi, Mississippi, and into the rip-roaring energy of New Orleans, our hotel was filled with parties, dances, and maître d's, coming and going in shiny shoes and fancy brass-buttoned uniforms. I soon discovered Bourbon Street and the French Quarter, where I came to life. Along the Mississippi, I watched the swell of steamboats and barges sailing by, lapping up the rivery smells, the sweet sounds of bluesy jazz sliding off the waterway. As I roamed the avenues of cobblestone, laced with wrought-iron filigree and shotgun houses, every breath I inhaled filled me with joy. A steam-boat called the *Natchez* surged downriver with a steam organ trumpet-ing, "When the Saints Go Marching In." I juked along with the bustle of folks with places to go, slipping off to a part of the French Quarter where they drowned the beignets in powdered sugar and served them up with steaming cups of café au lait. I lusted after every beignet bite, suspecting Mary-Louise would have too, but, of course, she never would have admitted it either.

Occasionally, I wished she were with me, but I was used to solitary time, though I sometimes ached to join even the tables of strangers, the nonfootball people sipping red wine, eating their muffulettas and po' boys, having animated discussions about all sorts of topics other than the game. They probably didn't even care who won the Sugar Bowl. *I could be you,* I breathed toward the lively tables, *I could be you.* But when they glanced up, they looked right through me, as though I were invisible.

I peeked inside Bourbon Street bars that revealed caches of throbbing stripteasers, jamming to the low-down smoky beat of salacious sex, making a reading of *The Happy Hooker* seem amateurish. Through the cracks in doors, I glimpsed the bawdy dancing of women, men, and men who were women, unable to peel my eyes away. While Bourbon Street proved not only a great education, I also used it as an escape from the redneck Georgia fans, who wheezed down the corridors of our hotel, whooping to bellhops and anyone else within earshot, "How about them Dawgs!"

"How about 'em," I would whisper, praying to get to my floor before they attacked. I learned fast to get out of their way whenever I saw a herd of them coming. Fortunately, Pitt creamed them on New Year's Day, which I found sweet justice against their red-eyed, beer-induced *Dawg patriotism.*

"The Pitt fans might be a little football crazy," I explained to Peaches one morning, applying a mouthful of lipstick before setting off on another New Orleans adventure. "But at least they have class."

"Exactly," she said, watching me closely in the mirror. "Liz?"

"What?"

"Can I try some of your lipstick?" She tickled the back of my neck, giggling.

"Sure," I smiled, feeling like a generous big sister. "Take all you want, sugar."

Our football fortunes seemed endless. After the Sugar Bowl, Daddy and Coach Mac were enticed to go to Hawaii to coach for the All-Star Hula Bowl. As we landed in Hawaii, the jazz of New Orleans faded into a hazy paradise. However, instead of soaking up the glory of the tropics, I felt like a snooty brat because all I really wanted was to return home to St. Joan's and my friends.

"Forget St. Joan's," Mama ordered me, as I paced the hotel room.

"But I could fail algebra. I'm horrible in it."

"How can you think about algebra in Hawaii?"

"I don't know. I miss my friends."

"We'll be up to our asses in snow soon enough. I'm sure they miss you too, but there's not a thing you can do about it now, except go enjoy yourself on the beach."

"Okay." I grabbed a towel, lotion, and my new book, *You Can't Go Home Again*.

For the next few days, I gorged on fresh pineapples, drinking virgin mai-tai's on the sandy shores. I felt more alone than ever. Lovers walked hand in hand at sunset, best friends splashed each other in the blue water, old folks sat together playing cards under the trees. Everybody in the world seemed to have somebody but me. Sometimes Peaches was with me, but mostly she and Beth Mac hung out together in their hula girl skirts and orchid leis.

Then the evil rumors I'd only heard whispered in Mississippi and New Orleans began to circulate in full force: Coach Donny Mac was returning to his alma mater to coach the Tennessee Fighting Game Cocks in Big Tangerine Country. I wanted no part of the southern, strutting macho Game Cocks, and I suddenly detested all shades of orange. I knew if I could just get back to Pittsburgh, I could command time to stop. The Tennessee gossip made my stomach ache, my eyes burn. Who knew how the twisted mind of a football coach worked? We had just won the National Championship, Pitt surely wanted us to stay, so I kept my ears closed to any talk of the south. Instead, I concentrated on the crystal shores of Hawaii; I learned to be careful near the rocky coral on the ocean floor; I even waxed a surfboard. But I only floated on it in the water, since my sense of balance was suddenly gone.

*Dear Diary,*

*We get on the plane tonight. The boys spent most of their time in the hotel room, watching* Blazing Saddles. *I've seen it once, but 10 times in a row is too much if you ask me. Last night the Hula Bowl hosts took us to the Don Ho show, where a bloated pig roasted in a pit, while belly dancers shook around up on stage. Don Ho himself invited all the ladies to come up to say aloha, "Hawaiian Style." Mama and Mary Martha pulled me up with them, behind a long line of tourists. I was soon deeply French-kissed by one of Don Ho's big Hawaiian men, in front of a massive audience of nasal cheers, flowered shirts, and bongo drums. It was by far the slobberiest moment of my entire life. I am so ready to go home, I could scream.*

# *19*

# HELLO, STINKING CREEK ROAD

*"Blocked Punt"*

**A Blocked Punt is caused by either a poor snap, poor timing by the punter, or a defensive scheme that frees up a defender at the line of scrimmage and permits an open lane, in which he is able to drive to the block point and take the ball off the punter's foot. The result is an excruciating feeling of devastation for the punting unit and Special Teams Coach.**

"Well, y'all have had a helluva trip," Daddy grinned, leaning over our seats on the airplane. "Biloxi, New Orleans, Hawaii. You folks are a pack of damn sojourners."

"I loved New Orleans." I smiled at Daddy, trying to steer the conversation away from potential bombshells.

"But folks, let me say this," he continued, "don't unpack those valises too soon."

"Valises?" asked Peaches.

"Don't say it, Daddy," I pleaded.

"What?" he laughed, swilling some of his Johnnie Walker with a splash.

"Knoxville," muttered Joe-Sam. "She thinks if you don't say it, it won't happen."

The words of Thomas Wolfe began to blur on the page.

"What's Knoxville?" asked Peaches.

"Where've you been?" Leo inquired.

"In Hawaii, la de da," crowed Peaches. "So what's Knoxville, Daddy?"

"Home of the Tennessee Fighting Game Cocks." Daddy grinned. "Peaches, the state of Tennessee had more volunteers during the Civil War than any other state."

"It means they're racist," I spat.

"What the hell are you talking about?" Daddy glowered. "For your information, slick, they volunteered for both sides, but the larger corps of volunteers was for the North. How about them apples?"

"So what? I'm not interested in Tennessee history or the stupid Game Cocks. It's not my state. It has absolutely nothing to do with me."

"Hey, hey now, Aunt Gertrude, don't get your panties in a wad over this move."

"My damn panties are not in a *wad* over anything"—I took a deep breath—"because I'm not going."

"The hell you're not. We just won the Sugar Bowl."

"Then why are *you* moving to Tennessee?"

"You might love the Fighting Game Cocks," whispered Peaches.

"Shut up."

"Well, at least she's gotta good attitude," Daddy sneered.

"She's eight years old. What does she care? I'm fifteen. I'm sick of this."

"You'll like the south if you give it a goddamn chance. You've always loved going to Nashville to visit Peter and Meemaw and all the folks."

"Pittsburgh is my home. I moved with you from Florida, Mississippi, Kentucky, North Carolina, Iowa, Kansas, and Pennsylvania. No more."

"Shhh," Mama warned. "You're causing a scene."

"Goddammit, Liz, we're going to Knoxville as a family."

"Wrong again, Coach." I got up, pushing my way past him to go to the second deck of the plane. In an empty seat, I stared out the window into the inky blackness ahead, to *my* home, Pittsburgh.

The future smacked us head-on like a steamroller. The first day back we dragged our suitcases through a blanket of snow in the front yard, while Mama vaulted into the house barefoot, having lost her high-heeled sandals in a snowdrift. Daddy immediately banged downstairs to start washing all his clothes for Knoxville; it was time to pack for prime recruiting season down south. A few days later, when I had turned in all the assignments I'd missed, Mama put the house on the market. A week after that the phone rang, and within a few seconds, Mama shrieked from upstairs, "Clean the house. The Realtor is bringing people through tonight."

"I don't want anyone to look at our house. They might buy it." I tossed cookie ingredients across the counter: flour, eggs, chips, sugar, vanilla, soda, salt. I planned on trashing the kitchen to turn off prospective buyers.

Mama yelled from upstairs, "I couldn't be so lucky as to have the first people through make an offer. Now get dusting, Liz. Put everyone else to work, too."

When she appeared in the doorway of the kitchen, witness to the cookie preparations, she raged, "For God's sakes. Put this junk away. Joe-Sam, vacuum. Peaches, rake the rug. Leo, clean the bathrooms."

"I can't stop, I've cracked the eggs."

"Elizabeth Frances Donegal, I don't give a flip what you've cracked."

I gave up and fed Bear Bryant the eggs, stuffing the rest of the ingredients back in the cupboard. We scoured the house in minutes, the doorbell rang, and the mousy couple who appeared with the Realtor made an offer on our beloved home that very night. After they left, Mama exclaimed, "I can't believe it. Our house in Ames, six months, our Kansas place, two years."

"I hope you're satisfied." I got out ingredients again for cookies.

"You're going to bake tonight? It's nine o'clock. You have school tomorrow."

"It's still my house, and I can bake in it if I want."

# Hello, Stinking Creek Road

★　★　★

Two weeks later, the movers arrived: three white-trash brothers from the Allied Van Lines of Tennessee, who resided in Pigeon Forge and looked like they could be related to Cynthia Elspecker. Their names were Wayne, Billy, and H. T. Shannon, and Wayne Shannon was the screw-off. They were the slowest movers in creation, according to Mama, which was fine by me. Every day when I returned home from school, I could hear H. T. yelling, "WAAAAAYNE. Where are you? Git hup here, boy. . . ." Wayne was usually off throwing the football with Joe-Sam and Leo in the front yard, even though there was at least a foot of snow in it.

"Little lady, it's our job to move ya," H. T. grinned, smoothing his hair back whenever I blocked the path to my room.

"I don't care. Keep out."

Mama took them aside, asking them to please pack up Peaches and the boys first, which eventually left my room as the only one untouched by rebel paws. When Daddy flew back to town to help on the last day, he cornered me, whispering, "Hell, Liz, those poor bastards are only trying to do their goddamn job, so by God, you let 'em."

I didn't care what their job was, I just wanted them to get the hell out of my house. I ignored Wayne, who was always getting in my face, trying to be Mr. Southern Hospitality. On one of his long lunch breaks, he hooted, "Y'all's family is gonna like hit in Knoxville. Why, hit's just as pretty as it can be."

"I don't really care, Wayne."

"Why, hit's real close to Pigeon Forge and Sevierville. Now you know who's from Sevierville, don't you? Why, Dolly Parton herself."

"So?"

He wouldn't stop. "And it's near Gatlinburg too, which is right in the heart of the Smokies. You know, Pigeon Forge has got some big old water slides, and Gatlinburg's also got the best mountain water taffy you ever tasted."

"So?"

"Shoot, they got this big old machine that yanks and twists the stuff into what looks like pink or green ropes."

"Who gives a damn?"

"Shitfire, I do. See, the ropes go into another itty-bitty part of the machine that spits it right back out into perfect little pieces of wrapped taffy. Say, you think your daddy might could get us Game Cock tickets on the fifty-yard line for the Tennessee games? Game Cocks are hot! I'm telling ya!"

"You can have mine, I won't be needing them." I turned up the radio to escape the persistent twang.

"I sure do appreciate that. I surely do. I'm gonna be calling ya now," Wayne yelled after me. I didn't answer.

The day Wayne and his brothers departed with all our stuff, my "big sister" Meghan picked me up to take me out to Red Lobster for a good-bye dinner. Afterward, she announced we had to stop by her house, and when I followed her inside, all my St. Joan friends jumped out, screaming, "Surprise!!!" I swooned, hazy with love. They gave me friendship plaques, pillows, and sonnets, along with James Taylor, Beach Boys, and Karen Carpenter records. Another one of my closest friends, Bess Ryan, even wrote a poem that began

> We sure will miss you, "Grits,"
> And that is not no lie.
> Cause all your friends around you
> Just hate to say good-bye.

They had anointed me Grits as soon as they learned of my move south. I loved her for writing that poem, which went on for pages. I also got a wooden plaque:

> Friendship

> There's a wonderful gift that gold cannot buy
> A blessing that's rare and true

# Hello, Stinking Creek Road

*And that's the gift of a wonderful friend*
*Like the friend I have in you.*

Anne gave me Kahlil Gibran's book *The Prophet,* highlighting the special chapter about "Friendship." Then later, Meghan pulled me aside, whispering, "Hey, Liz, I gotta date tonight. With a guy who's not a complete loser? So, I'd hang around the party, but I don't get dates often enough to turn them down . . . not even for yoonz."

I understood, but it meant that I had to say good-bye to her first, which made me feel like my heart was being laminated. The party lasted for hours, but since it wasn't a sleepover, Bess Ryan's big sister gave me a ride home. As we stood in the icy cul-de-sac of Brookseed, hugging good-bye, it started snowing. I kept praying they would offer me a home to live in for the next three years while I finished high school, but no offer was forthcoming, and I was too afraid to ask.

"I don't know who I'm supposed to be in Knoxville. Any ideas?"

"Why not be yourself? That's who I like," Bess smiled.

"I'll think about it. Will you write?"

"Sure, if you send me some grits."

When they drove away, I noticed Beryl Merzlak's grandmother's head peeking at me from her doorway. I blew her a kiss as I walked to my front door. I let myself inside the house, which was cold, empty, and lonesome. Bear Bryant was the only soul home to greet me. It didn't look like our house anymore with all the furniture gone and everybody else asleep across the street at our neighbor's house.

I unwrapped all my friendship plaques, posters, cards, books, records, and poems, reading each one aloud to him. I rolled out my sleeping bag on the shag carpeting, placing everything around it so I could sleep in the middle of my love shrine. I felt like Aunt Betty as I remembered something in the far corner cupboard of the kitchen, a leftover bottle of sloe gin the movers had missed. As I unscrewed the top, I thought of my aunt, who was said to have been permanently placed with the nuns of Saint Bridget. She never wrote except at Christmas, when we received crocheted pot-holders or doilies. I decided to become the old Aunt Betty by taking a few swigs of the gin. The stuff tasted terrible, but I drank what I could, trying to understand if this was what it felt like to be my aunt. Grief. Solitude. Gin. As Bear Bryant sniffed my friendship plaques, the room began to spin, and I stepped out into the crunchy snow on the back deck to fling the bottle over the gully. I heard it crash on an abandoned tractor below, smashing to slivers. I jammed breath mints into my mouth before I fell on my sleeping bag. Bear Bryant lay down, too, groaning. I sang him Peaches's favorite song, "You Are My Sunshine."

We both passed out, but sometime in the middle of the night, Daddy loomed over me, whispering, "Jesus H. Christ, you're gonna freeze your ass off in here. The heat's been turned off. Come on over to Bob's where it's warm, honey."

"This is still my house for one more night, Coach," I slurred.

"Have you been drinking?"

"Drinking. Ha. Are you kidding? I don't believe in it. I play field hockey. St. Joan hockey players don't drink."

He eyed me closely, but I burrowed farther down in my sleeping bag.

"You sure you don't want to come over to Bob's where it's warm? Last chance."

"Coach Donegal, I don't know if you can understand this, but this happens to be my very last night in this house, and I'm not going to waste it sleeping at Bob's."

"I'll come get you in the morning when it's time to go."

I woke with a pounding headache, feeling as if my brains were all hammers and Jell-O, but Mama appeared by my pallet with a steaming mug of tea, looking concerned. "Did you sleep well on this hard floor?" she began.

"Okay." I reached for the tea. "Look at my presents." I tried to speak, but a wave of nausea hit me. I fought it back as I gulped the scalding tea.

"They're nice, honey, but let's pack them in some newspaper, so they don't get broken on the trip. Are you feeling okay? You look awful."

Daddy bellowed from outside, "Hey, hey, folks . . . Let's get our ass on the road."

I combed through my home one more time, upstairs, downstairs, trying to memorize it. I scoured my teeth, splashed cold water on my face, scrubbing it with soap, patting it dry with paper towels, trying to sense if I was dead or alive.

"I'm sorry, Pittsburgh. Forgive me for being so weak. I couldn't stop it. I tried." As I stepped outside, I sniffed around for the familiar smells of steel mills, the aroma of the bread factories. They were still there; proof that I was alive. I listened for the woodpeckers tapping away in the gully. As I crept into the car, Joe-Sam's, Leo's, and Peaches's eyes were wide.

"Now listen here, folks, listen here," Daddy railed with only a true coach's enthusiasm. "Knoxville's a helluva town. I'll even check into the field hockey scene for you, Aunt Gertrude. I'm sure the university has a team even if the high school doesn't. And we've got a nice new house to move into . . . and by God, we all better get ourselves some tangerine clothes. Everything in Tennessee is tangerine."

"Tangerine?" sighed Mama. "That's worse than purple."

"Let's be positive, Sally." Daddy gunned the car out of the cul-de-sac, honking to all the Brookseeders. When I looked back, Bob was standing in his yard, waving good-bye forlornly. Bear Bryant chose that moment to smear up my new friendship pillow with his goddamn mucky paws. Mama screamed at him before I could throw him off, but it was too late. The damage was done.

"It's ruined," I shrieked at Bear Bryant. "You're dead." He panted in my face, thumping his tail.

"Liz, we'll get it cleaned. . . ." Mama tried to scrub the pillow with Handi Wipes. "For God's sakes, we'll get the friendship pillow professionally cleaned."

"You say that, but we won't." A knife of sorrow plunged in and out of my breast.

"Geez," sighed Leo, reading the sports. "Aren't you used to moving by now?"

"Shut the fuck up." I dug my nails into his thigh. He flew out of the seat, whacking his head on the roof of the car.

"No fair using girl claws."

Daddy squealed on the breaks at the entrance of Brookseed. "Get out, Liz. Get out of the car. Now!"

I pushed open the car door. We stood face-to-face in the snow, squared off, my tears freezing to streamlets of ice.

"How long is this insurrection going to go on?" he reproached me.

"What?"

"You know the hell what. Piss-poor attitude. You're not the only one who had to say good-bye, goddammit."

The nausea hit me again, stronger. "Coach Donegal?" I whispered.

"No more bullshit. You can leave it right here and now."

I turned away to vomit at the sign of our plan, WELCOME TO BROOK-SEED. HOME OF THE BABBLING BROOK.

"Feel better?" he asked when I was through.

I didn't answer.

"Good, now get your ass in the car. Remember, when I say, 'Jump,' you don't ask, 'Why?' You ask, 'How high?' "

"Yes, sir," I said, staggering through the snow. "But by the way, Coach. This is my last move. I swear to God you will not make me do this again. I'll kill myself first."


Somewhere in Kentucky, Daddy pulled into a truck stop, a cacophony of crashing dishes, fluorescent lights, and hot food. Mama ordered coffee for her and Daddy, and for the first time in my life, I ordered some too. The waitress poured the scalding black liquid into thick mugs, and I cradled the warmth in my hands. It was steaming and pungent, making my red eyes water, but suddenly things seemed more in focus, my head awake and alert.

A waitress drawled, "Howdy, y'all. For veggies, we got corn, okra, and sprouts."

"What are sprouts?" asked Joe-Sam.

"Why, son, you know . . . them little itty bitty cabbages. Sprouts."

"They'll have hamburgers and chocolate milk shakes," Daddy sighed, picking up the sports section of the Kentucky paper. When the milk shakes arrived, Peaches picked hers up, announcing, "Cheers, everybody. Cheers."

I groaned at her grotesque good humor.

"What?" she said. "Don't you like milk shakes now either, Liz?"

"Peaches, just lay off," I warned, reaching for Mama's bottle of aspirin.

"You lay off. Why can't everybody just be happy?"

Leo asked, "Can me and Joe-Sam have some quarters to play Pac-Man?"


One of the first signs we saw past the Tennessee state line advertised the next exit: STINKING CREEK ROAD. Daddy nearly drove off the freeway with excitement, "Hey, hey . . . Welcome to Tennessee, folks. Home of the Tennessee Fighting Game Cocks. Home of the most men who volunteered for the—"

"You already told us about a hundred times, Daddy," Peaches reminded him.

"Now remember, y'all"—Mama sat up—"don't be talking about how wonderful Pittsburgh is to your new friends in Knoxville. Nobody down here gives a rip or—"

"Cares," I finished her thought. "They'll just say, 'Why doncha go back where you came from then?' So everybody, just remember, your new life begins now. Your previous one doesn't exist."

"I didn't say that, Liz. You can talk about your memories at home, just not—"

Joe-Sam interrupted, "Yeah, just shut up, Liz, wouldja? Daddy, can we go to see the stadium when we get there?"

"Is that all you can ever think about—stadiums?" I asked.

"Dad, can we?" he said, ignoring me.

"You bet your ass, son. First thing. As a matter of fact, you can see the stadium from the hotel where we'll be staying, that is, until Wayne and the boys get our furniture to town. It's a real pretty motel called the Game Cock Inn."

I didn't reply to his edict, nor did I cry or protest or laugh. I left my tears in Pittsburgh, so I could face Knoxville, Tennessee, with cold fury roiling through my veins.

# TENNESSEE CATHOLIC
*"The Stunt System"*

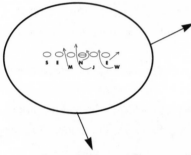

**A stunt is the predetermined movement on the snap of the ball
by one or more DEFENSIVE LINEMEN and/or LINEBACKERS, designated by
call,
e.g.: *MAD DOG/WILL FIRE***

First day in Knoxville, winter, 1977: I meandered along the Game Cock campus strip, stumbling upon places like Old College Inn, the Torch, the Last Lap, and a doughnut dive called Krispy Kreme, next to Pick & Grin, a guitar shop that ran a commercial of a barefoot hillbilly, yodeling in a hick voice:

*"Pick and Grin, Pick and Grin,
Choose your teacher, and then begin."*

Joe-Sam and Leo sang it constantly, strumming their "air ukuleles" to the point where I couldn't shake the tune out of my head.

The next morning in Knoxville, Daddy and the boys hit the Bubble, a canvas superstructure filled with air, containing weights, tackling dummies, and other football facilities, while Mama dragged me and Peaches to Cas Walker's to go grocery shopping, since the Game Cock Inn had a little refrigerator for storing stuff. In the parking lot of Cas Walker's, a bluegrass band performed on a flatbed truck, whinnying, "When I use my Bible for a road map to Jesus, my vision is forever clear . . ." One of the good old boys winked at Mama as we went inside.

"We're not made of money," Mama informed us, as we combed the aisles. She loaded the cart with items like Martha White grits, Cas Walker frozen pizza (four for a dollar), Cas Walker white bread (five loaves for a dollar), Big Rebel Yowl peanut butter, and dog food. The girl at the checkout was named Tammy-Jean, and when she gave us the receipt, she grinned through serrated teeth, "Have a good'n."

While we were unloading the groceries back at the hotel, Mary Martha swung by in her tangerine sweatsuit to welcome us to town.

"How was the trip down, y'all?" she asked.

"Let's just say we made it," Mama replied, stuffing groceries onto the shelves.

"Sally, don't tell me y'all shopped up at the Cas Walker's?" Mary Martha asked incredulously, implying she knew the etiquette ropes of Knoxville, being one of the former Game Cock homecoming queens of Tennessee.

"It was Cas something or other, I think."

"Honey, you need to be shopping up at the Winn-Dixie or the White Stores. Everyone knows Mr. Cas Walker is a racist. Why, he used to have a commercial of two little colored boys eating hunks of watermelon, yelling, 'Yum. Yum.' "

"Is that a fact, Mary Martha?" Mama sounded tired.

"Shoot, you're going to get used to everything. Now, how about we head up to Gay Street to see the sights? They've got some wonderful shops up there. Y'all want to come? We can go look at the stadium after. Seats ninety-six thousand fans."

"I'm positive that I don't want to go shopping on Gay Street now," I declared. "I want to write in privacy."

"Okay, but I just can't bear to imagine how you're describing your poor parents these days in that little diary." Mama shook her head.

"Journal," I hissed.

"Whatever," she laughed. "Lord, I can't do or say anything right these days."

"Aw now," Mary Martha gurgled. "Liz is too full of sugar to be hateful."

I winked at Mary Martha. Of course, I was too full of sugar to be hateful or cruel. No way would I call my parents "low-down fuckers" for dragging me south.

I flopped on the bed, watching them leave. Click. Gone. Good. I drop-kicked my journal against the wall, snapping on the television. I didn't feel like writing about misery at the moment. I was living it. On TV, the Pick & Grin commercial was just ending, followed by one about a Tennessee candy bar called a Goo-Goo Cluster, with a quartet of men singing in harmony, "Go get a Goo-Goo. They're goooood."

I stared through the venetian blinds at the rain-slicked streets. Across the road was a Baptist church with a sign that said, UP, UP, UP WITH JESUS. The pastor's name was Reverend Eddie Scruggs, officiating on Sundays at 9:00 A.M. Down the street was a tiny Church of Christ with a sign that read, FAMILIES SHOULD PRODUCE GOOD FRUIT, NOT NUTS. That pastor's name was Reverend Buck with services at 8:00, 10:00, and 12:00, plus a Sunday revival meeting.

A hunch of desperation licked my soul as I felt trapped in the land of Goo-Goos, Pick & Grin, and Bible road map folks. I turned off the TV, grabbing my new journal. I'd always written to myself in the past, but I needed to do something different. I needed answers, and I needed them fast. Who was the one person who would understand? I thought for a while before it hit me: Peter, of course, who, even though we seldom saw each other, always understood, or at least tried to. So scratching my Game Cock pen across the clean white page of my new journal, I began to compose my words to my uncle. I would fill the journal with letters to him about a place called Knoxville and who I was now. Then, when it was done, I would send it to him for some speedy replies and remedies for my out-of-control life of dictators and football.

*Dearest Peter,*

*You know I haven't seen you since Papa Sweetheart died. At least a year. How are you? I guess you heard we moved again. You know, Peter, I never asked you why you cried when I was sewing up the baby rabbit (it lived by the way) and I'm also wondering if you still miss your father like you did. It's hard to ask these things face-to-face, which is why I hide behind the pen and paper, but the questions are just as real, and I feel closer than ever to you. Why is it that you're so different from all the other men and boys I've known in my life?*

*I know that you're living an exciting life at Notre Dame, having art exhibits of your brilliant photography and paintings, but I miss you. In fact, I sort of hate you for living your own life so completely or at least having the freedom to do so. I surely hope to have a taste of it someday. Freedom. I'm at the mercy of coaches who blow with the wind, as they try to figure out which team is the next winner. Do you know that Tennessee is the eighth state I've lived in? I feel like a freak, always on the outside looking in. I can't just turn off one state and pick up another. The life of a football family devours faces, friends, and state lines as quickly as it does football seasons. I try to reach into my soul to be brave and stoic. When I was a kid, I used to try to be like one of the saints. In eighth grade, the nuns used to show us slides of blissful religious orders to encourage us to consider having a vocation. They'd always play the "Theme from Mahogany," sexy Diana Ross asking us if we wanted to enter the church. "Do you know where you're going to?"*

*Now, I really don't know where I'm going to or even where I am. Tomorrow, I have to go to a new school and be the new girl all over again. Everyone always stares, and they're impressed for about an hour that Daddy's a coach. Then it's just me, and so they quit being impressed, because I'm nothing, just the new tall girl. I want a dee-vorce from football. What's the country song? D-I-V-O-R-C-E. That's me and football, honey. I intend to be in control of my destiny, Peter, the way you're in control of yours. What do you do for fun up there? I hope to God it's more than football and that damn Touchdown Jesus they got painted. Knowing you, it surely is. I miss you so much. Your loving niece, Elizabeth Frances Donegal*

The next day, for the first time in our family's history, Daddy accompanied us to help with school registration. A miracle, and I suspected Mama had twisted his arm, but at least he agreed to be there in the flesh. I yanked on corduroys and a black sweater, shuddering at the memory of my last new school where I entered as Francie Nolan. Thank God those days were over, and I had a few more shreds of sense.

We first dropped off the kids at the only Catholic grade school in town, Holy Ghost on Northshore Drive near the state mental hospital, a facility encompassed by iron bars. On the way over, I pretended to be a concerned big sister by asking Peaches, "Are you scared, honey, to be going to a school near a mental institution?"

"What's a mental institution?" she asked, smoothing out her yellow dress.

"That's about enough of that crap." Daddy flipped on the all-sports station.

"I'm going to make lots of new friends, right, Mama?" Peaches predicted, popping her knuckles. She had become such a pro at knuckle-popping, snapping each joint in each finger, that Mama had nicknamed her the Castanet Kid for the rhythms she created.

"That's right, darling." Mama teased her hair in the mirror to make it poof.

Feeling particularly cruel, I whispered, "Do you know what crazy people's favorite color is?"

"Nope," she said, staring out the window as we sped past the mental home. "Yellow."

"It is not!" she screamed, covering her ears.

"I'm just repeating facts. No need to get all huffy, Mary Clancy," I said, using her real name to drive her nuts.

"Goddammit, Liz, this is bullshit. Yellow, my ass!" Daddy snarled, gunning it into the Holy Ghost parking lot, a few altar boys scampering out of his way.

"Hey, Mama, can I have my hair permed like Olivia Newton-John?" Peaches stuck her tongue out at me.

"We'll see, honey."

I turned to Leo and Joe-Sam. "Are you guys excited?"

"If they have football I will be, and if we can stop at Krispy Kreme on the way from school. They got the best glazed doughnuts," replied Leo.

"It's just another school," commented Joe-Sam. "Maybe they'll have some cute chicks."

After getting them plunked down in the correct grades, we drove along Magnolia Avenue, passing the Greyhound Bus Station, First Tennessee Bank, and the Little Debbie factory, zipping over to the one Catholic high school in all of East Tennessee—Tennessee Catholic.

"Now let's give the sumbitches a fighting chance," Daddy pep-talked.

"This place looks like a dump," I whispered, my heart sinking fast at the sight of the squatty brick structure with a glittering green Virgin Mary perched out front. I'd never seen a green Mary before. At her feet, the words FIGHTING IRISH were etched in stone. "Can't I please go to a public school for once?" I pleaded to Daddy.

"Hell, no," he answered. "You can't beat a parochial school education."

"Daddy? Why didn't you try to become the head coach after Coach Mac?"

"I did try, goddammit, but they didn't hire me."

"Oh," I replied, feeling a little sorry for him. I hadn't known he'd even tried.

"Assholes," Daddy muttered. "Limp dicks."

"Jack. Shhh," Mama hissed as we emerged from the car. A drunk with buzzy red eyes was sucking on a bottle of cherry vodka, loping near the green Virgin Mary.

"First day a school?" he snuffled as we trooped past him.

"How's it going, partner?" Daddy ducked his head in pity.

"Name's Harley," he croaked, collapsing in gasping sobs.

"Class of '60," Daddy quietly joked to Mama. "Poor bastard."

"Good luck to you, Harley," Mama called, prodding me into the school.

The bell rang shrilly, and students flocked everywhere. Perfect timing. We had to walk through the Smokers' Pit, plus the lockers of the seniors, juniors, and sophomores. I ignored the stares as I slogged after my parents down the corridor.

We found the principal's office with a poster of a smiling Jesus on the door, hanging below the Pope. "Y'all come right on in," chortled Miss Kitty, a tanned secretary who greeted us at the door. "This is so exciting to have a coach's daughter coming to our little old school. Father Haggerty will be with y'all in two shakes." She never stopped talking or smiling, her fingers twirling through the air. They were covered in rings with white stones, which I later learned were Tennessee pearls.

As Father Haggerty lumbered out of his office in black vestments, Daddy extended a handshake. "How do you do, Father Haggerty? I'm Jack Donegal, and my wife, Sally, and my daughter Liz: The Reluctant Freshman."

Father Haggerty pumped Daddy's hand. His face was a flabby, sunless alabaster, his eyes the color of peeled green grapes, matching the green Virgin Mary out front. I shuddered.

"Welcome. Sit down," he ordered. Looking over at me, he chortled, "Well, may I say that you certainly look happy to be here?"

Mama and Daddy laughed gratefully, but I snubbed the priest's attempt at levity by checking my watch. Only 10:15. Rats.

"Now, Father," Daddy began, "Liz wasn't real happy about leaving Pittsburgh."

"Is that a fact?" Father Haggerty glanced through some papers on his desk.

"You talk about a serious case of red ass," Daddy barked.

Mama was mortified, but Father Haggerty didn't even blanch.

"Jack, please." she choked. "Father Haggerty, I do apologize."

"That's all right. Well, Elizabeth, you'll have to be our southern transplant."

I didn't answer, for I was silently reading the names of the graduating class of 1927 from a plaque: "Frida Clancy. Xavier Bettlefinger. Aurelia DeWine."

"But I told her we'd get settled, and she'd make friends in no time," Daddy was saying. "This kid has more friends in more states."

"It's true, Father Haggerty," Mama echoed. "She's such a letter writer and insists on keeping in touch with more people. And she loves to read."

"Good for her." His voice was flat.

I began studying the names of the class of 1928. "Dorothy Stooksbury. Ruth Cox. Edna Valentine."

"Father Haggerty," Daddy plunged on, "right now we're staying at the Game Cock Inn until our furniture arrives. We'll be in a brand-new subdivision in West Knoxville. The moving boys are just a little slow."

"Excuse me. Do you have a field hockey team?" I interrupted.

"Field hockey? No, ma'am, we do not. But the girls do play half-court basketball." Father Haggerty tipped back in his chair, which was squeaking ominously.

"Half-court *what*?"

"The boys play full-court, the girls play half-court." Father Haggerty leaned forward, his chin resting on his palms.

"Why?"

"Half-court is not as strenuous as full-court."

"That's sexist. You must be the only state in the entire nation with that rule."

Father Haggerty coughed, Daddy expelled a "He, he, he," while Mama shot out, "Liz!" gripping my arm. I shook her off.

"In Pittsburgh, the girls play full-court basketball just fine and field hockey too, and we run ten minutes twice a day without blinking an eye," I informed him.

"That's quite remarkable, but you're in the south now, young lady." Father Haggerty's eyes gleamed, unimpressed, before turning back to Daddy to inquire, "Now are y'all having any trouble getting information about things here in Knoxville?"

"Not at all," Daddy replied. "We've got a woman calling us to give us all kinds of advice about the bus, uniforms, tuition, Girl Scouts, and even a music job for Sally."

"I'm actually thinking of going back to work after fifteen years of raising children," Mama admitted proudly.

"Good for you, Mrs. Donegal," smiled Father Haggerty. "Now that woman calling you . . . I believe that would be Mrs. Mally?"

"That's right, Father."

"Let me assure you good folks," Father Haggerty warned, "if Mrs. Mally had been the Pope in the fifteenth century, Martin Luther and his sorry Protestant Reformation wouldn't have stood a chance."

Well, that absolutely cracked up Jack and Sally Donegal. Haw. Haw. Haw. They were ready to bust a gut, but I didn't even smile. I waited for them to calm down, drumming my fingers on the arms of the chair. Then Father Haggerty had to leave for a minute to go deal with a student. The second he left, Daddy whipped around, sniping, "Aunt Gertrude, give the guy a break. The poor bastard's told every joke he knows."

"I can't stay here, Daddy. I can't breathe. Don't leave me here."

Before Daddy could utter a reply, Father Haggerty brought a girl into the office. She had bright red hair, the color of rich tomato soup.

"Miss O'Donnell will show you the routine, Elizabeth. She's fairly new, too, a freshman. An Irish redhead from Fort Lauderdale."

"Strawberry blonde," the girl corrected Father Haggerty. "Geez, Father, I know it's flaming, but I prefer to be known as a strawberry blonde."

"Kathleen here is studying to be a eucharistic minister, and she volunteers in the home for abused children."

*Great, a do-gooder was going to show me the ropes.* Mama and Daddy were already standing up, getting ready to depart.

"Hey. How are you?" The girl took my hand.

"Fine," I mumbled, pulling it away to put in my pocket.

"Well, it's very good to meet you, Kathleen." Mama was all gracious. "You have lovely hair. With that color, you look more like Jack's daughter than Liz does."

"Red on the Head," Daddy laughed.

"You'll have to come over to our house sometime. I'd love to hear about your work with the unfortunate children of Knoxville," Mama added.

*It was Beryl Merzlak all over again. No, thank you, Mother.*

"I'd love to." Kathleen was all smiles.

"You girls have a good day, okay?" Mama sang.

"Knock 'em dead, Gert." Daddy winked.

"Wait!" I called, hoping for a last-minute reprieve, but they were gone, so I had no choice but to follow Kathleen. My Earth shoes squeaked as we walked down the corridor. I asked her, "How come the girls play half-court basketball here?"

"Beats me. I think full-court is supposedly too tiring for our ovaries," she explained with a shrug. "You know? For all the babies we're going to have down the road. No doubt, some dumb fat-ass male came up with that commandment."

It was the first sensible, and funny, thing I'd heard all day, but I didn't laugh. I didn't want to her to get any ideas that we were going to be great friends or anything.

"Do you play basketball?" I asked her.

"No way. Do you?"

"No, not really. Field hockey's my sport. But where I'm from, St. Joan's in Pittsburgh, the girls would laugh if somebody tried to force them to play prissy half-court in order to preserve their organs."

"So your dad's a football coach? Are any of his football players hot?"

"I haven't met any Tennessee ones yet. I don't really care."

"How were his other players hung?" she giggled.

"Hung?"

"Yeah, you know, *hung*?" She waved her hand across her crotch and winked.

I swallowed, understanding but completely shocked. I'd never even thought about it, and suddenly I was being queried by a eucharistic minister who devoted her spare time to abused kids?

"I . . . I . . . I don't know that," I stammered, chewing my nails for the first time.

"Too bad. You should try to find out sometime."

197

I offered back a flimsy grin, praying to get to French class before she could ask me any more embarrassing questions.

Instead of conducting French class that day, the teacher, Sister Mary Josefat, had decided to give an impromptu lesson on Health and Human Sexuality. She was already in the middle of it when Kathleen pulled me through the door, introduced me to the class, and plopped me into the desk next to hers. I looked up at Sister Mary Josefat, who craned backward on her heels, arching her neck, spiraling on her toes to emphasize her many points.

"All right. Take dating. Question Number One. Who knows why they should carry a geometry book with them at all times on dates?"

I stared at my desk, having no clue. Apparently, no one else did either. Sister Mary Josefat was not to be thwarted. In fact, she seemed pleased by our reticence.

"Think about it. Suppose you have to sit on a boy's lap in a crowded car? What do you need between you and him? A geometry book. It's thick, and it works."

Nobody said a word. I wondered if we were going to have French class anytime soon.

"And what about when it's just the two of you in a car? A boy and a girl," she continued. "First the hand-holding, then the kissing, then the petting, then the buttons, buckles, zippers, and BANG."

I jumped. Trying to stop a terrible urge to laugh, I pinched the skin on my knuckles, digging my fingernails into my flesh.

"Before you know it," she thundered. "You have smacked head-on into the point-of-no-return. Then what are you going to do? Because, by then, it's too late."

A few students shuffled in their seats. The boys in the class were dead silent. Sister Mary Josefat clapped her hands, giving a few more jittery bounces. "Beware," she cried, "the point-of-no-return. You should never do anything on a date that you wouldn't do with your own brother."

There were a few gasps of disgust, mingling with disbelief. Kathleen leaned over, breathing in my ear. "Incest is best."

That did it. I coughed, then snorted into gales of giggles. After all my tears of good-byes to Pittsburgh, I roared with sidesplitting glee. I felt giddy, giggly, loose.

"What strikes you as so remarkably funny, Miss Donegal?"

"Nothing is funny; it's all very very very serious." I punched my thighs hard under my desk, trying to sober up. My face felt skinned.

"What did Kathleen O'Donnell say to you?"

"Nothing," I squeaked out, but then a baby snatch of cackles escaped. I was horrified. I'd never lost control like this. The eyes of the class were affixed on me.

"Maybe you would find it even more amusing to return to Father Haggerty's?"

"No, Sister, I'm heartily sorry for having—" I began whispering the Act of Contrition, replacing God with Sister Mary Josefat.

"Get quiet this instant."

"Yes, Sister. I am so so so sorry," I whispered, toiling to think of awful things: Moving all the time. Being born ugly. I breathed deeply, feeling sanity return.

Sister Mary Josefat kept one gray eye leveled at me through her rimless spectacles. In a monotone, she warned, "Girls of this class . . . On your wedding day, do you want all the men in the church to snicker at you up on the altar, the beautiful virgin bride, and whisper, 'I've had her,' 'I've had her too?' Is that what you want?"

A chorus of "No, Sister" wrangled the atmosphere.

"Remember, you were made in the image and likeness of the Virgin Mary. Remember your geometry books. And most of all, remember the point-of-no-return."

"Sister," asked Kathleen, raising her hand.

"Yes? What is it?"

"Is it equally important for a man to be a virgin as it is for a woman?" Kathleen posed her question with way more audacity than I had.

"Yes, it is, but it's up to the girls to decide how far things go."

"Why?"

"Because men simply cannot control themselves the way women can," Sister wheezed, sensing the sticky direction the questions were taking. "Now enough of this. We must have French class,"

I ingested a deep breath; memories of Bourbon Street in New Orleans flickered in my brain, the sex dancers bopping around on stage in seedy bars. Could that be what she meant? The darkness? The glitter, tassels, and spangles of illicit sex. The point-of-no-return? And what about the boys? Why were girls picked out to shoulder the guilt and weight of sex? Would no one whisper about them on the altar if they whored around prior to marriage? Could men whore around? We never discussed stuff like this in Pittsburgh. I felt drained. I looked at my watch. 11:15.

"Class," Sister Mary Josefat ordered, "please consider what we've discussed at home tonight with your parents. Now we're going to study the future tense of irregular French verbs. Kathleen O'Donnell? You share with Miss Donegal, Class Comedian."

I was relieved to focus on something as mindless as French verbs, while Kathleen scooted closer with her book. She smiled at me, I smiled back. She leaned into me and whispered, "Slut."

"Tramp," I scrawled back in her French book, as we managed to suppress our laughter, gazing at the verbs. She was both witty and intriguing. She had everyone fooled with her Samaritan act. I'd never had a fun friend before. I'd had serious ones, passionate ones, competitive ones, uptight ones, and athletic ones, but this girl seemed like pure fun. Buoyant sunshine. She'd made me laugh. I didn't know I had any laughter left in me. Sulky old Aunt Gertrude. What a concept. I also suspected I could get into a lot of trouble hanging around her. An even more exhilarating notion.

# 21

## IF YOU WANT TO BE A CHRISTIAN—YOU CAN! (AND THE FOLKS ARE FRIENDLY!)

*"The Audible"*

**We want to use a simple, yet competent audible system to check out of the BAD PLAY versus some of the different defensive looks we will see. Whenever a LIVE AUDIBLE changes the original play, our starting count will remain the same as called in the huddle—which is also being repeated on the line of scrimmage. Example: If Red is called in huddle, Red will be repeated on the LOS.**

"We got rats!" Mama screamed over the phone to Daddy, who was at the football office. "What do you mean, what am I going to do about it?" She slammed down the phone in a rage, shivering. "I can hear 'em squealing in the trash can, can't y'all?"

Peaches climbed up onto the counter, hugging her knees, horrified. I stared out the window at the trash can, which seemed to be vibrating with dancing rats. *Rats. How disgusting. Pittsburgh didn't have rats. The new house smelled of wood and paneling, like all our other houses. Yet what kind of place were we in?*

"I could beat 'em to death with my baseball bat," Leo offered.

"I could drop my weights on them," Joe-Sam added.

"Oh, for the love of God, would y'all get quiet so I can think?" Mama stepped out on the back porch where our neighbor, Owen Goodnight, was working on his Chevy.

"Yoo-hoo!" Mama called out. "Hello, Mr. Goodnight? Sorry to bother you, but I was just wondering if y'all had rats and what you do about it? I'm about to lose my mind."

Mr. Goodnight climbed out from under his car and strolled over, straightening his baseball cap, spitting out tobacco into a jagged Coke can. "Where are they, lady?"

"There." Mama pointed at the trashcan.

Mr. Goodnight leaned over to peek inside, cocking an ear. His pants swung across his bottom like a grin. "Yep, them's are rats," he nodded, straightening up.

"What should I do?" Mama looked ready to cry.

"Tell you what, lady"—he looped his thumbs in his belt—"git yourself a cat . . . feed 'em gunpowder . . . makes 'em mean." His eyebrows touched his hairline.

Mama had no reply as we all watched him mop his brow with a grease rag and head back to work on his Chevy.

"Hey! Mr. Goodnight?" yelled Joe-Sam after him. "How old were you when you first started chewing tobacco?"

"Old enough to know not to ask permission from nobody." Mr. Goodnight spat.

Mama laughed like it was a joke, before shoving Joe-Sam back inside. "Don't get any ideas, boy. That stuff rots your gums and teeth. I won't have it in my house."

"Are we getting a cat?" I asked.

"I'll name it Snowflake if we get one," sighed Peaches.

"I don't have time to fool with some old cat." Mama rubbed her hands together. "I'm calling an exterminator this instant. Gunpowder! Good Lord!"

★　★　★

# If You Want to Be a Christian—You Can!

The days moved swiftly at Tennessee Catholic. With the help of Kathleen, I grew somewhat accustomed to the girls of the school, but as to the selection of male creatures, Sister Mary Josefat had no need to fear the point-of-no-return. I knew it wasn't because I was such a devout Christian, but rather because I thought too much of myself to be pawed at by some horny football player (who just got trounced by Wartburg), in the ratty parking lot of Tennessee Catholic, where Harley might slink up to the window, begging for a dime. I began viewing the issue like a sick multiple-choice test: Who was the worst choice to lose your virginity to in Knoxville?

a. Bret Lankowitz: greasy-haired class brain with huge flakes of dandruff rolling off his skull, who performed Nixon impersonations on the bus

b. Pete Shanner: the worst student in French class, who slumped in his seat, winking, "Weee. Weee. Vawla Mademoiselle Teeboat. Wooo. Wooo."

c. George Mellon: Mr. Key Club, Eucharistic Minister, Boy Scout, Boy Wonder, Altar Boy, who gave everyone weepy hugs during the kiss of peace at mass.

d. A redneck Game Cock fan with a beer belly and buzz cut ready to go at it after swigging down salty tequilas with lemons, biting the worm to impress you.


The lack of choices was sickeningly clear, but what amazed me most was that certain girls seemed happy to pick a parking lot to "do it" in. Every so often, usually on a Monday, rumors would begin to circulate about "who did it," "where," and "when." I didn't consider myself a great romantic, but I wanted the hymen-breaking ritual to be more than rutting around in the backseat of a Mustang with beer bottles on the floor.


*Dear Peter,*

*Now I'm going to talk to you about sex. What is the big deal? Some girls in my class are desperate for guys, but the guys they settle for are reedish creeps with fuzz on their chins, who drive souped-up cars, and use double-negatives. Ug. Since you and I kissed under the Christmas tree all those light-years ago, I feel I can be honest with you by telling you that I am sure of only one thing: I have no intention of losing my virginity in Knoxville. If I am going to lose it anywhere, then Europe seems like the most appropriate place on earth. But then I can't imagine letting anyone see me naked. I don't have the greatest body on earth. Men don't exactly turn in the streets when I pass, plus I have hairy knuckles that I've been shaving. Isn't that sick?*

*If I ever do decide to sleep with someone, how should I go about it? Maybe on the moors of Ireland? Have you lost your virginity, Peter? Of course you have, probably years ago. Was it magical? Did it transport you to new lands and infinite horizons? I'm very curious. I envision steamers and Europe and bells and sirens and those gargantuan pillows from Dr. Seuss books. Mama talked about sex once when I was ten, and the subject hasn't been brought up again. She just says to watch out for "cheap" girls, and no matter what, "Never call a guy. Wait for him to call you."*

*When I get married, I hope my husband wants to stay in bed for days. I don't want to rush, but I would like some practical advice. I'll be sixteen soon. I guess that until I travel to Europe by steamer to find both great love and sex, my virginity is safe, not so much by good Catholic virtue, but by an absolute sense of superiority to the sea of males beneath me. Does that make me cheap or a snob or both?*

*Don't take this wrong, but I hope that cracker Cynthia Elspecker wasn't your first. You deserve better. Your Loving Niece, Elizabeth Frances Donegal*

I continued to persevere in trying to understand the rhythms and expectations of my new southern peer group in general, but I was slow. All the students had been together for so long, they weren't sure what to do with a new girl either. Even their parents and grandparents had graduated from Tennessee Catholic. All along the walls of the school were graduation pictures dating back to the 1920s, and students were always bragging, "There's my aunt. Class of '50," or "Here's my mom. Class of '55," or "There's my grandpa, Class of '20."

One thing the Tennessee students did was greet each other with "Hey" or "Howdy" every single morning in enthusiastic voices, as if they hadn't seen one another in five years. When I tried to repeat it back to be friendly, the actual word "Howdy" got stuck in the back of my throat.

Naturally, the rim of hope in all this adjustment was Kathleen, for we quickly evolved into best friends. I knew we had reached the status of "best friend" when I began hearing my name linked to another's.

The questions "Liz, where's Kathleen?," "Are you and Kathleen coming to the Y-Teen Rally?," and "Liz, can you and Kathleen buy extra M&M's?" were simple inquiries, resonating like Mozart to the ear. No longer was I just plain old ugly Liz, alone, adrift, or one in a pack of girls; for the first time, I had one special friend to stroll with to class, to be with after school, to chat with on the phone at night.

We ambled along Magnolia Avenue, arm and arm, catching up on our lifetimes apart from each other: *Her life-threatening car wreck on the way home from Brownies in the third grade, leaving her fragile pug nose without cartilage; my teeth getting knocked out; her collection of frogs: stuffed, posters, glass; my collection of books, lining my shelves; her desire to become a ballerina in New York City; mine to become a writer; her weird crush on a dancing priest with a mustache, who she thought was hot; my desire to be Annie Hall for a day so I could smoke cigarettes and walk the streets of New York in great clothes; our vision of being saints when we were kids.* She was also as determined to move back to Fort Lauderdale as I was to return to Pittsburgh, so we offered each other islands of understanding in our grief at losing friends. We also loved thinking up disgusting names to call each other, using this safe arena for testing our more carnal natures.

"Why did your dad want to leave Fort Lauderdale anyway, whore-bag?" I asked her one afternoon, the canopy of dogwoods and magnolia trees blustering above us in a bloom of southern spring. I loved the way she talked, her words dancing out of her mouth. I absorbed each of her looping syllables with adoration.

"Well, you sleazy harlot, he was sick of all the Cubans moving in. The Christian Knights have already awarded him Father of the Year."

"Wow. And he hates Cubans?"

"He claimed they were polluting Fort Lauderdale. He runs the Roy the Boy, Your Iron Works Biggest Joy Company out on Kingston Pike. Do you think your dad will coach here long?"

"As long as they win, and the head coach is happy."

"How come?"

"They kind of influence everything. All they think about is winning and becoming heroes with millions of bumper stickers that say WHEN DONNY COMES MARCHING HOME AGAIN, HURRAH."

"What boners," she giggled.

We walked along quietly without saying anything for a bit. That was the nice thing about us; we could have silences and never think a thing about it. I felt like I'd known her forever. I watched her as she traipsed down Magnolia Avenue, gathering trash like she was collecting rare flowers, pitching it all lightly into garbage cans. After she tossed a few smashed Coke cans and candy wrappers into a Dumpster, she turned to me, whispering, "I was adopted." She linked her little finger with mine.

"You were?" I trembled, cherishing such a secret being divulged to me.

"My parents adopted me when I was four months old from a Catholic home," she continued. "I never knew my real mother."

"Really? Do you wish you had?"

"Yes," she murmured after a minute. "But I would never tell that to my parents. It would hurt them too much. My mother says when they picked me out I was real scrawny in a yellow dress with carrot red hair. They were supposed to get a boy."

"Are you ever going to try to find your real mother?"

"When I'm eighteen—legal, you know—I might."

"Can I go with you? To help you in your search? Please, oh please?"

"All right. When we're eighteen, we'll go to Florida to take a look." She smiled at me. I couldn't help it, I hugged her quickly, proud that she'd told me something so profoundly captivating. What secret could I fire back? Nothing that gripping had ever happened to me. Well, there was Aunt Betty's electric-shock therapy, but . . . Then something occurred to me. Maybe Aunt Betty was actually Kathleen's mother. After all, they were both from Florida. How far was Tallahassee from Fort Lauderdale? I had no idea. My mind began racing. Were we cousins? Was it a miracle? Maybe we were blood kin, or maybe we'd been reincarnated together from another life, over and over, as best friends or sisters or mother and daughter. The possibilities were endless.

"No matter what," I told her, "I bet you were a love child."

"Oh, be quiet." She blushed, grinning. "By the way, have you ever been drunk?"

"Sort of . . . I think . . . I've definitely been hungover. I remember that better."

"I know where my big sister keeps her Miller Tall Boys, and my mother drinks peppermint schnapps. My dad doesn't drink at all, except for Baileys Irish Cream during the holidays when he gets drunk and sings 'Sunrise, Sunset.' He says that song doesn't belong strictly to the Jews."

"I loved Anne Frank when I was a kid. I still do."

"That diary book? I think I started to read it, but I quit. It was really depressing already knowing the ending."

*Quit? You quit reading, The Diary of Anne Frank? But I bit my tongue. Okay, so, she wasn't one hundred percent perfect. I could handle it. I could. I would teach her about Anne Frank, and then she'd get it.*

"I think I'd prefer my sister's Tall Boys," Kathleen continued. "What about you?"

"Definitely Tall Boys. You're so lucky to have a big sister. I always wanted one."

"Don't be so sure. You haven't met mine yet. She's a flaming bitch on wheels," Kathleen smiled. "But I love her."

I laughed, unable to imagine how Kathleen could have a sister like that when she herself was *almost* perfectly perfect. We heard the bell peal from far away, calling us back to class. Late again. She grabbed my hand as we began to streak down Magnolia Avenue, so Sister Mary Josefat wouldn't punish us with another detention. As we ran, racing over cracks in the sidewalk, the breezes spiraling through our baggy uniforms, I glanced over at her. Her strawberry blond hair blew off her elated face, and in her fine, tapered fingers, she swung keys, which had more key chains than keys. I wanted to freeze her into memory forever, just in case anything ever happened.

★　★　★

It didn't take long to discover a very important clique in our freshman class, made up of four girls: Ellie, Mary Jo, Samantha, and Patsy. Kathleen had pointed them out as four best friends, whose mothers had all been best friends too. I studied them with respect for having such generational friendship longevity.

Though the school uniforms of Tennessee Catholic were shapeless gray dresses that zipped up the front, the girls of the clique made them look almost chic. It was the exact opposite with the tough senior girls, who spent break time in the smoking pit, chalking numbers on the backs of their uniforms to indicate how akin they were to prisoners. The boys had to wear a tie, something I would have much preferred over wearing the ugly uniform.

The uniforms of Ellie, Mary Jo, Samantha, and Patsy were always cleaned and pressed. They got straight As, wore add-a-beads and crucifixes around their necks, and loved-loved-loved Knoxville, Jesus Christ, the Tennessee Game Cocks, and getting high on "Mary Jane." They didn't even seem like members of the same species as the field hockey girls of St. Joan's. They were also Y-Teens, a kind of all girls' version of Junior League with Christianity attached. Most every girl at Tennessee Catholic automatically became a Y-Teen, including me and Kathleen.

On our first Y-Teen outing, we wore old-fashioned nursing pinafores to honor Clara Barton, Florence Nightingale, and Saint Catherine of Genoa. A bus driver picked us up in the school parking lot early on a Saturday to drive us to the Cordial Relations Home of South Knoxville, where we sang, "Blowing in the Wind," "If I had a Hammer," and "Amazing Grace" to people who looked like stroke victims, but weren't. After we finished, we shared our brownies with the ones who could still chew. On the wall of the home, above a stained couch, was a handwritten poster that said, IF YOU WANT TO BE A CHRISTIAN—YOU CAN! AND THE FOLKS ARE FRIENDLY!

Mrs. Nolan, the Y-Teen leader and mother of Patsy, pulled me and Kathleen aside after the songs. "Kathleen, I hear you do sacred dancing?"

"I don't know, Mrs. Nolan. I'm not that good, really." Kathleen swallowed some watered-down lemonade, her eyes traveling over the stained wood paneling, rickety rockers, strips of plastic runners slung across the linoleum.

"Believe me, these poor souls wouldn't know the difference." Mrs. Nolan moved away to say the rosary with an old lady who was munching on M&Ms.

On that note, we fled outside, gulping the fresh air, overjoyed at being released from the mildewed caverns of Y-Teen Christianity. Kathleen looked up into the white sky and belted out, "Eat me raw, Mrs. Nolan!" We ran back on the bus laughing.

On the way home, as Kathleen fell asleep on my shoulder, I began to wonder why the boys weren't asked to go sing songs in these run-down places? I guessed they were all too busy with sports to give a crap about the needy of Knoxville. Like maintaining the boundaries of sex, it was also up to the girls to cover the bases of humanity. The boys who weren't jocks belonged to the Key Club, but they didn't have to dress up. They were supposed to prove citizenship by planting trees and painting houses. A handful of girls belonged to the Key Club, but only as "Lovely Keyettes."


The girls of the clique were quite inseparable, but once they invited me and Kathleen to go with them to see a movie called *Audrey Rose,* about a reincarnated girl who burned to death in her first life. During the previews, Samantha, a curly blonde with a sprinkling of freckles, leaned over to ask, "So do y'all like Knoxville now?"

"Nope," I answered honestly, but I wished I hadn't as soon as I saw Samantha's dour expression. She whispered something in Patsy's ear, and they snickered.

Kathleen slapped my leg, answering for both of us, "She didn't mean that."

"Here's popcorn, y'all," squealed Mary Jo, a girl with flushed cheeks who was always on the verge of laughter, squeezing across the row of seats.

"I got the Goo-Goo Clusters too," hissed Ellie, a girl with white blond hair, who passed each of us one like free throws from the basketball line.

As we sat in the darkness watching the movie, I pretended we were lifelong friends, and I followed their cues, ducking at the scary parts. After the movie, we went to Baskin-Robbins where I ordered a double scoop of pralines and cream in a cup. As everyone speculated about the spirit of poor Audrey Rose, I felt like they talked more to Kathleen than to me, but I figured it was just my own paranoid imagination. I studied the girls, allowing their sweet southern accents to fade away, thinking, *I could be sitting here with Sarah Camp and the Bangers or Jo or any of my field hockey friends.*

"Hello in there?" Mary Jo poked me after Kathleen got up to go call her mother.

"What?" I flinched. A car roared by, braying, "Cat Scratch Fever."

"Hey, Liz . . . Doo-do-doo-do-doo-do," Ellie laughed, humming the *Twilight Zone* theme, flicking a cherry at me, looking just like Lacy from track camp.

"I'm sorry, I was thinking of something else," I said, my pralines and cream sloshing around in my stomach.

"That Kathleen is so sweet," Patsy sighed, watching Kathleen doing arabesques while chatting on the pay phone.

"Can we ask you a question, Liz?" Mary Jo probed.

"Sure," I answered, my neck growing warm.

"Why are you always following us around at school?" Ellie wanted to know.

"Do I? I mean, no, I don't." I whacked my head against the wall, trying to stand.

"Y'all, don't be mean." Patsy rolled her eyes to show she was half on my side. She pulled me back down beside her. "You can't help it, right? You're new."

"I mean . . . it's okay if you want to be with us"—Ellie slurped on her strawberry malt—"but sometimes we need our privacy, even in school, you know?"

A train thundered through my ears as I tried to find words. "I'm sorry if it seems like I do that," I bumbled. *Fuckers, fuckers, fuckers.*

"Like Ellie said, it's no biggie, but—" Samantha wiped her cream mustache.

I interrupted, "I'm sort of legally blind, not Helen Keller blind, but I can't see where I'm going if I don't have my contacts in. . . ."

"That's really sad," clucked Patsy.

"We all have twenty-twenty vision," Samantha bragged.

"It's pretty important for basketball and cheerleading," Ellie informed me.

"Well, I can see fine when my contacts are in," I explained, not adding that my contact lenses were never out. Yes, I did eat lunch at their table, but Kathleen did too, but they were on to me.

Kathleen pirouetted back to the table on her toes. "My sister is coming in twenty minutes for us, Liz," she smiled.

"So, Kathleen, tell us when you started dancing. We hear you're great."

"No way," she protested. "But I started when I was three."

"That's amazing," they all chirped with wonder, wooing my best friend, who was immediately sucked in by their false charms.

"Not really, my mother . . ." and Kathleen started to explain the history of her ballet, diverting all the attention from me, but I was grateful to her. My skin felt scorched, desiccated, the lights of Baskin-Robbins psychedelic. *I tried to appear normal, no tears, no fucking tears. Never would I follow them around again. Ever.*

After they left, Kathleen gushed, "They were really nice, weren't they?"

"They hate me, Kathleen," I mouthed the words.

"I'm sure they didn't mean anything, Lizzie. You have to give people a chance is all." Before I could reply, Kathleen's big sister, Mandy, the Bitch on Wheels, peeled up to the curb outside, laying on the horn for us to hurry up. A boy behind the Baskin-Robbins counter shook his head and said, "Dang, she can sure drive fast for a girl."


After the *Audrey Rose* evening, I kept my distance from the clique, but then Kathleen persuaded me to attend my first Y-Teen Rally in the spring with her, though at the last moment she got sick, so I was stuck with the Y-Teens alone.

"All right, y'all are going to be bumblebees," Mrs. Nolan chirped.

"Put on these big black plastic Hefty garbage sacks first. Stuff yourselves good with newspaper."

"Then what?" shouted Mary Jo.

"Poke your arms through the Hefty sacks for armholes. Okay? Everybody understand? Help each other now. That's the Christian Catholic spirit now."

After we taped ourselves into our bumblebee bags with plenty of newspaper, we piled into a bunch of cars to go to an empty stadium in East Knoxville to compete with girls from the public schools in town. Our main cheer was:

*"We've got spirit. Yes, we do. We've got spirit. How about you?"*

We were judged on talent, costume, and cheering, but we didn't win jack.

At the end of our freshman year, Kathleen tried out for cheerleading and made captain. I auditioned for half-court basketball and got cut. A girl named Big Faith rammed into me during a lay-up shot, horning her elbow into my eyebrow with such force, I needed six stitches. The girls' coach drove me to the emergency room, since Mama and Daddy were out of town at a spring game. I was hoping she'd feel sorry for me and put me on the team for loss of blood. No such favors, but on the table while I was getting stitched up, she said I could run the clock or keep statistics.

Kathleen surprised everyone by giving up her position on the cheerleading squad so she could spend more time in dance class. I loved her for her choice even more. She was a true, gifted artist. I didn't feel like a true gifted anything, so I spent my days out on the track learning to run the 880. I attended Kathleen's recitals of *Giselle, Swan Lake,* and *The Nutcracker.* She went to my track meets when they didn't interfere with her work schedule. I remained wary of the clique, but Kathleen was so nice to everyone that they were forced to put up with me as much as I had to put up with them. I wasn't about to give up Kathleen just because she was adored by the masses. We were the best of friends. Nothing could ever change that, even if I didn't belong in Tennessee.

# GETTING INTO THE
# TENNESSEE SPIRIT
*"Split Jet"*

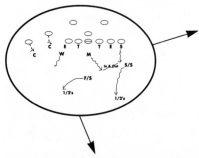

**A secondary coverage with the CORNER BACKS, employing man-to-man coverage techniques. The FREE SAFETY employs Zone Coverage in the Strong Side Half. This permits the CORNERS to be more aggressive in their coverage techniques with deep help from the FREE SAFETY.**

During the scorching summer between freshman and sophomore year, I found a yellowed clipping, dated 1960, at the bottom of an El Producto cigar box.

MISS SALLY THOMAS WED TO COACH JACK DONEGAL

*The bride wore a gown of chiffon velvet. The fitted bodice came to a soft point at the waist and also featured a scooped neckline and three quarter length sleeves. The skirt was softly shirred at the waist and cascaded into a full chapel sweep. The bride's fingertip veil of silk illusion fell from a pillbox hat made of*

*the same white chiffon velvet as the wedding dress. She carried a cascade bouquet*
*of white roses and holly.*

The box was filled with rolls of undeveloped Kodak film, dating from 1964 to 1975. The memories and proof of our family existence were sealed in tiny Instamatic caskets.

"Why didn't you get these developed?" I accused Mama, as she was hanging up her decoupaged posters of Big Eight teams. "This is our family history."

"For God's sakes, Liz, we've lived in eight states. I can't think of everything. What would I do with a bunch of photo albums anyway?"

"And look at the article about you as a bride."

"That clipping? It's as old as the hills. Keep it if you want. I don't need it."

"I will. Geez."

"Sweetheart, look, I'll take you to the Smoky Mountain Market to get those rolls of film developed and buy some photo albums if it means that much to you. Then you can put it all together. That'll be your little project for the rest of the summer."

"Can we do it today? I doubt any of the pictures will turn out, but we have to try."

"Let me finish hanging this stuff up. We want the rec room to look nice. Why don't you brush the dust off the pool table, clean the wet bar, and straighten up the pool sticks? Then we'll get the pictures developed. I promise."

I watched her drive a nail into the new paneling to hang up another decoupaged mascot. Pictures of players blanketed the walls. I yearned to see art hanging up instead: a van Gogh or Picasso or Frida Kahlo or Diego Rivera or, even better, Edward Hopper. Though I hadn't yet mailed Peter my journal, he had sent me a picture of himself in his college dorm room, the walls covered with art, his own plus all the others, which he explained in detail in his letter: murals, abstract, surreal, expressionist, impressionist. I didn't understand it all, but I wanted to know more.

"Can I visit Peter when he moves to New York after his graduation next year?"

"That would be nice," Mama replied, putting the wine bottles in the wine rack.

"Do you think we could buy some real art? You know, different pictures other than football players?"

"I wouldn't know what to buy."

"Peter would." I slipped outside to escape the home decor process, carrying the cigar box of film. Behind our house was a farm with cows where I liked to walk. Whenever I studied the picture Peter sent, he seemed so grown-up, confident: his roommate standing next to him, a handsome guy with curly hair, Peter's arm draped over his shoulder. They looked like best friends. I bet they talked about art all the time. I shook the cigar box with the reels of film, feeling sad, like I'd lost something. I didn't have much hope for their rescue. I decided to send Peter my journal as soon as possible, but I wanted to fill up all the pages first.

Going back into the past, in Mama's opinion, meant you were either brooding or you weren't trying your best with the present. She positively believed in getting into the spirit of things, and though she missed Daddy, since he was at the football office hours and hours a week, she refused to let that fact of life drag her down. After she organized her sheet music for her new elementary school job, practicing songs like "Old Dan Tucker" on the piano (the boys secretly changed the words to "Old Dumb Fucker" whenever she was out), she sewed matching tangerine ponchos with fringe balls for Peaches and herself (I vowed never to wear it if she made one for me) and decided to jump even more into the Tennessee spirit of things, by slapping down roots for the time being, trying to do what other Tennessee folks did. She joined the Game Cock Singers, bought patchwork quilts, and even attended the Dogwood Ladies' Luncheon to get properly welcomed to town as a Game Cock Wife.

By her fortieth birthday, I had finished putting together all the photo albums. Some of the pictures were faded, but many had held up remarkably well for years in a box. I gave her four photo albums for her birthday present. They held pictures of my First Communion, Peaches's baptism, Joe-Sam's play at the age of five when he walked on his hands, Leo in a baby swing, Christmases, Easters, summer vacations, and first days of school. Our lives did exist. It was documented right there in black-and-white and Kodachrome. Finally, she smiled at me. "These are lovely, Liz. You were right." She kept looking at them, her eyes tearing up, as if she couldn't quite believe what she was seeing. "Thank you," she said, putting them on the coffee table. "You know what I'd really like to do now?"

"What?"

"Go out to the farmers' market in Shooks Gap. I want to experience something really southern on my first birthday in Tennessee."


It seemed to take forever to get to Shooks Gap over the back roads, past little white clapboard churches, ascending on cinderblock foundations. Next to the farmers' market itself was a body shop that resembled a shack more than anything else. It was entirely ensconced in dazzling hubcaps with a sign that said, POKEY REED'S BODY SHOP. FREE ESTIMATES. Somewhere near the top of the hubcaps, a white cross stuck out with the words READY OR NOT, HERE HE COMES! Whenever I saw signs like those, it made realize where we were living, and that being Roman Catholics in East Tennessee, we were probably considered papal freaks, but I also felt above the born-agains and their tacky religious trademarks. I didn't need to get dunked into the waters to know where I stood on the path to eternity. As a Catholic, you were pretty much guaranteed a spot, as long as you received the Last Rites before death and apologized for your sins on the way out.

At the farmers' market, Mama bought tomatoes, okra, squash, peaches, and three bushels of corn, and when we got home, we shucked it for her as a present. She boiled it, ready to sink her teeth into creamy white corn, dripping with salt and butter.

"How long you been boiling that corn, Mama?" Peaches asked, cutting out paper dolls from a pad of construction paper.

"About thirty minutes. I guess Tennessee corn just takes a little longer, sugar."

A few minutes later when she checked again, the corn was still uncooked. She stabbed at it, "This is just a little bit ridiculous."

216

"What is?" hailed Mary Martha from the window, Beth and Buster trailing behind. "How y'all doing?" She breezed in wearing her tangerine tennis outfit. "I just thought we'd drop by after our tennis lessons."

"Look at this corn, Mary Martha. It's as hard as a rock."

"She's been cooking it for about three hours," Leo chuckled, grabbing Buster by the neck. Joe-Sam shoved them both outside. Beth lurked in the doorway. "Hey, Peaches. Let's go play in your room."

Mary Martha walked over to the pot to inspect the corn. "Darling, they have sold you field corn. What they give to pigs, barn animals. You know!"

"Field corn??? Dammit to hell and back . . ."


An hour later, we pulled back into the dusty farmers' market in Shooks Gap where Mary Martha and Mama approached the field corn culprit.

"Listen, you . . ." Mary Martha got right up in his face. "You sold this lady field corn. Now she may not be from Tennessee, but, by God, I am, and I know what's what. Furthermore, my husband is the head coach of the Tennessee Game Cocks."

"No fooling?"

"Now you can't give my friend back her time or her children's time spent shucking and cooking this crap, but you can give her back her money, dammit."

"Yes, ma'am. I do apologize, ma'am. Is your husband really Donny Mac?"

"He is, but I sure wouldn't be asking for any tickets if I were you."

"No, ma'am."

"Thank you, sir." Mama grabbed the money, leaving the soggy bushels of corn at his feet. On the way home, we stopped at a McDonald's in Fountain City to eat Big Macs. After the field corn experience, the only Tennessee thing Mama wanted to do was to go up to Gatlinburg to ski down the snow carpet.

★   ★   ★

"Kath, whatever time you want. No problem. Two? I'll meet you there. You're kidding. Oh, big time. All right, *dang it*." I hung up the phone from Kathleen.

"You know you talk just like her these days." Mama smiled, doing bills.

"Oh, please." I walked out of the room, embarrassed. Even if she was right, it still made me despise her comment. In a matter of months, Kathleen had been catapulted into the most popular girl in the sophomore class. She was adored not only by the clique but by the underbellies as well. In addition to imitating her speech, I also tried to make my handwriting look like hers, cheerful and loopy. She also dotted her *i*'s with fat hearts and added extra vowels on words for emphasis, like "You are sooooooo special." She hated French, pronouncing *huit,* the word for eight, "hoot," instead of "hweet," even though I told her at least a hundred times how to say it right.

Throughout all her budding fame, Kathleen remained loyal, very proud of the fact that I was a writer. She noticed it more than anybody, including teachers, Mama and Daddy, other people at school. Kathleen ate up what I wrote, staring at it hard, until she finally handed it back, whispering, "Gosh, I wish I could write like you. You are the best. A storyteller."

"You think so, you low-down dirty streetwalker?" I touched her hair, which was so thick and red.

"You'll be famous, you twat. I'll be a famous dancer, and you'll be a famous writer. We'll live in New York. It's the perfect place for dancers and writers."

In English class, I wrote a story about two young women, best friends, residing together in New York City, surviving on the most delectable desserts in town. Kathleen showed it to everyone at lunchtime, reading the funniest parts out loud.

*Dear Peter,*
*Have you ever loved somebody so much you thought you would die without*
*them? Have you ever loved somebody so much that the more you loved them,*

*the more uptight you became around them? That's how I feel about Kathleen. Most of the time, it's normal, but then I get afraid of losing her. Since she's pretty perfect, I try to be perfect right back, but my adoration is making me tongue-tied and possibly ruining our friendship. Our silences are now sometimes strained, because I'm afraid if I say the wrong thing, she won't be my friend anymore.*

*I am at a loss, and since you're on the verge of graduating with honors from Notre Dame University, you've got to have more answers than I do. Did being popular matter to you? I hate to sound shallow, but it does to me. I want to be liked. I don't want the room to get quiet when I walk in, like they've been talking about me. How can I make them like me?*

*When I don't worry if Kathleen likes me or not, our friendship is steady, but when that's all I can think about, we run out of things to say. Can you understand what it's like to be best friends with someone who is perfect? The pressure is so intense. She is still considered my best friend by everyone, but she has vaulted into such demand that I am in awe of why she wants to remain my friend. I mean, she could have anybody now. Why would she still want me? But I can't lose her. She's the best thing about Knoxville. I love her so, I can't swallow, and my stomach flip-flops whenever she's around. Your loving niece, Elizabeth Frances Donegal*

I sent Peter the completed journal after the last entry dealing with Kathleen. It was getting to the point where I couldn't wait for answers anymore, and I'd spent more than a year filling up pages to him. On the manila envelope, I printed his name in big block letters with a Magic Marker, sticking lots of colorful stamps on it, adding the words "Special Delivery." I held the package in my hands for a moment before I dropped it in the mailbox, debating. It scared me to send it, kind of like tossing my heart off a cliff, but I did it. Naturally, I expected an immediate response.

What also made my best friend so popular was her fabulous dancing. At the Homecoming Dance, most of us were without dates, but it didn't matter with Kathleen as our fortress. She led the girls to the pumping

Pointer Sisters' beat under the flashing lights of the mirrored ball, sashaying to "We Are Family." As our finale, we followed Kathleen's cue to shimmy off the gym floor, while the opening chords of Lynyrd Skynyrd's "Free Bird" struck, igniting everyone to mate up. Eric Lankowitz asked me to dance, but I turned him down flat, preferring to watch the tribal ritual of Lynyrd Skynyrd love. As the music gradually crescendoed, the guys wrenched away from their girls, lunging into the middle of the gym floor with their air guitars, caterwauling, along with Lynyrd Skynyrd. They pulsed, heaved, and slid across the floor in a frenzy, eyes glazed, necks twitching in fierce rhythm. When Lynyrd's "Free Bird" hit its zenith, shattering fluorescents illuminated the rank gymnasium. We sluggishly exited the basketball court, sweat soaking into our nylon shirts, ears ringing.

Kathleen pulled me aside, "You want to go to Jam and Andy's?"

"Sure," I whispered, excited, realizing it was a college bar on the strip.

"Are you coming, idiot?" Kathleen's sister, Mandy, shoved her hard from behind.

"Yeah," Kathleen laughed, rolling her eyes, not at all angry. When we got in the car, Mandy floored it to Jam and Andy's. Three cars actually moved to the side of Magnolia Avenue to let her pass. When we arrived, she ordered us four Miller Tall Boys, since she was eighteen, then departed with strict instructions for us not to follow her. We breathed a sigh of relief when she left. Kathleen explained, "I'm with Bitch on Wheels so she won't get into trouble. My parents trust me way more than they trust her. So cheers, you trollop."

"Cheers back, horny cock-tease," I smiled, clinking my Tall Boy against hers.

"Good one. Okay, chug it," she dared, sucking hers fast. I began gulping mine, checking around for any waitresses who might ask us for ID, but we were in a dark corner, so we felt safe.

"Remember when we went to the locker room during the fourth quarter of your dad's game and naked guys kept walking right by the door?" Kathleen giggled.

"All those jiggly little penises wagging behind tiny team towels . . . sick!"

"Those players think they're hot shit. How pathetic," she sighed.

"In their dreams," I agreed. "Hey, Kathleen, why is Mandy so mad tonight?

"Mad? She's not. That's just her personality. Let's make mountains."

"Okay," I laughed, pouring salt and pepper into neat hills and valleys.

The more beer we sucked, the woozier the night grew. The Tall Boy fizz lapped at my face; my ears burned. Kathleen blurred into a strawberry blond haze.

"You're my first best friend," I told her in a rush of love.

"You're not my first best friend, but you're my best friend now."

"Are we drunk?"

"We'd better be," she giggled.

When Mandy came back a few hours later, she prodded us into the car, unrolling all the windows. "Time for a freeze out, you trashy little sophomore alcoholic whores." Mandy hit the gas. The cold wind blasted through our clothes, but we huddled together to keep warm. Kathleen started wailing "Rocky Top," and I joined her. We sang it at the top of our lungs.

I realized that we were becoming more and more like Tennessee girls all the time. As Mandy floored it, Kathleen suddenly sat up, cheering, "Faster, Mandy, faster." Her big sister pressed the gas pedal to the floor. I gripped the back of the front seat in horror, my life flashing before my eyes, as Mandy began hooting, "Haul ass and fuck you! Haul ass and fuck you!" into the curdling wind.

"Go, baby, go!" Kathleen's eyes were on fire at the thrill of the ride.

We hit three mailboxes going fifty miles an hour, splintering them off in the darkness, before Mandy slammed into a tree stump. She whacked her head on the front windshield. We were safe but shaken in the backseat, but Kathleen was laughing and crying wildly, so I leaned over the seat to check on Mandy. She was coming to, still muttering, "Fuck ass, haul you." I gently scooted her over, climbing into the driver's seat. I'd hardly driven before, but I put the car in reverse, and by a miracle, we unhitched from the tree stump. As I jerked it into drive, I crawled at a snail's pace up the black road, wheels wobbling, engine wheezing.

"My dad's gonna shit bricks," Kathleen slurred from the backseat.

"Yeah, probably," I agreed, dreading Roy the Boy's reaction.

"I love you," Kathleen screamed at me.

Mandy clutched her head in the darkness, moaning softly. I prayed she wouldn't die on me.

"I love you too," I breathed, feeling like her bodyguard, because suddenly I wasn't drunk anymore. I had to get my friend the dancing movie star safely home.

# ''DANNY BOY''

*"Hail Mary Long Bomb"*

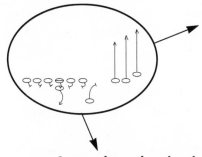

**Commonly employed at the end of the game (or first half)
when a touchdown is needed to win or tie the game. The offensive
formation involves three wide receivers aligning in a cluster to one side
of the formation. Obviously, they all sprint toward the goal line on the snap;
however, their assignments vary. The INSIDE RECEIVER when reaching the
reception point lags behind to play for a tipped ball. The OUTSIDE RECEIVER
sprints past the reception point and plays for a tipped ball. The
MIDDLE RECEIVER goes for the reception and if he cannot
catch the football, he attempts to tip it up in the air.**

Mandy didn't die, but her father took the car away from her for six months, and made her baby-sit at Holy Ghost on Sundays in the nursery for the ten A.M. mass. Sometimes Kathleen and I baby-sat, too, but I preferred not to with Mandy around, since she seemed just as likely to swing a baby against a wall as not. Kathleen never got angry with her sister, which I could not understand. If she'd been my sister, I'm sure I would have gone for the throat. Being around Mandy and Kathleen made me begin to rethink my own relationship with Peaches. I was certainly no prize, but I did not want to become a "Mandy" in my little sister's eyes either.

On a Sunday in the fall of my sophomore year, I was in my room writing a Christmas play for my best friend to star in, when I heard the usual "Liz, come down here." I resisted, working for another few minutes on Kathleen's opening monologue.

"Liz. We need to talk to you," Mama yelled. "Now!"

I ambled into the kitchen, noting that she and Joe-Sam were sitting at the table, with Daddy pacing. It was an odd time for him to be home; usually he was at the football office on Sundays, breaking down film of the next week's opponent.

"Where are Peaches and Leo?" I asked, uneasy.

"I sent them outside to play. At least for the moment."

Daddy chose his words carefully. "Sweetheart, your uncle Peter is missing."

"What do you mean, missing?" My stomach seized up. Then I remembered my journal I'd sent him three months earlier. There'd been no response at all.

"The thing is," Daddy continued, "Meemaw found his wallet in his room. The whole goddamn situation doesn't make a lot of sense at this point. The long and the short of it is, he took off in his car, the Gold Duster."

"About three days ago," Mama explained, vigorously drying glasses with a dish towel. "Not a word since."

"Where do you think he is?" I twisted the pen top around in its barrel.

"I wish to God I knew. His psychiatrist said he might be on a plane to visit his girlfriend or . . ."

"His psychiatrist?"

"He'd been feeling some pressures since graduating. . . . A psychic's been brought in, too. . . . She keeps picturing a car in her mind."

Joe-Sam was intrigued. "They brought in a psychic?"

"Everyone's desperate to try anything," Daddy trailed off helplessly.

"But you just saw him, Daddy," I accused. "How was it?"

"Fine, goddammit. I was too busy; I mean, it was a recruiting trip. We didn't have much time to talk, but he was fine. Maybe a little depressed, but that's normal. A young man has to decide what he's going to do with his life."

"He already knows. He's an artist."

"Yeah, well, an artist still needs to eat. He had an art job, doing layouts or some such crap. They called Meemaw when he didn't show up for work on Thursday."

"Maybe he took a trip," Joe-Sam offered.

Daddy lashed out, "I don't care if the sumbitch is lying naked in a field of lilies; he could pick up the phone and call somebody. He's got us all worried sick." He pitched his coffee cup into the sink, stomping outside. Mama followed him.

Joe-Sam drew pictures of sharks on his pad. I watched him sketch the thorny teeth, opaque eyes, followed by a rigid gray body gliding across the ocean floor.

"Joe-Sam?" I ached to share my connection with Peter, to make someone understand that he belonged to *me*. "Peter and I used to kiss when I was little. A lot."

Joe-Sam stayed very quiet, sketching his sharks.

"What are you thinking?"

"I guess it's okay. I mean, after all, we're related . . . or wait a sec. Doesn't that make it weirder?"

"He had very wet lips. I told him that. So before he'd kiss me, he'd dry them off with the back of his hand. I was supposed to visit him in New York."

"Me too."

"You were not."

"I was too. He wasn't just *your* uncle, Liz."

The trembling started from my shoulders and worked its way down. "Joe-Sam, we need to go to a museum. Now. Are there any museums here in Knoxville?"

"I've never seen one."

I pulled down the phone book. My stomach was convulsing, my mouth as dry as the Sahara. Short breaths, I reminded myself as I tore into the Yellow Pages. *Maybe it's not too late.* I kept thinking if I found a museum with art, I'd find Peter. Stupid, but possible. He'd left clues to his disappearance. The last time I talked to him on the phone, he'd said, "Look at art. Find out for yourself. How it makes you feel." I didn't listen to him then, because he hadn't said a word about my journal.

"But why didn't he tell Meemaw where he was going?" Joe-Sam remarked.

"And why did he leave his wallet in his bedroom but take his car?" I felt my blood begin to throb. Joe-Sam was as calm watching me as I was agitated.

"Well?"

"It sounds bad, doesn't it, Joe-Sam?"

"Yeah, I think maybe it does," he answered, shutting the pad on his sharks as I threw the phone book across the table.

I went to my room. I'll write to him, I thought. If I write to him, he can't be gone. So what if he never answered before? He probably had a lot on his mind and was waiting until he saw me in person to give advice. I picked up the new journal I'd bought and peeled away the cellophane. With the softest touch I could manage, I creased down the first page, smoothing it back against the cover.

Dear Peter,

Why can't I find any museums in Knoxville? I know there must be some. I don't know why I didn't check before now. More importantly, where are you? Why didn't I go to Notre Dame the weekend you invited me to see Crosby, Stills, and Nash last spring? I should have gone. I was busy being with my best friend. I knew you and Notre Dame would always be there. I should have gone to see you. I had no idea time was so short with you.

I put down the journal. I already knew. I took down the massive *History of Art* book he'd given me, attempting to gather traces of him. I opened it to a picture of Vincent van Gogh's, titled *Self-Portrait*. Studying the *Self-Portrait*, I remembered that Peter's own latest self-portrait had also been a desolate, shadowy painting, resembling van Gogh's. Meemaw had hung it up in the living room, and folks commented from time to time on how brilliant it was, but secretly labeled it "morbid." I took out the slide he'd sent me of his self-portrait, aiming it into the sunlight filtering through the gritty window. His eyes had the same haunting sorrow, the wavy eyebrows, the creased face full of introspection, the mouth closed, repressing all spoken thought. What could Peter have to do with Vincent van Gogh? Comparing the two portraits side by side, it seemed like almost everything.

He had included four other self-portraits in his package of slides. I dug out Daddy's ancient football slide projector from the hall closet. After setting it up in my bedroom, I put each of Peter's slides into the projector, watching his van Gogh–like face infuse the wall of my friendship plaques and posters. The rather corny *"Friend, no matter how far"* script scrawling beneath his face seemed somehow laced with vicious irony. I removed all the plaques, placing each one under my bed, so I could study Peter's portraits without hokey messages bleeding all over them.

As I absorbed Peter's slides, scrutinizing the brush strokes, the colors, the expressions, I noticed that in each of them, his eyes were inky, but luminous. They were locked inside faces full of suffocating secrets. Why hadn't I seen this before? I always took him for granted, a whiz kid artist who loved me and would always be there. Why not? He was only five years older. He had just graduated on scholarship with tons of friends. Meemaw couldn't say enough about how all the priests of Notre Dame thought the world of him.

Then it came to me—all his sketches were of the men in the family. Never the women. It's true the men did the exciting things: hunting and coaching. What did the women do anyway? Meemaw had spent her life catering to the men. My most vivid memory of her was of her in the kitchen, chasing down the live crabs Papa Sweetheart had brought home in bushels for a seafood feast. She picked off the crawling crustaceans from her kitchen curtains, pitching them into boiling vats of water to steam them, their claws waving in protest, Papa Sweetheart's voice bellowing from upstairs, "Meemaw, get me a beer. Jesus, Mary, and Joseph." Peter's brothers married women who then had babies. Hunting and coaching were more exciting than cooking, fetching, and birthing babies. Anyone would tell you so. Was it approval then? Was it love?

I went further back in my mind to the night Peter cried at the kitchen table way back in Pittsburgh just after everything fell apart with Aunt

Betty. What had he said? "*I put on a good show anyway. . . . It's all part of the act.*" I was too wrapped up in her electric-shock therapy to question him. Besides, I was only thirteen, and his tears embarrassed me. Was it real or did I dream it? Sections of my brain must be cast about in a million places. *Peter, where are you?*

In the same package of slides, he'd also sent two other subjects, which were very different. For the first time, I saw Edward Hopper in his work. The first was his painting of a craggy-faced man in a ribbed undershirt, grinning uneasily from an overstuffed easy chair, acting like he wanted to get up but couldn't quite manage it at the moment. A bowl of potato chips rested on the arm of the chair beside him, next to a glass of orange juice with slivers of melting ice. It seemed like the man was watching the fights or baseball on TV.

The second painting was of an elderly lady propped up on a pale chintz spread, resembling a very comfortable queen. She was wearing a house-dress, bobby socks without shoes, and her slender ankles were neatly crossed. Unlike the fat guy in the undershirt, she was really smiling, per-fectly content to stay right where she was.

I remembered Meemaw saying Peter painted from old photographs, not with the person in the room at all. Thoughts thumped through my head. How was Peter trying to be like Vincent van Gogh? What about Edward Hopper? By painting very ordinary people in rather extraordinary ways? At that moment, the face of his handsome best friend loomed into my mind, his roommate at college.

Peaches waltzed into my room, donning her new ballet costume. "Am I beautiful, Liz?" She was a rainbow with glittery sparkles.

"Nope," I answered.

"Yes, I am."

"Then why did you ask me?"

"Forget you." Her bottom lip bulged out dangerously.

"I'm sorry . . . of course you're beautiful. You always have been. I'm just worried."

"Who's that lady?" she asked, pirouetting as she stared at the portrait.

"Somebody Peter painted. Peaches, has anyone told you?" I asked her softly, wishing she were fifteen instead of nine, so we could discuss everything heart-to-heart like true sisters. "Did you hear about Peter? What's happened?"

"I don't want to talk about it."

"Peaches, get back here."

"Sorry. I'm a sparkling rainbow at the moment," she crooned, tripping out of the room on her toes.

When we received the actual word of Peter's suicide, Donny Mac flew our entire family to Nashville on a tiny chartered plane, compliments of the University of Tennessee Fighting Game Cocks football team. When we arrived, Meemaw's house was crammed with food, flowers, and relatives. She was in her bed, but she pulled each of us down to her into tight hugs, uttering, "God love you and I do too."

Peter's bedroom was so full of life and Peter. It seemed inconceivable that he wouldn't walk in the door any minute, treating us to a Zoo at Farrell's, like old times. His books, his cartoons, his paintings leaped out at me, along with all of his men-things: piles of loose change, a money-clip, aftershave, weights, a basketball, chapstick, shaving cream, big sweaters, tweed hats from Ireland, Notre Dame yearbooks, art history, Norman Rockwell, Edward Hopper, and Vincent van Gogh books. My eyes lapped it up, memorizing every artifact for clues. Was my journal in here, too? As I scanned the room, feeling Peter's presence everywhere, Uncle Whitey entered.

"How would you like to stay out at the farm with us, Princess Loving Cup?"

I smiled at the nickname I hadn't heard in years. He'd given it to me when I was around four years old. It made me wonder what made my uncle see me as Princess Loving Cup, when to my father, I was Aunt Gertrude.

"I'd like to stay here, Uncle Whitey," I answered him, looking at him, realizing that we didn't look so much alike anymore except for the eyes. They were Peter's eyes too, and Daddy's, slate blue.

"We need you at the farm. Just for tonight. I'll bring you back in the morning, I promise. Please?"

"Okay." I looked at his sweet, haggard face as he stood in the room of his dead brother. In the stillness, I ventured my question. "Uncle Whitey? What happened?"

"We'll talk about it later, darling." He left the room, sneezing. His sneezes were wild explosions from his head. I flinched with each detonation. As I moved to Peter's bureau, I found some pictures of him as a little boy in a bow tie. I slipped them into my jeans as I followed my uncle downstairs.

I hated staying at Uncle Whitey's even for one minute, for I wanted to talk to Mary-Louise, so the two of us could get back into Peter's room to poke around, figuring things out. To pass the time, I attempted to watch *West Side Story* in the family room, but it was impossible even with my ear next to the volume, because the room was filled with the giddy shouts of ten kids, who were unable to comprehend that we were in a time of mourning. I couldn't even scream "SHUT THE FUCK UP," the way I would have done at home, since Aunt Little and Uncle Whitey were sitting right there, discussing the funeral arrangements.

Aunt Little yelled over the hubbub to me, "You're the cream of the crop as far as good baby-sitters go. Real responsible, your Mama says. Hell, I say it, too, the way you took care of the kids at the beach that summer."

"Oh, yes, ma'am."

"You think you could sit for all the kids while we go back and forth to the funeral home and what-not over the next few days? We're gonna be real busy."

*Oh, so this was the plan? One night was what Uncle Whitey said. Ha.* Trying to act like I didn't hear her, I was propelled into being Maria weeping over Tony's body on TV, me weeping over Peter. Once started, the cascade of tears wouldn't stop.

"What about it?" Aunt Little asked again.

I turned to her, unbelieving, my words punctuated by sharp sobs.

230

## "Danny Boy"

"Aunt Little? You want me to baby-sit while y'all run back and forth to the funeral home?"

"Didn't you tell her, Whitey?"

Uncle Whitey just sat there, tearing up as the swells of *West Side Story* music wafted through the hysterical din in the family room.

"No, ma'am"—I wiped my face with both hands—"I'm sorry, but you're gonna have to hire somebody else. I'll do your dishes tonight if you need help, but that's it."

Uncle Whitey didn't say a word. Aunt Little didn't know how to respond, having never seen me in a grown-up light since I'd always been so repulsively agreeable around her. Aunt Little wasn't a bad person at all; in fact, I'd always enjoyed her wry sense of humor. Now she couldn't fathom that I was no longer Miss Conviviality of the Year. I'd plain caught her off guard. She pretended to be interested in Tony's death, too. Her newest baby, the tenth one, toddled over to hand me a gummy cracker. I kissed her sticky face. Then the pack of boys wrestled into a lamp, slamming it over, sending sparks shooting through the air.

"Goddamn it, men!" Uncle Whitey howled, skyrocketing out of his La-Z-Boy, knocking their heads together, but in practically the very next second, he was kissing them, howling, "God love you. Say it! Say 'God love you!' and 'I love you.' "

I couldn't take any more, so I sneaked out of the room to call Mary-Louise, who, by a miracle, answered on the first ring.

"You gotta come get me," I told her. "I'll meet you on the road at midnight, and we'll go back to Meemaw's house. I have to see Peter's room again."

"I love you, Liz."

"I love you, too, Mary-Louise."

When we hung up, I could breathe easier. I knew she wouldn't let me down. This was too important. Though we couldn't save him, maybe we could find something to help us understand.


At midnight, Mary-Louise got out of the car, and we stood there for several minutes holding each other up on that black country road some-

231

where in Franklin, Tennessee, steaming mist rising like gossamer ghosts. For a few seconds, I felt like we were in Ireland, home of our ancestors, instead of some country road in Tennessee. I cried again, huge sobs wracking my ribs, so relieved to see my lovely cousin, who was as outraged as I was about the whole tragedy. I knew if anyone could find answers, it would be Mary-Louise. She no longer smelled like grape lip gloss, but rather a mixture of Ivory soap and Noxzema. As we got into the car, I whispered, "I left a note for Whitey and Little, so they wouldn't worry."

"Uncle Whitey was the one who found him," she sighed, starting the car.

"Really?" I suddenly felt very sorry for Uncle Whitey. It seemed like he was the chosen one in the family to discover the tragedies and make the "bad news" calls.

"Did you hear the story?"

"I know it was suicide. In a garage. But no details."

"He drove his Gold Duster into the garage behind his house," Mary-Louise continued, driving on into the darkness. "He told Meemaw he was going to mass, and he never came back. He must have shut the garage door, leaving the engine running. It took them a week to find him. No one ever thought to look in the garage."

"I saw Meemaw, briefly."

"Have you heard her theory? Brain tumor. Since he'd been having so many headaches lately."

"A brain tumor?" I gasped, amazed.

"Can we talk *denial*? None of this shit makes any sense."

"No, it doesn't."

We drove on for a few minutes in silence, before Mary-Louise commented, "You know, they think he changed his mind at the last minute."

"Why?"

"He was half out of the car, like he was trying to get to the door."

"Fuck."

"Well, not to sound unsympathetic, but it's a good thing he did it in cold weather. It could have been a real mess if he'd done it in July in that hot garage. Not finding him for a week and all."

# "Danny Boy"

I couldn't answer Mary-Louise, forever practical even in the face of tragedy, but I was glad for her sensibility. It kept me steady from drowning in the sorrow of the years and years ahead of me without Peter.

*A brain tumor? I felt like I was getting a brain tumor, I had such a headache. How could they call it that? A boy of twenty-one drives his Gold Duster into his garage, leaving the motor running until he dies. That's a brain tumor?*

I stared at the blackness rushing past, longing to feel dead for a while to survive this time. If I could do that, I would be all right. Mary-Louise held my hand in silence even as she took the curves on the back roads. I'd pretty much lost my favorite aunt, who had faded from our lives like a living ghost down in Florida; now I had to lose my favorite uncle in suicide. What a waste. What an absolutely senseless waste. What was I supposed to do with my bitterness? *Peter? Come back, and I swear to God I'll pay attention this time. I swear. I swear.*

Mary-Louise had a key to Meemaw's house, since she often stopped by to visit on her way home from school, so we were able to let ourselves in quietly in the middle of the night. As we crept upstairs, she whispered in my ear, "There has to be a suicide note in his room, and we're going to find it." We poked around, paging through books, digging in his closet, until Mary-Louise discovered a folded note wedged into a corner of his mirror, out of sight behind a pile of folded T-shirts. It had been there all along, but it was as if no one had wanted to dig too deep to find out the awful truth. To be honest, I hadn't really expected to find it, but Mary-Louise just knew without a doubt.

*Dear Friends,*
*I'm not good enough for you . . .*
*Please understand . . .*
*I'm not worthy of your love . . . I'm deeply unhappy . . .*
*Mama, I'm so sorry . . . but it really is better this way, and*
*Jack and Whitey, my brothers, please accept my decision and know that I*

*love you . . . you'll always be my brothers. A man could not have asked for better brothers.*

*Patricia, please go on with your life and find someone who will love you for the special person you are . . . raise a family with him the way you want . . .*

*I just couldn't be that person . . . I'm sorry.*

*Mick, travel again someday the way we did last summer . . . back to Ireland . . .*

*And Liz, I'm not who you think . . .*

*You're better off without me . . . I'm not good the way everyone thinks . . .*

*I've done what I've had to do.*

*Please find it in your hearts to forgive me and go on with your lives.*

*I love you all very very much.*

*Your son and brother and friend, Peter*

My heart cracked reading those words. I turned to Mary-Louise, "Well, for someone who was supposed to be so smart, he sure left one helluva cliché note."

"Liz!" she was shocked.

"It's true, fuck him, it's true." *How dare he leave me?* I read the note over and over, but then Daddy walked into the room in his boxers.

"What the hell? It's two A.M. Liz, you're supposed to be helping out at Whitey's."

"I'm not staying at Uncle Whitey's, Daddy. I'm staying right here."

Mary-Louise handed him the note, which he read without saying a word. It took him a long time to read it. He finally looked at us, his eyes full of inconsolable sorrow, his shoulders bowed in pain. After what seemed like hours, he breathed, "Well, that's that. Y'all don't stay up too late. We got a long-ass day to get through tomorrow." He walked out of the room, taking the note with him. We never saw it again.

I moved to Peter's window to survey the tiny white garage, glowing below like a tomb, offering no answers. From Meemaw's room, I heard the record player begin. *What was she doing up?* The haunting strains of Ethel Merman singing "Danny Boy" crooned from underneath her door. Mary-Louise met my eyes as we listened to the music, and I saw him,

# "Danny Boy"

Peter Donegal, standing alone on the moors in Ireland where he'd spent his last summer after graduation from Notre Dame.

In my mind, a clan of all the Donegal relatives stood in the distance, watching him, loving him, adoring him, banishing him, hating him, disapproving of him, afraid of him—for what he was. At that moment, it hit me. Peter was gay. I didn't know how I knew; I only knew that I did. It made perfect sense. What would be the one thing that the Donegal family of proud Irishmen would not and could not tolerate? The Donegals produced podiatrists, lawyers, and football coaches. Not gays, not homosexuals, not faggots. The Donegals begat good Catholic Notre Dame boys. The Fighting Irish.

*It's a mortal sin against God and Man. Not in this house. Not while you live under my roof. Not in this family, buster, not on your life.* Call it a brain tumor, and pray for the repose of his soul in heaven. Our brother. Our son. My uncle. My first kiss.

# 24

# BEAM AND STREAM
*"Controlled Stationary Scrimmage"*

**Vital for the DEFENSE as well as the OFFENSE. Both have definite responsibilities. Wear and use all equipment assigned. Move with your opponent. Have a controlled charge, flow with the play.**

By the next morning, Peter's room was packed with all his friends from Notre Dame. They arrived in droves, hanging around his room, browsing through his books, his clothes, his art. Uncle Whitey put Peter's new girlfriend, Patricia Weiner, in charge of giving away Peter's things to his closest friends. Patricia resembled Dorothy Hamill, only she was more of a tomboy. I liked her. She was certainly several million light-years above and beyond Cynthia Elspecker, but I decided not to speculate with her about my theories on the suicide of her boyfriend.

Over the next crazy days, while Meemaw was still in bed with her sorrow, Patricia Weiner, like a collegiate widow, gave away everything of Peter's; his buddies hoarded the articles, wearing his sweaters, vests, scarves, and coats like trophies. They took his paintings, his photography, his sketches. In all the stuff, I never found my journal, and I was sick at the thought of someone else discovering it.

Uncle Whitey spent the next year trying to track down all of Peter's things, because when Meemaw got out of bed one week later, there was virtually nothing left of her son. Everyone believed they were helping Meemaw by getting rid of all evidence of Peter. They each wanted a little piece of him. I got his Irish hat, a wrought-iron golfer, and some art books, but when I offered to return them, Meemaw said I could keep them.

Mary-Louise deemed Patricia Weiner a royal pain, because the night before the funeral, over a plate of corned beef and cabbage, Patricia wailed, "We were supposed to get married. All my friends expected me to have a rock on my finger by this time. He promised me a rock by Easter. I can't take any more suicides."

I allowed Patricia Weiner's euphemism for an engagement ring to roll over in my mind. *A rock.* I caught Mary-Louise's gaze as she mimicked gagging at Patricia's outburst, but I was fascinated by her sorrow. When Patricia wasn't looking, I watched the way she washed her face in the bathroom, the way she buttoned her coat, or pushed her hair off her forehead. To me, she was a tragic figure, because not only her first, but her *second,* boyfriend had committed suicide. Her boyfriends didn't just break up with her; they went out and killed themselves, while they were dating *her.* Patricia, with her easy smile and Dorothy Hamill looks, just didn't seem the type to drive men to their deaths.

All that week, Peter's friends were really nice to me and Mary-Louise when they hung out at the house; they comforted us by teaching us to drink Blue Whales, a drink that turned our tongues bright blue. They also gave us hot Irish whiskeys, which kept us tipsy-turvy for days.

I couldn't face seeing Peter in the casket, so I refused to go to the funeral home. I begged off at each invitation, preferring to sit with Meemaw in her dark room, where the family doctor kept her heavily sedated. She had me play "Danny Boy" over and over. The coach in Daddy just flat-out died, and he kept away from conversation. He had a way of standing, folding his arms across his chest, thumbs up, his lower lip protruding just the slightest bit. Aunt Little and Uncle Whitey took over, giving orders. Meemaw never got out of bed, not even to go to the funeral.

Peter's handsome roommate, a proud-to-be-Irish-kind-of-guy, Mick O'Doherty, finally showed up on the third day for the mass. He got drunk quickly beforehand, even taking down his pants to reveal a tattoo on his butt: a green leprechaun, with his fists clenched, ready for victory. Mick told us Peter had the same symbol on his butt too. They'd had it done together at a tattoo parlor near Notre Dame. I had a dream of Peter that night, a long twisted dream. I could see him in his coffin, moons up, with the green leprechaun growing larger until it jumped out of the coffin, chanting: "When Irish Eyes Are Smiling."

Mick cried the most at Peter's funeral, even more than Patricia. I suspected he loved Peter more than Patricia ever could, and I was betting Peter loved him back, but I mentioned my thoughts to no one, not even to Mary-Louise, because I had no proof.

Father Albert, a frail priest from Notre Dame, arrived by train to say the mass, dazed and disheveled. I had always been instructed that the Catholic Church wouldn't bury a suicide, but since the official word on Peter was "brain tumor," his funeral went off without a hitch. When Father Albert delivered the sermon, he had no answers either. You could tell this whole event had really caught him off guard too. Six months earlier he had given the sermon at Peter's graduation mass from Notre Dame. For the funeral, he recited from Emily Dickinson, Thomas Wolfe, and James Agee, but he didn't talk much about God or trying to understand. He hurt as much as the rest of us. When he left to return to Notre Dame, he gingerly clutched an oil painting that Peter had done of him a year earlier, nodding good-byes before he was out the door.

At the wake right after the funeral, many of Peter's friends asked me if I was his sister. I said no, but I knew the question wasn't stupid as I stared at the framed graduation pictures of Peter. If I'd been a man, we could have been twins. We had the same eyes, same nose, our face the same oval shape. We even had the same tooth chipped in the same place. I never noticed any of this when he was alive.

Uncle Whitey insisted a group of us follow him out to the stream running along Meemaw's farm. He gave us each a glass, insisting we fill them half full with creek water. Then he went around pouring Jim Beam into our glasses, decreeing, "Y'all take a sip now. What you're about to delight your tongue with is Beam and Stream, and it don't get any better. Cheers to Peter in heaven with Jesus. God love him."

I wandered away from the Beam and Stream gathering alone. It was a November day, wind-slicing, but I felt warm with whiskey. I ambled up to the barn, where I found Mick O'Doherty sitting on a broken motorcycle, pretending to ride it. As soon as he saw me, he began making rumbling engine noises. I moved toward him. By the time I reached the motorcycle, he was crying. He toppled off the bike into the dust and hay, swirling lint into the gray air. He bawled into my shoulder as I rocked his huge body back and forth. Through the soft powdery dust of the stables, I thought I distinguished the filmy shape of Peter, standing there in a corner, watching us. I blinked, shaking off the apparition, fearing it. When I opened my eyes, he was gone.

I longed for sleep. I ached to see Kathleen again, to go back to Tennessee Catholic to do nothing more than have an ordinary French class. I wanted life to be normal again. Mick's sobs finally slowed to gasps, then to even breathing.

"He loved you best, Mick," I whispered. "Last summer, he sent me a picture of the two of you. He never looked happier."

"You know, don't you?" He stared at the ground, then at me, his eyes searching.

"Yes."

"He was afraid, Liz. He was terrified of hurting people. I tried to make him see, but he couldn't get past his family. What they would think."

"He could have made his own family . . . with you."

"He couldn't see that far. Every time he tried, he'd see his father, his brothers. I think I'm going to have to get far away from here. By the way, he loved your journal."

"He did?" I felt the tears crowd into my eyes.

"It meant a lot to him the way you loved him. He wanted to give you his Gold Duster, too, since he was planning on moving to New York and he didn't need a car in New York. He wanted you to have it."

"I don't want his car, I'm sorry, Mick. He died in that car. I don't want it, but do you know where my journal is?"

"It's in his car. Under the seat. I saw him writing in it once, and I asked him what it was. He said he was trying to answer some sex questions from his niece, but frankly, he was having a hard time." Mick smiled as I reddened.

"Liz, please take his car. It would be nice to know you're the one driving it."

I cried then, harder even than Mick. I wept convulsing sobs, missing my uncle, afraid to see his car, to own it, to drive it.

Finally, the two of us made our way back down to the house. The place was packed with even more people and voices. Daddy was standing watching a football game on television with the sound off; Uncle Whitey, plastered, was playing "Danny Boy" over and over, intercutting it with "Für Elise" on the piano. Mary-Louise and Joe-Sam were slow dancing. Mick O'Doherty wolfed down some roast beef, sent one wave across the room to me, and left. I never saw him again.


When we returned to Knoxville, I still couldn't stop thinking about Peter. Whenever I brought him up, Mama would comment, "What a waste. Did you fold the clothes?" It was impossible. Both she and Daddy remained resolute in putting the past behind them. Even when Joe-Sam failed his classes for the next six months, nobody ever thought to attribute it to Peter's death. They just told him he'd better get a better attitude if he planned on playing quarterback next football season.

The more I tried to slip into my uncle's skin, to live what he must have endured, the more I began to understand him, especially since I realized that Peter craved for approval the way I did. Why had I been such a good and responsible daughter for all those years? Not because I had a great calling to the domestic way of life, but because I loved the pats on the head. He had been the perfect boy, the perfect artist, the perfect scholar, before he finally cracked. I tried to think of what it meant to be gay. To love a man if you were a man. To love a woman if you were a woman. I thought of Daddy's football world. *"Get after that ball. What are you? A fairy? What's the matter with you? Homo."*

It was also gospel that the boys of the Donegal family proclaimed themselves "pussy-whipped," drooling over any hot babe in a bikini. Farrah Fawcett was tacked up in Joe-Sam and Leo's room, but she wasn't ever hanging in Peter's room. Being different was lethal in our family. I ached to tell Peter that he didn't need to die over his family's disapproval and sorrow, but it was too late. My life, my whole adult life to come, would be less engrossing, less alive, more status quo without him or Aunt Betty in it, for I knew that for all practical purposes, Betty was gone too. Not exactly like Peter, but she was unreachable, forbidden, and would probably remain so for the rest of her life. All my other relatives were kind, normal people, but Aunt Betty and Uncle Peter were extraordinary; in their living, they had reached out to a lonely awkward girl and made her feel special. That was their gift to me. They were rare souls of mercy and love. I didn't believe that just because one was dead and the other shut off from me. It was really true.

"Suicide is the most selfish act a person can perform," Mama sighed one day, sitting at the piano, playing Brahms.

"They don't look at it that way," I told her, sitting down on the bench next to her.

"How do they look at it?" She took her fingers off the keys.

"I've been thinking . . . and it's like their sadness gets so deep and so wide, they've got to end it. They don't think about death, they think about ending the pain."

We sat there quietly for a minute, staring at the black and white keys on the Yamaha.

"Mama," I began. "How's Aunt Betty? Does all this stuff with Peter make you want to go see her?"

"No," Mama replied. "Anyway, the nuns write regularly and she's doing as well as can be expected."

"Oh," I said, disappointed, wanting more.

Mama must have read my thoughts for she said, "You know what Betty did once? Joe-Sam was a newborn . . . Betty was there for all my births . . . but anyway, Joe-Sam woke up for a feeding, and I was so tired . . ."

"Where was Daddy?" I asked, knowing the answer.

"Who knows? Recruiting, I'm sure. Anyway, Betty came into the room and said, 'Sally, you sleep, honey. I'll feed him.' God, I was so grateful, and when I looked up to see her sitting in the rocking chair feeding him, you know what else she was doing?"

"What?"

"She was eating a big chicken leg. I thought it was the funniest thing. She had Joe-Sam on her lap, and his bottle in one hand and a big chicken leg in the other."

I smiled, thinking of Aunt Betty enjoying her chicken leg. "Sounds like she was more a night person," I said.

"Hell, I guess she was," Mama retorted. "Since she didn't get out of bed until afternoon most days. At night, my sister came alive."

I put my head on her shoulder as she began to play again. I recognized Mozart.


A month after Peter's death, Daddy drove the Gold Duster to Knoxville from Nashville after a long recruiting trip. He handed me the keys, and told me to go put gas in it even though I only had my learner's permit. I sat in the front seat alone, waiting for a sign, a voice. Finally, I reached underneath the driver's seat, and just as Mick had promised, I found my journal. After each of my entries, Peter had written something. A comment, a phrase, but his pain was evident in his responses. After the one about Kathleen's perfection, he wrote, *Love your best friend, Liz, but don't worship her. She will love you more for not adoring her. Adoration is hard to keep up. I've tried for too long, trying to be the adored one. What I really am would tear the family apart, and I love everyone too much to do that. Anyhow, it's too painful to keep it all perfect. To pretend. Whatever you do, keep writing. Promise. I want to say so much more, but my mind is off these days.*

# Beam and Stream

\* \* \*

I didn't read all the entries at once. I wanted to savor them, reading them one by one over the months to make Peter last longer. I grew used to driving his Gold Duster. The muffler fell off after three months, and then one of the front seats collapsed, but it got me around Knoxville. Sometimes I pretended Peter was riding along with me in the car. I pointed out things to him, or I asked him questions. I played all his 8-track tapes full volume: Steely Dan, Chicago, the Beatles, and more than anything else, "Proud Mary" by Tina Turner or Creedence Clearwater Revival. Mama claimed that with the loud music and no muffler, she could hear me coming from miles away.

# BIG FIGHT AND A FROZEN DOG FUNERAL

*"Tackling"*

**In a ball game, we tackle any way we can to get the
BALL CARRIER down. Nothing sets the tempo like a good, sharp hit, and
gang tackling. Be under control and cocked. Get close. Put face in opponent's
numbers. Explode up and through the ball carrier. Use your whole
body to pop him. Grab anything you can get hold of.
Wrap him up and continue to run through him.**

I hated my strident, fishwife voice, which I trumpeted several times
a day at home, but it seemed I had no place to shelve my growing anger
after the funeral. I kept it swallowed at school, gracing strangers with blank
smiles, but in our house, I was a shrew, lashing out toward everyone.

Everyone except Peaches. I decided to become a better big sister to
her. I was certainly no saint by any stretch of the imagination, but I didn't
turn into Angela anymore, nor did I terrorize her on our walks together.
She was getting to be fun to talk to because, in spite of her girly-girl ways,
she was an excellent listener.

"My hair looks like shit," I told her, getting out the ingredients to
bake cookies.

"You should grow it long," she declared. "You've had a pixie forever. Your teeth look pretty now since the dentist fixed them. It's time to pay attention to your hair."

"Really?" I asked, while my old resentments thought, *Hey, I'm almost seventeen, you're ten. What do you know anyway?* But I knew she knew style. She studied the girls on shampoo commercials with an eagle eye for detail.

"Lizzie, I have a favor to ask." She popped her knuckles rhythmically.

"What?"

"Can I be your maid of honor when you get married?"

"No, of course not," I told her. "Now grease the pan."

"I always have to grease the pan. Why can't I be your maid of honor?"

"Because Kathleen will be. That is, if I ever get married. I doubt I will."

"Rats. I wanted to wear the prettiest dress." She slapped a hunk of shortening down on the cookie sheet, rubbing it in swirls.

"But in case I do, Peaches," I explained, "Kathleen has to be my maid of honor because she's my only best friend." I watched the corners of her mouth curl down. "Uh . . . look . . . you can be one of the bridesmaids." I threw that in as an afterthought.

"Kathleen may be your only best friend, but I'm your only sister," she retorted.

"Well, I know that," I replied, even though it hadn't actually occurred to me. She did have a point. *Could Peaches actually be right?*

"I'll think about it, Peaches, I promise." I watched her pick the Crisco out of her nails. "Do you want to crack the eggs, honey?"

"Can I?" She got all excited.

"Sure," I said, handing her the carton.

"You're going to be my maid of honor," she sighed, cracking four eggs into the batter. "I don't care how many best friends I have."

"Really? Why?" I asked.

"Because you're my sister," she laughed, hugging me with her buttery fingers. Where did her love come from after all the torture I'd put her through?

I began taking my sister to the library on Saturday afternoons, afterward crossing Kingston Pike to go to Arby's, each of us carrying about seven books each, to eat a roast beef sandwich and a cherry turnover. She read everything I instructed her to, since she knew I had excellent taste in books for girls her age. I read *A Tree Grows in Brooklyn* out loud to her, and *Harriet the Spy,* and we began reciting the parts of Blanche and Stella in *A Streetcar Named Desire* for I was just beginning to discover plays. Peaches was dying to play Blanche, but the part belonged to me, so she patiently read the lines of Stella, the loving sister.

Occasionally, I tested the waters by broaching the subject of Peter with her, but she consistently clammed up. I knew she was thinking about him, too, but I didn't force her to bare her soul. I didn't want to make Peaches obsess about Peter. I had railroaded her into doing so much else for my good, and I knew he would have hated me doing that. I let his death build up alone inside my heart and head. There were days when I automatically went to write him, forgetting. Then I would read one of his answers in the journal to ease my grief.

> *Dear Liz,*
>
> *What makes you think I'm living the high life at Notre Dame? I think many people's lives look good to those who aren't living them. Just remember, perfection doesn't exist anywhere. As for your escape from football, don't come to Notre Dame if that's your heart's desire. Football is huge here. Do you know what typical art students do? They use their Student Activities Book to get their free season tickets, and then they sell the book of tickets for two three hundred dollars. That way they can use the money to buy more art supplies. I guess I'm not a "typical" art student, since I've never missed a game. I suppose it's because all my friends know my brother is a coach and I'm expected to be there, but I wish, just once, I'd sold my tickets to get more art supplies. I have plenty . . . it's not that . . . but I just like the idea of it. You know? Anyway, don't think you're the only one who doesn't care about football. And whatever you do in*

*your life, rebel. It's good for the soul. I'm still trying to figure how to do it. I'll write more later.*

Rebel. The word stuck in my brain. When I passed my driver's test and was officially registered as the sole driver of the Gold Duster, Mama was freed up from her role as the family chauffeur after more than a decade of carpool hell. From then on, I drove everyone to school, to football practice, to ballet—all over the place. I loved the freedom of open-road driving, chatting with the phantom Peter if I was alone, complemented by the pulsing decibels of Harry Chapin or Fleetwood Mac. I also welcomed the rush of this responsibility because it got me the hell out of the kitchen.

The only chink in the armor of the new routine was the battle to get everyone to school on time. With Mama teaching music at a new private school and Daddy at the football office, it was up to me to get everyone up and dressed and out the door. Peaches dawdled, but at least she paced herself. The boys, on the other hand, moved in slow motion: Leo because he didn't give one flip about being on time, and Joe-Sam because he stood forever in front of the mirror, combing his hair over and over, studying the effect. He spent hours in the bathroom, grooming himself, checking for whiskers, of which he had none. I already had seven secret chin whiskers of my own that I plucked out religiously. It wasn't fair.

As the weeks passed, both boys became my nemeses in different ways. I tried everything to get Leo out the door with Peaches, but he refused to budge, lagging over cereal, unable to locate his socks. When Leo was finally in the car, I'd go after Joe-Sam in the bathroom, who'd look at me with sleepy eyes, grin, and murmur, "Hey. Chill." Then he'd saunter out of the house in his tight uniform pants, a studly, practiced stroll. He made me sick.

One morning, with everyone finally ready to go in the Gold Duster, Joe-Sam snoozing in the back for his beauty sleep, Peaches studying her lines for a role as Juliet, Leo scowled at me as I frantically sped out of our subdivision, squealing tires.

"Just drive me up the hill to the church, man, when we get there. I gotta serve mass today," he snarled.

I ignored him, flooring it over Middlebrook Pike to get to Holy Ghost.

"Could you roll up your window, Liz? I'm in a wind tunnel back here." Joe-Sam cracked open one eye.

"Forget it, Joe-Sam, I'm boiling. And the answer is, no, Leo, no."

"Just do it. You won't be late," Leo wheedled, poking his finger into my arm.

"It's one minute to eight, Leo. I have to be at school in five minutes."

"Joe-Sam doesn't get detention if he's late," he shrilled.

"That's because the football coach teaches his first-period class," I fumed.

"They're not going to give you detention. It's not going to take you one more second to drive me up to the church."

"Get out of the car!" I squealed up to the curb.

Peaches jumped out, running up the hill, calling, "Romeo, Romeo, wherefore art thou Romeo," while Leo leisurely opened the passenger door.

"Hurry up," I foamed, hoping it was possible for a sixteen-year-old to have a heart attack, proof of the agony I was put through each day.

"I'm going, I'm going." He pushed the door open as wide as he could.

"GET OUT!!" I became a hag, a crone.

"Don't get your panties in a wad," he grinned, sliding out but not shutting the door behind him.

"SHUT THE DOOR."

"No way!" He lollygagged up the hill in order to watch me fume, altar-boy outfit flapping behind him.

I hurled my body across the seat to close the door, but it was swung so far out, I couldn't reach it. Joe-Sam couldn't reach it from the backseat, nor did he bother to try. Raging, I climbed out of the Gold Duster to go around the car, slamming the passenger door shut myself. As I stormed back to the driver's seat, I heard a voice hail across the Holy Ghost parking lot, "HAVE A SUCKY DAY, YOU QUEER. . . ."

I entertained the fantasy of roaring after him in my Gold Duster until he disappeared beneath the wheels, but then Joe-Sam spoke up. "Can you adjust the rearview mirror so I can see myself a second?" I roared off to Tennessee Catholic, ignoring Cary Grant in the backseat.

Tension also continued to escalate between Joe-Sam and me. Perhaps it had something to do with his trying to be such a "man." Nearly every girl in school came up to me at one time or another to coo about what a "cute butt" my brother had. How was I supposed to respond to that? In grade school, they'd inquired about my cute brother; now we were on to his "cute" butt. What was next?

When Cute Butt wasn't playing football or lifting weights, he was in the living room doing strange Elvis Presley and John Travolta imitations. He dragged a full-length mirror into the living room to watch himself convulse across the shag rag, flexing his biceps with admiration. He also used Mama's mascara to make sideburns, continuing to perform Travolta dancing long after the *Saturday Night Fever* craze was out of style. Mama, Peaches, and Leo slipped on their "boogie shoes" with him, and so the four of them were often wiggling it to the *Saturday Night Fever* soundtrack.

Joe-Sam and I also had an ongoing feud over our new puppy, Halfback, the son of purebred Bear Bryant and a mutt named Trixie. Even though both dogs had fleas, Joe-Sam kicked Halfback out of the house, while Bear Bryant stayed in like a king. Every time Joe-Sam tossed Halfback out, I'd let him back inside. We'd go round and round about it, arguing wildly about treating both dogs fairly, but Joe-Sam didn't care about fair. He just hated the fleas attacking his legs. He had even begun taping garbage bags to them when he went to bed at night so the fleas couldn't bite him and mar his hairy legs with bulging muscles.

One evening, when he tossed Halfback out into the front yard for the millionth time, I immediately let him back inside.

"Keep that fucking mutt outside," he yelled, meeting me at the door.

"No, it's not fair to him."

"I'm allergic to his fleas. Look at my legs."

I didn't give a crap about his legs. Or his hair. Or his cute butt.

It wasn't a fight that built. It mushroomed like a nuclear explosion.

*"He's staying inside."* Then I threw the first blow, dragging my fingernails down his neck, but I also seemed to step out of my skin, watching my maniacal self wreak havoc on the household.

Peaches cried, "Don't hurt him, Liz," but I continued swinging, while Leo demanded, "Deck her, Joe-Sam."

As I took nail-digging swipes at Joe-Sam's face, Peaches and Leo ran upstairs to find Mama, who was already flying down the steps to break it up. She jumped between us—"What is happening?"—but her words meant nothing. I was a demon, going for the kill, pummeling the crap out of the hotshot football player. I had slaved my entire life, but all this Adonis had to do was show up and be admired. I jabbed him; he kept backing up as I whaled, and scratched, round and round the house. The more he pushed me off, the more I came at him, going for his face. The part of me that was watching noticed he wasn't punching back, but the other part of me was out for blood.

Mama followed, hovering at a safe distance, "Stop this right now. Or I'll call your father and have him come home this second. I mean it! I damn well mean it!"

Laying another bash into Joe-Sam, I hissed, "Go fuck yourself, old lady."

Her voice hit the ceiling. "How dare you!"

Her shock and horror thrilled me; the adrenaline rushed. I was in a fight to the finish. Mama tried to push the phone into my hands, informing me, "Your father wants to speak to you! They have called him from the practice field! I told them it was an emergency! Your father wants to speak to you right now!!!"

I ripped the phone from her hands and winged it across the room, watching it land, splat, in the dog's water. Then I lunged for the old metal coffeepot off the stove, full of cold coffee and grounds, and hurled it against the wall. Coffee and black grounds dribbled down the pumpkin-colored wallpaper.

Mama ran out of the kitchen away from me, yelling, "You crazy person . . . Do you hear me? I am your mother, and I am telling you right now that this will cease. . . ."

As I headed for Joe-Sam again, he ducked, yelping, "Help. She's a lune."

I amazed myself at my pure brutality. Who was this person? As I flung myself at Joe-Sam, knocking him to the linoleum, he still wasn't hitting back. Then I looked at his red face—no anger, just fear, tears, nicks, and gashes. The fight washed out of me, spent. I quit, rolling off him.

Mama sidled back in the room, "Nuts. Absolutely nuts." She picked the dripping phone out of the dog water, wiping it dry before hanging it back up. She got out some rubbing alcohol for Joe-Sam, who hobbled to the kitchen table. Peaches and Leo crept back into the room, silent. No one in our family had ever defied a parent with such absolute abandon. I whispered, "I was sick of him acting like Sylvester Stallone on a disco fever high. He thinks he's God's gift to women."

Joe-Sam stared at me with a mixture of surprise and respect, before he whimpered, "It's not just my legs, Liz. I got fleas, I really do."

Mama's voice sounded high and far away. "You're lucky he didn't hit you. I swear to God I would have decked you one good if you'd come after me like that."

What was there to say? I thought about it, staring down at my wounded brother with the fleas. He should have hit me, but he didn't. He just kept pushing me back, blocking my blows to his head. In the past, he would have come back at me full-throttle. A fight was a fight to him, no matter what.

"Why didn't you hit me back?" I asked him.

"You're my sister, Liz, and men don't hit girls." He slowly extended his hand to shake mine. We shook, truce.

Mama started crying. "Aren't you the sweetest boy? Your brother is so good."

"I know, Mama." I gulped water straight from the faucet, I was so thirsty.

When Daddy called back a minute later, the receiver spit fuzzy sounds from landing in the water. "Well, did you two sumbitches work it out?" he laughed.

"We did," I spoke warily.

"Good. You obviously needed to get that out, so you did. Now forget about it."

"Daddy, I have something to tell you. Peter was gay."

"What the hell are you talking about?"

"He was gay. That's why he killed himself. I thought you should know. Just in case one of your children decides he or she is gay one day, too."

"I gotta play the Bulldogs on Saturday. I don't need this bullshit." He hung up.

As I replaced the phone in its cradle, Mama whispered, "That was cruel."

"Well, how else am I supposed to tell him? He's never here."

"It's his brother, Liz."

"I'm sick of never talking about things."

Mama sat down heavily at the table, sticking Band-Aids on Joe-Sam's wounds. "You know," she sighed after a moment, "I always thought Peter was gay too."

We were all dumbfounded at this calm and incredible revelation.

"You did?" I asked finally.

"It's not the kind of thing you can ask, but I do believe you." She looked weary.

"What's gay?" asked Peaches.

"You're too young to understand," Leo told her.

"No, I'm not," she yelled. "What's gay?"

"He was gay?" Joe-Sam wiped the blood from his neck.

"What's gay?" Peaches screamed. "Dammit." We stared at her in disbelief.

Mama reached out to hug Peaches. "Well, sugar, 'gay' can mean 'happy.' "

"It means Peter liked guys," I interrupted her.

"I like guys," she answered, confused.

"He likes them the way Joe-Sam likes girls. Get it? Like instead of a girlfriend, Peter had a boyfriend."

"Ooooohhhh." Peaches nodded her head, fearful.

"Do you understand?" I asked.

"Yes, but I don't want to talk about it." She got up. "I'm going to go play in my room for a little while," she added, before creeping upstairs.

"She's too young for all this mess." Mama got up to start supper.

"She should know the truth."

"Well, Liz, I've had about enough truth for one evening. The truth is it's time for supper, and that's about all the truth I can handle at the moment."

I let it go, tossing down napkins, plates, and silverware, aware a small miracle had occurred. Joe-Sam studied his face for scars, Leo poured the milk into glasses, and Mama swallowed three aspirin.


Kathleen and I met by our lockers after school the next afternoon. I had whispered the fight to her earlier. Her eyes grew wide as I filled in the details.

"Way to go. You needed that." She hugged me tightly.

"Guess I did."

As Joe-Sam strolled up, she kissed his cheek—"How you doing, buddy?"—not mentioning the brawl. He glanced at her appreciatively. I noticed he'd pulled up his uniform shirt and tie, as high as he could, to cover the scratches on his neck.

"I'm sorry. I'm really sorry," I whispered.

He smiled, forgiving me, shaking his head in wonder.

"Did you tell anyone?" I asked, suddenly thinking, *I'm a Y-Teen. What kind of Y-Teen viciously attacks her brother that way? I give talks on Catholic womanhood, and I've been elected to the student council. I know it's all kind of petty, but it would be mortifying if the truth got leaked to anyone at Tennessee Catholic.*

Joe-Sam threw some books at the bottom of his locker, "I didn't tell anybody anything. You think I want guys going around saying my older sister can lick the crap out of me? I got my pride, Liz. Understand?"

"So you said nothing to anyone?"

"Well, I told my coach that I was holding a cat and a dog chased me."

Kathleen got tickled at that, and the three of us were still laughing as we climbed in Peter's Gold Duster to go home.

Right after the brawl, Bear Bryant died of heartworms. Talk about deaths in the family. It was like he was saying, "Keep fleabitten Halfback; my turn's up. No more fighting about it."

Mother woke me up early the day of Bear Bryant's funeral, urging, "Come on, Liz. Let's you and me go get him."

The day we'd found him stiff in the wood chips, we couldn't think clearly, so we drove him to the vet, even though he was already dead. When we decided to bury him in the backyard, we had to go back to the vet and get him. The vet told us to wait in the waiting room while his assistant put Bear Bryant in the trunk of our car. As Mama and I stood around inside, watching people bring in their living pets, it soon got to be too much for her, so we went outside. That was when Mama noticed the large freezer and the vet's assistant trying to lift something out of it. A pair of rigid black paws appeared.

Mama cried, "My God, is that where they've got him?"

"Don't look." I tried to shield her view.

The boy was struggling with Bear Bryant, halfway out, when he slipped. There was this dull thud as Bear Bryant hit the bottom of the freezer.

"Do you want some help?" Mama wept.

"No, ma'am, I can do this," the boy answered cordially, climbing inside the freezer where he was able to get more leverage by shoving Bear Bryant up over the side. The poor frozen dog bounced once as he hit the ground.

The boy hopped out of the freezer, hoisting him into our trunk. "Guess I'm getting my exercise today, ma'am," he grinned.

"There's a blanket inside the trunk. Cover him up good."

"Yes, ma'am," he said.

She shuddered. "I just gotta keep reminding myself that it's not him anymore. He's in heaven, right?"

When we got Bear Bryant home, the kids were still sleeping, which really upset Mama. How could the clods just sleep?

"Have some feeling, for God's sakes," she said. "We are going to bury our beloved dog today. If y'all want to be a part of it, get your lazy ass out of bed."

Mary Martha, Buster, and Beth arrived with their dog, Hobo, and Kathleen showed up with her new Chinese pug, Saint Mark, for the funeral in our backyard.

"He loved his ears being scratched," Mama smiled. "His ears still feel the same." Then, at her request, we said the rosary and sang "Be Not Afraid."

Joe-Sam and Leo stuck Bear Bryant in the grave. The two of them had been up late digging it the night before. It wasn't a very good one, but maybe that was because the yard was on kind of a slant. Part of the grave was deep, the other part shallow. We covered him up as best as we could, but his back paws still nosed out of the soil. As Peaches put flowers on the grave, we cried our hearts out. I think we cried all the tears we couldn't when Peter died. Somehow Peter and Bear Bryant got mixed up together in a sorrow that just wouldn't quit.

The afternoon we buried Bear Bryant, we had a visitor stop by. She arrived in a tangerine Cadillac. As she stepped out, she called, "Howdy, y'all, my name is Joetta Falcon of Tangerine Realty."

"Hey," smiled Joe-Sam, since Joetta wore a tight tangerine top of soft popcorn material, revealing large bouncy boobs.

"What can I do for you?" Mama asked.

"Well, I know you coaching families are in the business of moving a lot, so I wanted to offer you my card. Since the Fighting Game Cocks didn't have a very good season, well, just in case . . . keep me in mind."

"We'll do that." Mama's voice was frigid.

Joetta glanced around, her gaze landing on the cross and flowers in the backyard. "My, my, look at that pretty spot. What's all that for?"

Peaches said, "Our dog, Bear Bryant, died. We had the funeral this morning."

Joetta stared at us, looked at the grave, and back at us again, before answering, "Well, I'm real sorry to hear that. What kinda dog was he?"

"Lab," answered Joe-Sam confidently, squaring his shoulders. "Black Lab."

"They're full of sugar," Joetta answered.

"Is there anything else we can help with, Joetta?" Mama wanted her gone. "As far as I know, we're not moving this year."

"Here's a hint, anyway. Free of charge. It's a real pretty grave and everything, but you might want to consider taking that cross down, just for whenever people come to look at the house. That is, if you do decide to put it on the market in the next year or so."

"We'll keep that in mind." Mama was about to shut the door in her face, but Joetta stuck her tangerine-heeled shoe inside.

"I mean, y'all don't have to," she gushed nervously, sensing she'd lost any hope of being our Realtor. "It's just something for y'all to think about. Okay? Y'all are just so sweet the way you loved your dawg. You're just sweet."

# PRAISE THE LORD

*"The Chapel Program"*

**The purpose of the Game Cock Chapel Program
is to make a spiritual investment into the life of each player
that will in turn improve the character of the team. The focus of the Chapel
Program is on Jesus Christ, the God-Man, and Savior of the World. A life in
Christ is the ultimate lifestyle and will produce quality living. The Christian
principles taught in each chapel service and Bible study will assist
each player in the areas of spirituality, character, personal
dignity, courage, confidence, endurance, motivation, family
enrichment, and maturity. The overall Chapel Program
is designed to make the team more successful in life.**

During my junior year, two significant events occurred simultane-
ously: Coach Donny Mac decided to part ways with Daddy and the other
assistant coaches, and Kathleen stood me up several times in a row. Daddy
refused to elaborate on what had happened with Coach Mac or on his
future football plans, only that he was going to have to start sending out
résumés to other university and professional teams.

Knowing football the way I did, I figured out that Coach Donny Mac
was under formidable pressure to succeed at his alma mater, petrified of

following in the footsteps of his predecessor, who'd had moving vans and exterminators sent to his house by rabid Game Cock fans who wanted his ass fired. From my vantage point, Coach Donny Mac dumping the men he'd coached with for years seemed to be his weak-kneed solution to the creation of another National Championship football team.

I was not particularly upset by Coach Mac's decisions, because I'd already warned Daddy in Pittsburgh that I wouldn't be moving again, and because I was in the process of divorcing myself from football permanently. I rarely attended the games anymore, neither Joe-Sam's nor Leo's nor Daddy's. I told myself that I respected Coach Mac and Daddy for doing whatever they had to do but, as far as I was concerned, I'd done my duty as a coach's daughter. At the age of seventeen, enough was enough.

"Do you miss not seeing Mary Martha?" I asked Mama early one evening as we sat sipping coffee, reading the paper, realizing it had been months since we'd seen the Macs socially: no barbecues, no breakfasts at the training table, no Sunday picnics.

"Yes, I do," Mama replied a bit wistfully. "But I love teaching. As boring as Knoxville is compared to Pittsburgh, at least I found music again."

"Is that why you're not hanging out with the *coacheswives* as much?"

"I suppose so. Besides, music takes my mind off football and losing seasons."

"You think we're going to move, don't you?"

"I know we are, and so do you." She rubbed her forehead.

"I'm a junior in high school, you know," I replied after a few seconds.

"I'm aware of your age, honey," she sighed, reading a headline in the paper about Donny Mac's plans for new coaches.

"I'm also not moving my senior year. Are you aware of that?"

"Well, I hope you have a place to live if it comes to that, but the last thing I want is for you to have to move your senior year."

"Do you mean that?"

"We'll do our best to figure out a way for you to finish here. Okay? By the way, where would you live if we moved?"

"With Kathleen, of course."

"I see," Mama hummed, knowing the routine of Kathleen's broken promises.

Peaches skipped into the room, announcing, "Kathleen's going to be Liz's maid of honor, right, Liz?"

"Would you be quiet?" I snapped.

"You told me a long time ago." Peaches stood with her hands on hips. "Unless you changed your mind and you want me? I'm still available, you know."

"My, my. When's the wedding?" Mama smiled.

"Mama, we were only talking *hypothetically*," I assured her, tying on my uniform skirt for my new job out at the South Knoxville Dinner Theater. It was my job to pour sweet tea and dish up the bacon-sizzled vegetables and slabs of roast beef to the "blue-hairs" who enjoyed watching anything by Neil Simon, plus musicals like *Oklahoma!, Annie Get Your Gun,* and *South Pacific,* after a hearty supper. I often spied on the green-room where the actors played gin rummy before their entrances, listening to them talk, so I felt hip to know the theatrical lingo. For instance, when *Macbeth* opened at the university, I knew to refer to it as that "Scottish play" whenever inside the hallowed walls of the theater. As I stood grinning from my serving post, dishing up heavy food, watching all the action and drama go on without me, I longed to write plays of my own. I wanted the actors to speak my lines, to bring my stories to life with real sets, lights, and props. Someday.

Kathleen did not offer any explanations for her behavior, except to gush apologies with such passion that it was hard to believe that she'd ever pull the same crap again . . . until she did. Kathleen's continued string of broken promises stung a lot more than the threat of Donny Mac firing Daddy, but I never showed the extent of my pain to her, still not wanting to risk our friendship. I did my best not to adore her, as Peter had instructed me, but I still let her get away with murder. I used to watch in amazement as she'd say yes to five different people (one right after another), to five contrary plans on the same night, rather than tell any one of them no. People learned not to expect her to show up or keep her word, so when she actually came through, it was a miraculous surprise, and she was welcomed with open arms by everyone.

*"Kathleen's here, everybody. By God, Lazarus rose too. No kidding? Alleluia."*

The only time she ever said no was when she was getting paid a compliment, in which case, she'd blush, protesting, "No way, I'm not a good dancer, you're crazy," even though she was one of the best in Knoxville. She always received an honorable mention at the Junior Miss contests down at the Knoxville Coliseum or Bijou Theater.

We used to laugh about it together, her habit of breaking promises, until she began doing it to me. The first time it occurred, I was stunned. I was positive that I was different from other people: Never would she blow me off like she did them.

After the first few times, I said, "Kathleen, if you can't make it Friday, just tell me."

"I'll be there, swear to God, our Mother in Heaven." She crossed her heart, repeating her usual promise that she came up with awhile back, after she decided God was a woman.

"I'm not mad at you"—I struggled to be offhand—"but you can tell me the truth."

"I am so so so so sooooooo sorry about all the other times," she interrupted. "I'm going to stop making promises that I can't keep."

I said nothing, letting the silence speak for itself.

"I really am," her voice rose. "That's going to be my New Year's resolution."

"Um, sure, whatever," I responded like the spineless feeb I was. To my sick horror, I realized I was becoming the jilted lover. Her actions were shoving me into that role. I desperately wanted to believe her each time, yet knew I should stop trusting her; but the ties between us kept twisting us together.

We had our first double date with two brothers, Mark and Matt, who took us to a Y-Teen formal and on the way home skidded 360s for us in the Cas Walker parking lot in their station wagon. Before they dropped us off at my house, they kissed us good night, ramming their tongues down our throats. As they sped off out of the subdivision, she and I held hands, gagging in disgust, mortified.

"What did Matt's kiss taste like?" She elbowed me.

"Sangria," I shuddered.

"That's better than Mark's . . . I got ketchup," she laughed.

"Ew!" I shivered.

"Come on, let's rack em up," she announced, as I followed her into our rec room, where she began scooping pool balls out of the pockets.

"Did y'all have a good time?" Mama's voice called from upstairs.

"It was great," Kathleen answered.

"Good. Now don't stay up too late," Mama sighed. "And if you get anything to eat, clean up the dishes."

"We will, Mrs. Donegal. Good night," Kathleen sang, yanking off her mauve formal, flinging it over the rattan furniture, as I threw my sky-blue one with spaghetti straps in the corner, glad to exchange it for a football jersey. We talked and shot pool until three in the morning, slept until noon curled up side by side in my double bed with the canopy, and together, we went to the guitar mass on campus at five-thirty. I couldn't ever get enough of her, I loved my best friend so much.

Religion continued to throw us together more than anything else. I convinced Kathleen to do one of her sacred dances for All Saints Day, which nearly brought down the gymnasium. She appeared before us like a barefoot goddess, filmy skirt over a turquoise leotard, to begin her dance to the music of Simon and Garfunkel's "Bridge Over Troubled Water." She whirled, swung, and spun in front of the altar, rendering us silent, as she extended her arms to Jesus Christ in time to the ballad. She was so utterly magical to watch that I forgave her for every broken date and promise.

She plunged herself completely into the music, swaying faster and faster, which sent her skirt flying high above her waist. I glanced around to see how others were reacting. Most of the boys tried to look serious, but from the way they shifted around on the bleachers, changing positions, elbowing each other, it was pretty obvious which part of them was *most* moved by Kathleen's sacred dancing.

After mass, one muttered, "Man, those girls' uniforms sure do hide a lot. Kathleen is one hot babe."

"Whoa. Fuckin'-A!" agreed the lunk next to him.

"I sure would like to have my own fucking sacred dance with her sometime." Guffaw, guffaw, yuck, yuck, yuck, snort.

When I later repeated their remarks to her, she twirled her rosary, gyrating her hips, snickering, "Baby. Whip it out. Bring 'em on."


Our Catholic good girls' personae fooled all the adults, including Father Haggerty, who viewed the two of us as potential candidates for sisterhood. I didn't try to dissuade him, because I enjoyed being the pseudo-religious director of the students, creating theatrical liturgies for our little school, using special effects like lighted candles and slide shows of nature to accompany songs like "I Want to Live" by John Denver.

Word also spread about Kathleen's sacred dancing, and a nunnery in Atlanta nabbed us, with the help of Father Haggerty. They even sent a holy car to Knoxville to whisk us off to a retreat at the Motherhouse. However, the Dominican Sisters definitely didn't have it in mind for me to plan any masses for them or for Kathleen to do any sacred dancing, but to spend the weekend, instead, exploring the mystery of Jesus Christ. I didn't mind going in the least, because I had Kathleen all to myself. Kathleen and I had to sign up for a time to keep an eye on the Eucharist in the middle of the night. It was pretty exciting, sneaking down from our virgin metal beds to baby-sit "Jesus Christ" up there on the altar. Some nun with a walker crept along the hallway, following one of the many brisk sisters who kept the chalices polished for the priests. We sat there in the smooth darkness of the pews, smelling the candle-wax drippings, waiting for Jesus Christ to do something, but He never did. We'd both been crammed full of miracle stories about how the Holy Ghost might fly down and pat you on the cheek if you sat real still, but nothing like that ever happened. One night, after we slipped off to the bathroom to talk, I heard her yelp from the stall next to mine.

"Gross. I dropped my crucifix necklace in my pee. How am I going to get it out?"

"Just reach in and get it."

"I can't put my hand in it. That's sick."

"Here, open the door. I've got a hanger," I said laughing, as she let me in. Together we dragged the hanger across the bottom of the toilet to hook the crucifix, but we couldn't catch it. Suddenly the bathroom door flew open, and one of the postulants marched in.

"You're both making too much noise. What's the problem?"

We were struck dumb; I flamed red, while Kathleen pointed to the toilet. The postulant peered in, noting the crucifix at the bottom of the bowl. She stuck her hand right in, picked out the tiny cross, handing it to Kathleen.

"Thank you," whispered Kathleen, holding the cross in her hand.

The postulant eyed us severely, saying, "If it's your time to be watching the Eucharist, you should be in the chapel or else go back to bed."

"Yes, Sister!" we nearly shouted, standing up straight.

She gave us one more look before breezing out without even washing her hands. We were in shock.


After the Dominican House in Atlanta, Father Haggerty chose us to be leaders at Quest, another religious retreat, not for potential nuns but for committed Catholic teens, held in the new gym at Holy Ghost where Peaches and Leo still attended school. Quest signified a weekend of teenagers seeking Jesus Christ without wearing a watch, so time would be irrelevant in their search for grace. Communication games were played, "Praise the Lord" banners were glued together for Sunday mass, and we leaders delivered talks on the meaning of faith in God.

It was essential that our talks reveal some personal tragedy, exaggerated or not, and they had to end with rousing tearjerkers from John Denver or Neil Diamond's album about Richard Bach's *Jonathan Livingston Seagull*.

With Peter and Betty, I had built-in tragedy to spare and learned to use my experiences to reduce the entire gym to tears. I had a gift for that. My evil Angela days behind me, this drama inside me found a new outlet. I still wasn't popular, but I could make a hundred teenagers cry at once. In front of a crowd, I found myself emerging into the gentle side of Angela, reaching out to the lonely, molding them into my way of thinking at a retreat. It was a sick high, and I loved it.

During the retreats, Kathleen expanded her sacred dancing repertoire to songs like "Sunshine on My Shoulders," "May the Lord Be Good to You," and "Gentle Woman." Late on Saturday night of the retreat, we also blindfolded little groups of Questers, leading them on a trust walk around the gymnasium, through the playground, until they ended up at the candlelit altar of the smiling Jesus portrait. It was rigged up to be a kind of spiritual surprise party for them: to have their blindfolds lifted, finding themselves at the altar with the Almighty grinning at them at midnight. At the end of the weekend, all the retreaters had to open love letters from their parents, and they sobbed reading them, clinging to each other in a kind of euphoric haze of no sleep, Jesus Christ, and eternal friendship.

The parents' letters were designed essentially to be the capper, but when I made my first quest as just a participant, Mama sent my letter with Leo to school, instructing him to give it to Father Haggerty to give to me. Of course, he lost it, so I never received my parental eulogy of love on what a great offspring I was. Later, Mama tried to make a joke out of it, but it pissed me off, so I made sure Joe-Sam got a real letter to read from them when he made Quest the following year.

Whenever it seemed like Kathleen and I were securely back on the best-friend track, blessed by God and respected by all, something else would happen. The clincher occurred when she went to Myrtle Beach with the clique for Thanksgiving, without breathing a word to me. When she returned tanned and glowing, more a part of them than ever, I asked her, "Why? Why didn't you tell me?"

Her voice oozed concern, as she lamented, "Geez, Liz, you know, I just didn't want you to feel hurt. Okay? Dang it. I love you. You're my best friend, and I just didn't want you to feel sad, especially after all you went through with Peter."

I was headed out to the field behind the school to hit balls for fifth period, since Daddy had taught me to golf the previous summer and loved my powerful swing so much he persuaded Father Haggerty that I had the potential of LPGA pros. He was so excited about my future as a golfer that he convinced me I needed driving practice way more than I needed French III if I was going to be the next Nancy Lopez.

"Oh . . ." I said to her, yanking my golf clubs and shag-bag out of my locker. "I'll see you later," I mumbled, moving past, but she stopped me.

"You know, it wasn't fun at all. It was boring, Liz. Even the water was cold," she sighed, taking her art supplies out of her backpack.

"Too bad." I headed down the steps, banging the golf bag on my back. She followed me to the bottom, where I sat down to put on my golf shoes.

"So gosh, how was your Thanksgiving, Lizzie? Did you go to Gatlinburg with the Macs like last year with the football team? You are so so so lucky to be around that many gorgeous football players. What hunks. Even if some are only this big," she cackled, stretching out her pinkie.

"Kathleen"—I jerked the laces of the cleats hard, suddenly sick of her humor—"my father is getting fired after the Copper Bowl, and you're changing the subject."

"Am I?"

"Yes. Tell me about Myrtle Beach. I want to hear about *your* Thanksgiving."

"It was nothing. The guys were boring too."

"Oh, so guys went? Why wasn't I invited?"

"I'm sure they just forgot. Mary Jo, Patsy, Samantha, and Ellie, they're all really sweet and nice and religious. They just forgot. They really like you. They can't believe how many books you've read."

"That's such fucking bullshit, Kathleen."

"God, Liz, I didn't ask them why they didn't ask you. It's not the kind of thing you can ask." She grabbed my arm. "I brought you back a present."

"Oh?"

"A Praise-the-Lord pin and a Peppermint Pattie." She thrust the gifts at me.

"Thanks. Whore," I said, meaning it this time. I wanted to smash the stupid presents in her face, but I held them tightly in my hand.

"Praise the Lord. You slut," she hissed, before ducking off to art class.

I hit several balls high into the air, feeling my body loosening into the swing. *Back to the hole, front to the hole.* When I took my first drive, I saw her face on the ball. I hit the Spalding two hundred yards.


I began showing up places alone, and people never failed to ask me where Kathleen was, but I always made up a cheerfully elaborate lie of her distinct location. *She's helping her grandmother who's incredibly ill go to mass for the last time. Oh, she's working triple shifts at Casa's restaurant out on Kingston Pike, and it's really tough, but she's saving her money to study dance therapy in college or move to Broadway and become a star. She's busy writing pen-pal letters to a prisoner on death row.* The last excuse, in fact, wasn't a lie at all. She really did write regularly to a prisoner on death row in Alabama and only abruptly quit when he requested that she enclose some pubic hair in her next letter to him. She ditched him cold after that solicitation, and instead chose to do volunteer work on the cancer ward at St. Mary's every other Saturday.

Anyway, with such an array of truths and fabrications, I knew no one would ever surmise our friendship was toppling toward the brink of disaster. If only Kathleen had been my boyfriend, the rules would have been more clear-cut. I could have just said, "Hey, we broke up," but she was my best friend, and nobody officially "broke up" with best friends. Plus, she really did have a social conscience, so how could I complain about getting the shaft when she was spending some of her extra hours with the truly needy of Knoxville. I couldn't compete with Kathleen's love for the most popular girls in the class, much less a cancer patient, so I kept quiet and was grateful for the crumbs of affection she tossed my way.

I began to wonder if Peter had broken up with Mick O'Doherty, or if he'd even had the nerve to kiss him. I hoped he and Mick had fucked their brains out at least once, so Peter could have experienced that *supposed* joy before his death. But I really suspected that my uncle was so deeply dug into the closet that he never emerged. If he had come out to at least one person in his family, I don't believe he would have killed himself. Mick probably tried to convince him that they weren't the only homosexual couple on the planet, but Peter couldn't see past the judgment of his family or the ghost of Papa Sweetheart turning over in his macho Catholic grave at such a revelation. The thought of hurting anyone was reprehensible to Peter—what others thought and felt about him mattered more to him than his own life.

Was I gay? I didn't think so. I was crazy for Kathleen, but I found myself looking at men, not women. I did understand how self-loathing felt, though. I had plenty of that to go around. The more popular Kathleen became, the more lies she told that I accepted, the more I felt like nothing. I tried all the tricks to thwart her rejection. I thought, if I'm more loving around her, more forgiving, more apologetic, more humorous, give her no guilt, she'll stop. Nothing, however, worked. I couldn't change her. I tried to comprehend her actions, thinking . . . *If I were something, she wouldn't do it, but I must be nothing, which is why she can get away with it.* Did I ever want to kiss Kathleen? Not really. I wanted to slap her face, shake her, wake her up. I also longed to snuggle in her glorious red hair, holding her for days, begging her to be my eternal friend for life, "my Francie Nolan, my Anne Frank," my one true, bosom friend along the trail of moving so goddamn much.

I began to ache, too, for a real boyfriend, a guy with jeans, strong shoulders, messy clean hair, and white teeth, to drive me up to the Smoky Mountains and share a bottle of red wine by a rushing river. Someone who loved to read as much as I did. In my new journal, I wrote about someone who would wrap me in a blanket, kissing me so long and hard, it would erase the reality of Kathleen's weaknesses and imperfections, which I couldn't forgive her for, and who would make me stop missing Peter so much. Why couldn't it happen? I didn't look so ugly anymore, since I'd grown my hair long at Peaches's insistence. Sure, the back of my hair was tangled most days, but even I knew how to put on makeup, though I wore only a little. I was seventeen, and I wanted to live. In truth, I think what I really wanted was sex. I was getting ready to jump somebody's bones. I ached for love. The last entry from Peter in my journal tried to be of assistance in the love arena.

*Dear Liz,*

*You asked me about sex in this entry. Good God, I'm the last person to ask, plus your father would kill me if I tried to advise his daughter. Sex? Make sure you love the person. Love them well, body and soul. Don't lose your virginity (I'm blushing as I write this) for the sake of losing it, but find someone with whom you feel . . . I don't know . . . ready for this intimacy. Someone who loves you for all the things you do, not just someone who wants to get you in bed for the hell of it. (Though that can be nice.) Scratch that. What am I trying to say? Don't be afraid of love, and don't be afraid to find it in very unexpected places. And for God's sakes, don't let guilt eat you alive. My words are easy for me to give, but I don't know how to follow them. No clue. Would like to see you sometime. Would like to show you some of my books. Find out what you like. Would like to . . .*

I stared at it, willing the sentence to complete itself, but it didn't. Like Peter, his last words remained unfinished.

# CHAPTER 27

# TRUE CATHOLIC LOVE
# UNDER THE MAGNOLIAS

*"60 Counter Gap—No Penetration"*

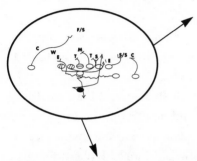

**Initially provides a misdirection read to the DEFENSE by the blocking scheme and the backfield action. The Counter Step by the BACK will misdirect the defense with enough influence to permit excellent blocking angles for the OFFENSIVE LINE at the point of attack.**

I was chipping golf balls on the practice field behind the school, when Father Haggerty walked toward me with what looked like one of his priest-wannabees for the diocese of the Nashville-Knoxville-Chattanooga region.

"Miss Donegal, this is Robert McCoy, a former Quest leader from Chattanooga who's a freshman at Tennessee."

"Hey." I shook his hand, not bothering to remove my golf glove.

"Miss Elizabeth Donegal is our resident golfer and vice president of the student council," Father Haggerty continued.

"Hi," Robert smiled, his hands folded across the back of his head, his elbows like wings. "You've got a good swing."

"Thank you," I replied, noting he had thick dark hair, which fell into his warm brown eyes. His nose was smaller than mine, but his teeth were strong and white, and he had broad shoulders. I couldn't tell if he was exactly handsome or not, but I liked his smile. It was also the way he was looking straight at me, not past me, which was utterly new in my experience. My stomach fluttered.

"Robert, now remember, I want you to at least consider Minnesota." Father Haggerty slapped him on the back. "As a seminarian you'll have your tuition and books paid for by the Diocese of Tennessee."

"I'll think about it, Father," Robert answered, never taking his eyes off me.

"Good," replied Father Haggerty, turning to walk back into the school. "Miss Donegal," he added, "I believe sixth period is about to start. Religion class, isn't it?"

"I'll be right there," I assured him, as Robert and I watched him waddle away, black robes billowing behind him. From the back, he resembled an enormous sea lion in holy vestments, treading up the steps.

"So you're going to be one of his priests?" I asked Robert, shagging my golf balls on the field. "I've heard about you seminarians."

"What have you heard?"

"That you get to go to college for free and date and live a regular life until you decide at the very last minute if the priesthood is right for you."

"What's wrong with that?"

"Nothing at all . . . except that if a girl decides to be a nun, she's a nun the second she crosses into the convent walls. Take the Dominican order? The first year postulants give up their lives entirely, wearing habits, living all shut up together, scrubbing floors and banisters. They don't have the freedom the seminarians do."

"Not all orders are as strict as the Dominican sisters."

"And how come priests take only two vows, of chastity and obedience, but nuns take three vows, of chastity, *poverty,* and obedience? I never understood that. Have you ever seen a nun driving a new Buick? Father Haggerty gets one every year."

"You sound like a feminist."

"I am."

"You can't be a feminist and a Catholic."

"Who says so?"

"It's just a known fact. And I never said I was going to be a seminarian, much less a priest. Father Haggerty would like me to, but I'm definitely not."

"Well, that's a relief," I beamed, straightening my visor, as though the winter sun was shining in my eyes.

"Why?"

"Because I'm sure you'll make some nonfeminist Catholic woman a very happy husband someday with a slew of kids. I gotta go. It was nice to meet you, Robert."

"Nice to meet you too." He looked perplexed.

I swung my golf bag onto my back, striding into the school. When I glanced back, I noticed he was still standing where I left him. I waved before dashing into sixth period, a dull religion class taught by the porkish baseball coach. The coach was talking about the seriousness of cheating, especially on a religion test. I glanced over at Kathleen, who winked at me as she guiltily ripped up a tiny cheat sheet she'd spent hours preparing.


I ran into Robert again on the campus of the university. I had a library card Daddy had gotten for me that was still valid, even though he was no longer officially a coach for the Game Cocks. On the steps to the library, I heard a voice ask, "So how's the golfing, Catholic feminist?"

I turned to see Robert coming up the steps behind me, wearing his backpack, eating an apple. "You want some?" he offered me a bite. I bit into the delicious sweetness. He was better-looking than I'd remembered, and he was a good three inches taller than me.

I smiled. "Thank you."

"So why are you at this library if you're still in high school?"

"It has a better selection."

"A reader . . . and you're the student council vice president?"

"Yeah, but only because I ran against two idiot guys; one hadn't written a speech, and the other only talked about raffle tickets. I give good speeches."

"I bet. You know, you're the first girl golfer I've ever met."

"My father wants me to play professionally," I explained. "I'm a junior, but when I graduate, he wants me to join the women's golf team at the University of Alabama, since he knows the coach." I was afraid I would never be able to stop talking.

"What do you want?"

"What do I want?" I had to stop and think, since no one had ever asked *me* that question before.

"Yeah, what do you want?" He leaned toward me, his eyes meeting mine.

"I . . . don't know. I keep thinking I should give it a shot. I mean I want to be a writer, but . . ." What I wanted was to just keep staring into those brown eyes of his.

"We should play sometime." He moved closer to me.

"Yeah, sure," I said, my heart walloping my ribs. "What sport do you do?"

"Wrestling," he grinned. "In high school anyway."

"Oh, a wrestler." My smile was getting wider, because I could imagine myself wrestling with him, him pinning me down, me pinning him down. *Good God, I had to stop right now.*

"Why are you smiling?" He seemed to read my thoughts.

"Am I?" I asked, patches of blood creeping into my face. "Well, I'd better return these books." I felt lightheaded as I walked toward the library.

"Hey, do you know a girl named Kathleen?" Robert called after me. I turned back to him. "Kathleen O'Donnell? She's my best friend."

"Well, tell her Robert said hello. I met her at a CYO camp last summer."

*Great, he wants Kathleen. I might have known. My books turned to barbells.*

"Yeah, sure, see ya," I replied, ducking inside the library. *Fine, I don't care. I'm going to get a great book that will make me forget all about the wrestler. Who needs the sow sucker? I got a lot more important things in my life. Like hell.*

★   ★   ★

After Mama finished typing my major term paper on multiple per-sonalities, inspired by the movie *Sybil,* she vowed that she was never going to type another one of her kids' papers. Ever. "Not after deciphering your scrawl. Don't the nuns teach y'all kids penmanship anymore? I used to get As for my handwriting."

She even forced me to sign up for typing, though I balked at the idea, vowing I had no intention of winding up some stupid secretary.

"Yes, of course." Her voice dripped sarcasm. "We all know that secretarial skills are beneath you."

"I just don't want to pour some guy coffee and type his letters. Okay? Is that a crime?" I retorted, knowing that the secretaries at the football office were pretty much indentured servants to the football coaches.

"Honey, you want to be a writer, don't you?" she grilled.

I waited a minute before answering, realizing it was a trick question.

"Then trust me on this one. Writers know how to type. They don't have their mothers type their stories for them, comprendo?"

"Okay, okay. I'll take typing. . . ."

Naturally, I was a horrendous typist, so I practiced every night on our antique Underwood, trying to improve my coordination without peeking at the keys, but it made me crazy. The pungent smell of correction fluid mixed with typing ribbon gave me a headache, and the "m," "k," and "s" keys always stuck to the paper.

One evening, as I was struggling to unjam the keys *again,* the phone rang, bringing me back to reality. When I answered it, Kathleen asked, "Hey, Liz? Robert McCoy just called to get your zip code."

"Did you give it to him?"

"Of course, what do you think? He's great. Everybody likes him."

"Who's everybody?"

"He was one of the leaders of the CYO camp last summer. Do you like him?"

"I've just met him twice."

"But you have to have an opinion."

"He has very thick hair."

"Look, if a guy asks for your zip code, he really really likes you. I bet he sends you something. And get this?"

"What?"

"He wants to meet us for mass on Sunday. Guitar mass. Five-thirty. I told him yes."

"Guitar mass?"

"Yes, yes, yes!" She sounded ready to hyperventilate.

"Kathleen, why are you so excited?"

"Because I think this guy is going to be your first boyfriend."

"How do you know he doesn't like you? It's very possible."

"A guy calls me up to talk only about you? Come on, it's not me he wants."

"You never know."

"He was like a brother, dang it. He did have a girlfriend, but they broke up. She's my sister's friend. I heard from her that he's an excellent kisser, among other things." Kathleen snickered a dirty chuckle. "He has the right kind of lips for it."

"I wouldn't know," I replied stiffly.

"You will, baby," she giggled. "Come on, admit it. You know you want him, twat."

"Shut up."

"I knew it. See you at guitar mass, dang it."

*Twat?* Could it be I was getting my best friend back? She sure sounded like her old self again. Could I actually have Kathleen and get a boyfriend at the same time? It all seemed too miraculous. In my imagination and longing, I figured I was pretty much ready for everything that had to do with a boyfriend, but suddenly this was way too real . . . too close . . . too physical. *My zip code? Guitar mass? The right lips? Dang it.*

When we met at the guitar mass that Sunday, Robert was with a bunch of his friends from Chattanooga. Afterward, we piled into one car to go to a deli, and I wound up having to sit on his lap. All of a sudden, I felt something stirring underneath me, and it dawned on me, *So this is what Sister Mary Josefat meant about the geometry books.* As the driver hit the brakes, I got thrown back against him, and Robert grabbed both my hands, interlocking our fingers together. It was pure white-fire heaven.

# True Catholic Love Under the Magnolias

A week later, he showed up unexpectedly at a Tennessee Catholic dance, slipping his arms around me from behind. The girls of the clique were amazed that I had a college boy interested in me. I watched them as they tripped into each other, following Kathleen around in a line dance. Robert and I weren't dancing. We were just watching the dancers, but with his arms encircling me, liquid lightning zapping back and forth between us, I thought, if I'm not careful, my brain is going to explode.

It didn't take long for me to fall hard for Robert Samuel McCoy, which made me a person truly changed for the better. I kept my mouth shut about him at home, but I couldn't stop singing and dancing, and basically coming to life. I dropped all former hints of the bossy, vile demeanor of my younger days, trying to become the perfect big sister I knew I was meant to be.

I began by driving Leo right up to the church steps every morning without so much as a single impatient word.

"What's wrong with you? Geez!" Leo inquired as I kissed him good-bye on the cheek, wishing him a wonderful day at school.

My good deeds flourished unceasingly. I bought several tubes of flea cream for Joe-Sam, and I even disco-danced with him in the living room to *"Do the Hustle."* I swore to Peaches that yellow was not the favorite color of insane people, and I taught her all the Karen Carpenter songs, plus a few Diana Ross, so we could put on our own concert just for ourselves.

As for Mama, I couldn't do enough for her either. I whipped up dinner, tornadoed through the house on a cleaning frenzy, folding towels, scrubbing the tub, and damp-mopping, not only so she'd let me take Peter's Gold Duster to visit Robert on campus but because she was my mother, and, by God, I was going to respect her for giving me life. Oh, what love could do. I even practiced my golf game more than ever to impress Daddy, which seemed to cheer him up, since he was on the phone a lot to head coaches trying to find a job.

*    *    *

275

I felt tense the first time Robert came over. I had no idea what he'd think of my family, so I lovingly, but firmly cautioned everyone to fly right or there'd be hell to pay.

As I stood in the kitchen introducing him around to Leo, Joe-Sam, and Peaches, we heard Mama screaming bloody murder out on the deck.

"Help, Jesus. Get out here now. Halfback's digging up Bear Bryant again."

"Bear Bryant?" Robert asked.

"Our dead dog," Peaches explained. "The boys didn't make a very good grave."

"Shut up, you girl," said Leo.

"Yeah, man, the grave was fine." Joe-Sam was drawing whales in his art pad.

"No," she insisted. "Our other dog smells him and keeps trying to dig him up."

I stammered, "You . . . you . . . know dogs."

"Oh, my God," Mama's voice came stronger. "Hail Mary! Somebody!"

I backed out of the kitchen, explaining, "I'd better go check."

"Should I come?" Robert asked.

"No, you just kick back and . . . relax. This won't take a minute." I dashed to the backyard to Bear Bryant's grave, chasing Halfback away, ready to kill the little bastard.

Mama was crying, "Look, I see a paw, oh God, I see a paw. My poor baby. Damn you, Halfback!"

Halfback ran around the yard in delirious circles, tongue flapping, thinking it was a great game.

"It's okay, Mama, I'll take care of it!" I yelled, praying that Robert was still inside, not witnessing this bizarre event. But as I went to gather more dirt and rocks, he appeared beside me with Peaches tagging behind him.

"Can I help, Liz?"

"No, I got it, Robert."

"Come on."

"All right, sure, just grab some dirt and rocks if you like. I know this must seem a little odd . . . stuff like this doesn't happen around here much." I winced, winging hunks of dirt on the grave of Bear Bryant.

"It's okay." He dumped rocks on the burial mound.

"Peaches," I instructed her. "Run in the house and get some red pepper. We need extra precaution, so he doesn't do it again."

"I told you that dog is a fleabitten piece of crap." Joe-Sam began doing chinups on a branch above the grave.

Leo, bouncing a basketball in the driveway, clarified the situation. "Joe-Sam has fleas . . . that's why he hates Halfback. You shoulda seen the fight he and Liz had awhile back over him. Talk about claws, she . . ."

"Leo!" I warned, making my voice low and severe.

"I don't have fleas, you pussy!" yelled Joe-Sam. "I'm allergic to them."

"Here's the red pepper, Liz." Peaches skipped out, smiling at Robert.

As I was sprinkling it on the grave, Mama opened the screen door, looking exhausted but in control. "How do you do? I'm Liz's mother, Mrs. Donegal."

"It's very nice to meet you, Mrs. Donegal." Robert wiped his hands on his jeans before taking my mother's.

"Sorry for all the excitement on your first visit," Mama smiled.

"That's okay," Robert assured her, but I had my doubts. They were confirmed when the next thing we heard was "Where are the sumbitching towels!" Then Daddy shrieked from the window. "Goddammit, my ass is freezing."

"Look in the hall closet," Mama blasted back.

"Uh . . . my father," I explained to Robert. I shot a pleading glance in my mother's direction. "We were planning on going to the movies."

"When will you be home?" Mama asked.

"I'll call you after the movies," I said.

"Have a good time, hon," Mama smiled, but her eyes seemed sad.


The more I learned about Robert, the more I respected and liked him. It was soon apparent that he was smart as a damn whip. After all, he was studying engineering, received a 32 on his ACT tests, and 1,500 on his SATs, plus he typed my research paper on John Steinbeck when he saw I was ready to throw the Underwood out the window. I was beginning to believe I'd struck boyfriend gold. By week three in our friendship, he gave me his class ring, which fit perfectly on my index finger without tape, since I had pretty chunky fingers, and I began emphasizing conversational points with my hands, so everyone could see I was attached at last. *Me. Old maid Aunt Gertrude, the greatest dishwasher in these here United States. Ha.*

Almost every week, I received poems through the mail from Robert of dreams and port-wine sunsets. I hadn't realized that guys liked poetry, much less wrote it. For St. Patrick's Day, he gave me a necklace with half a heart, and he wore the other half. The pieces fit together with the tender inscription "May the Lord keep us safe while we're apart from one another." I could have wept and died of happiness. We even had our own song, "Babe" by Styx, which we kissed to for the first time in the dark. Whooooeee. There was no going back.

Kathleen felt my absence for the first time in our two years of friendship. She brought it up on the eve of another Dominican retreat.

"So now you're the one ditching me?"

"I'm not ditching you. I've never broken a promise to you about anything."

"Yeah, but you can never do anything anymore."

"I get to see Robert only on weekends. He doesn't have a car. He always has to borrow his roommate's, so it's just easier for me to drive to see him."

"You're coming to this Dominican retreat with me, aren't you?"

"No. Robert and I are going to the Smoky Mountains to climb the Chimneys."

"What am I supposed to do with all those nuns by myself?"

"Come with us to the mountains," I urged, mentally pleading, *Say no. Say no.*

"I already promised them."

"When did that ever stop you?"

She gave me a chilly look of reproach before replying, "You know I'm really trying to change. It was my New Year's resolution."

"That's been your New Year's resolution ever since I've known you."

"So will you come with me?"

"I can't."

"Can't? Or won't?" Her eyes narrowed. "Have you guys gone further than first base?"

"What? No!"

She didn't blink. Her eyes stayed glued to mine.

"We've just kissed. A lot. Okay?"

"French-kissed?"

"Yeah, of course. What do you expect?"

"Is it good?"

"Yeah . . ."

"How good? Slut." She winked.

I got tickled. "It's . . . It's very good, hooker." As we looked at each other, we began to giggle, trading our usual insults of, "Bitch, whore, slut," back and forth, seeing who could say it fastest, which cracked us up, tears streaming down our faces.


I lied to Kathleen. French-kissing? That was only the beginning. I was greedy for more than that. Robert and I did spend the first weeks kissing only, but the night his hands drifted down the front of my sweater, I immediately wanted them underneath. I craved him with a hunger that I hadn't known existed. In the back of Peter's Gold Duster, Robert's kisses eager and warm on my mouth, all I wanted was to drink him up under the spring fragrance of magnolias. I wondered where all my modesty of the last seventeen years had fled, as he feasted on my breasts, nibbling, sucking, rolling them around and around. I didn't recognize my body, which seemed to have its own language with Robert nearby. I loved his full lips, his hard lean torso, and his gentle hands and, if the truth were told, Peter's Gold Duster had become a haven of luxurious, lapping, orgasmic heaven in every dark parking lot of Knoxville. Was it possible to lust after another person the way I used to crave blueberries?

Before each date with Robert, I took a long hot shower, soaping up three times, washing my hair twice, using an apricot cream rinse. I brushed my hair, blowing it dry, rolling it in hot curlers. Sometimes I blow-dried my face too, so my cheeks looked radiant and rosy. I rubbed lemon lotion all over my body, sprinkled baby powder, slapping at myself until the powdery clouds stopped wafting everywhere. After I brushed my teeth, I put in my contact lenses, lightly applying touches of rich blue eye shadow, black mascara, rose blush, and a coral lipstick. I usually wore a turtleneck, a blue sweater, and jeans. For the grand finale, I sprayed a hint of Cachet on my wrists and neck. Then I emerged . . . ready for Robert.

Mama was freaked out, afraid to look me in the eye. The more Robert and I saw each other, the more closets she cleaned with a look of sickness smeared across her face. Daddy had recently left for Cincinnati to become the special teams coach for the Titans, his first professional football team, and she was putting the house on the market. Daddy kept calling me from Cincinnati to check on my golf game. "Goddamn! Are you still practicing even though you're in love with that limp?"

"He's not a limp, believe me . . . and yes, I play every day."

" 'Cause you're not gonna be worth shit if you don't practice. Professionals practice. Nancy Lopez—"

"I know, Daddy, I know."

"I'm looking around for high schools up here with girl golf teams. There's a lot."

"I'm not moving my senior year."

"What are you going to do? Stay in Knoxville?"

"Yes."

"I don't think that's a very good plan."

"Well, I'm not going to talk about it. I warned you that I was not moving again."

"Liz, just 'cause you think you're in love with that sumbitch now, don't throw your life away at seventeen. For the love of Saint Jude, don't do it."

"Yes, sir."

"I mean it. 'Cause if you do, you may as well piss on the fire and call in the dogs, 'cause it'll be over, baby. I'm telling you. You got more pride than that. At least I hope you do. Now put your mother on."


I missed Robert terribly during spring break. Peaches tried to cheer me up, slipping into my bed next to me to cradle my hand.

"He'll be back soon, Lizzie."

"I know, I know. But my heart is heavy." I felt the drama of my words.

"Do you love him very much?"

"Very, very, very much," I whispered, trying to picture his face. "You'll understand when you're older."

"I understand now," she answered snappishly. "Nobody thinks I do, but I do."

Mama's voice honked, "I could use some help around here. I could use some help. The Realtor is bringing folks. I wish y'all would get off your ass and clean up."

I tuned out the endless nitpicking drone. Who cared about Realtors?

When Robert returned after spring break, he brought me a dozen red roses and an Irish Prayer picture that said:


*May the road rise to meet you,*
*May the sun always be at your back,*
*And until we meet again,*
*May God hold you in the palm of his hand.*


We immediately went to bed in his dorm room, doing "everything but." The fact that I was still technically a "virgin" said nothing about my control, and everything about Robert's not wanting to get me pregnant. However, there was such intense pleasure in everything we did do that I didn't miss penetration. At the moment of glorious climax, John Denver's voice sprang from the stereo, his "*I want to live,*" song. I saw that Robert's face was wet with tears of love as he gazed into my eyes.

"Do you know how much I love you?" he gasped.

"I love you so much." I cradled his face in my hands.

"Oh God, I love you. Forever." He held me so tightly.

"Forever and ever." I hugged his neck, as I lay in his arms, snuggled up afterward. How I adored his sweet face in slumber. I would have gone anywhere and done anything for him, my wrestler, my lover, my joy, Robert Samuel McCoy. He was the love of my life. The real thing. With him, I was finally alive.

# 28

# VOCATIONS

*"Taking a Safety"*

**In a game-ending situation when we are ahead by a minimum of six, we may choose to take a safety. When taking a safety, make sure you retreat into and through the end zone.**

"It's pretty hard, Liz, when you're a mother, to think about your children having sex." Mother exhaled, dissecting me with her eyes, as she yanked dandelions and stickweeds out of the back yard.

"Mother, we're not having sex. I'm still a virgin, if that's what you're worried about." I poured gas into the lawn mower, the fumes licking the air in shimmery waves. "At least, technically." I muttered the last part under my breath.

"All I know is that you act very differently now."

"Oh, brother," I sighed with exasperation. Why couldn't she just be happy for me? Why couldn't she just rejoice in my first true love like other normal mothers?

"I want you to grow into a strong woman with morals."

"I have morals. I'm a good person."

"I never said you weren't a good person, but there's a difference between being a good person and a good Catholic."

"Why does Catholicism enter into everything?"

"How can you even ask me such a question when you're the ringleader of all those holy roller retreats for teenagers?"

"Why do you hate him? For God's sakes, he's an A student in engineering, he goes to church, he types my term papers, which is more than I can say for you. He doesn't do drugs, and he's not a redneck with a chaw of tobacco who drinks six-packs and beats me up!" I blinked back the tears, refusing to cry in front of her.

"I never said that!" She rubbed her coiled ringlets off her forehead, her new permanent from The Tangerine Curl frizzing with humidity and stress.

"He's my best friend. He likes me just the way I am." Couldn't she see that he was the best thing that had ever happened to me?

We were both quiet for a few seconds, but I yanked the lawn-mower cord with such ferocity the machine revved up the first time.

"I don't hate him," she squalled over the roar, wagging her arms. "He's a nice boy, but every weekend is with him. He spends the night on our couch all the time."

"Do you know he got a fifteen hundred on his SAT? That's a great score, in case you didn't know that," I screeched, the tufts of grass gusting out the sides in neat rows.

"What is a college boy doing still hanging around high school?" she bawled.

"We're only a year apart," I cried back. "Because he's young for his grade, and I'm old for mine. He skipped a grade because he's so smart."

"He has a weak face."

"What?" I howled over the motor.

"His bone structure. He has a weak face."

"I'm not having this conversation."

"Look, we're moving to Cincinnati."

I turned off the lawn mower. "I'm not going to Cincinnati. You promised that you would do your best to let me finish my senior year here."

"That was before you fell head over heels in love and lost your sanity," she announced, getting right back in my face, her voice dropping low in case Mr. Goodnight was peeking out the kitchen window to catch the theatrics.

"I haven't lost my sanity. I've gained it."

"I didn't know you loved the south so much that you wanted to spend the rest of your life here." Mama began raking up the grass near the lawn mower.

"I don't." I flashed a placating smile, pretending she was a stranger who needed a thorough explanation of the situation. "However, it's my home for now . . . But I'm going overseas for my junior year in college as an exchange student."

"What will your true love say to your living in another country?" she snarled.

"What can he say, Mother? If he truly loves me, he'll understand." I spat the words to get her off my back, strolling out of the backyard. *I am detached, I am detached, I am detached.*

"We're not finished discussing this, young lady," Mama warned, barreling toward the driveway, rake in hand.

"Yes, we are, Mother." I hopped into the Gold Duster, backing it swiftly down our steep driveway. I needed to bust loose from that voice.


My lover prayed often, attending daily mass, thinking about his relationship with God, the saints, the life ever after. He was by no means sickeningly religious, but he insisted we go to church together on Sunday evenings, holding hands, listening intently to the homily, singing our hearts out to the guitars of the college folk group. I tried to stay focused, but I usually drifted, thinking about what we would be doing *after* mass. Would we go to the Gold Duster or his dorm room? I craved him most on Sundays because I had to wait until the following Friday to see him again. I needed our lovemaking to tide me over through the weekly tedium of lockers, uniforms, classes, and the boring discussions of earthworms in Wendy's hamburgers or backwash clotting in the bottoms of bottled sodas. High school was becoming so intensely passé. Books barely interested me at all either. They couldn't hold my attention, because my own life was now finally full of love, drama, and excitement. I even made Robert a huge collage of our deep love for one another, cutting and pasting colorful pictures of sunsets, oceans, mountains, stars, rainbows, hands, fingers, eyes, mouths, hearts, ears, and unicorns.

At the end of May, after nearly five months of bliss together, we had our first fight. It was a Sunday night, and we were in bed after church, planning for my prom, where we would both be wearing tuxedos, when he asked, "So did you get your ACT scores back? You should have by now."

"I don't know." I quickly buttoned my blouse, pulling on my sweater. My jeans were still on because I had my period, and I wasn't about to try to figure out how to get around that messy obstacle.

"What do you mean, you don't know? You either got them back or you didn't. Which is it?" He looked at me quizzically.

"Who cares." I stood up, jamming a brush through my hair, looking in his little dorm mirror above the built-in bureau. The brush stuck fast in the snarls.

"You do too. That was the second time you took the test to see if you could improve your scores. You got them back, didn't you, Liz?"

"I can't remember. I get a lot of mail, you know. I get mail from Iowa, Kansas, and Pennsylvania. Did I tell you I've started writing all my old friends, and I've already gotten some responses. I didn't live in a dinky town like Chattanooga my whole life the way you did. I was on the move."

"Is that right?"

"My friend, Sarah Camp? She's studying to be a minister. Her dad was a minister. Presbyterian. We used to ride our bikes to hear him preach."

"What about your test scores, Lizzie-Liza?"

"And my other friend, Jo? She coaches track for the Kansas State Bobcats."

"You're changing the subject."

"All right then, I got them back. Two weeks ago. Okay?"

"So what was your score?"

"Could we just drop it?"

"Why won't you tell me?"

"Why do you have to know?"

"I helped you study. I invested time too. I love you. No matter what your score, it's not going to change the way I feel about you."

"So why do you want to know then?"

"Just forget it," he snapped loudly. The blue vein in his jaw flexed, and I wondered for a second, *weak face*?

Suddenly, I was afraid. I had raised my voice to him. What would he think of me? I'd never seen him angry before, but I was outraged too. My brain, for all my years of devouring books, constantly betrayed me when it came to taking multiple-choice tests, and the last thing I wanted to do was discuss this ultimate failure.

"Twenty, I got a twenty, okay?" I threw the brush down on his bureau. "No, wait, it's even better. I got twenty the first time I took the fucking test, and the second time I got eighteen. Now you know. I suck at standardized tests. Happy? Mr. Thirty-two and Mr. Fifteen hundred SATs?"

"Test scores don't prove a thing, sweetheart."

"Tell that to any university. Tell that to any Ivy League University."

"You can still get into Tennessee. Fifteen is the cutoff."

"Gee, I feel so much better."

"Come back to bed. I know some other things you can do that are a lot more important than standardized tests."

"No."

"Please. I love you. Anyway, it's more important for guys to do well on those tests than girls."

I saw red. "Oh, really, why?"

"Guys will have to support families one day."

"What about women supporting families?"

"They support them in a different way."

"What way?"

"It's just different. Now come here, before this gets totally out of hand."

He sat naked on the bed. I was dressed and in no mood to get back into the bed with the male chauvinist pig. How could I have been so blind and stupid?

"Robert, I'll call you." I edged toward the door.

"You can't walk downstairs unescorted in a men's dorm." He looked hurt, and more than a little irritated.

"I'll be fine."

"I could get in trouble. Just give me a second to get dressed." He jumped out of bed, throwing on his wrestling sweats and tennis shoes. Silently, we got onto opposite sides of the sixth-floor elevator, which stopped at every floor to let loving couples push on. As we walked outside, he accompanied me to the Gold Duster, which sat in a remote corner of the parking lot. I slipped into the car, and Robert climbed in after me. We sat there watching the orange glow from the stadium, a night practice.

I whispered, "All I've ever wanted is to be considered intelligent. I'm not pretty, I never will be, and if I'm not smart, what am I?"

"Elizabeth Frances Donegal, you are smart, you're bright, and you're lovely. You write good stories. Test scores can't measure what you have. I'm serious. Besides, Liz, you look fine. Why would I date a moose?"

I froze at the word *moose,* realizing that barely five years earlier he, too, had belonged to the throngs of short boys who lived to humiliate tall girls.

"You're very sexy and pretty." He kissed me gently, again and again. "And you've got great eyes, especially when your contacts aren't in."

Not knowing exactly how to respond to that *compliment,* since I wore my contact lenses fifteen hours a day, I allowed myself to be coaxed into the backseat, thinking *we'll just kiss;* but, as usual, the kisses grew more and more hungry. Robert shoved the boys' football pads and Peaches's shimmery ballet costume to the floor, all my overdue library books stacked beside us. I prayed no frat guys in chinos and Izods were lurking on their balconies with beer kegs, observing the Gold Duster bucking urgently under the starry night sky of Knoxville. *Catholic dry humping as usual. God, I was weak. Where was my womanly pride that Aunt Betty spoke of so long ago?*

# Vocations

★   ★   ★

When I dropped by to see Robert after school the following Friday afternoon, he informed me that he felt he had a true vocation to the priesthood and was planning to enter a Catholic seminary in Minnesota. As I tried to digest this piece of news and remain conscious at the same time, I asked, "Why? Why? The first time we met you said it wasn't for you. You said—"

"I just have to try. I think it's what God wants for me."

"Oh, so you two have sat down and talked about it?"

"I'm going to Minnesota. I want to help people."

"For free, right? Your college tuition will be free. Room, board, everything."

"It's where the seminary is for the Diocese of Tennessee."

"What about me? What about us?"

"It'll be hard, and if I don't make it, I'm coming back to you for the rest of our lives. Will you wait for me? We could get married, if it doesn't work out for me."

"If it doesn't work out . . . ?"

"I don't want to lose us." He moved toward me, his eyes misty with longing. Enough already. I backed off. But then I thought, wait, if I kissed him now, if I touched him, would it mean making love to a priest? Would it make God angry if I fucked one of his prospective apostles? I hoped so. I pushed him toward the bed, taking the seminarian by force. By God, I wasn't going to let him go without a battle.

As we tore at each other's clothes, I tried to make him go all the way this time, but he wouldn't. He exploded on my stomach, soaking my uniform skirt and blouse. Afterward, I sat up stiffly, smoothing down my skirt, yanking up my kneesocks, lacing my saddle shoes, as he gently dried me off with a towel. I begged him to change his mind. He held me closely, rocking me. I wept in his arms, hating God for trying to woo my love away. At that moment, Robert's roommate, Mark, sauntered in, wolfing down a greasy slice of pizza from the cafeteria. I quickly pulled on my navy blazer, acting upbeat so Mark wouldn't think I was some whiny, clingy loser.

"Hey, Mark, how's it going?" I tried to fix my hair, which seemed to be shooting out of my head.

"Hey, Liz." He smiled to himself, sitting at his desk. "Hot day, Robert?" he inquired since Robert didn't have a stitch of clothing on.

Robert blushed and pulled on his sweatshirt, jumping under the covers. I then noticed a new book on Robert's desk called *Saint Vincent's Seminary of Minnesota*. On the cover, a few college guys in regular clothes were standing under an elm tree chatting with a gregarious priest. Everyone rested Bibles and theology books on their hips, rosaries dangling from their front pockets.

"I'll see y'all later." I flashed a forced grin, hurriedly escorting myself downstairs without the help of my wannabe priest, the words to our song, "Babe" by Styx, burning in my brain. I glanced at my watch. Shit, I was almost late to go lead another Quest retreat weekend with Kathleen. Shit, shit, shit. We were to guide the sophomores into the love of Jesus Christ. In the Church. I was supposed to give a speech on Catholic womanhood. What I really preferred to do was vomit, so I did, in the parking lot of Robert's dormitory.

In our sleeping bags that night, I whispered this cruel twist of fate to Kathleen as all the retreaters snoozed under spiritual posters of waterfalls and a smiling Jesus. Her eyes widened as she gripped my hand, whispering, "Boy, Lizzie, is that ever ironic, dang it, 'cause you see, I've got something to tell you too. I've decided to enter the Dominican Order in Nashville this September, and I was thinking maybe that you—"

"What?" I couldn't believe what I was hearing. Had the world gone crazy? *A nun? Kathleen, a nun? Was that her destiny? Wait a minute. Was it mine? Were we supposed to enter the convent together to save the world? Robert was just a secular detour, and now I was back on track with my childhood of saints and martyrs? The Motherhouse was so much like the boarding schools of my Jane Eyre dreams. Me and Kathleen as Dominican sisters? Traveling to India to work with Mother Teresa? Going to New York to help the poor? Two sisters in habits and rosaries and black boots opening up an orphanage for all the girls in China who needed our love?*

Then, *Reality* . . . the faces of Sister Mary Analise and Sister Matilda and Sister Josefat loomed up.

"What about your dancing, Kath?" I hissed. "As far as I know, I've never met a ballerina who was a nun."

"I don't feel like I'm praising God with my dancing. Besides, all the other dancers are so competitive. They fight to get seen in the front row. There's no love."

"But you're an artist. You can't be a nun. I won't let you."

"It's not your decision, Lizzie," Kathleen murmured. "I haven't told anyone else. I almost told John a couple of nights ago."

"That guy from the restaurant? You're not still dating him, are you?"

"Sort of. He's really sexy. Anyway, I was going to tell him after we finished, you know, doing it, but it seemed kind of out of place."

"Kathleen, how much sex have you and John had?"

"It's not sex," she hissed. "It's everything . . . but."

"That's sex, Kathleen. Do your Dominican sisters know about him?"

"We've only been going out a few months. Off and on. Besides, I wanted to live it up a little before I enter. You know?"

"When do you go in?"

"In September."

"What about us trying to find your real mother? We were going to do that when we were eighteen. Remember?"

"I have a mother. The woman who raised me is real enough for me."

"You'd give up your senior year and dancing just to be a nun?"

"I really feel like Jesus is calling me. It's about sacrifice and love. I also want to go to a place where I can just be quiet for a while. Everybody's always at me, but I need some peace, and the convent is about the quietest place I know."

"Can't you just back off from people for a while?"

"I can't say no to one person, but by entering the convent, maybe I can say no to everyone for a while. I also know Jesus wants me with him."

"When do you feel that? Before or after screwing John."

"We're not screwing. I'm still a *Virgin*. Dang it."

"Kathleen, come on . . . Maybe we have goddamn hymens, but neither of us are virgins anymore."

"Lizzie, don't get mad or anything, but it really bothers me when you say 'Goddamn.' "

"Oh, then forgive me, Sister Kathleen. Or what will your new name be? I bet anything it will be a guy's, right? All those nuns are Sister Joseph or Sister Jude."

"You can visit me in the order."

Self-interest raised its head. "All right, so where am I supposed to live if you're in the nunnery. My parents want me to go to Cincinnati before next football season."

"You can have my room to yourself now."

"I don't want to live in your house without you."

"I just have to try. If I don't like it, I'll come back to be with you."

"You and Robert both. Can't you go in after we graduate?"

"They have a special program for high school seniors. I would still go to their school for girls, but I would sleep in the convent at night."

I got up and began rolling up my sleeping bag. I was exhausted, but I knew I couldn't stay and lead a bunch of sophomores into the love of Christ when his love had so betrayed me, and I was certainly a huge fake in His eyes.

"Where are you going?"

"You're the one who's going to be a nun. You lead this retreat. Tell Father Haggerty I have scarlet fever. Here." I handed her the speech Robert had typed for me from my notes. "You can give it if you want."

"Wait, wait!" she whispered, but I was gone. I dashed out of the gym to my car. I drove out of the church parking lot, vowing never to return. I blasted Patsy Cline from Peter's tape deck, having recently discovered that Patsy was the kind of music you ached for late at night, especially when it was almost summer, driving the dark roads of Tennessee. As I rolled down my windows, the midnight sounds of frogs and cicadas came shrieking out of the buzzing humidity.

I wasn't sure where to go. I had heard if you drive out Kingston Pike, the main drag in Knoxville, eventually you'll hit California. I didn't aim to go that far, but I planned to travel far enough. In the past, I was the one who did the leaving, but now my two closest friends had made decisions that would take them about as far as they could get. They might as well be going to China as to the Holy Orders of Atlanta and Minnesota.

Fury stepped into my sadness. Their fathers hadn't dictated to them the way mine had always done. *Get your ass in the car. We're gone. Let's go. Let's go. Let's go.* Kathleen and Robert were choosing for themselves, and in their choices, they didn't care they were leaving me, since they obviously figured they were heading to something much better. God, Himself. Or Herself.

I passed lonesome town signs—Lenoir City, Oak Ridge, Wartburg, and Harriman—the words blurring together. Occasionally, a Church of Christ sign would crop up in front of a white church with more new sayings like JESUS IS LOVE, BLESS THE BEASTS AND THE CHILDREN, and HAVE Y'ALL PRAYED TODAY?

I longed for an ice cold Miller Tall Boy, the kind Kathleen and I used to get drunk on after dances and football games before we had guys in our lives. I even considered stopping at a Weigels Convenience Store to get one, but I wanted something stronger, some Lem Motlow, a sipping whiskey named after the nephew of Jack Daniel. I passed a bar called The Round-Up, where I saw a bunch of guys in flannel shirts driving pickups, and I figured I wasn't so thirsty after all. As I drove on, I wished I were a man. I looked too womanly to pull it off anymore, the way I did when I was a kid to impress Daddy. Being a man sure had its advantages. A man had the freedom to walk into a strange bar alone and get a drink, snatch up good conversation and tingling stories, but if a woman walked into a bar alone, they said she was either lonely or asking for trouble or both. I wasn't either.

First Betty and Peter, now Kathleen and Robert. A whole life of leavings and being left. Finally, I came upon a rock quarry, the kind where Blanche DuBois and her friends hung out, drinking and diving, only there was no polka music. I didn't hear a sound except the screech of cicadas from a cluster of sugar maples leading into a forest. As I crept down the craggy rocks, I took off my clothes. I pulled off my crucifix and Quest cross from around my neck and flung them far into the water. I took off Robert's ring and the half-hearted necklace, put them in the pocket of my jeans, and went skinny-dipping for the first time in my life. Floating, I felt free, soothed in the cool water. I wondered if I'd become a heathen. I sure hoped so. I'd never done anything so daring in my life, and I felt shivers of joy as I swam back and forth across the lagoon of the lake, thick black mud seeping between my toes whenever I stood on the bottom. I was alive, and it was God enough for me.

# 29

## K U D Z U

*"40—Gut . . . Running to Daylight"*

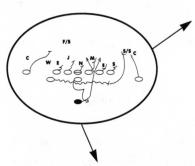

**A dive play with Power Zone blocking. If this play is
to be successful it is imperative that the offensive line create movement
off the line of scrimmage to permit the RUNNING BACK to find
the crease and run to "DAYLIGHT."**

I wish I could say I stopped seeing Robert, that I kept my pride by
not returning his calls or dropping by to see him. The truth was, we leaped
into bed nearly every chance we got until he left on his priestly mission
to Minnesota. He wanted it all, and an insidious part of me continued to
crave him. Like a good lapdog, I figured if I overflowed with kindness,
love, and indulgence, he would come to his senses and choose me over
the Church. I was also convinced that no other boy could ever make me
feel the way he did. Once he was gone, I would dry up, forced back into
the domestic role as oldest girl child. Sucking up life with him would
sustain me through the drought that was surely ahead.

Though it may have appeared to some (his mother in particular) that

I was chasing my first love too hard, the Seminarian was also hanging on to me until the very end, even persuading me to visit him once more at his home in Chattanooga. As we interlocked fingers on the front porch one Saturday evening, his mother and a close family priest friend, Father Ed, stepped outside to be with us. After a few minutes of forced coughs, Father Ed tweaked the back of my neck, "So, Miss Donegal? When are you going to release our tormented seminarian from your charms?"

Mortified, I flashed a glance at Robert's kind mother for a support signal, but her stony eyes revealed it was she who had solicited Father Ed to pose the question. Robert just sat there, *weak-faced*.

Anger welling up, I shot back, "Why don't you pose him the same question?"

Nobody answered. Robert's little sister, Eppie, bounded out, banging the screen door. She was the only other McCoy who liked me.

"You want to go climb trees, Liz?"

"Sure." I slipped off the porch, relieved to escape the web of piety to scale the lush tulip poplars in the backyard. As Eppie and I edged near the treetops, swaying back and forth, she dug at the bark with her fingernails. "Liz? Nothing against my brother," she hummed, "but you can do better. He's your run-of-the-mill mama's boy." She stretched a leaf over her mouth.

"You think he'll be a priest?" I asked.

"Hard to say, but I kind of doubt it." She blew the leaf to make a sighing sound.

"Why?" *Tell me the future, you wise old girl. I gotta know.*

"I guess," Eppie reflected, " 'Cause nursing homes give him the shivers, and he's also been looking at *Playboys* since he was twelve."

"Liz," Robert's voice churled up through the branches. "*The Jerk* starts in twenty minutes over at Red Bank Cinema. Come on down now."

"I'd rather see *The Rose*," I replied, clinging to my teetering perch. I also wanted to keep gazing toward Lookout Mountain, listening to Eppie's insight. This kid had the eyes of Anne Frank and the braids of Francie Nolan.

"We'll flip for it in the car. And Eppie," he whined, "you need to get down too. You both are just a little old to be climbing trees."

"Shut up, Robert, you're not a priest yet," Eppie ordered.

"Yeah, *shut up,*" I echoed, giddy as I swung from the limbs of the tree.

He turned and walked out of the backyard. I didn't have to peer down through the leaves to know the blue vein in his jaw was arched.


I saw the Seminarian for the last time when Kathleen and I decided to attend the graduation pool party at Suppa Nolan's house, Suppa being the oldest son of Y-Teen leader Mrs. Nolan, and Patsy Nolan's brother. Suppa always hosted the party for the graduating class at Tennessee Catholic. He ran a liquor store out on Middlebrook Pike, but every year he closed down shop to play host to the senior class, which invariably included a sibling or two. Juniors were allowed to attend if they had friends of the family who were seniors, like Kathleen, whose sister, Mandy, was graduating with a softball scholarship to Valdosta, Georgia. Mandy, as usual, was feeling none too generous about sharing her celebration with her sister.

"I'm warning you now, Kathleen. Y'all better not show up. This is my party," Mandy snarled, her eyes shooting sparks from under her 1979 cap and tassel.

"We won't come. I swear." Kathleen hugged her sister. "Now Happy Graduation. I love you."

"Yeah, Happy Graduation," I echoed, but Mandy was already bitterly gunning her Mustang at full throttle.

"So?" Kathleen turned to me cheerfully after Mandy careened out of the parking lot. "When do we get there?"

"I'd say in about an hour or two," I chuckled.


The graduation festivities would be my last chance to be with both Robert and Kathleen. Mama thought I was spending the night at Kathleen's house, and her mother thought she would be at mine, so we were free until morning. When Kathleen and I arrived at Robert's dorm room, all his belongings had been packed, boxes ready to be shipped to the seminary, his engineering exams flawlessly concluded. While he showered, we listened to Supertramp gliding through the window, mingling with the scent of jasmine and glad shouts of students. I pretended it was just any cement dorm room, not the one that had held such rapture for so many months. Kathleen squeezed my hand. "How about I brush your hair?" she suggested, taking a hairbrush, attempting to comb out the knots that insisted upon forming in my lengthening hair.

"Liz"—she worked on a hunk of hair—"I think we need to get drunk tonight. Drunker than we ever thought possible."

"Kath, you've got to promise not to become a nun. I'm begging you."

"I promise not to take my final vows unless it's absolutely the right thing."

"And one more favor?" I asked, studying her eyes in the mirror. "Don't leave me alone with him tonight."

"I won't." She crossed her heart.

" 'Cause we've already said good-bye about ten times this month."

"I won't leave your side . . . slut," She winked lovingly.

"Thanks, cock-tease," I whispered without enthusiasm.

"You know it." Kathleen licked her lips. *God, she could be disgusting— for a nun.* Suddenly, she stopped herself, staring at her reflection in the mirror, "Geez, you know, I've got to quit talking this way. I'm leaving for the convent in three days."

Robert drove the Gold Duster over to Suppa Nolan's with Kathleen sitting between us. Nearing the party, we pulled onto a dirt road. *Sounds of splashing, squealing, and Lynyrd Skynyrd. God, how I hated Lynyrd Skynyrd.* The spare tire proved the perfect surface for a makeshift bar. Robert shook up a gallon-size milk jug overflowing with gin and lemonade, a drink called Yellow Suicides. *Whooo-doggie.* He poured that sweetly sour concoction into plastic cups.

"All right, girls, let's get drunk." Robert winked at us, big man bartender.

Nobody said anything for a few minutes. The three of us chugged our drinks, surrendering our tongues from the grip of sobriety and etiquette, so we could spill our guts and not think about it until sunrise.

"I just realized something, Kathleen." I grabbed her after swilling my second Yellow Suicide, my brain befuddled. "I've finally figured out who we're like. The movie *Julia*. You're the character of 'Julia' helping everyone, and I'm 'Lillian,' the writer. Only Julia never did become a nun. It's imperative you know that. I'm trying to save you. I want to give you back your destiny," I insisted, not knowing what the hell I was talking about. My knees buckled under me into a tangle of kudzu vines near an embankment.

"Liz!" She staggered down beside me.

"What?" I screeched hopefully, ready for her revelation regarding my future.

"You are so dramatic sometimes. Dang it!" she roared.

"So I've been told."

Kathleen reached for my fingers across the damp vines. We inhaled the moist earth, filling our nostrils with summer.

Robert squatted down beside me, "Where does that leave me?"

"Well," Kathleen ventured, "I think it leaves you in Minnesota, Robert."

"With the priests," I added, sliding down the wet slope. Kathleen followed me as we tickled each other all the way down the kudzu, laughing hysterically. As Kathleen and I neared the bottom, we heard a struggle and a yelp as Robert tumbled past us down the incline, followed by silence.

"Robert?" I hissed, wondering if he was hurt or . . . ?

"Robert?" Kathleen yelled.

Eventually, we heard a cross voice say, "What?," which relieved me terribly. As he crawled toward us, Kathleen and I tackled him. The three of us were covered in mud, and we laughed, linking arms, singing over and over with pure euphoria: "Michael, row your boat ashore, Alleluia."

As I looked at their faces swathed in moonlight, I realized I still loved them best out of anyone in the whole world. But I would never do to them what they were about to do to me. A madness welled up inside, making my face feel loose, rubbery, and full of yellow suicide. I began slugging Robert, beating my fists on his chest, sobbing, "How could you? How could you do it?"

Tears streamed down his cheeks, as he cried, "I'm sorry. It's just God works—"

"Don't you dare give me that bullshit, Robert, fuck you. You're not a priest any more than I'm the Pope! I hate you," I wailed, watching my hideous self bloom in the night. Kathleen backed up in fear. Robert wept, ducking my blows. *Stop it, stop it, I told myself. Robert wasn't Joe-Sam, what was I doing?* It was all so ugly, I was monstrous, I was Martha in *Who's Afraid of Virginia Woolf?*, vile, but I couldn't stop. *This kind of behavior would convince him to stay? Slug, punch, hit. I'd been so good to him for months, loving, gentle, empathetic. No more. Fuck me and my politeness, my newly acquired southern-girl demeanor of being so understanding, holy water and hot sex.* I became a bully, a creature Robert could no longer love. I tried to crawl away from my fury, from those two traitors who were hell-bent on breaking my heart, but immediately got violent head-rushes and began throwing up. Robert stayed beside me like a good priest-to-be, comforting the drunken, but I waved him off. I didn't need his pity as I clawed up the hill back to the Gold Duster to vomit in privacy.

After I reached the top, I felt better. I rinsed my mouth and washed my face with club soda, the bubbles cleansing my skin, fizzy and warm. I became keenly aware of the summer world of Knoxville. Ghostly branches of leaves chafed the night as I dug around for a towel in the trunk. Near the spare tire, I noticed a sketch pad underneath some rags. I pulled out the pad, and holding it under the street light, saw the name "Peter Donegal!" etched across the front. I was instantly sober. I could hear Robert and Kathleen crawling up the hill from down below. I slowly opened the pad and the first drawing was of Peter, a self-portrait, smiling a devilish grin, eyes sparkling. How could he make his eyes shine like that?

A stab of longing. I clasped the book to me with relief and guilt, flooded with Peter who had dimmed tremendously in the gush of my first love. I felt his presence completely, reminding me of who I was, giving me back my courage. I slowly turned each page, black-and-white pen sketches of the family jumping out at me: Joe-Sam and Leo as football players, Papa Sweetheart bearing a rifle in a collage of wild animals. My heart beat wildly. What else would I find? There were Daddy and Uncle Whitey in their bathing suits as little boys, boxing gloves draped over their baby shoulders. I drank them in, studying their features. Suddenly, I saw me and Mary-Louise that summer at the beach, me scowling, her laughing into the sun. There were others of Mama and Aunt Little as shy brides, Cynthia Elspecker applying toenail polish, and Patricia, his Notre Dame girlfriend, a winking Madonna. He hadn't forgotten any of us.

"They're Peter's, aren't they?" Kathleen breathed, standing behind me.

I jumped back, startled.

"The uncle I typed up your talks about for the retreats?" Robert asked.

I held them protectively against me, not answering.

"Liz?" Kathleen began.

"It's a sign," I murmured, transfixed by the drawings.

"Oh. Well, of course, you would know all about those kinds of signs," Robert drawled sarcastically.

"Get away from me," I wept, unable to look at him, for his presence represented every single weakness pulsing inside me.

"Come on, y'all. Let's be nice," sputtered Kathleen. "It's our last night together."

"You're right," Robert grinned. "Sorry, Liz." He traced my shoulder blades, trying to rein me in close to him. I pulled away, thinking . . . *Who am I? Peter knew.*

"Have it your way," he shrugged, waltzing off toward the lights and music of the party, swinging the milk jug of Yellow Suicides alongside him. Kathleen tipsily followed. I carried the sketch pad with me, gazing at the portraits as I walked. The pictures were alive, breathing. I was reeling in the memory of Peter, the proof that he did exist, but even more, the proof that I existed. I had existed before Robert, and I would continue to exist after him. I would even exist after Kathleen, as impossible as that seemed. It was a tremendous gift. I wanted to carry it with me all night, drinking in the drawings. As I walked up the Nolans' driveway, I watched several people splashing in the pool, the science teacher chewing on a lobster claw.

I spoke to no one as I sat on a porch swing and found another picture of me in the sketch pad. I was about seven, holding baby Peaches, Mrs. Beasley, and books near a Christmas tree. At that moment, Mary Jo and Ellie stumbled up to me, snickering, "Hey, Donegal. We're drunk, so what are you?" Their thick mascara streaked spidery markings across their flushed cheeks, as they limped into the house. When the swimming pool crowd applauded noisily, I glanced up to see Robert and Kathleen dancing to Blondie on the diving board, *shaking, swooning*. I turned the page, and there I was gripping my swan, ballet dancing with a more grown-up Peaches, both of us beaming, the room piled high with books: Alcott, Salinger, Wolfe, Chekhov, Baldwin, Welty, Smith, Neruda, cummings, Williams, Márquez, and Shakespeare . . . so much I hadn't read yet. *What had I been doing with my life?* What had I read since Robert? *The Grapes of Wrath,* "The Darling," and "Dear Abby" columns, but that was it. I was starved for stories again.

"Welcome," Mrs. Nolan cooed, stepping out onto the porch. She eyed me more closely, "Darlin,' did you fall down in the kudzu out back?"

"No, ma'am, I'm fine." I smiled harder, realizing for the first time my muddy white shorts, grass-stained knees.

"Do you want a soda?"

"I'm fine for now."

"Good for you, sugarpig," She patted my cheek, disappearing back inside.

On the last page of the pad, I discovered an unfinished sketch, revealing the contours of Mick O'Doherty's face, but only a shell of the body of the man standing next to him. Suppa suddenly loomed before me in Fighting Game Cock swimming trunks, his hairy belly spilling over the elastic waist band. He was holding hands with Mandy, who was looking demure for the first time in her life. I noticed a raspberry hickey pitted near the strap of her floral sundress.

"Hey, Mandy!" Kathleen waved to her, as she and Robert did the bump.

It took a second for Mandy to register, but all she said to Kathleen was "Hey, sweetie." Then she smiled at her sister for the first time since I'd known her.

"Anybody want plum wine and chips and dip and M&M's?" Suppa's lips stretched across his gums. "I got a stash in the basement fridge."

"Sure," yelled Kathleen, hopping off the diving board, Robert tagging after her. It was getting chilly on the porch swing, so I carried the sketch pad inside.

For the next few hours, as I grew more sober, everyone else became more inebriated, polishing off several bottles of plum wine to games of pool, rounds of darts, dancing to Abba and Fleetwood Mac. Around three in the morning, the partyers either passed out or went home. I drove Robert and Kathleen to the Game Cock Inn, where we spent the night with about twenty drunk Y-Teens who'd rented the hotel room. Robert was positively plastered, as was Kathleen. I felt a million years older than they, as if I were their baby-sitter. *You can't escape your destiny.*

As we stepped into the hotel room, I made Kathleen drink water. Robert lurched to a corner, keeling over, and I covered him with a blanket. I loved him, but I could let him go now. Neither he nor Kathleen belonged to me any more than I belonged to them. I was never going to be like them, one of the rowdy Catholic gang. I doubted, as I had many times before, that I could ever be part of any gang. But instead of feeling horrified, I felt a twinge of jubilation. Maybe being on the outside looking in wasn't such an awful place to be.

Somebody put on a medley of Diana Ross, and as I studied the clusters of besotted Y-Teens, I felt my blood burn with energy. Clasping Peter's sketch pad to me, I began to dance and sing along with Diana, a slow whirling, picking up speed, faster now, faces blurring together. Stepping over bodies, I stoked the air, belting out the song, free, my voice exploding with music. In the glorious heat of singing my heart out to the confused Y-Teens, I saw that the hotel room was identical to the one we'd stayed in when we first moved to Knoxville, when I'd first begun my journal to Peter.

★   ★   ★

I woke before anyone else, the sketch pad still in my arms, realizing my hard contacts were glued to my eyelids. I stepped over Robert and poured solution into my eyes, trying to soften the dry sockets. The room was crumpled with bodies, the smell of liquor and feet pickling the air. I took a shower to wash away the dirt and alcohol, the scalding water cleansing me. After I dressed, I dug around in my bag for an old pair of eyeglasses, which I put on, placing my sunglasses on top of them. As I woke Kathleen and Robert to drive each of them home, Robert grinned, "Morning, Diana," and heaved himself out the door to the car.

I dropped him off first. Kathleen and I watched as he wobbled away from the car in the muggy sunlight, his skin a clammy green.

She yawned. "Your first boyfriend."

"Yep," I replied, turning on the radio. I waited to see if the ex–love of my life would turn around—a wave, a salute, anything—but he never did. I had prepared for this moment to be the worst, but I felt surprisingly little more than relief.

Kathleen fell asleep on the way to her house, and I shook her awake as we pulled into her driveway.

"Gosh, are we home?" She stretched.

"Kath, will you call me before you leave for the nuns?"

"Sure I will," she laughed. But at that moment, I knew she wouldn't. She couldn't. She would probably spend the rest of her life saying yes, but meaning no.

"I'll always love you, Kath," I sighed as the weight of grieving good-byes turned into peace.

"Me too, Lizzie." She rubbed her head, checking her watch.

I drove away from her house slowly, leaving my best friend in the driveway: standing, waving, fading . . . in the rearview mirror. *Good-bye, Kathleen.*


When I got home, I crawled gratefully into my own bed. When I awoke late that afternoon, Mama was sitting on its edge.

"Enjoy yourself last night at Kathleen's?"

I huddled under the covers, peering up at her. "Yes, ma'am."

"Here, drink this."

"What is it?"

"Tomato juice. It helps."

"I don't need it."

"Sure you don't. I had a few of my own during the glory days of Daddy's coaching. Trust me."

"I do, Mama."

"By the way, Robert called from Chattanooga."

I gulped the tomato juice without stopping. "We already said our good-byes."

"You mean it? It's finished? Oh, honey. Alleluia." Her face lit up. "I'm so happy. The end of your first boyfriend. I can't believe we survived it."

"It wasn't that bad, was it?"

"I suppose not, but hell, what a relief. Thank ya, Saint Jude."

"Your prayers were answered." I smiled. "Mama? Do you ever miss Peter?"

"What?" she flinched just the slightest bit.

"Do you ever miss Peter? And how about Betty?"

"Of course I do. What kind of question is that?"

"How do you miss them?"

"How? Look, what are you talking about? We've been through this, and I told you what I thought. Maybe you need to sleep some more." She stood up.

"No, I'm trying to see—"

"Liz, I've got a lot on my mind," she laughed. "You know, you'd better get packed for Leavenworth. Catherine and Poppy can't wait to see you. We leave soon." She waltzed out, making the sign of the cross, whistling Scott Joplin.

I pulled out the sketch pad from under the bed. I had wanted her to crawl in bed with me, so I could share it with her. I wanted to tell her what it felt like to be Diana Ross. I wanted her to hold me. I climbed out of bed, the late afternoon sun creeping through the room. From the window, I watched Peaches and Leo doing bike races in the street, looking like a drawing of Peter's.

"Don't be such a girl," Leo ordered, staring up at Peaches, who was now five inches taller than he, despite Leo's being a year older.

"I am a girl. Deal with it, jerk." She mounted her banana seat bike.

"Well, don't be so much of one then," he barked after her.

Joe-Sam was sitting on the front-porch steps, trying to figure out the fingering on his new guitar using a Willie Nelson big-note guitar book; Halfback snoozed at his feet. There was a For Sale sign in our front yard. I decided to take Peter's sketchbook downstairs, so I could share it with my family. I would go to the library in the morning. Peaches and I were going to need tons of books for the long trip to Leavenworth. I couldn't wait to start reading again. I had so much to do and catch up on. I felt like I had finally come out of a long sickness, whole and strong. I was positively starving.

# LEAVENWORTH

*"Target Points of Offensive Line Play"*

**Whenever possible, strive to make the defender take the
path of least resistance (the way he wants to go), then wall him. Make
your escape around behind you so he is forced to take the long path for
pursuit. Each player must have a good understanding of the total play. It is
impossible to position yourself properly or to anticipate your man's
reaction if you do not have a good understanding of the play.**

Long after the era of Kathleen and Robert, when I was a mother
myself for the first time, my grandmother Catherine Thomas lay dying in
a hospital bed, a death rattle choking each breath, her throat trembling
like antique castanets.

"This is awful," she gasped, her fingers searched the salmon-pink
rosary beads.

"I know, I know," I whispered, leaning over her.

"Like—hell—you—do!" she wheezed.

My mother stood on the other side of the bed, murmuring, "Shhh,
Mama. Sleep," attempting to quell the flailing arms.

"Don't — you — tell — me — what — to — do — !" Catherine railed.

"I'm just trying to help, Mama," Mother sighed. "I'm sorry."

"Oh — you're — all — sorry. Every — last — one — of — you!" Catherine looked disgusted, outraged to be dying at the age of ninety-one.

I slipped out to the hallway to bury my face in the doughy body of my eight-month-old daughter, Hannah, where my husband, Michael, was holding her. I touched Hannah's blond curls, inhaling her scent of rose petals and talcum. God, she smelled so good. I couldn't stop kissing her, drinking her up with kisses; chubby arms clasped my neck as she slimed me with baby goo. With my grandmother dying on the other side of the wall, I only desired to sniff her neck, breathing her in like fresh baked bread and sunshine. She reminded me so much of Peaches at that age.

Mama poked her head out into the hallway, "Get back in here. The priest is about to give her the last rites."

"The—hell—he—is!" Catherine's voice exploded.

"Now, Mama," I heard Mother say as she receded back into the room.

"Drink this, Liz." Michael handed me a carton of orange juice. *Dear Michael. The first man in my life to cook for me, who couldn't have cared less about football or golf, who went to China with me our first year of marriage to teach at a new university eclipsed by rice fields.*

I gulped the juice as Hannah greedily began nursing, my breasts dripping with milk. I closed my eyes, feeling the tug of Hannah's mouth, listening to my mother in the next room trying to convince her dying mother to see a priest.

"No, no, hell, no," Catherine ordered.

Later, when Michael took Hannah back to the house for a nap, a tentative priest stole into the room to perform the last rites, but Catherine awoke, mumbling, "Get him out!" As he sidled to the door, an elderly nun inched inside wearing a cardinal and gold coat. Mama said to her, "I like your coat, Sister. I had one just like it once."

The nun replied, "Thank you, it was a gift from your mother." It was then Mama recognized her old Hurricane coat from Ames that she'd given to Catherine twenty years earlier, but had never seen her wear.

"How are you doing, Catherine Thomas?" the nun nasally hailed my grandmother, but received no answer. She turned to me, "God love her . . . She'll be with her daughter, Betty, in heaven very soon. And you are the granddaughter?"

"Yes, Sister," I answered, immediately riveted back in time, squirming before Sister Matilda, as I prepared to sing for the Wednesday funeral mass. Aunt Betty's face also came to mind. She'd died while I was working odd jobs in Ireland after college. I'd visited her once before graduation. She seemed happy to see me, but she was much older, changed. When I tried to tell her about my Shakespeare class, she reminded me that *Benny Hill* was about to start, followed by *M\*A\*S\*H*. She also wanted to make sure she didn't miss supper, so I didn't stay very long. I left her laughing uproariously at *Benny Hill* as one of the nuns brought in her tray.

"I was just talking to your father," the nun interrupted my thoughts, splaying her broad hands in front of her buttoned Hurricane coat. "Now let me tell you. . . . Your father may have been a coach, but mine was the finest butcher this side of Kansas City. He knew . . ."

I glanced over at Catherine, who was seemingly oblivious, but I remembered that hearing was the last of the senses to go, so I moved away from the nun's empty chatter. Mama leaned over Catherine, trying to cradle her. I saw out of the corner of my eye my father in the hallway, swinging an imaginary golf club. Poppy sat in a low chair, announcing for the tenth time, "I think we'd better eat. How about the A & W?"

A howl erupted from the deathbed. "Loooord-a-God!" Mama tried to soothe her mother's agitated fingers.

Poppy clattered on, "Maybe Kentucky Fried Chicken. You know, there's a terrible sound around here. How about Taco Bell? It's true that you can get about anything you want in Leavenworth." His eyes fell on me. "You look mighty familiar. Didn't you used to work for me at the theater in Kansas City?"

"I'm your granddaughter, Poppy," I explained gently.

"No kidding?" He nodded.

"Hail—Mary—full—of—grace!" came the second banshee cry.

Poppy squinted. "Is that my little wife, Catherine, making that awful noise?"

"Yes, Poppy," I answered. Mother looked sick.

"I'd better go to Food-4-Less. Get her some Tylenol," he replied cheerfully.

"Daddy, it's okay. We're under control." Mama smoothed back Catherine's hair.

"I think we'd better eat," Poppy began again. "How about the A & W?"

Mama, now rubbing her mother's skeletal feet, sighed, "Liz, for God's sakes, run buy us lunch at the A & W and bring it back here. I don't want to leave her."

I jumped up, relieved to be sent to buy root beer and chili dogs. "Should I get you something, Mama?"

"I couldn't swallow a bite, but buy Poppy at least two chili dogs, and get something for you and Daddy, too. Okay? Wait, what about Michael?"

"He took Hannah home. They'll be back later."

"That's good. Oh, and Liz?" Mama pushed her dark curls off her forehead.

"Yes, Mama?"

"I'm glad you're here." Tears of exhaustion rose in her eyes.

"Me too." I embraced her before escaping the hospital room. As I stepped out into the hallway, I heard Poppy's voice repeat, "I think we'd better eat. How about the A & W?" Mama didn't even answer him, overwhelmed at losing her mother and her father's worsening Alzheimer's.

I tried not to think of my grandmother dying as I glided down the spotless corridor of the hospital. I had never expected it. Death hadn't happened in our family since Peter and then later Betty. I had wanted to grow up so much back then, but I never realized everyone else was going to get old and change too. I figured they'd exist in a sort of time warp, while I was the one who grew and changed and did exciting things—the wisdom of Peter and Aunt Betty guiding me along the way. I slipped out of the hospital into the warm daylight of Leavenworth, which was shimmering just like the summer of ten years earlier.

# Leavenworth

"You're telling me," Daddy ranted on the golf tee at the Leavenworth driving range, "that you're going to live in Knoxville by yourself even though your two best friends are gone? What the hell are you? A masochist?"

I watched him concentrate on his ball, head and shoulders hunched, fingers folded around the shaft of the club. Snatches of midwestern sun bled through the whipping winds, stinging our faces, leaving our lips cracked and parched.

"I told you I wasn't going to move again. I'm done."

"Liz, for Christ's sake. You can't—"

"I can stay with Kathleen's family or in our house. It isn't sold yet. I'd be happy to live in it and take care of it. I could be your Realtor. I've had enough practice."

"No, no, no!" he gripped his club, taking a few more practice swings. He looked very stressed. Mama had been after him day and night to convince me to move with them, since she'd had no success. He was also living alone in a motel (which he hated) near the stadium in Cincinnati, prepping for his first professional football season in Special Teams. He had never said anything about not becoming a head coach, but occasionally I wondered where that dream had gone. Hadn't we spent our childhoods praying for this wish? *Please Lord, help Daddy get a good head job.* But my childhood was over, and somehow we'd missed it. Was there still time left? I shifted my position under the tree, trying to write a letter to Kathleen.

"You'd pick Tennessee over your family?" Daddy mopped his face with a towel.

I stood up, placing a rock on the half-written letter. "Daddy, have you ever imagined that you could split into different people?"

"What are you talking about now?"

"That the fractions of your soul you left behind in each town are still hanging around like ghosts?"

"Hell no!" He whacked a worm-burner.

"Or that maybe the leftover molecular bits evolved into a real person,

311

and picked up where you said good-bye, and suddenly a person who is you, but isn't you, is still there living the life you could have lived had you stayed?"

"Now, that's crap. Crap!" He practiced his swing again, head down.

"I feel like part of me, the Iowa Liz, is tasseling corn this summer, hanging out with Sarah Camp, skimming through the green stalks."

"Suppose we get a goddamn grip on reality here?" He positioned another ball.

"Or the Kansas me is working at the Dairy Queen out near Bobcat Country Drive. It's just a summer job, since I'm about to join the Peace Corps in Africa."

"Jesus Christ."

"Or the Pittsburgh Liz just accepted a field hockey scholarship to a local college. Or Peter's alive in New York, painting, and I'm visiting him, or—"

"This is a load of horseshit. This is my life, the one I'm living, here and now. I can't stand that sort of limp dick analogy of who I might have been if only—"

"But I need to know who I was then, what I might have become if I'd stayed in those places."

"What the hell for? I can tell you who you are right now. You're a very talented, intelligent seventeen-year-old girl who's tougher than anyone I know, and who just so happens to be moving to Cincinnati. End of story."

"Not the end of story. I'm also figuring things out to know who I'm supposed to be five years from now. Ten years from now. I want to be ready for it."

"What about the golfer in you? Where the hell is she?"

"Where's the head coach in you? I thought you were supposed to be a head coach by now!"

"Goddamn, I thought I was too. But I made mistakes. I made . . . mistakes."

"What mistakes?"

"It's none of your goddamn business!"

"Why do you have to yell at me?" I breathed, keeping my voice from cracking.

"Jesus H. Christ, who's yelling?" he railed, waggling a seven iron through the air. "I'm not yelling. We're having a discussion here is all. I don't know why I'm not a head coach yet. . . . You think I haven't asked myself the same question? You think it doesn't hurt like a sumbitch? It does, but what the hell am I supposed to do? Cry about it? But I will tell you one goddamn thing—I'm not about to quit trying! You can bet your ass on that one, chief!"

"Daddy?"

"What?"

"I truly hope it happens for you, but I can't come along for the ride anymore. You've decided our lives for seventeen years. I'm only doing what you taught me. To do what I believe in. If I move again, my brain will crack open, trying to guess who I'm supposed to be in Ohio."

"Aw bullshit!" He hit a line drive, a perfect two hundred yards. "That was pretty. Whoooeee. That was pretty now, folks."

"I'll be home in the summers."

"Sweetheart, this conversation isn't finished. Not by a long shot."

I picked up my pages to Kathleen, thrusting them into my backpack. What else was there to say?


Catherine smiled at me as I walked in, propped up in her crushed-velvet chair in her cotton robe, sipping a cup of tomato soup, watching *The Young and the Restless*. She patted my hand, announcing, "You know, your mother has two Crock-Pots set up in my little kitchen. Two. There's no room to turn around in there. Why don't y'all go home? I'm too old for all this company."

I sat down to look at the soap opera. "Anything good today?" The air-conditioning was blasting arctic air, chilling me after the dusty walk.

"That lady there, Liz"—she wagged a finger at the TV—"she wants us to think she's young, but just look at her hands. If you want to know how old a person is, just look at the hands. She's sixty if she's a day."

I stared at the woman's face, which seemed middle-aged enough, but her hands were mottled with liver spots. My grandmother's razor-sharp perception amazed me. I studied her spindly legs, which she still shaved once a week.

"You know, you're pretty." She looked me straight in the eye. "I mean that."

"Thanks," I smiled, then seized the moment. "How'd you meet Poppy?"

"For God's sakes, that was a hundred years ago. Who cares?"

"I'm curious."

"A priest fixed us up. Now drop it. Lordy, it's awful getting this old."

"I know, I know," I clucked sympathetically.

"No, you don't *know*. And don't even think you do."

"I want to try to understand."

"Well, don't."

I kept quiet, watching the soap in silence with her for a few minutes. Victor and Nicki were having an argument as usual. When a commercial came on, I spoke fast before she could cut me off, "Catherine, I need to know your past. Where did you go on your first date? What was your mother like? And your father? And you were the baby of nine. I want stories of your childhood. Growing up in Purcell, Kansas. All your sisters?" I was practically panting.

"Lord have mercy. Everyone's dead and gone. You're not going to do this."

"Do what?"

"You *know* what!" she snapped.

"I just want things to tell my grandchildren."

"Well, tell them about your past, then, and leave mine out of it."

"But you will be my past and—"

"Oh, *God*. Hand me my lemon lotion."

I handed it to her, massaging her skinny shoulders. She was like a bird. "I'm sorry," I whispered.

Rubbing the lotion into her hands, she sighed, "You know, there's nothing left but to smell good." As she sipped her soup, her eyes remembered something. "When I was young," she began, "I played Portia in a school play, and after one of my monologues, I heard somebody in the front row say, 'She likes the sound of her own voice.' And you know something? Back then, I did," she laughed.

I smiled, trying to picture this frail lady as Portia over sixty years ago.

"Do you pray, Liz?" she asked after a moment.

I studied the framed portrait of Aunt Betty hanging on the wall, her eyes full of love. *Did I pray? What was she thinking now? Did she still pray?*

"How's your faith these days?" Catherine set her cup of soup down cautiously, picking up a white fingernail pencil.

"I don't know," I replied, honestly. "My ex-boyfriend's becoming a priest. Does that count?"

"Of course not. Why should it? Don't lose your faith, Elizabeth. Don't lose who you are."

I leaned over and kissed her again, whispering, "Catherine, I want to go out to see all the relatives' graves later."

"Lord have mercy, what for? They weren't that interesting in real life. I can't imagine they'd be any better company now."

"I bet your sister Hannah was a kick."

"Hannah was a spinster with a screw loose," Catherine retorted, a fondness in her voice.

I laughed, thinking of the stories I'd heard about my great-aunt Hannah. She ran a candy store in Leavenworth and threatened to horsewhip kids who tried to snitch jelly beans whenever her back was turned. One Sunday she got bored, so she gathered eleven kids and made them all walk with her to Kansas City—twenty-nine miles away. Afterward, they took the train home. I liked Aunt Hannah's spirit. Poppy often spoke of how she had a "thing" growing straight out of her forehead, and how it just kept getting bigger, until one day Aunt Hannah decided she'd had just about enough of it, so she took a razor blade and sliced it off in the bathroom. Apparently there was some blood, and she fainted, but that was Hannah. She took care of things in her own way.

"I want to look at the graves," I explained to Catherine, not knowing what answers I'd get in a cemetery, but I wanted to see it just the same.

"Say," Catherine spoke up, looking at me. "Do you think we'll be young in heaven? I'd like to be about thirty when I'm there. Wouldn't that be nice? To feel good and have my own young body back?"

"Yes, it would."

"All right, now go help your mother while I watch the rest of this. Tell her to get rid of those Crock-Pots." Her eyes fixed again on the soap.

"I love you, Catherine." I stood in the doorway. I lifted one of the doorbell pipes on the wall, letting it bang and ring.

"I know you do, Liz. I've always known it. Now leave those chimes be. Drives me nuts." She picked up her rosary, the beads clicking together like pebbles.


The Cincinnati Titan move hovered around us like the saint statues and the *Reader's Digest* condensed books in the house. Mama kept giving me long, searching looks that seemed to say, "You gave up your boyfriend. Now come to the rest of your senses and move to Cincinnati with us." I avoided her eyes as we stalked past one another, tight-lipped, both of us determined to keep up the pretense of tranquility so as not to disturb Catherine, who hated noise and even nicknamed Daddy "Noise" whenever she heard him coming. "Here comes Noise," she'd sigh, sipping a Manhattan, watching Johnny Carson.

As the days passed on our three-week vacation, I roamed the rooms, trying to fit the pieces of my life together. Nothing about the Leavenworth house ever changed. It was the one constant in all the uprooting moves of my life. *Look* and *Life* magazines from the 1960s were still spread across a coffee table in a sitting room at the side of the house. Stacks of *Popular Mechanics* magazines from the 1940s and 1950s were bound up in the room off the attic. The sister portraits of Catherine and Hannah, of Mama and Aunt Betty, and even of Peaches and me, never aged or varied, since Catherine hadn't hung new pictures since 1970. I wondered if the stasis of this house was the main reason Mama now so willingly picked up and moved every few years of her life. With her childhood of quiet sitting rooms, she was ready for parties by adulthood. I wondered if I would be the opposite in my adult life. Would I be content with quiet sitting rooms and rosaries? Definitely not. I wanted my own life, without either football or rosaries, plus I yearned for Peaches and me to have lives we could share—even when we were old ladies.

As I devoured *Madame Bovary* and *Lady Chatterley's Lover,* I waited patiently for the mail each day, but Kathleen never answered any of the letters that I mailed faithfully to the convent. I didn't know if this was because she wasn't allowed to or she never received them, or because she simply couldn't be bothered. Although I hadn't written him at all, Robert wrote often. I wasn't even sure how he got my grandparents' address. There was usually a letter every other day, making silly promises. I couldn't write back. I wanted to quit him cold turkey, ignoring the ache in my heart. I also kept seeing his mother's eyes grow small with contempt for me, and I never wanted to be looked at like that again. Whatever Robert decided, I had already made up my mind that he had no place in my future, except as a friend.

On our last evening in Leavenworth, a plan in mind, I drove all the kids to the Dairy Queen in Poppy's Buick. Holy scapular medals swung from the rearview window. Catherine had hung them up to ensure against car accidents, but they'd had about one a year for the last five years anyway. Fortunately, no one was ever seriously hurt, which Catherine attributed to Saint Jude watching out for them. Next to a magnet of Saint Jude on the dashboard was a compass. *That's what I needed: a compass.*

After the Dairy Queen, we took our treats and a bunch of roses out to the cemetery. They were pink, white, and red roses, and I had them wrapped in foil and wet paper towels, so the thorns wouldn't prick us. We sat in the Buick in the graveyard eating our ice cream, its syrupy coldness soothing us from the sweltering evening.

"Remember when Daddy threw our ice cream out the car window," Leo reminisced to Peaches, taking a chomp out of his chocolate-dipped frozen banana.

"I hated that," sighed Peaches, sipping her lemon–lime Mr. Misty.

"It was Joe-Sam's fault," Leo said. "He spilled his first."

"Where was I?" I asked, slurping my blueberry sundae.

"You were there," Joe-Sam spoke up. "It was just a long time ago. But remember when he used to chase us underwater like he was a shark?"

"I loved that," Peaches smiled.

"Me too, that was great!" Leo licked the chocolate off the sides of his mouth.

"It was fun," I admitted, remembering all the hotels we'd stay in on trips or moves. The first thing Daddy did was take us swimming, and the games would begin: *chasing us, dunking us, throwing us high into the air; Mama calling from the side of the pool, "Not so rough. Not so fast. Be careful. Someone is going to get hurt. Fine. Go ahead, but don't come running to me crying."*

"Which ones are our relatives' coffins?" Peaches opened the car door.

"Graves," I corrected her, wondering where the family lay.

"Let's get out and go find them," suggested Leo.

I gathered all the ice-cream trash, cramming it into a garbage can, then checked the faces of my brothers and sister to see they were clean enough to visit the dead. Old habits die hard.

"You have a glob of chocolate on your chin," I whispered to Leo.

"So?" he whispered back, wiping his chin with the tail of his shirt.

"Don't be such a mother hen, Liz, come on," said Joe-Sam. "I think it's this way."

We followed him around the graveyard. He began walking on his hands, and pretty soon, all we could see were his two feet sailing past the various gravestones. Then he popped up, yelling, "I found them, I found them."

Peaches and Leo scampered toward his voice, but I saw I'd forgotten the roses in the car. As I turned around, it dawned on me . . . *Roses. That was it. The flying roses. All the things Aunt Betty and Peter had forgotten at one point or another in their lives: love, connection, and finally allowing others to let them slip away too. The answer is in remembering who you are and claiming it, like Catherine had said. Then others will see it and know it too. For in that moment in time, Peter forgot he had the brilliance to be a great artist, striving so much to please other people. When he knew he couldn't do it any longer, he had to reject life, because he couldn't bear the pain he might bring to his family, not realizing that his death would be the ultimate hole that would never close. And Betty tried to hang on to who she was, but she got caught in the trap of marrying the wrong man and living too much in the present, forgetting how magical she was—and later, letting others decide her course of treatment, no matter how dangerous. Even in his short, unfinished life, Peter was an effervescent teacher and lover of life. Before Aunt Betty got sick, she too had offered me her incandescent gifts.* It was almost as if I could feel them beside me, and it was a sensation of bliss. I was alive, and they were as real as ever.

As I traipsed back to the car to get the roses, I heard a voice behind me say, "I thought I'd find y'all here." It was Mama. She was wearing white pants, a red T-shirt, and sandals, looking radiant and, for the first time all summer, relaxed. Daddy was parked behind us, reading the sports page in the driver's seat.

I pulled the roses out of the backseat. "How'd you know we'd be here?"

"We used to bring you up here when you were little." Mama's face was soft. "You'd run looking at graves, trying to find ones with creepy names." She smiled. "Those roses are lovely."

"They're for the great-grandparents. Joe-Sam found their graves."

Mama glanced around. "Catherine and Poppy will be buried up here someday."

"What about us? Where do you think we'll end up?"

"God only knows," she said. "I guess Daddy and I will be buried in whatever football town we happen to retire in. I hope that's not for a long time."

"Me too."

"Well, sugar, I've made a decision." Mama tested the waters.

"Let's talk about the move later, Mama," I urged, not wanting to break the first moment of peace between us in a long time.

"Now listen. You've stated your position over and over, so let me state mine."

"Fine." I waited, expecting to hear the Knoxville house had sold, which was why she was in such a good mood.

"Here's the thing," she explained. "You have one more year of high school. You've lived in eight states already. Our house hasn't sold."

319

I chewed hard on the edge of my thumbnail, gnawing into my skin.

She plunged on. "I still have a job in Knoxville that I like very much. I even have a chance to direct the children's school choir in *A War Requiem* by Benjamin Britten at the Coliseum this fall."

"Yeah?"

"Of course, the thought of leaving Daddy alone for a year in Cincinnati isn't my most favorite, but since you've absolutely decided that you're not moving, I've decided I'm not either."

"What?"

"We'll all stay the school year in Tennessee and visit Daddy once a month, and he'll come down and see us during the off-season."

"You're kidding, right?"

"Daddy wants Joe-Sam to repeat his junior year, anyway, so he can have another year to grow before he plays college football. It makes sense to stay."

"You mean it?"

"Yes. Cincinnati is only a five- or six-hour drive away. What do you think? We'll move up officially after you graduate. It'll be good for everyone, especially you."

"Oh, Mama." I wanted to dance with her across the gravestones.

"My darling daughter. I have one more year with you. One more. I am entitled to that. Selfish as it sounds, I can't let you go yet. That'll happen soon enough."

My tears blurred her into streaks of red and white.

"Come on, you guys," Leo bellowed from the middle of the cemetery. "They're all up here. Tons of headstones of your dead relatives, Mama!"

Mama squared her shoulders. "They're yours too, young man!"

Peaches waved. "Hey, I picked daisies. Liz, you can put them with the roses."

"Okay," I called back, walking hand in hand with Mama to see the family plots. As we drew closer, she squeezed my hand, and then I saw my great-grandmother's name on the headstone: SALLY ELIZABETH, with the inscription YOUR LOVE IS OUR STRENGTH. Next to her was HANNAH MARY, with the word BELOVED.

# Leavenworth

I closed my eyes, remembering the young Aunt Betty in her royal-blue scarf and bright red lipstick, throwing roses up to Mama from beneath the hospital window, her worn copy of *The Heart Is a Lonely Hunter* heating up on the dashboard. When I opened my eyes, I saw that Peaches was making a daisy chain to drape over the headstones. She smiled at me, her fingers braiding the daisies with excitement, and I recognized Aunt Betty in the eyes of my sister.

The air smelled sweet; lilacs and blackberries bloomed along the walls of the Leavenworth cemetery. Leo and Joe-Sam were arm-wrestling on a grave a few rows over. If Peter were here, he'd be sketching them. Mama knelt down, tracing her grandmother's name with her finger. A mockingbird trilled from a tree nearby. As I gently placed the sprays of roses on my great-grandmother's grave and on my great-aunt's grave, I glanced down the sloping hill toward the sunset that was bathing Leavenworth in a ruby glow, and saw that Daddy was walking up the curling path to join us.

# ACKNOWLEDGMENTS

Special thanks to my father, Joe Madden, and his football diagrams and definitions, and much love to Keely, Casey, and Duffy Madden for their support, and to Gwyneth Kerr Erwin for her editorial skill and to Zachary Schisgal, my editor at William Morrow, and to my agents, Lee Kappelman and Ling Lucas, and to the others at William Morrow who have been so helpful, Anne Cole and Joan Amico, and to Diane Keaton and Bill Robinson.

A deeply heartfelt thank you to. my dear friend Heather Dundas for her patience in reading the book in its every incarnation and also to Jose Rivera and his glorious plays, and the members of the Silver Lake Fiction Writers' Group and their careful advice and suggestions: Judith Dancoff, Denise Hamilton, Marlene McCurtis, Eileen McMahon, Celeste O'Dell, Donna Rifkind, Lienna Silver, and Diane Zaga.

I also want to thank my relatives: Mary P. Madden, Lefty and Judy Madden and their children, Sally Pilkerton and her family, Ben Lueke, Nan Finkle, Mary Margaret Kelly, Catherine and Joe Kelly, Monica Kelly Zaworski, Sally Toland and all the McLaughlins for their love and generosity, and Tomi Lunsford.

For all our dear Los Angeles and New York friends: Jess Lynn and Theresa Rebeck for the Notre Dame connection; Terri Seligman for her sage advice and George Hagen for his inspired letters; Joe Purdy, Diana Wagman and Todd Mesirow for Ling, Julie Singer and Charles Fleming, Faith Kelly and Andy Schneiderman, Sabrina, Laura Berry and J. T. Allen, Roetta Lee Collins, Jillian Boyd, Ann and Chuck Cochran, Patty Radcliffe and Kirk Phillips, Jane St. Clair, Allegra Swift and Reuben Gonzalez, Nanette Anderson and Mark Heidmann; Leslie Hope for her "moving" stories; Caron Salazar, Rene Hahn, Luis Beccera, Lourdes Garcia, Sally Thomas, Red Guillen, Gabby Moreno, Luly Perez, Christina Lopez, Fabiola Hinojosa, Ana Pearson, Lily Alcaraz, Dan Duling, Betsy Amster, Tunde Tekete, and our Dillon Street neighbors.

# Acknowledgments

I would also like to thank those whose friendship has helped along the way: Paula Vogel for her encouragement, Marian Beth Khoury for her Boston edits; Doug and Marjorie Kinsey for their insight; Joan Griffin McCabe, Ruth and Sarah Campbell, Anne Monteverde Haus, Nancy McNeese Marchus, Evelyn Powers, James Grimaldi, Mary Sullivan, Patty Flynn, and Dan Morris, "second favorite son."

Special thanks to all the coaches and families whose memories have helped in the writing of the book: Mary Lynn and John Majors, Marian and Larry Beightol, Lorraine Harrison and the Harrison family, Norberta and George Haffner, Diane and Joe Avezzano, Nancy and Bobby Jackson, Sally and George Perles, Dot and Tiger Johnson, and Sue and Joe Paterno.

For all the schools and Tennessee people who have been a great inspiration to me: St. Cecilia's, St. Teresa's, Vincentian Academy, Knoxville Catholic High School; Patricia Chandler, Nicki Nye, Judy DiStefano, Al and Mayme Harris, Patrick Schmitt, Faye Julian, Bob Mashburn, Craig Gillespie, Keytha Graves, Rich Connelly, Joe McCain, Cappy Yonker, Sherry Todd, Sandy Suchomski, Berry and Buck Barta, Pat and Dan Murphy, Anne Ayres, Rebecca and Jim Barry, Dale Dickey, Tina Shackleford, Skip Dye, Don Stephenson and Emily Loesser, Jon Vandergriff, Julie Jackson, Tommy Keeney, Mary Ellen Lyon, Johnson West, Page Phillips and Dennis McCollough, Cindy Hatchett, Beth Free, Jonathan Krueger, David Thompson, Mary Jane Harville, Jason and Cindy Hunt, and Mike Thomas.

For the actors, directors, and writers of Los Angeles: The Met Theatre; Moving Arts Theatre; L.A. Theatre Works; Leon Martel, April Vanoff, Beth Rusio, John Rechy, Terri Cavanaugh, Megan Butler, Leah Applebaum, Joel Polis, Paul Redford, Max, Ann, and Mark Goldblatt, Erica Horn, Anne O'Sullivan, P. B. Hutton, Cedering Fox and Steve Abbott, Carol Schlanger, Doris Baizely, Kerstin Dahl, and Carla Conway.

For all the teachers: Inge Wacker, Uta de Lara, Lisa Krizek, Paul and Mary Vandeventer, the Eagle Rock Montessori staff, Dietrich Bradford and the Manhattan Place Elementary students and staff and the Garfield and Southgate Community Adult School students and staff.

For my Manchester University friends: Meera Syal, Mike Tait, David Mayer, John Pearson, Jem Warr, Janet Wallis, Ali Jeffers, Tony Johnson,

# Acknowledgments

Fiona Copland, Michelle Flatto, Mark Sproston, Eileen Grimes, Diana Keeley, Susan Egan, and Patrick Tilbury.

For Frances Lunsford and her thirteen children, most especially her seventh child, my husband, Kiffen, for his great affection, encouragement, and love, and our two children, Flannery and Lucy.